The End Of The Sixties

The God of the Bottle

The End Of The Sixties
Rescue of the invisibles

Neil Woodhall

The End Of The Sixties, 2nd Edition (1st print version)
Published in the United States for world wide distribution

Cover design by Doug Holcomb
Cover art by VividCovers.com
Font used throughout is Bookman Old Style

Self Published by Gomonish Entertainment LLC
Copyright control number 1-8136059011
Package A, through Amazon, starting October 2019
Print   version ISBN 978-1-7324568-2-2
Ebook version ISBN 978-1-7324568-5-3
Audio version ISBN 978-1-7324568-8-4

This book is lovingly dedicated to my wife Tina and our three sons Mark, Chris and John. Her encouragement, and their advice, have been invaluable in the creation of this story.

Preface

The sixties were a time of great hope, as well as enormous rage. I was in my teens and twenties back then. To me, to us, to a small group of people all around the world, it felt like a fresh cosmic breeze had blown in from somewhere out there in the great beyond.

That sixties feeling mysteriously disappeared early in the seventies.

Maybe every new generation feels the same way but I'm not so sure. Whatever the reason, when I was right in the middle of it all, back in 1968, I tried to write down how it felt to be there at that time. I couldn't do it. Feeling this joy, this connection, this transcendent wonder was one thing. Expressing it in words was like trying to capture a fog in a butterfly net.

Life happens, I got married, we had kids, they grew up.

During all those years I scribbled away. It was never my intention to be a professional writer. One idea after another got written, rewritten and reconsidered. Then I came across a fresh approach, which was actually the most ancient approach.

Rather than trying to rationally describe something larger than ourselves, I decided to use a particular style to reveal this as a quest. The best approach to the great mysteries seems to be a tall tale which everyone knows is a key, not a truth.

After I retired there was finally enough time to put the finishing touches on my book. It's not at all like what I started off with when I was twenty years old. I've changed, the world has changed, the story has changed.

This mysterious cosmic consciousness will return, for different reasons, in a new disguise, during some distant future, at an unknown place. This is the story of what it felt like to be there at the end of the sixties.

Neil Woodhall
September 10, 2019

Introduction

Throughout human history there have been countless tall tales told about people and invisible beings. The variety of these stories is truly astonishing. During the past hundred years advances in astronomy have changed how we visualize our place in the grand scheme. New styles of invisible beings should be included in this upgraded view of things.

In the 1920s astronomers began uncovering inconvenient facts about the universe we live in. Outer space, which had always been considered some sort of divine constant, was not at all what we had previously imagined. The space-time continuum was expanding. Hmm, what does that mean?

As the 1990s slid into the early years of the third millennium the debate surrounding these vexing observations began to show some results. Not only was the actual fabric of space itself expanding, but it was doing so at a zigzag pace.

The part I found to be fascinating was that the clusters of galaxies we identify in sky surveys today ... will not be visible in the future. In other words, the majority of what we see now, will no longer be seen then, because the expansion of space will have moved our neighbors so far away that their light will never reach us. Hmm, what does that mean?

One of the responsibilities of a storyteller is to visualize the uncomfortable problems we encounter and then create tidy fictions which give the reader useful information to consider. By giving names to the things which confuse us, it becomes easier for us to confront them.

At first glance, the expansion of space may not seem like a boffo plot line for a picaresque adventure story. On the other hand, if you ask a common question that writers must have in their repertoire - what is our destiny - then this odd expansion cannot honorably be avoided. The tricky part is coming up with a decent story to fit this esoteric theme.

Another idea which emerged during the early millennial era gave me something I could work with.

We do not live in a simple three dimensional world. According to one report there are eleven necessary dimensions. The fascinating thing is that some of these dimensions remain "folded-up" while other dimensions become "unfolded." You and I see and feel the dimensions that have unfolded for us. Other beings experience other unfoldings. Wow!

These recent ways of imagining such things provided a method for combining science with folklore to create updated versions of our invisible beings. Everyone "*knows*" that ghosts can fly through walls but they also sit in chairs. Taking what might be called "ghost physics" I set about the task of cobbling together a tale of the unseen.

The following simplifications emerged slowly.

There's a whole lot that we *don't know* about the Big Bang Universe but what we *do know for sure* is that it is expanding. So why don't we just go ahead and call it an Expansion Region? As a storyteller, an expansion region just sounds so much more realistic than a big bang universe.

And, if we are sure there is at least one expansion region, then why not two. Why not many. Why not make expansion regions the norm for the eternal universe. Doing so makes it easier to resolve the ancient philosophical problem of ultimate beginnings and ends.

Having settled on these fundamentals, I began looking for ways to take these mystical musings and make them amusing for the reader.

Somewhere in the middle of this project I created the term "anca" for the invisible characters. As would be expected, I gave them names and personalities, then began experimenting with how they would behave.

After struggling with this for quite some time, a fresh idea emerged suddenly from nowhere. What if anca are invisible to us but there are also other beings who are invisible to them? It took some fussing around but eventually I called those new characters the "soto". More names, more personalities, bigger plot.

Then came the insight that made this story work for me. What if *They* needed *Us*! What if both anca and soto needed human beings for some grand purpose?

I felt comfortable with this convoluted story line so I decided to go for it. During development I created a "fictional geography" based on recent results from astronomy. As a guide for the reader, the next section will describe how these story locations fit together.

##

Planets orbit stars, which wheel around in galaxies, that are clustered into vast gravitational structures, surrounding voids of astonishing proportion. That is what astronomers detect. The ancients knew about the planet but thought it was flat.

Grafting an ancient quest story onto this recently revealed visualization of our cosmic neighborhood became my goal. We will begin with what science tells us, and then we will move beyond that to consider our cosmic future. I have given anca names to this expansive geography.

Our starting place will be good old planet Earth. We orbit a star with the anca name Darimia. Associated with Earth is an artificial anca sphere named Paliyur. We are located in the Roshomon star cloud, which coils its way through the majestic spiral arms of the Ostramona galaxy.

At another location in Roshomon is a planet named Zog. Earth and Zog share a soto colonization project. At a different place in Roshomon is the Sagonish star system. That is where the headquarters of *Valdaria Colonization Enterprises* can be found.

At the next higher level we will take a look at the Ostramona galaxy. In the west this is called the Milky Way. Any reader who has ever watched the Star Wars movies will be familiar with galaxies.

Our galaxy is located in a small local cluster named Tromolea. Two other notable neighbors are the Andromeda galaxy and the Phorlom void. The headquarters of *Sylumini Consulting Services* is in Andromeda. The *Phorlom Research Foundation* is headquartered in the Imbotil dwarf galaxy.

Millions of galaxies, including Ostramona, are bound into a vastly larger gravity group known as Gomonish. In the grand scheme of things, this is our natural home. While the space-time continuum continues to expand, gravity and atomic forces will hold our home region together. But it won't last forever.

Sharing Gomonish's place in the cosmos are other gravity groups such as Argulen, Mezna, Vartog, and Zibbot. The expansion is pushing all of them away from each other.

These huge clusters of galaxies, and many more, are in Nimulos.

What is called the Nimulos expansion region in this story is exactly the same thing that technical writers refer to as the Big Bang Universe.

At this point in the fictional geography lesson we have reached the end of what science tells us. As a storyteller, I felt the need to expand the backstory to more levels. These larger levels, fractal like, are similar at increasing sizes.

Of a type similar to Nimulos is a neighboring expansion region named Jeshmol. Nimulos and Jeshmol are invisibly co-expanding through each other. The intrepid heroes of our story have figured out how to cross the gap.

For reasons which higher beings understand far better than our limited human minds can comprehend, these two regions can be combined to create a more durable home that will take us through the next phase of eternity.

There is no magic which makes these things happen mysteriously. All you need is a clear understanding of cosmic reality, plus good skills.

The fundamentals always remain the same. What exists now will eventually fade away. And yet, by some process we can barely understand, there is always renewal.

Enjoy this tall tale.

Table of Contents

Chapter 1 - The Wanderer

Scene 1 - Hamil and Hamine

In the utter darkness of the void the pale glimmer of the Fobimini sphere seemed unnaturally bright. As Captain Rakari steered the cruiser toward the docking station, Hamine had a clear view of the sphere from her seat in the passenger cabin. Hamil sat across the aisle, so he had to lean down to see. This would be their last stop before entering the most dangerous part of the void.

"Prepare for docking," announced Copilot Jagh.

Hamil and Hamine were nearing the end of a long journey to take over as co-leaders of the Earth Anca Corp. They had decided to take this journey into the Phorlom so they would have a better understanding of the problems and solutions their mission to Earth was facing. On their previous evolutionary planet, the region where they worked was crowded and high tech. This new assignment was in a remote region where the technology was still under development.

These beings were anca. They have well proportioned bodies with a head, body, arms and hands but - instead of two legs - their bodies slim down to one single taper. They glide to get around so they don't need to walk. Aside from the fact that their billowing colors are constantly shifting, they resemble sleek humans.

Co-leader pairs are matched to combine the characteristics of Ur and Um, who are the life patrons of our Lengtor life zone. From the unique natures of our foundational beings, every individual is known as either an urbie (male) or umbie (female).

##

The officer at the docking station waited until Hamil and Hamine regained their sense of balance. After being cramped in the cruiser for so long they needed to do special exercises. When they were ready she said, "Hello, my name is Eliam. I will show you to your hotel."

"A pleasure to meet you," said Hamine.

"Do you have any baggage?" asked Eliam.

"Very little," said Hamil, touching his side pockets. "We always travel light between assignments."

"Very well," said Eliam, "please follow me."

Fobimini was an isolated sphere where anca did cutting edge research in the supreme scientific stillness of the Phorlom void. The interior of the sphere was more elegant than would be expected this deep in uninhabited space. Every precious bit of construction material had been hauled in by caravan.

In the distance was a tall spire, glittering with bright windows. "The Grand Palugan Hotel," pointed out Eliam, "I think you will find your stay there quite comfortable."

When Eliam opened the door to their suite it was nothing short of phenomenal. The rooms were small, as would be expected on a sphere, but the subtle elegance of detail was perfect.

"This will do nicely," said Hamine.

Hamil turned to Eliam and asked, "Are there any messages for us?" This would be their last chance to exchange messages over the anca network.

"Three," said Eliam calmly, watching for their reactions.

Both co-leaders went on alert. "Who are they from?" asked Hamine.

Reaching in her pocket, Eliam handed them three code-cubes, "Mical and Macel, Sarkon and Sarena, and of course, Celene."

Mical and Macel are co-leaders of the Ostramona galaxy, which includes Earth. Sarkon and Sarena are co-leaders of the anca assigned to Earth. Celene had been the Prime Minister of Hamil and Hamine on their previous planet of assignment. Three code-cubes meant trouble.

"We need a few moments," said Hamil, in a steady voice.

"Of course," said Eliam. She moved away to give them some privacy.

Hamine opened her travel case, inserted each of the cubes, authenticated the codes, and both co-leaders examined the messages.

"That's horrible," whispered Hamine.

Hamil got an angry look on his face. "We were told to not trust the Sylumini but this is despicable."

Eliam thought that now would be a good time to inform them of an option. "You should know that Tahra and Noom are here at the hotel. They would like to speak with you concerning this matter."

"Ah yes, the ishmili project leaders," said Hamine. "We've heard so many wonderful things about them."

"Please take us to them as soon as possible," said Hamil.

"Follow me," said Eliam.

Tahra and Noom were ishmili, who are quite unlike anca. They are majestic beings who live on an entirely different plane of existence. As project leaders for the Roshomon colonization efforts, these two ishmili had learned to speak with both anca and soto. To do this, they projected communicator bodies from the vastness of their true forms.

Eliam led the co-leaders down the hall and knocked on a door.

"Please enter," said a voice, which had the booming resonance of an ishmili.

Eliam said, "It is my pleasure to introduce you to Hamil and Hamine. Please meet our project leaders, Tahra and Noom."

Seated in two chairs were the bright fuzzy communicator bodies of the ishmili.

"Greetings and good fortune to you," said Tahra.

"Greetings and thank you for meeting with us today," said Noom.

"We just received a disturbing report ... " began Hamine.

Noom rose from her chair, "Would that be about two human evos named Cynthia and Wendy?"

"Why yes," said Hamil, "it says right here ... "

Noom held up her hand. "I was an eye witness to their murder."

3

Hamine said, "So it really was murder. Anca never harm evos."

"Anca rarely harm evolutionary beings," said Noom, "but sometimes it happens. I watched it happen. The Sylumini do not know I was there. We ishmili are not permitted to testify in your anca courts. May we make a suggestion?"

"What would you recommend?" asked Hamil.

"The issues are complex but we propose a simple solution," said Noom. "Put Celene in charge of the rescue. Sarkon and Sarena have been compromised by the Sylumini."

"That would require a top level diplomatic exchange," said Hamine. "We will soon enter the zone of silence."

"We understand," said Noom. "We have available a diplomatic courier who knows how to do the jump."

"Absolutely not," snapped Hamil. "Not one of their kind. Anca who claim they can do the jump are tricksters and frauds."

"The courier we have in mind is an exceptionally skillful trickster," said Noom, "but he has never been a fraud. We have found him to be quite useful in situations such as this."

"It sounds as though you've thought this through," said Hamine. "The least we can do is interview this courier."

Noom replied, "It is important that we contact him immediately. He's on an extremely tight schedule at the moment."

Eliam got up and opened the doors of an enormous cabinet at the back of the room. Hamil and Hamine had never seen an ishmili dome so strange. The five of them pulled their chairs over in front of it.

After Eliam made the connection she cautioned, "Don't be surprised by anything you see."

Scene 2 - Dene

Dene was in a deep swamp. Surrounding him were slimy things like fanged eels, crawly things like spiky lizards, and creepy things like giant spiders. The vegetation was clingy and, if he wasn't an anca, the heat and humidity would have been unbearable.

He was in a bad place and didn't know how to get out. It wasn't like one of those predicaments he'd been in so many times before, with shrewd schemers intent on bringing him to personal and professional ruin. No - it was all very simple - he had no idea where he was.

The last thing he remembered was jumping from the Mezna gravity group to an assignment in Argulen. Then, all of a sudden, it was as if he was in a mist. That's how he ended up on this doomed planet. The local star was about to go supernova. Since he didn't know anything about this region, it was too dangerous to jump into the unknown. This might be the end of his grand trek across Nimulos.

Quite unexpectedly, Dene felt his taper device buzz - twice. That meant someone was trying to reach him over an ishmili network. He put it to his ear.

"Hello hello, who's there?" asked Dene.

"Is this Dene?" asked Eliam.

Dene got suspicious. He didn't recognize the voice and the directional coordinates made no sense. "Yes, as a matter of fact this is Dene. How do you know who I am?"

"Your coordinates were given to us by the ishmili," Eliam said, in a soothing voice.

By now Dene had identified the voice as that of an anca speaking over an ishmili network. "What do you want from me?"

"We have a special project we'd like you to consider," said Eliam.

"I'll take it," said Dene.

"You don't even know what it is," said Eliam.

"Doesn't matter," said Dene, "I take whatever life throws my way. I accept full responsibility. Now get me out of here."

Eliam fiddled with the controls until the image was clear. "I'm going to put you on with those who need your special skills."

Hamil put his face to the ishmili camera. "We are co-leaders traveling to our next evo planet. We need a diplomatic courier to exchange messages with the current administration."

"I'm a fully certified Hierashu Diplomatic Courier," replied Dene. "Where do you want me to go?"

5

Hamine replied, "We were told you are currently at the edge of Vartog. We are at the edge of Gomonish, facing your location across the Sautur void. How long do you think it will take to get here?"

"I can't give you an estimate without a grid map," said Dene.

"The ishmili just told us they can send someone with maps," said Hamil.

"That would be wonderful," said Dene, with an enormous amount of sarcasm.

At that moment the fuzzy glow of an ishmili appeared, leaning against a thorn tree, which was crawling with poisonous spiders. "Greetings and good fortune to you," said Frang, "I've got the maps."

"I'm going to put you on speaker," said Dene. He placed his taper device on a rock and adjusted it for full audio and live video.

"Let's get this out of the way first," Dene growled at Frang, "why did you hide me on this doomed planet?"

"We changed our minds about your next assignment," answered Frang. "We know how impetuous you can be so we put you in a place where you couldn't get away."

"Another couple of days and my soul-seed would have curled up," hissed Dene. "That star over there is about to go supernova."

"We know that," said Frang, "but you're not dead yet."

"Fine," snapped Dene. "Let me see those maps."

Frang created an interactive map, in multi-mode colors, with standard locator marks. He explained, "This is Mezna - where you were, and Argulen - where you were going. Nearby is Vartog, where we put you in a safe place, here on planet Eetor. Over there is Gomonish, where Hamil and Hamine are currently located. We want you to find a grid line you can use to get there in a hurry."

At the bottom of the ishmili map were virtual controls. Dene zoomed in and out, rapidly adjusting the view, while calculating jump conditions. Then he faced his taper device on the rock, "It'll take me 14 or 15 months to make that jump."

"That seems extremely optimistic," said Hamine.

"You wanted an estimate, I gave you one," said Dene. "What's the name of my destination?"

Hamil said, "It's an evolutionary planet named Earth, in the Ostramona galaxy."

"I'll send you a confirmation message as soon as I get there," said Dene.

"That won't be possible," said Hamine, "we're on a research mission in the Phorlom void. We will be beyond the reach of any anca network. Our destination is a lost planet named Cazouni. Go to Earth, get instructions, meet us on Cazouni."

"I can do that," said Dene. "Who do I ask for when I get to Ostramona?"

"Jenissen will take care of everything," said Hamil. "Frang will show you where to find him."

"No problem," said Dene. "Always glad to help. Is this Jenissen an anca or an ishmili?"

"He's an anca," said Hamine. "Jenissen is the Director of Special Operations for the Ostramona Galaxy."

"I look forward to meeting him," said Dene. "Bye."

"Goodbye."

"Thank you."

Turning to Frang he said, "Show me what I need to know."

Frang zoomed in until Tromolea, a local cluster of galaxies, could be seen. "This is the Phorlom void, where Hamil and Hamine are being trained for their next assignment. Over here in the Ostramona galaxy is planet Earth. Between the Ostramona and Andromeda galaxies is the Avilia sphere. That's Jenissen's base of operations when he's in this region."

Dene took the controls and slowly moved around, carefully considering any dangers. "Can I get a copy of my search patterns?"

"Of course," said Frang. Even though Frang was an ishmili, who are enormously different than anca, they used the 'palm-dome/image-exchange' method to shake hands and upload the search patterns directly from one mind to the other.

"Got it," said Dene, after thinking his way through the uploaded files.

"I'll be following you until you find Jenissen," said Frang. "If you need me just call my name."

7

"I appreciate that," said Dene. "You ishmili aren't usually this cooperative."

"We want to make sure you get to your next assignment safely," said Frang. "It's important to us." Then he faded from sight.

Dene was all alone, on a doomed planet, waiting for the right moment to jump to his next adventure. He reached over to the rock, shut off his device, and put it back in his taper pocket.

Scene 3 - Jenissen

The Avilia sphere was stationed along a strategic route in the Tromolea local gravity group. It was parked between Ostramona and Andromeda, monitoring freighter traffic for suspicious activities. The pilot was maneuvering to the next observation post when he looked up and saw an anca waving his arms from the sterile zone. "Take a look out there and tell me what you see," he said to the copilot.

She glanced up and said, "That must be the one they told us about."

"He got here early," said the pilot.

"You never know what to expect from these characters who know how to do the jump," said the copilot. "Each one is different."

"I'm going to let him in," said the pilot. "Take over the controls." He gave a hand signal to fly around to the docking station.

Ten minutes later the dock lock closed behind Dene. The chamber got repressurized. When the door opened Jenissen was waiting for him.

Dene shook his hand. "Is this the right place? They told me to ask for some urbie named Jenissen."

"I'm Jenissen."

"Pleased to meet you. I'm Dene."

"You got here fast," said Jenissen.

"If you play it right, you can get a nice kick from a supernova," said Dene. "I had good tailwinds on the trip over."

"Did you have any trouble finding the Avilia sphere?" asked Jenissen.

"Nah," said Dene. "Some ishmili named Frang showed me some maps. This is the only surveillance sphere I found parked between the two big galaxies so I figured it must be the one."

"Welcome aboard," said Jenissen.

A few days later Jenissen was having a private conversation with Dene.

"We got the report on you from Hierashu Headquarters," said Jenissen. "Your diplomatic credentials are impeccable and your jail record is quite impressive."

"I've spent some time in jail," said Dene, "but I've never been convicted of a crime. When you make powerful enemies, these things happen."

"Why do you make powerful enemies?" Jenissen asked.

"If nobody stands up to the bad guys they just get worse," said Dene.

"How'd you get into this line of work?" asked Jenissen.

"Not exactly sure," Dene told him. "One day I was on vacation while traveling to my next assignment as an architect. Next thing I know the Mysterians of Zibbot were teaching me how to do the jump."

"What were you doing on Zibbot?" Jenissen asked.

"It was one of those exotic vacation packages they offered at the grid cruiser terminal," replied Dene. "I had some time on my hands so I figured I may as well see something interesting. My life has been more than interesting ever since."

"Do you enjoy this line of work?" asked Jenissen.

"I take whatever life tosses in my direction," said Dene. "Sometimes I wonder what it would have been like if I'd kept working as an architect."

"We've spoken about many things over the past few days," said Jenissen. "Now I want to make sure you understand what my main goals are for you."

"Job number one," said Dene, "the rescue of the jeshies must not fail."

"Job number two," said Dene, "to make that happen, get Riana's Plan up and running."

9

"Job number three," said Dene, "dig up all the dirt I can on the Sylumini. When I meet with Hamil and Hamine, I will need to explain what's really going on."

"Very good," said Jenissen, "Do you have any questions?"

"Yeah," said Dene, "you're hiding something from me."

Jenissen gave him a sidelong look. "Your biggest problem is Riana. She's the only one who can make this rescue a success. Riana is impossible."

"The reports say she's a brilliant loner," said Dene. "What's her weak spot?"

"She won't take orders from anybody," said Jenissen. "She will only do what she believes is right."

"Then I won't give her any orders," said Dene.

Chapter 2 - Underground Highway

Scene 4 - Riana And Melona

Riana floated above the sidewalks of Greenwich Village. Melona was with her mother and father. It was graduation day. The streets around New York University were filled with students strutting in their proud graduation gowns. Larry and Renee Geffion had not seen their daughter in three years. There had been a family argument. For this special occasion they had flown in from western Kentucky to attend their daughter's big ceremony in the big city.

Riana was worried that Melona wouldn't be strong enough to anchor the east coast terminal. The underground tunnel couldn't get sealed unless the atmosphere bubble was tightly bound. How the daughter got along with her parents today was the plan's biggest weakness.

Their family feud had started off as an ordinary classroom assignment. The professor gave his freshman English majors the same project every year. Greenwich Village was famous for its freethinking bohemians, as well as its NYU academics. He told his class to interview some hipsters and write a paper comparing their way of thinking with what the university expected. It was the type of assignment which tagged students deserving special attention.

Melona's paper caught the professor's eye and he put her in touch with a small publishing house in The Village. A slim volume of interviews with beatniks was published during the winter of 1959. "Beatnik Village" consisted of verbatim quotes from local nonconformists, as well as catchy pen and ink sketches done by a colorful character named Sandal Annie. As luck would have it, the beatnik

11

craze was huge right then so the book became popular with the tourists.

When she proudly mailed a copy home, her father went into a rage. He didn't want his daughter associating with known beatniks, in the sinful city, far away from their decent home. Larry Geffion burned his daughter's first published work in the family fireplace. Until yesterday, they hadn't spoken to each other.

Melona stopped in front of the Paradise Regained Bookstore. She faced her mom and dad. "It's really important to me that I buy you a gift in here." Defiantly turning around, she marched through the door, parents trailing behind their daughter.

Noutashi was inside the bookstore, surrounded by a posse of Guardian Anca. Melona was Noutashi's regular client. The guardians were gathered to make sure that no harm came to this evo.

Riana ignored them.

An expectant hush descended upon the room.

Melona, who knew nothing about any of this, led her parents to the Local Interest section in the back. Turning to face them, she reached for a slim volume on the shelf.

Riana touched Melona's hand at the same instant the girl touched the book. Power flowed from anca world into human world.

"On this special day I want my loving parents to have a fresh copy." She held it up and read the cover out loud to them, "Beatnik Village by Melona Geffion." Then she boldly strode to the cash register and paid for the book, using royalty money she had earned from this very same book. Handing it to her father, she got a stubborn glint in her eye.

Larry took it in his big hands and said, "I still think you ought to stay away from those beatniks but you've grown into a fine young woman. I'm going to take this home and put it on the bookshelf next to The Blue Princess." Tears rolled down his tanned cheeks.

"Thank you daddy," she said, giving him a great big hug. The Geffion family was whole again.

To the utter astonishment of every guardian in the room - Riana vanished.

##

A NimuTrak Observatory van was parked inside the bookstore. Only Riana could see it. The table marked Best Sellers was in the engine compartment. Melona and Riana were in the equipment bay. Two alien beings sat in the control cab. Mom and dad were outside the door.

Xen was a soto. She had pale blue skin, was short, with thick legs and enormous feet. Her place was behind the steering wheel, in the supervisor's seat.

Wun was an evolutionary being from Jeshmol, or evojesh. He had lush green skin, was tall, and showed signs of getting along in eons. He sat in the technician's seat. In front of him was the dashboard dome.

Melona sensed that something fantastic was happening all around her. That feeling was so far beyond anything she had been taught that her mind rejected any notion of it actually being a separate reality.

"how does evonim look now" asked Riana, speaking the soto language.

"need gooder results this way" said Xen, pointing at the display in the dashboard dome.

Riana studied the image, then put one hand on Melona's neck and the other at her elbow. With a quick flick of Riana's wrists, Melona's human body shifted deeper into jeshie world.

"that much gooder" said Xen.

Wun said, "ready for anchor".

"do it" said Riana.

Wun's hands were a flurry of activity on the dashboard dome. When he stopped he said, "solid anchor east coast".

Xen checked the readings, "approval go".

For the first time in several years Riana had a look of enormous relief. "me shift back now".

Riana disappeared from their sight inside the NimuTrak.

At the same instant she became visible again to the guardians in the bookstore. None of them could think of anything to say.

Melona turned to join her parents. The fact that invisible beings had just transformed her life was too strange to be taken seriously.

Same bookstore - three different realities.

13

"Tell Vint the jeshies locked in the east coast terminal," said Riana.

"I'll do that," said Noutashi. "What's going to happen to Melona?"

"She'll be in danger from now on," said Riana. "The Sylumini will notice that she's become an active part of our plan."

Noutashi winced. Melona was her favorite client. There were persistent rumors about what the Sylumini had done to Cynthia and Wendy. "That's your choice but it will never be mine."

Riana said sternly, "Gotta do what I gotta do." Then she flew through the ceiling and left them wondering.

Noutashi asked the other guardians in the room. "Did Riana just disappear and then reappear?"

"Yes."

"Do you know how she did that?" asked Noutashi.

"No."

"I don't like this," said Noutashi. She was trembling.

Scene 5 - Riana And Andy

Eberli was waiting for Riana, wondering how things had gone in New York.

Floating through the front window of the BeBop BookStore, in San Francisco, Riana didn't even bother saying hello. "I've got to get rid of that one first," she said, floating through the back wall.

A minute later Diane Rishi, owner of the bookstore, came storming out of her office to declare, "I'm going out for office supplies."

Andy glanced at the clock. It was 12:09. At least she had made it until lunch time today. "Cash register tape," he called out. "We need more paper tape for the cash register."

"I'll bring some back after lunch," she yelled, as the door slammed, and the bells on the cord jangled.

Andy knew she wasn't coming back after lunch and it was better that way. When she returned to the store after she'd been drinking it ruined his day. He would buy more paper tape at the stationary store on his way in tomorrow.

Riana glided back into the store and hovered next to Andy.

"How'd it go?" asked Eberli.

"The east coast terminal is solid," answered Riana. "Hopefully, the west coast terminal will be easier."

"Mmmm," said Eberli. He had learned to leave her alone when she was in one of her shadowy moods.

Andy, who had been sitting sullenly, because of no customers, suddenly looked alert. This "on" feeling was something he had gotten used to over the years. Other people might think he was crazy, but sometimes he felt an invisible presence, and it seemed like they needed him for some reason. He always cooperated, as long as it felt right.

"If the jeshies get this underground highway built then we're going to need to get the two of them together some day," Riana said.

"I've already got that set up for you," said Eberli.

He zipped through the front window and came back a few minutes later. Two tourists followed him through the front door. Getting behind Andy's shoulders, Eberli spread out his arms, ready to beam an image into his client's imagination.

"Howdy," said the husband.

"Welcome to the BeBop BookStore," said Andy.

"We're looking for a book on those beatniks," said the man. "Down at the hotel they said you had that sort of thing."

Andy didn't consider himself a beatnik, although he did have shaggy hair, a sculpted beard, and was dressed in black. "Are you looking for a book of poetry by beatniks, or maybe one of their novels, or perhaps something of a historical nature?"

"Well, I don't know about any of that," said the man, "we just want to try and understand em. You know, they've been all over the newspapers and magazines and we just can't get em figured out."

Eberli projected a picture into Andy's mind.

"I think I have just what you're looking for," he said.

As they walked away from the cash register the wife said, "We don't want anything with filthy words in it. We want to take this home."

15

"Take a look at this," said Andy. He pulled a slim volume from the shelf and held it up for them to see. "Beatnik Village by Melona Geffion. This is a nice work by a researcher in New York. I've read it and can assure you there are no filthy words."

The husband took the book in his hands and turned it over. A stylish young woman was pictured on the back cover. She was wearing a black and white striped blouse, sunglasses, and a beret was perched on her head at a jaunty angle. His wife snatched the book away from him. She flipped through and read a few lines. "Looks alright to me."

They went to the cash register. The man paid for it. The woman put it in her purse. They left the store. The bells jangled.

Eberli turned to comment on how well that had gone. To his complete surprise, Riana had vanished.

The NimuTrak surrounded the cash register. Riana hovered behind Xen and Wun's seats. Eberli and Andy were in the cargo bay, but neither of them knew that.

"him strong today" said Xen, glancing at the dashboard dome.

"he sold book" said Riana. "make him feel proud".

Wun's hands were a flurry of activity on the dashboard dome. When he stopped he said "terminal west coast look steady".

"you monitor bubble for pim" said Riana. "me stay here" "set up continental portal".

"we on it" said Xen.

Started the engine, she drove straight through the front window of the BeBop. Making a quick turn, straight up in the air, she headed off to find a suitable halfway point between Andy and Melona.

Eberli could see Riana again. She had a strange look in her eye.

"How'd it go?" asked Eberli, feeling nervous.

"Both terminals are solidly anchored," said Riana. "Now they're driving out to the Midwest to monitor the bubble for the tunnel crew."

16

"Mmmm," said Eberli. He wasn't sure who 'they' were but he knew better than to ask.

Riana also felt nervous. The two jeshies had a test they were going to run for her. It might be impossible.

Up in the sky, Ulta was spying on the NimuTrak as it left the bookstore. She was Chief Technology Officer of the Sylumini and they were desperate to steal more secrets from Riana. The blue blur of unknown origin was on the move again.

Pressing the intercom button she said to her pilot, Yori, "Follow that blue thing."

California to Nebraska - the chase was on.

Ulta had no way of knowing that Xen and Wun were intercepting every spy signal she beamed down on them.

Scene 6 - Xen And Wun

Xen and Wun had been searching Middle America since the earliest days of the first rescue. It's a bad idea to rely on only one plan. They always have fresh ideas so they had built a test device, on the sly, just in case. The first rescue got cancelled. If this test worked today, the second rescue might have a chance.

Pim, their soto boss at Wamilla Emergency Services, had not been told about this because he didn't have a security clearance.

This rescue could not work unless all three types of beings - anca, human, and jeshie - worked together. But they wouldn't know how to work together until after this test.

Pim's part of the project was simple. A long thin jeshie bubble had been anchored between the terminals established by Melona and Andy. Inside this transcontinental safety zone, a work crew would finish sealing the tunnel sections. A highway would eventually be built inside. That would connect the old west coast colony to a new east coast colony.

At ground level in Nebraska was a boy in his late teens. He was driving a tractor, plowing the fertile topsoil of this remote prairie region.

The dual atmosphere readings inside the protective bubble were stable. Deep in the underground, jeshie construction crews worked at top speed. At ground level Xen and Wun were getting ready for the Nebraska Kid. In the sky above them circled Ulta's spy cruiser.

"conditions goodly" said Xen.

"me go" said Wun, grabbing his bag.

Inside the bag was a little blue toy. It had been given to Wun by his aunt when he graduated from the Wamilla Observatory Academy. They sold these little mementoes at the campus dome store. After the mode-quake hit, he was searching through the rubble of his home and the blue toy was one of the few things he could carry away.

For Riana's Plan they needed a small test object to check out a radical portal design. Riana was out in San Francisco with Andy. Noutashi monitored Melona from New York. The little blue toy was a scale model of the big blue NimuTrak van that both jeshies were sitting in. Built inside the toy was a high tech portal circuit.

Crawling into the back of the van, Wun put on his atmosphere pack, adjusted the jeshnim goggles, and slung the bag over his shoulder. Quickly opening the side door, he jumped out and slammed it shut.

Near the middle of the field was a green tractor. Strange noises came from it. Wun adjusted the audio levels on his headphones. Driving the tractor was this young man, who was wearing faded blue jeans and a plain white t-shirt. On his head was a red baseball cap.

When he got closer, Wun understood where these strange sounds were coming from. The Nebraska Kid was bopping his head to the tractor radio. Top 40 Hits of 1963 were blaring into the dusty field at loud volume.

Taking a calculated risk, Wun slipped aside his breathing mask. The air was fine. He shut off the valve to the atmosphere pack and adjusted the rest of his gear for comfort.

It was kinda weird - the Kid and the Jeshie were both breathing the same air.

While the tractor was making turns, Wun prepared the test. In his hand was a mode-shifter he had redesigned for this purpose.

##

Up in the sky, Ulta's cruiser dipped lower. In her spy dome were images which would please the Special Board when she reported her findings.

They had known about the planetary bubble for a long time. Now she had evidence of a local jeshie bubble poking up through the ground. The unidentified blue blur was inside the mid section of this bubble. From the coordinates, Ulta could tell that the terminals were connected to Melona and Andy. Apparently something really big was happening down there in the terran underground. This news was huge.

Wun methodically adjusted the settings on the experimental mode-shifter. Suddenly the readings jumped into the green zone. He pressed a small red button on the side.

A few minutes later the farm boy switched off the loud radio. Sounds of cosmic consciousness were playing inside his youthful head. Nothing in his short life had prepared him for an experience like this. The dual atmosphere, amplified by the mode-shifter, had made the boy feel bubble fuddled.

After breathing more of this strange air - fit for humans and anca, plus jeshies - the Nebraska Kid shut his tractor down. The mechanical noise interfered with his new insights. Dust from plowing got swept away by a fresh breeze. Somewhere in the distance a cow mooed. Bird calls seemed to be a language all their own. The wind made soothing whoosh sounds through the sparse trees.

Wun walked right up to the boy. Reaching in his bag he took out the toy.

The Nebraska Kid was leaning against the tractor, one cowboy boot in the soft soil, the other propped up against the huge black tire. His t-shirt was dusty. He took off his baseball cap to wipe the sweat from his brow.

Cool air on his forehead put the Kid over the top. He felt like everything in the whole wide world was just the way it was supposed to be.

Wun had the mode-shifter in one hand, the blue toy in the other. The Nebraska Kid had the perfect soto colors for this exotic test. With sublime skill, Wun made adjustments until the Kid blended with the soto colors of Melona and Andy, far far away.

Poof - the little blue toy disappeared.

He wasn't sure where it went but the test might have worked.

Wun looked over at the NimuTrak van. Adjusting his jeshnim goggles, he could see Xen in the cab, giving him two thumbs up, shouting something he couldn't hear.

Turning his attention back to the Nebraska Kid, he decided to remain right where he was until he was absolutely certain that this young man was going to be safe. 'Do no harm unless necessary,' was an old saying he firmly believed in.

Wun powered down the mode-shifter. Looking into the farm boy's eyes, he watched as the bubble fuddle effect began to wear off. Dual atmosphere was being pumped out of the long bubble, into the highway tunnel, which had now been sealed. The big bulge in the middle sagged. Their role in Pim's project was over. The results of Riana's test would not be known until they figured out where the blue toy had gone.

Wun waited, standing on his thin green legs, squishing his large toes in the freshly plowed earth, at a place he had never touched before.

The Nebraska Kid nodded his head and grinned. Whatever odd thing had just happened to him, he felt good. Real good. Putting his baseball cap back on, the young man climbed up on his tractor and started plowing again. On a farm there's always more work.

A few years later they would be calling this bubble fuddled effect the 'sixties zap.'

Wun stayed where he was until two complete turns had been plowed with no signs of trouble. Then he slowly walked away.

Inside the van, Xen asked, "how it go".

"goodly" said Wun. He had set foot on a new world for the first time. Someday, if this rescue went the way they all hoped it would, they would be living in one those jeshie tunnels, down there in the terran underground.

##

In her spy cruiser the only thing Ulta could see was that the local bubble had faded from sight. It sank beneath the ground, as if being deflated. The big blue blur drove away.

She said to Yori, "Let's head back to home base." Ulta had a rare smile on her face.

Chapter 3 - Double Duty

Scene 7 - NimuTrak Observatory

After driving away from an obscure farm field, on an alien planet, Xen and Wun felt odd about being back in the familiar cloud island of Kemong.

They were observatory technicians. Most of what they knew about the expansion region named Nimulos, where Nebraska was located, came from data displayed on their dashboard dome. Today they hadn't merely mapped conditions on Earth, using state of the art equipment. Wun had explored the planet with his feet.

They were also homeless. The mode-quake in Wamilla had destroyed where they lived, as well as the place where they used to work. Their van, and temporary housing, was all that remained in their shattered world.

As they got closer to Wamilla, the practical matters of everyday reality began crowding in on their minds.

"pim be mad at us" said Xen. "we be late".

"you boss" "pim yell at you" said Wun. "me not care about you" "me care about test kid".

Pim was a political appointee who had been given this job, far away in the remote vacation paradise of Wamilla, to get him out of the way. After the mode-quake hit, what remained of the NimuTrak observatory fleet had been shifted over to Pim's emergency services department. It was a lot different but at least it was something.

Xen slowed down as they approached the Wamilla Medical Center. Signs of devastation were everywhere. According to the schedule Pim had given them - they were eleven minutes late. When they pulled into their parking space at the Norovio Mansion they got out, slammed both doors, and trudged inside.

##

"where you jokesters been hiding," growled Pim.

"not hide" said Xen, "check safety".

22

"you work late" snapped Pim. "good workers always on time".

Xen and Wun were not allowed to say a word about the blue toy test.

"make sure bubble deflate safely" said Xen. "want highway workers be safe".

"bubble they problem" "you problem be prompt" said Pim. "governor zeb not like overtime".

"governor zeb promote safe work environment" suggested Xen.

"you get back late" snarled Pim. "you make me look bad".

Xen resisted saying what was really on his mind. "you look good to me".

"you not count" said Pim. "governor zeb count" "her in charge".

Xen recalled something that one of the long time emergency services workers had explained one day. "we get overtime for being yelled at" "it rules".

Pim knew they had him beat. The rules clearly stated that emergency services staff got paid overtime for extra service, regardless of the reason for that extra service. By yelling at them for earning overtime, Pim had to pay them more overtime.

"go upstairs" "stay out of trouble". With a wave of his hand he dismissed them. Their boss began plotting ways to make them pay for their little rebellion.

Xen and Wun didn't dare look each other in the eye, or they would have burst out laughing.

##

The Norovio Mansion was the fanciest place any of them had ever lived. The fabulously well connected family who owned it used to vacation here twice a year. After the mode-quake, an evacuation decree forced them to abandon their vacation estate and return to safety on the mainland. Those NimuTrak workers who had lost their homes, and careers, had been assigned here to live, so they would be located near the hospital.

For the rescue, NimuTraks were being converted into AmbuTraks.

As punishment for their notorious lack of servility, Xen and Wun had been banished to the attic. The elevator didn't work, so they had to walk up eight flights of extravagantly elegant stairs.

After reaching the top floor they could speak openly about their plans.

"when we sneak portable soto dome out of van" asked Xen. "we got bigly meeting tomorrow".

"not need entire dome" said Wun. "only need memory drive" "that in my pocket".

"we got no soto dome up here" said Xen.

"not need soto dome" said Wun. "we got ishmili dome".

"that not read soto dome data" said Xen.

"me write data converter program" said Wun.

"when you do that" asked Xen.

"when me mad at you" said Wun.

"how long it take convert anca spy baddie data" asked Xen.

"all night" said Wun.

"must be ready for earth meeting tomorrow" said Xen. "we no let sylumini figure us out this time".

"no problem" said Wun. "we be ready" "anca spy baddie be smart but we be tricky".

Without another word they went to their own rooms. The leftovers of luxury were stored in the attic. Surrounded by these glamorous castaway items, they had started rebuilding their lives. While the employees downstairs relaxed or played, these two worked far into the night, at tables lit by emergency lanterns.

Scene 8 - Chephra Observatory

Next day, at the appointed hour, Xen setup the ishmili dome and made the trans-world call to the Chephra Observatory on Earth. Two full time employees worked there, Honat and Qusheem. Riana had teamed up with them as a consultant. Those three from Nimulos had a meeting scheduled with Xen and Wun from Jeshmol.

"observatory here" said Riana, speaking the soto language.

"norovio here" said Xen.

"me translate for honat" said Riana, "him got something he need say".

Honat put his face in front of the ishmili camera. The soto language was something he was going to learn someday but he hadn't gotten around to doing that yet. He spoke directly into the camera, while Riana translated from the side.

"Lumbia wants me to tell you that the jeshie tunnels are safely connected coast to coast. The work crews in the underground colony are very excited about that," said Honat.

Lumbia was Honat's committed partner. She was an administrator for the terran pumps, which provided dual atmosphere for the jeshies in the Earth Rescue Colony.

"lumbia say tunnels goodly" said Riana, translating into soto.

"we glad to hear" said Xen.

Honat obediently continued on the promises he had made. "And she also says she wants me to make sure that I say thank you for all the fine work you have done for us. Lumbia says that I am often rude and forget to say how much I appreciate what others have done for me."

"honat lumbia say thanks" translated Riana.

Honat then scooted his chair away from the camera, having fulfilled his promise to his spouse.

"anything else you want hear" asked Riana, teasing them.

"blue toy" said Xen, who was desperate to know.

Qusheem could no longer contain his excitement. Sliding Riana's chair out of the way, he put his huge face in front of the ishmili camera and said, "Wfgejnaclz", using one of his big-words. Holding the little blue toy in front of the camera, he laughed gloriously.

"hoopa hoopa hoopa" yelled Xen and Wun, jumping up from their chairs, slapping their hands together. Both of them were perpetual cynics but this news was awesome. If they could get a toy NimuTrak from one world to the next, then they should be able get a massive AmbuTrak ambulance over to the other side.

"Mqibof," suggested Qusheem.

Xen said, "we work on design for that" "send you when finish".

Riana slid her chair in front of the camera. Honat crowded in on one side, Qusheem on the other.

"last question" said Riana. "did you get ulta spy data".

"anca spy baddie super busy on us yesterday" said Xen. "we got lots" "when you want we send it".

"right now" said Riana.

"take long time upload" cautioned Xen.

"we got plenty time" said Riana.

Honat and Qusheem both giggled. They didn't have any bosses, except Ing, who was never there. They could do whatever they wanted, whenever they felt like it.

"data start receive on our side" said Riana. "what you plans".

"not make plans" said Xen. "you know why".

"not really" said Riana.

"when something go goodly" said Xen, "next thing go badly".

"Zegyjicl," Qusheem added.

Xen laughed cheerfully. "you right" "trouble always find us" "we no go look for it".

Chapter 4 - Diplomatic Courier

Scene 9 - Hoshambelan Tower

In the Nimulos expansion region, for a certain class of planets, it is the custom for an artificial anca sphere to be built nearby. The sphere linked to Earth is named Paliyur. Planet and sphere are connected by a flexible tunnel.

Coming down the tunnel were Jenissen and Dene. They had spent the past few days on Paliyur meeting with Ing, who heads the Ishmili Colonization Bureau.

Jenissen was much respected - and greatly feared - throughout the entire Ostramona galaxy. Several of the commuters who saw him ducked to avoid his piercing gaze. Traveling with him was an anca who none of them had ever seen before. He was lean and tough, with colors of cold gray and somber blue billowing in his body. They would soon learn that this was Dene.

As soon as they reached the exit in Greenland, the two of them zipped up to a medium speed lane - flew across the Arctic Ocean, over Russia, China and Indonesia - then descended into the Perth Basin off the western coast of Australia. Diving into the clear blue waters they approached the capitol city of Hoshambelan, center of all political power among the earth anca. Jenissen brought Dene to the diplomatic entrance at the back of the headquarters tower. From there they were escorted to a private meeting room.

Seated at the head of the conference table were Sarkon and Sarena, co-leaders of the Earth Anca Corp. To their right were three anca who had legitimate, but conflicting, interests in the emergency rescue. To their left were Jenissen and Dene.

"On behalf of the Hoshambelan Administration, I would like to welcome all of you to this hastily arranged meeting," said Sarena. "A year ago we received a request

27

from the incoming administration to participate in a co-leader to co-leader exchange concerning the jeshie rescue mission. Celene received the request at the same time."

"Why wasn't I informed of this?" interrupted Khaletora.

Sarkon answered him coldly, "Mical and Macel sent instructions for us to wait until the diplomatic courier reached Earth. Jenissen will explain."

Mical and Macel were co-leaders of the entire Ostramona galaxy. Jenissen reported to them as Director of Special Operations. He was in charge of straightening out problem planets.

Jenissen had a frosty look in his eye, directed toward Khaletora, who was Chief Executive Officer of the Sylumini Consulting Group, Earth Division.

"There is a serious matter we must attend to today. We have little time and I will not tolerate *anyone* who interrupts me," Jenissen began. "Co-leader to co-leader exchanges are an extremely serious matter. They are also quite rare. The fact that one has been called for is why the galactic leadership sent us here today. I would like to introduce you to Dene, who is a Hierashu Certified Diplomatic Courier. His mandate is to investigate the cause of the delays holding back the rescue, then deliver diplomatic code-cubes to Hamil and Hamine."

To emphasize how serious he was, Jenissen took a hard look into the faces of everyone in the room. His gaze had a commanding presence - even to those who were accustomed to wielding enormous power.

"There are many nagging problems plaguing this rescue," continued Jenissen, "but one fact remains perfectly clear. Vulnerable refugees need our help and we will give it to them. Universal custom demands it of us. We must not fail. Mical and Macel gave me strict orders to deal with this matter firmly. Having made these preliminary remarks, I will now turn this meeting back over to the co-leaders."

Sarena said, "Thank you for reviewing the essentials. A full report will be forwarded to the Sylumini and the Valdarians. Time for this meeting is running short but we should hear a few brief remarks from each of you, for the benefit of the courier."

Khaletora had been bursting to have his say. "As always, the Sylumini are prepared to provide a full range of services for all situations." He smiled with enormous self satisfaction.

Sarkon said, "Larush, do you have a few words ... "

Larush was the Chief Executive Officer of Valdaria Colonization Services, Earth Division. She replied, "It has been my position all along that Hamil and Hamine should be included in these rescue plans. They will bear the consequences when they take over the administration of this planet. We will examine the report and provide a public response."

Sarena said, "A quick word from Celene, then we must go."

Celene's current title was Chief Transition Officer for the Ayamara Administration. She had been Prime Minister for Hamil and Hamine on their previous planet of assignment. "We need clear instructions. This diplomatic exchange should take care of that."

"This meeting is adjourned," said Sarkon, rising from his seat.

Five powerful leaders rushed out the door.

Jenissen and Dene sat alone, in an ornate conference room, at the top of the Hoshambelan Tower.

"Now that you've had a chance to meet the big players what do you think?" asked Jenissen.

"I think this is going to be fun," said Dene.

They both laughed that hardened chuckle of tough professionals.

Scene 10 - Wamilla Medical Center

The next morning Dene woke with a soft pillow under his head. It was only then that he realized how long it had been since he'd had a good night's sleep in a comfortable bed. Stretching out beneath the covers, he relaxed.

Being in odd situations on strange planets was what he did. Jenissen had raced off to another crisis, which meant that Dene would be on his own for awhile. None of the leaders he met yesterday would expect him to do anything bold during his first full day here on Earth. The question was, how was he going to do it?

29

Dene reviewed what Jenissen had told him last night. The argument between the Valdarians and the Sylumini was the part you could see. That's the part Dene was to work on in public. Behind this aggressive power play, ugly shadows were on the move. Find them. Neutralize them.

Snuggling his head in the pillow, Dene let his mind wander.

After some daydreaming he had a sudden hunch. He never knew where these hunches came from but he had learned to trust them, if they felt right. Throwing the covers off, he decided that Beel, the concierge of this apartment building, was the only anca he could trust right now. Jenissen would not have introduced them, the way he did, if that wasn't true.

Opening the door to his new apartment he floated out into the hallway. Carefully he looked around. He wanted to make sure he remembered which door was his when he came back.

Down at the end of the hall was a standard up-arrow/down-arrow sign. Because anca glide through the air they don't need elevators. One vertical shaft is for up traffic, the other is for the down direction. He dropped down to the lobby. Beel's office was on the right.

Dene stuck his head inside the door.

"Ah yes," said a mellifluous voice, "welcome to our lovely little planet, Dene. I would remind you that my name is Beel and I am here to help."

"Thanks," said Dene.

"Please have a seat," said Beel.

He sat down in a guest chair and took a look at Beel. The concierge was wider than most anca and considerably shorter.

Beel smiled. "I hope our apartment meets your expectations."

"Oh, it's much nicer than the place I was staying before," said Dene (thinking of the doomed planet Eetor, with its poisonous spiders on thorn trees).

"What can I do for you today?" asked Beel.

"My goal for this morning," said Dene, "is to get a solid feel for this planet. No tour guides please. I want to see things for myself. Would you direct me to one of the high speed lanes so I can take a look around."

Low speed lanes are where anca fly to travel locally. High speed lanes are used mostly by messengers and athletes.

Beel replied in a scholarly tone, "The diplomatic zone, where you are staying, is on an uninhabited continent called Antarctica. There are two major land groups in the mid latitudes. We call one the sunrise lands, and the other the sunset lands, because that's the way they appear from the capitol city of Hoshambelan. I will take you to a suitable launch site."

"Most excellent," said Dene.

##

Dene circled Earth thirty six times at high altitude. The pattern he flew made it look like he had gone out to get some vigorous exercise. It was his intention to make everything seem perfectly normal.

During his high speed tour he spotted an area which suited his plan perfectly. Over the Pacific ocean was a vast stretch with no islands - therefore few anca. High above this vast expanse of water he made a quick jump.

##

In the blink of an eye, Dene was so far above Earth that it looked like a blue and white ball, floating in the void dark sky. From Jenissen's maps he knew the exact location of the Wamilla Peninsula, in Jeshmol. Because of his jump training he could see, dimly, into worlds beyond ours. It took only a few precious seconds for him to find what he was looking for.

Near the middle of the peninsula was the Wamilla Medical Center. Its buildings were blurry to his eyes but the pattern of their outline was unique. When he got closer he could see blue rectangles higher up on the cloud hill. At the bottom of the hill, lined up neatly in the hospital parking lot, were white rectangles of the same shape.

The blue blurs were the old NimuTrak observatory vans, parked around the Norovio Mansion. The white blurs were recently converted AmbuTraks down at the medical center. These were going to be used for the rescue of seriously ill patients.

Wamilla Hospital was famous for treating allergic disorders. Many evojesh, and the occasional soto, were allergic to the air in Kemong. Getting them away from here was of the utmost importance.

It wasn't much to see but it was enough. Dene was a great believer in looking at things with your own eyes. Don't trust a report. Don't believe an image in a dome. See for yourself.

As fast as he had arrived, he jumped away.

After popping back into the Earth's atmosphere he kept flying in the same pattern, going slower. No other anca were near. Continuing his tour, he got a wonderful view of this delightful gem of a planet. It would be his home until this mission was brought to a conclusion.

A few minutes later, Dene returned to Beel's office.

"That was fast," said Beel, with a perfect smile on his face. His sharp eyes noticed that the colors of Dene's body had shifted.

"Now that I know what my new neighborhood looks like," said Dene hastily, "I need to begin my investigation. Perhaps you can advise me."

Beel asked, "Where would you like to begin?"

"Setting up a meeting with the Valdarians and the Sylumini would be helpful," said Dene. "I assume you would know who to contact, or could find out for me."

Beel got a frown on his face. "I can easily arrange for you to meet with the Valdarians. That shouldn't be a problem. I would advise you, however, that the Sylumini are unlikely to agree to a meeting. Naturally, I will put in a request on your behalf."

"That's their loss, not mine," said Dene. "From what I hear, the Sylumini don't like outsiders, and I'm the ultimate outsider."

"I will do my best to make those appointments," said Beel.

"Whatever you can get is fine," said Dene. "Thanks for offering."

Chapter 5 - Chephra

Scene 11 - The Valdarians

Chephra was a strict high security area. The Valdarians had agreed to allow Dene in for one meeting. Nothing had been acknowledged by the Sylumini.

The overall shape of Chephra was like a huge section of pipe. There was a circular outer shell which housed the engineering facilities, offices, and laboratories. The inside of the shell was empty. Colonization cruisers from Jeshmol were designed to fly through mode-tunnels such as this one. At the entrance they arrived from Jeshmol. At the exit they emerged into Nimulos. They shifted from their old world, to the new, inside the mode-tunnel. After the transformation the jeshie colonists would be taken to their new permanent colony between Earth and Mars.

Unfortunately for the emergency rescue, Chephra was still under construction.

The tunnel itself was buried beneath the shifting sands, west of the Nile River, in Egypt. The rocks and sand which filled the tunnel - from a human point of view - were nothing more than a light brown fog to jeshie pilots and anca support staff.

Getting through Chephra security took two hours. After getting his clearance, Dene was issued a visitor's badge, and escorted to the Portal Analytics Group. This was where Riana used to consult for the Valdarians. This was where the Sylumini had stolen priceless portal secrets from her.

Seated at the conference table were three anca. Gervaie was at the head. To her left were Cami and Farli. They had a happy glow about them which was entirely absent from their boss's demeanor. Cami was a design engineer and Farli was an instrumentation specialist. They were a committed couple who had met here at work.

33

"Welcome," said Gervaie, "you may sit there," pointing to the chair on her right.

Dene knew that Gervaie wanted nothing to do with him. She was a professional manager who ran her organization according to strict guidelines. It was bad enough that Riana had been a consultant here. Dene had a reputation for trouble. Gervaie did not like trouble.

The presentation that Dene had prepared did not go well. Gervaie tried everything to find some excuse to get rid of him. After he figured out how she was playing the game, he set a verbal trap.

During a particularly heated exchange Dene snarled, "It's not my fault your laboratory is riddled with Sylumini bugging devices."

Gervaie's head whipped around and she glared at him with hostility. "Captain Behchel sent his top security team in here and they removed those bugs."

"Stop right there," demanded Dene in a stern voice.

Gervaie was shocked. She did not like being spoken to in that tone of voice - especially in front of her subordinates.

"Questions are always welcome," she mumbled, with obvious irritation.

"This is not a question," said Dene sternly. "This is a statement of fact. I don't work for you. I'm a special ops professional. You're the one who follows the rules. I'm the one who finds clever ways of bending those rules."

"They told me you would be difficult," growled Gervaie.

"Riana gave you trouble. I'll be a more trouble than she ever was. Without my unwanted interference - your project is doomed," said Dene, in a loud voice.

"Our project is right on schedule," Gervaie began ...

Dene cut her off with a snap of his finger. "Take me to the lab where Riana used to work," he demanded, rising from his chair, pressing his knuckles on the table. "I'll show you what I mean."

Gervaie wanted to throw Dene out but her boss had told her to hear him out.

The Design Lab was in the back section of their suite of offices. The four of them left the drab conference room

34

and entered a place filled with highly sophisticated equipment.

"Now, I want you to reenact a typical day working with Riana," said Dene.

This took some time because Riana never had typical days.

Eventually they agreed to have Gervaie sit in Riana's seat, facing an imposing communicator dome. Cami took her usual place at the design dome. Farli went straight to his workbench so he could get some real work done while this charade was playing itself out.

"I will now perform a radical action," said Dene. "I will face in the same direction that Riana used to face." He hovered directly behind Gervaie, which irritated her enormously.

After making a visual survey Dene announced, "There's another one."

The four of them floated across the room to a standard piece of lab equipment.

"Can you see it?" asked Dene.

"See what?" asked Gervaie.

"Take a close look at the front panel," said Dene. "See the control knobs in this row. That one little knob at the end is a slightly different color and it's a teensy bit larger than the others. Now watch this."

With powerful fingers he pulled the knob off.

"See," said Dene, "it's a bugging device. You told me they had all been found. Well, here's another one. It was right in front of where Riana would have been explaining her strategy to your technical team."

Gervaie muttered, "I don't see how that could have gotten past our security team."

Dene laughed. "Be careful what you say. This is probably a live device and the Sylumini might be listening to everything we're saying. I brought along a silencer box." He reached in his pocket. "Goodbye Sylumini," he said, in a mocking tone. Then he snapped the bugging device inside the silencer.

"I should have noticed that," said Farli. "It didn't quite fit with everything else."

"You *could* have noticed it but most anca see what they expect to see," said Dene. "Let's go back to the conference room so we can discuss this in private."

Gervaie had a sinking feeling that her reputation was damaged. She trailed along behind the others so they couldn't see the pain on her face.

After the conference room door shut, Dene placed the silencer box on the table - to focus their attention on failure.

"All organizations have weaknesses," began Dene. "I'm going to turn this little device over to the Watchers so they can add it to their vast collection of circumstantial evidence against the Sylumini. The fact that I found it doesn't really change anything."

"That was pretty slick," said Farli, "the way you saw it and none of the rest of us did."

"I'm trained to do that," said Dene. "Let me ask you a few questions. After you order spare parts what happens?"

"Well, I send in my order," said Farli, "and the delivery cruiser comes to the back entrance. Our warehouse anca open all the boxes and inspect them."

"Where do you pick up the parts?" asked Dene.

"They're delivered right here to my work bench," Farli replied.

"What happens after that?"

"I sign for them and the delivery anca goes back to the warehouse," said Farli.

"What happened to the employee who delivered parts when Riana worked here?" asked Dene.

"Uh, now that you mention it, she got a job on another planet," Farli said. "It was a great opportunity for her."

"When I was being briefed for this assignment that topic came up," said Dene. "Someone with access to your lab could have gotten in here when none of you were around. The anca you mentioned was a long term employee with a suspicious work history before she got this job."

"She was really friendly," said Farli.

"Let me tell you something," said Dene, "that's the oldest trick in the book. I've used it myself. Jenissen explained to me how the Sylumini run their operation. At the top they have the best and brightest. At the bottom they have a flexible army of contractors who haven't done very well in life. If they are willing to risk doing something a little bit wrong, the Sylumini will set them up with a cushy job far away, even if they get caught. Many of them have been working in deep cover for years."

"I shouldn't have allowed this to happen," said Gervaie. "I'm responsible for this failure."

Dene gave her a warm look. "From what I hear you're one of the best technology managers in Captain Behchel's organization. That's why you were sent here, to one of the toughest assignments. There's a lot of things I haven't figured out yet but there's one thing I know for sure. You and I are going to have to work together, whether we like it or not."

"To be honest, I don't see how that's possible," said Gervaie.

"While Jenissen's away, I report to Ing," said Dene. "Ing talks to Larush. Larush talks to you. How hard is that?"

"I suppose that might work," said Gervaie.

"Jenissen has a few things he wants me to accomplish," said Dene. "Naturally, there is the rescue. The other thing is to find out what's really going on. The Sylumini have grown arrogant. Sarkon and Sarena have been unable, or unwilling, to control them. I need your help so I can bring Hamil and Hamine up to date."

Gervaie slumped in her chair. "I'll cooperate."

Scene 12 - The Sylumini

In a commanding room at the top of Sylumini Headquarters the Special Board was holding an emergency session. Everyone present had just been told that this so called diplomat, brought in by Jenissen, had found one of their bugging devices. They were here for damage control.

Khaletora, as always, led the meeting. "There was an unfortunate security lapse yesterday. The new courier had a meeting with the Valdarians. I want all of you to hear this recording."

Lanmon, head of the legal department, and an old friend of Khaletora's, placed a small audio device on the table. "My staff has reviewed this recording carefully. There

are some concerns but no problems of major significance."
He pressed the play button.

##

"I will now perform a radical action. I will face in the same direction that Riana used to face."

"There's another one."

"Can you see it?"

"See what?"

"Take a close look at the front panel. See the control knobs in this row. That one little knob at the end is a slightly different color and it's a teensy bit larger than the others. Now watch this."

(Skreek)

"See, it's a bugging device. You told me they had all been found. Well, here's another one. It was right in front of where Riana would have been explaining her strategy to your technical team."

"I don't see how that could have gotten past our security experts."

"Be careful what you say. This is probably a live device and the Sylumini might be listening to everything we're saying. I brought along a silencer box. Goodbye Sylumini."

(Click)

##

Khaletora quickly took control of the situation. "A minor success for Jenissen's spy. I don't think this space tramp can match our superior organization. Does everyone agree?"

Everyone agreed.

"Having said that I want to make sure we're not being overconfident," Khaletora declared, with that peculiar wave of his hand. "We know that the Valdarians are working on a secret plan to build a new type of rescue portal. That's why they brought Riana in as a consultant. We have our own portal project and it's imperative that we succeed before they do. Colonization contracts are our richest opportunity for rapid growth. This emergency gives us the entry point we've been hoping for. We will move beyond this minor setback and we will gain control of those contracts. Are there any questions?"

Lanmon hesitated before raising his hand. "There are persistent rumors that Riana has been moved to the Ishmili Observatory instead. Do we have any information on that?"

Khaletora turned to Ulta. "What information do we have?"

Ulta had been close to Khaletora for as long as Lanmon. Putting a carefully controlled spin on her reply she said, "Our office services employees at Chephra have reported a significant increase in the amount of time Riana has been spending at the Observatory. Personally, I don't see how one dreamer, a bizarre techno wizard and a freak evonim can compete against our engineering excellence."

"Step up monitoring of this situation," instructed Khaletora.

"We will," said Ulta, relaxing slightly.

With barely a quiver, Ulta and Lanmon exchanged knowing glances. A long time ago the three of them had been good friends. Things were different now. Big-K was starting to crack up. The pressure had gotten to him. The other two were worried.

"Well," said Khaletora, beaming that winning smile of his, "let's talk about something more important. Strong personal relationships are the key to our success. I have noticed recently that our dear friends, Sarkon and Sarena, seem to have cooled toward us. That can be fixed, of course, but we must be cautious during these turbulent times. Make sure that nothing about this incident is mentioned to anyone. Any more questions?"

There were no more questions from the Special Board.

"Well," said Khaletora with a grand smile, "I believe that settles this matter."

Chapter 6 - Hikli

Scene 13 - Governor Zeb

A couple of months later, Xen and Wun were staring out the window of the attic, where they lived at the Norovio. Down on the mansion grounds, their fellow workers were rushing around, cleaning up the last of the mess which had accumulated from lax living conditions. Both of them felt that, since they hadn't made the mess, they weren't going to help clean it up.

Yesterday there was an announcement that Governor Zeb would be making a major speech today at the Norovio. Zeb was the leader of Sector Forty Two (which includes the Wamilla Peninsula), of the Kemong Cloud Island.

The crisis facing Wamilla was that it had broken off from the mainland. The mode-quake had severely weakened the narrow corridor which used to contain the only road between the small peninsula and the enormous bulk of the cloud island. Aftershocks had crumbled that connection. Now, Wamilla was drifting away into the death trap of outer space.

Zeb had something new to report.

##

Pim was strutting around on the front steps with a speaker-horn in his hand. "governor zeb on way" "all personnel assemble at vans" "look sharp".

There was no way they could get out of this. Their beat up old NimuTrak was parked in front of the mansion, along with all the others. Reluctantly, they trudged down eight flights of stairs and took their places.

In the distance they could see a small group of cloud copters approaching. As these got closer there were gasps of excitement. The copter in front, which was enormous, was painted the same colors as the AmbuTrak fleet down by the hospital.

Four copters landed on the lawn - the big one first - followed by three executive copters. Pim rushed over to greet them. When Governor Zeb stepped out of the big copter, Pim was the first one to shake her hand.

After the usual delays, it was time for the speech.

Striding up to the microphone, Governor Zeb tapped it, 'pop pop'.

"greetings all you" said Zeb. "amazing job done by every one".

Polite applause.

Zeb, like all politicians, could talk forever, and at first it seemed like she was going to. But Zeb was also skilled at working the crowds. After she rattled off the obligatory pronouncements, she began telling a story which affected them all.

"we got two goodly rescue plans now" said Zeb. "see big cloud copter over there".

The crowd shouted out "oooh yeah".

"that new backup plan" said Zeb. "we test it later today".

"aww right" cheered the crowd, breaking into applause. All that hard work, all that big talk, and now there was finally something to show for it.

"rescue copter pick up ambutrak with patient inside" explained Zeb. "smooth ride to mainland" "fantastic achievement".

Everyone in this crowd knew that when this rescue was over they could leave crumbling Wamilla to find new homes over in Kemong.

"earth rescue plan still our best hope" continued Zeb. "two among you make huge breakthrough" "big copter take them to government lab" "they finish important work".

The crowd was not sure what this meant, as Zeb had planned.

The governor waited until the right moment, then sprung her announcement.

"two among you xen wun" shouted Zeb. "they invent rescue technology" "join us now onstage".

Xen and Wun, who were goofing off, had not been listening to the governor's speech. Those around them had to prod them into moving toward the stage.

The crowd roared out their approval. Xen and Wun were their rebel heroes. Now they were onstage, standing between Zeb and Pim.

Xen and Wun shrugged.

Pim waved his arms in the air, hands clenched, as if he was the champion who had made all this possible. If pictures of that made it to the nightly news, then everyone would believe it was true.

"we hear it for xen wun" shouted Governor Zeb.

The roar of joy from staff and crew was enormous. Two of their own were moving up to something big. Maybe this rickety rescue was going to work after all.

The way the AmbuCopter worked was brilliant. For this first field test they were going to use a NimuTrak, because it was the same size as one of the recently renovated AmbuTraks. After Xen and Wun loaded everything they could possibly fit into their van, it was super heavy.

The big rescue copter was going to be tested by taking Xen and Wun to the government lab over on the mainland. The roads were out. The van was heavy.

Four claws descended from the copter and clamped it tight. Xen and Wun were inside. Then, in an amazingly smooth ride, they lifted off and headed away.

The governor had wisely decided to go back in her own executive cloud copter. Just in case something went wrong with the test. An eager crowd, clapping and shouting, watched as the rescue copter became a small dot in the sky, heading for Namoush, the capitol city of Sector Forty Two.

The copter set them down on a lonely road, retracted the claws, then abruptly flew away. The first AmbuCopter rescue test had been a stunning success. Xen and Wun were confused.

"read note again" said Xen.

Wun searched his pockets and read aloud what had been given to him by one of the governor's assistants. "find evojesh lon" "she show government lab".

Since Xen was the supervisor, she made the decision. "van pointed that direction" "we drive that direction".

"you boss" said Wun.

After they drove down the road some distance they saw a car parked in front of a wide industrial gate. A plum colored evojesh was wildly waving her arms at them. They pulled up next to her car.

"welcome to maintenance yard" said Lon, sarcastically. "we here top secret mission".

Xen and Wun got out. Plows and cranes and other heavy equipment were stored on the other side of the fence. A battered sign above the gate read ...

Emergency Services Warehouse District

Lon held up two keys. "me given these at office" "one say hikli building".

She opened the front gate, both vehicles drove through, then she locked the gate behind them.

After driving through the warehouse district a couple of times they heard Lon beep her horn. They stopped and got out. There, on a warehouse door they had driven past already, was a small sign. "hikli building" it read in faded letters.

Lon tried the second key and, with a bit of jiggling, the door swung open. She found a light switch. They stepped inside.

"oh joy," said Wun, in wonder, "we got our lab equipment back".

##

After the mode-quake, Xen and Wun thought they had lost everything. Xen's apartment building, and Wun's modest home in the country, were obliterated. The NimuTrak Labs were flattened. All of the observatory technicians were reassigned to emergency services. At Norovio they started rebuilding their lives.

Noom the ishmili had worked diligently with Riana the anca, and Zeb the soto, to make the best of a bad situation. While Xen and Wun stayed at the mansion, work crews had been sent to salvage all of the equipment from their old laboratory - damaged or not.

"you do us goodly big favor" Xen said to Lon.

"not know what me do" said Lon. "not know why me here".

"what you work schedule" Xen asked Lon.

"me off duty" "want go home" said Lon, anxiously.

"when we see you again" asked Xen.

"tomorrow morning" said Lon, reluctantly.

"enjoy pleasant evening" said Xen.

"only got one set keys" said Lon.

"not need keys" said Xen. "we get into anything".

"good night".

"see you tomorrow".

"enjoy".

Lon didn't notice but, as she was getting into her car, a figure in the shadows was watching her.

Scene 14 - Hikli Laboratory

When Lon came back from Namoush the next morning she was astonished at the transformation inside the Hikli Building. The equipment had all been put in order. In the middle was their NimuTrak, which was the command center. Usable equipment formed a wall in one corner. Broken equipment was stacked up diagonally opposite, to be used for spare parts. Behind those two walls were Xen and Wun's rough apartments.

"good day huh" said Lon, using a standard soto greeting.

"maybe" muttered Xen. She was staring at a box of connectors.

There was an uncomfortable silence in the room, broken by the occasional sound of boxes being thrown around.

Wun came back with an accusing look. "you disconnect cable for ishmili dome" " you leave convertor in wall socket".

"so" said Xen, taking a belligerent stance.

"ishmili convertor still there" said Wun. "ishmili dome here" "we got call to make".

"ooooh that bad" admitted Xen. "bad bad bad bad bad".

Lon wanted to be anywhere except where she was right now.

Xen got a sneaky look in her eye. "maybe that lurker got one".

Wun got a happy look on his face, "aha".

Without saying a word Wun snuck out the front door and tiptoed around to the side.

Lurker had been listening in on their conversation through a broken window. He walked straight up to Wun.

"me name trz" said Lurker. "me you contractor".

Wun got right to the point. "need 2743 ishmili convertor".

"me find that" said the stranger named Trz. He was getting old, so he hobbled around the corner because of a bad knee.

A few minutes later he came back.

"got goodly connectors" said Trz.

Wun shook hands, "me name wun" "go inside to introduce".

Trz nodded his head eagerly.

Lon, who was totally stressed out, was shocked to see an ancient evojesh walk in, as if he owned the place. "who that".

"like you meet trz" said Wun. "this lon".

"glad to acquaint you lon" said Trz.

"that xen" said Wun.

Xen was angry at the world.

Trz emptied the bag on the table. Picking up one piece he said "2743".

Two minutes later the ishmili network was fully operational. Government Lab Hikli was now connected to Observatory Chephra for their call between worlds.

"we got super secret call to make" said Xen. "trz welcome".

This pleased Trz immensely. "me happy".

##

Exactly on schedule the ishmili dome showed two images. On the left was Lon, in Jeshmol. On the right was Vint, in Nimulos. She was from the Soto Guardians. He was from the Anca Guardians.

"Hello, is anybody out there? This is Vint calling."

As she had been instructed to do, Lon answered, "lon here" "you call come through clear".

45

What an exciting thrill this was for both of them. For the first time in either of their lives they were speaking to someone from a different world.

Riana, who spoke both anca and soto, did the translating from her place at the Observatory.

"Vint, I would like to introduce you to Lon, who is your guardian soto contact on the refugee team," began Riana. "lon me introduce vint who guardian anca on rescue team".

"pleased to meet" replied Lon, who was feeling better now.

Vint had been working on pronouncing Lon's name "Pleased to meet you, Lon. I look forward to working with you."

Lon's face lit up when she heard her name pronounced by an anca. "that my name" "you vint" "we work rescue". She had been practicing his name too.

"We will do everything we can to bring you over here safely," said Vint.

"we talk each tuesday thursday" said Lon. She had been told that this was the right thing to say.

"Yes, that is right," said Vint. "You and I will meet every Tuesday and Thursday, local Earth time, for a one hour meeting."

Their bosses on both sides had told them to keep the first meeting short.

"say bye now" Lon said.

"Good first meeting," Vint said.

"sign off two side". "Signing off both sides," announced Riana.

For the next few minutes Lon jabbered excitedly to herself. Xen following her around to bestow words of praise. After the exhilaration of speaking to someone from an invisible world, her natural distrust of strangers returned. Pointing at Trz, she demanded "who that".

This is what Xen had been waiting for. "me not know" "him tell us".

"me been long time here" Trz declared.

"how that be" asked Xen.

As the morning wore on, Trz unfolded a short version of his long life.

46

Early on he had been an ordinary evojesh, born on a regular life cloud. The first few million years had been spent studying mode-hopping. Like many evos before him, he journeyed throughout Jeshmol in as many forms as he could fit. When he started feeling old, and wasn't quite as peppy, he decided it was time to find a job with better security. Trz decided to work for the government.

That's how he became a loyal employee of the Kemong Emergency Services Department for almost, but not quite, a full one billion years.

Trz always did his job well, took every assignment they gave him, and attended every mandatory seminar. Then he began to notice something they had always warned him about. As he neared retirement age they began looking for ways to make his life miserable, so he would quit before becoming eligible for full benefits.

It didn't matter that he knew every part number without having to look it up. The fact that he remembered where each and every piece of equipment really was, rather than what the soto dome said, just irritated them. Trz held on as long as he could but then came the inevitable. They forced him into early retirement. The old geezer was gone.

Or so they thought.

Then came the Wamilla mode-quake. All of a sudden, all of that emergency equipment in the warehouse district was actually needed for something big and important.

Governor Zeb hired Trz as a contractor to help Xen and Wun at the new government lab in the Hikli building. Trz's reputation as the best parts guy around got him the job.

And here they were, four jeshies, sitting together as new found friends.

Scene 15 - Riana And Dene

Dene was working at the communicator dome in his apartment, in the diplomatic zone, which surrounds the south pole in Antarctica. He was at a broad table, looking out a wide window, where he could enjoy the view of endless ice. Three months had passed since his assignment to Earth and his investigation was proceeding smoothly.

47

Seeing a blinking icon, he opened a message from Ing. Just two words. "See Riana."

Riana rarely had visitors. Plus, she was almost never at home. Besides, no one could ever predict what she might do next. Oh well, the best plan was to start with the obvious and see if she was in her apartment.

Dene lived at the South Pole, so travel directions always began with the same simple rule - fly north. Heading out to the windy commons area, he adjusted his launch angle and flew toward England.

Glastonbury Tor is a stately hill in the southwestern corner of the British Isles. When he reached his destination he landed on top. Sinking halfway into the hill, he approached her front door.

Dene had never met Riana before.

After a short delay, he was quite surprised when the door swung wide open and she said, "We've got to talk."

The living room - if you could call it that - was filled with exotic equipment. None of it was familiar to him. There were four plain chairs and no other furniture. She sat down in her favorite seat and said, "Sit anywhere you want." He sat opposite her.

"Ing asked me to ... " he began.

She silenced him with a flick of her wrist. "Let me get right to the point. We're techies. None of us want to waste our time on stupid political intrigue. Are you going to do that for us?"

"That's why the ishmili sent me here," said Dene.

"Good," said Riana, "you need to meet them."

"Fine," said Dene.

Without another word, she rose from her chair and headed out the door. He followed quickly. They flew over France, above Sicily, then descended into the desert sands of western Egypt. After reaching Chephra it was much easier for Dene to get through security this time. Ing had placed his name on the official contractors list.

On the other side of the main checkpoint, Riana took Dene down a long corridor to one of those circular hallways which lead to offices and tech areas. At the very bottom was a door marked "ICO." This was the Ishmili Colonization Observatory.

Riana palm badged in and they floated inside. Offices and storage rooms were on the left. On the right was a huge work area. They entered a wide door on the far side.

Dominating the observatory was the biggest ishmili dome that Dene had ever seen. Sitting in front of it were two nimulons, who were so absorbed in their work that they didn't even notice two others had entered the room.

Riana swiveled their chairs around to get their attention. "Dene, meet Honat and Qusheem."

Honat might have been an ordinary anca if it wasn't for the fact that his eyes were enormous and shined like sparkling galaxies. He said, "Glad you finally got here."

Unlike Riana and Qusheem - Honat could not travel between worlds with his body. With his astounding mind, however, he could visualize cosmic connections which are far beyond the limited imaginations of others.

Qusheem was the oddest looking evonim Dene had ever seen. As a matter of fact, he was so strange that Dene had to look twice just to make sure he really was an evolutionary being from Nimulos.

"Bhujvaq," Qusheem said.

Oddly enough, Dene seemed to understand what he meant. "Yes, I would like to see what the Hikli Lab looks like."

Honat dragged an extra chair over and the four of them sat before the grand ishmili dome.

At that moment no one could be seen in the Hikli. The ishmili camera was pointed at a NimuTrak, which had the side door wide open, with cables running everywhere. Dene recognized its style and blue color immediately.

"I assume Jenissen briefed you," said Riana.

"Very little," said Dene. "He doesn't understand what you guys are trying to do."

"Here's what you need to know," said Riana. "We've got two observatory teams. We map Jeshmol from the nimulon side. Xen and Wun map Nimulos from the jeshie side.

"What do you map," said Dene.

"Portal parameters," said Riana.

"That's a tricky business," said Dene.

"Yeah," said Riana, "but getting a fleet of ambulances through a portal is trickier."

49

"Nearly impossible in a region this thin," said Dene.

"See that little blue toy sitting there on the console?" Riana picked it up and handed it to him.

Dene turned it around in his hand, "This is a scale model of a NimuTrak Observatory van. Just like the one we see in the dome."

"It was sent to us from that van you're looking at in the dome," said Riana. "We're developing a new portal technique. The first half of the test was them sending this to us. The second half of the test will be for us to send it back to them. If that works, more technology will need to be developed."

"Sounds like you guys have a lot of work ahead of you," said Dene.

"*You* have a lot of work ahead of you," said Riana.

"I thought you said I was doing dirty political tricks to shield you guys," said Dene.

"You are," said Riana. "The blue toy is your second assignment."

"When do I start?" asked Dene.

"Monday," said Riana. "You and Eberli will be working with Andy."

"I'll adjust my schedule," said Dene.

Scene 16 - Ing And Celene

Once a month Ing had a regularly scheduled meeting with Celene. Celene's bosses, Hamil and Hamine, were going to have full responsibility for the Jeshmol Colonization Project after they took over the anca administration on Earth. In the current administration, Sarkon and Sarena wanted nothing to do with the colonization project - with its unnatural need for high tech solutions. Ing and Celene always had a lot to talk about.

Today's topic was especially exciting for them.

"How did it go?" asked Celene, the moment Ing was seated.

"Jeshie Guardians made first contact with our Anca Guardians," answered Ing.

"That's bigger than big," said Celene.

"Now that the rescue project has finally recovered from the 'accident,' we need to adjust our expectations," Ing said. "I'm assuming that the two Guardian groups will figure out how to work together in a professional manner."

"Guardians have shared values," agreed Celene. "There will be problems, of course, but I'm sure that Vint and Lon will be able to resolve any issues."

"The Combined Observatory Group is an entirely different matter," cautioned Ing.

Celene laughed, "That's putting it mildly."

"We've got two rebel jeshies, three ridiculously independent nimulons, and now they've thrown Jenissen's special ops agent into the mix," said Ing.

"I heard that Dene was seen leaving Riana's apartment and flying with her to Chephra," chuckled Celene. "Rumors are running wild."

"I asked Riana to bring Dene to the Observatory so she could introduce him to the rest of the team," said Ing. "That meeting went well. Tomorrow she's going to take him to meet Melona and Andy."

"Ooh, I hadn't heard about that," said Celene. "Do you think that's wise?"

"We need a distraction," said Ing. "If the Sylumini are busy following Riana and Dene around, they'll be less likely notice what the Guardians are up to."

"No matter what we do, it's a dangerous game," said Celene. "The more I learn about the Sylumini, the more I distrust them."

"That's why our galactic leaders got special ops involved," said Ing. "I don't think the Sylumini are Dene's biggest problem, though."

"Hmm, what do you have in mind?" asked Celene, who was curious.

The Sylumini are a nasty bunch, and the Valdarians aren't much better, but I think Dene is facing a bigger problem than both of those organizations combined," said Ing.

"What would that be?" asked Celene, who was now alarmed.

Ing answered, "When I spoke to Riana about meeting Dene, she said she was going to put him through every tough test she could think of. He has to prove to her that she can trust him."

"Ooh hoo hoo hoo," blurted out Celene, "I would not want to be Dene. Mmmm mmm mm."

They both laughed so hard that the office staff outside wondered what was going on in the boss's office.

Chapter 7 - Guardians

Scene 17 - Noutashi

In Washington Square Park, crowds of weekenders were playing folk guitars around the fountain. All sorts of hipster attitudes were on display down there in evo land. Riana and Noutashi sat on top of the Arch at the entrance to the park. The two of them met every Saturday to talk about next week's plans for Melona. Noutashi was a professional guardian anca and Melona was her favorite client. Riana was the odd outsider who was meddling in Melona's life, in order to build a special type of portal, but very few understood the reasons why. On this particular Saturday they had invited Dene to join them because they needed to sort out additional responsibilities for Melona and Andy.

The two umbies were chatting when Noutashi glanced up and asked, "Is that him?"

Riana looked over. Dene was flying toward them from the south - above the nightclubs of Greenwich Village. "That's him alright."

"Good morning umbies," said Dene, "it's nice to see you today." He was hovering in the air in front of them, with his back to the folk singers down at the fountain.

"I'd like to introduce you to Noutashi," said Riana. "This is Dene."

"Pleased to meet you," he said.

"Hi", Noutashi said. This urbie didn't look at all the way she had expected. He was lean and tough from doing all those jumps. By comparison, Riana was ancient and ethereal. Both of them were old, by anca standards.

"Let's go where we can talk this over in private," suggested Noutashi.

"That would be best," agreed Dene.

They flew to a poverty stricken neighborhood a few blocks away. Gliding gracefully through the crumbling wall of a brownstone building, they entered a one room studio apartment, which was all Melona could afford after finally getting a job.

Dene took a quick look around. It was packed tight with all the worldly possessions of a young woman just getting started in life. Pretty things were neatly arranged on rickety shelves. He felt comfortable here.

Melona was making a cup of tea. As far as she was concerned, she was all alone in her tiny urban home. There was no way she would ever understand that three anca had just invited themselves in, to decide how they were going to use her.

"Have a seat," Riana said to Dene.

There was a small table in the middle of the room, much battered but solidly repaired. Four unmatched chairs were placed around it. Dene picked the one where he had the best view.

The two umbies sat down, leaving Melona's regular seat available.

Noutashi asked, "Vint told us that you've been brought in on this project. Why is that?"

Dene had his answer ready. "When Jenissen assigned me to this planet I was expecting a different line of work. Since Jenissen is away on other business, he put Ing in charge of my day to day activities. Ing wants me to stop the Sylumini from shoving their way in on this rescue mission. What do you think I need to know?"

"There's only one thing you need to know," said Noutashi, "stay away from my girl. Riana is enough trouble."

"I've been told I'll be working with Eberli and Andy," said Dene. "Riana mentioned that you might feel protective about your client. On the other hand, if I need to understand how we're going to work with Andy, then I need to have at least basic knowledge of Melona."

"Stay away from my client," said Noutashi.

Just then, Melona joined them at the table. She sat in her regular place, facing Noutashi. They watched from the invisible realm while the young woman set down her cup of hot tea without spilling a drop.

"She's such a wonderful person," whispered Noutashi, "with warm feelings and worthy dreams. I don't want her to get hurt."

"Nobody wants her to get hurt," said Dene, "but there's more to this than that."

"What do you mean?" asked Noutashi, with a suspicious scowl.

Dene pointed his finger at the wall and asked, "Do you know what's over there?"

Noutashi turned her head, "Boston?"

Dene said, "I'm not sure what this Boston thing is but in that direction are jeshie refugees in need of our help. We don't want them getting hurt either."

"What does that have to do with Melona?" snapped Noutashi.

"I need to ask you a question before I give you an answer," said Dene. "Why was Melona chosen for this project?"

"Riana never tells me anything," complained Noutashi. "Ask her."

"I asked Honat instead," said Dene. "The jeshies chose Andy a long time ago. Then the jeshies matched him up with Cynthia. After Cynthia died, the first rescue plan died along with her. So they came up with a second rescue plan. Now the jeshies need Melona. That's their decision, not ours. They're the ones who need to be rescued."

"Andy and Cynthia lived together," said Noutashi. "Melona is separated from Andy by an entire continent."

"The Sylumini stole portal secrets from the first plan. That put them in a competitive position, " said Dene. " Look at how much progress they've already claimed. The second plan is designed to prevent the Sylumini from figuring out what we're doing."

"Why Melona?" demanded Noutashi. She wasn't letting go of this. Noutashi was going to protect her client.

"Through no fault of her own, Melona was born with the perfect soto colors to suit the second plan," said Dene. They need her because no other person, in the right place, has such a precise match. You've worked with portal people before. You know the drill."

Noutashi and Eberli had spent thousands of years working on people powered portals in the ancient days. Chephra was being built to replace those old portals with new machine portals. Chephra wasn't ready. This rescue needed people now.

A deep silence descended upon the room. Outside the window, the urban sounds of wailing sirens could be heard. Three anca, living on one planet, in a vast co-mingling of worlds, had deep thoughts.

Melona picked up her cup of tea and blew gently across the top. Taking a tiny sip she decided it was still too hot. Setting the cup down again, she leaned back in her chair, sharing the table with invisible beings.

Scene 18 - Eberli

In the North Beach section of San Francisco the Phoenix Coffee House had been a well known landmark since the 1950s. Walk in customers had slowed to a trickle. The lease was going to expire at the end of 1963. That would be a tremendous relief for the owner, Pika Pablera. The money just wasn't there anymore.

Pika was going to throw a "lease is dead" party at the end of the year. He was calling it The Last Grand Slam Poetry Jam. All their friends had been invited - the ones they could still find anyway.

At street level was the coffee house. Downstairs in the basement was what they called the Phoenix Poetry Center. It had been an informal clubhouse for the youthful hipsters of cool jazz existentialism, expressed in shades of black.

As a favor to a longtime friend, Andy had agreed to help get the place ready.

When Riana and Dene glided through the walls of the Poetry Center they saw Eberli sitting in a bright red chair. Andy was fixing something on the small stage.

"Hey, howya doing, you must be Dene," said Eberli, getting up to shake his hand.

"Nice to meet you," said Dene, "how's things."

"Doing alright," said Eberli. "Welcome to the Phoenix."

Glancing around, Dene saw evidence of a faded bohemian past. "Uh, Riana mentioned something about an evo party she wants you and me to work on. What's that all about?"

"Have a seat, get comfortable, no hurry," said Eberli.

Choosing a green chair, Dene sat down at a small bistro table with Eberli. Riana went to a yellow chair, two tables away, so she could listen in. She was testing Dene.

For the past month Dene had been working at the Observatory. He showed up during regular work hours. The other three came and went as they pleased.

"Have you heard that I've been working at the Observatory?" Dene asked Eberli.

"That's a hot topic these days," said Eberli. "The Other World Observatory is a hard place to get into."

"I've learned a lot about how the second rescue plan is supposed to work," said Dene. "Now I would like to do something which Riana never does."

"What's that?" asked Eberli, glancing at Riana.

"I want to tell you what you need to know," said Dene.

"Mmmm," said Eberli.

Dene got comfortable in his chair. "What do you know about the NimuTrak?"

"Nothing," said Eberli.

"A few months ago you and Riana were in the bookstore with Andy," said Dene. "She disappeared."

"She sure did," chuckled Eberli. "That's fine with me. Riana does all sorts of stuff. But Noutashi is still bent out of shape about that. Whooooeee."

"In both bookstores Riana simply shifted into the NimuTrak, then back again," said Dene. "She didn't go anywhere."

"I'm having trouble visualizing that," said Eberli.

"You were inside the NimuTrak too," said Dene.

"I was!" exclaimed Eberli.

"You and Andy were inside with two jeshies. Riana was working with them on the second rescue plan," Dene explained to Eberli. "At the Poetry Jam, that very same NimuTrak is going to be parked right over there, on that stage."

Eberli glanced over at Andy, who was installing new speakers. "Why?"

"At Chephra we have the Observatory studying portal conditions on the Jeshmol side," answered Dene. "Over on the Jeshmol side there are NimuTrak Observatories studying portal conditions on our side. Then the mode-quake hit. Around here I believe you call that an earthquake."

"Yeah, earthquake," said Eberli. "San Francisco got destroyed by one about fifty years ago. I was there. Those were tough times."

"Here's what you need to know so we can do this poetry jam right," said Dene. "Andy and Cynthia used to be the two portal guides. Then the Sylumini stole their information from Riana and used it to built their own portal. Our new plan uses equipment inside the NimuTrak to prevent the Sylumini from figuring out what we're doing the second time around. That's why the jeshie van is going to be parked onstage. Ulta and her team are clever but, as far as we know, they cannot spy on equipment inside an alien NimuTrak."

"Don't count on fooling the Sylumini," warned Eberli.

After listening in on their conversation, Riana came over to their table. "You've got this thing figured out. You don't need me." She flew through the ceiling.

Eberli and Dene were on their own.

Andy finished installing new speakers on the old stage.

Dene said, "Let's block out a preliminary plan. We can change it later."

"Ready when you are," said Eberli.

The two of them drifted over to where Andy was straightening up.

"What's this thing?" asked Dene, tapping a large wooden decoration on the backstage wall."

"That's the Wooden Phoenix," said Eberli. "It's become a mascot for the bopsies. Andy carved it with his chainsaw, then finished it with chisels."

"Who are the bopsies?" asked Dene.

"Uh, to simplify, the bopsies are Andy's friends," said Eberli. "On the east coast, fifteen or twenty years ago, they had a style of music called hard bop jazz. Out here on the west coast there was a mellower version called bopsie jazz. These kids adopted that as their nickname."

"Here's what we need to do," said Dene. "The van will be parked right here. My position will be this wooden thing on the wall. Andy will be in the cargo bay. Two jeshies will be in the cab, operating the experimental portal equipment.

58

You will be out in the audience with your guardian buddies. Ulta will have her spy portal somewhere nearby."

"Ulta?" asked Eberli. He despised the Sylumini.

"This event is bait for Ulta," said Dene. "My job is to trick her."

"You're being way over confident," said Eberli.

"You worry about getting the crowd pumped up for renewed portal duty," said Dene, "Ulta is my problem."

Eberli shook Dene's hand. "You got yourself a deal."

Scene 19 - Vint

Guardian Anca Headquarters is located high in the rugged mountains of South Island, in New Zealand. Vint is the Director of Human Cultural Creativity, North American Region. Among his many responsibilities was this special project with Noutashi, Eberli and Riana. Dene had now gotten involved. The time had come for Vint to make sure he understood what Dene was trying to accomplish.

A short jump got Dene from the diplomatic zone to Vint's office, unseen.

The early part of the meeting was devoted to timelines, milestones and gap analysis. Vint was a master planner but this particular project had dark corners which seemed impossible to illuminate.

At one point Vint mentioned, "You know what I can't understand? Lon keeps telling me we need these massive amounts of dual atmosphere. Why?"

"Because of the lawyers," said Dene.

"Nobody told me anything about lawyers," grumbled Vint.

"That's good," said Dene. "Ing wanted me to be the first one to explain this to you."

"How did Ing get involved?" asked Vint.

"As the ishmili representative for planet Earth, she's the one who filed a lawsuit against the Sylumini," said Dene. "There was a ruling in her favor last week."

"How does that affect us?" asked Vint.

"The Inter Regional Courts at Hierashu ruled that the Sylumini are guilty of obstructing the rescue of jeshies," said Dene, waiting for Vint's reaction.

"Oooof," said Vint. "The Inter Regionals give me a headache."

"Reconciling Nimulos law with Jeshmol law is a dry subject, suitable only for experts," agreed Dene. "To answer your question, though, that ruling affects what Eberli and I need to do at the poetry jam."

"Now you've really got me confused," said Vint. "Where does the poetry jam fit in?"

"Simple," said Dene, with a twinkle in his eye, "that's how we're going to sneak the lawyers in."

"If you want my personal opinion," said Vint, "We already have enough lawyers."

"These are jeshie lawyers," said Dene. "First time they've been assigned to Earth. Probably won't be the last."

"I thought we were bringing over construction specialists for the Gheney Hospital," said Vint.

"We are," said Dene. "We're also bringing in lawyers, along with their staff, and a large team of special investigators. When you add it all up, Eberli and I are expected to bring ten thousand jeshies over to our side, using a new portal technique of untested design."

"That's a monumental challenge," warned Vint.

"Let me fill you in on a few details," said Dene. "You need more facts so you can think this thing through carefully."

"Please do," said Vint, looking grumpy.

"As you are well aware," said Dene, "the jeshie rescue colony here on Earth must be temporary. We are legally required to transport them to the permanent colony, between Earth and Mars, after those facilities get built. Because the courts ruled against the Sylumini, we were issued a brand new colony permit. Now it's for thirty years, with up to fifty thousand colonists. The old permit, which is about to expire, was for ten years and ten thousand colonists. And that explains why Lon keeps telling you that we need such tremendous amounts of dual atmosphere."

"Thank you for explaining that to me," said Vint. "What the jeshies are investigating?"

"Cynthia and Wendy's deaths caused the delays which cancelled the first rescue plan. The jeshie lawyers are here to establish who was responsible."

Vint got a cynical look in his eye. "If, as some suggest, the Sylumini had a hand in that foul deed, then no amount of lawyers will be able to prove their guilt. They never get caught."

"In anca court, what you say might be true," admitted Dene. "On the other hand, in the inter regional courts - evidence from anca, soto, and ishmili can be admitted into evidence."

"The Sylumini are masters of deception," said Vint.

"Two can play that game," said Dene, with a gleam in his eye. "There's something else you need to know."

"What would that be?" asked Vint.

Dene smiled, "The Sylumini have not been told that our temporary colony permit just got upped because they are not allowed to know about this team of jeshie lawyers. It's an ongoing investigation. Nothing will be made public until the jeshie team reports their findings to the inter regional courts."

Vint seemed happy but cautious. "I hope this might be the tipping point."

"Could be, but isn't yet," said Dene. "It's up to us to make this work."

"I'm afraid to say this but, after all the disappointments we've had maybe, just maybe, we will finally be able to bring justice to this planet."

"That's why they sent me here," said Dene. "Eberli is going to help me do my job. The next few years will be tough and we must not be weak. An opportunity like this will never come our way again."

Chapter 8 - Grand Slam Poetry Jam

Scene 20 - River Of Life

Bopsie Lewis and the Redwood Hipsters were wailing. The crowd was in an ecstasy they hadn't experienced for years. Andy was in the sound booth with Bongo. Both of them were grinning because what was going down on tape was awesome.

Norbert the Poet, street eccentric extraordinaire, was at the microphone. He was reciting his endlessly scribbled epic, "The Death Of Hipness." Pika Pablera, owner of the coffee house, was mad at Norbert because the audience was wilting like lettuce dropped on a hot summer beach. Wilted customers don't buy strong coffee and sugary snacks. This was Pika's last chance to get some much needed cash before the lease snapped shut.

Eberli, along with dozens of his guardian buddies, were working the crowd. They'd been with these people many times before, opening portals here at the Phoenix. It was a well trained human crew. They'd been doing this since 1955. The citizens of the west coast jeshie colony had all entered the underground through this basement. Tonight would be their first attempt to start staffing the east coast colony.

Across the street, Ulta and her techies had set up their portable portal on the rooftop. Everyone knew they were spying. No one seemed to care.

In the corner of the sound booth, Dene worked on some mysterious plan. Riana was nowhere to be seen. On the audio desk was a soto dome, customized by Qusheem. With it Dene could see images from the dashboard dome in Xen and Wun 's blue van, which was parked onstage. Norbert the Poet sure did look weird in soto colors. Not that he wasn't weird anyway.

Alicia Hathaway, Cynthia's best friend from Frisco, was queen of tonight's crowd. Back in the day - when this place was really hopping - Bongo and Alicia, along with Andy and Cynthia, had been the force which kept this poetry center alive.

Xen and Wun, who sat quietly onstage, spied on Ulta while she was spying on them. They couldn't decrypt her signals but they could learn a great deal about her technique from the search patterns she used. Ulta wanted desperately to get in on the portal game. Xen was equally determined to keep her out.

Eberli was portal master for the evening, as he had been many times before. The North Beach Guardians had been getting ready all week. With Cynthia gone, they were going to use a synthetic portal tuner invented by the jeshies. He directed the guardians to play the people, according to tonight's newly devised techniques. When the mood felt just right, and Alicia was at the peak of her powers, Eberli whispered something to Alicia's guardian.

All of a sudden Alicia got a strong hunch. She sidled up to Pika. From her hip pocket she took folded papers and showed them to him. He nodded yes.

Alicia sauntered back toward the sound booth.

Pika plunged through the crowd to get at Norbert.

Bongo was in on the plan. When he saw Alicia headed their way, he turned to Andy and said, "You're on in one minute."

"On what?" asked Andy, who was tweaking the knobs on the sound board.

"On stage," said Bongo.

"What broke?" asked Andy. "The sound levels look good to me."

"You're not fixing anything," said Bongo, "you're reading something."

Alicia opened the door. "Andy - I want you to read Cynthia's poem. Don't argue with me. The bopsies need you. Do it now."

Andy was speechless. He hated being under the lights.

Pika was onstage with Norbert. Both were angry. Bongo muted the mic. Norbert began shouting out his poem. Two bulky friends of Pika's picked up the babbling poet and carried him offstage. Bongo turned the mic back on.

"Let's have a big round of applause for Norbert the Poet," Pika announced grandly.

Rude remarks and cat calls erupted from the audience.

Alicia dragged Andy onstage.

"Let's hear it for Andy and Alicia," shouted Pika.

Whoops and admiring whistles erupted from the audience.

Alicia held that paper high. "Do you remember The River Of Life?"

"Yeeeeaaaaaaah!"

"Who wrote it?" shouted Alicia.

"Cynthia! Cynthia! Cynthia!"

"I honor of her memory, I think we need to hear it one more time," yelled Alicia. "Andy is gonna read it for us."

Andy couldn't escape. These were his friends and they needed him. He took the poem from Alicia. Seeing Cynthia's curlicue handwriting made a tear appear on his cheek.

Dene took his position inside the wooden phoenix. Cynthia's poem was all about the camping trip where this phoenix had its origins. Dene merged with the wood. A soothing field of energy surrounded Andy.

"Whoop! Whoop! Raaaah! Raaaah!" shouted the crowd.

The Redwood Hipsters struck up the theme song. Sweet mellow jazz blossomed from their solid souls. When Bossman Jones finished the sax intro, the reading began.

Andy wiped away his tears on his shoulders.

The audience knew their parts by heart.

Hey bopsies!
Once upon a zany night
     we got a real bad case of restless feet
When the wine was shining
     and the morning sun was red
So we decided to seek the purity
     of the holy forest and go
        c a m p i n g
Cats and kitties piled into the big green van,

woody wagon, and mama jama car
We drove in enlightened madness
    to where the redwood trees are
        T A L L
A mysterious lake found us
    after guiding us down a wrong road
The lake sang to us
    from whispering cold stone shores
Let me hear it from you now
    what was it like in that forest
        (AUDIENCE) COLD
    what did we burn to stay warm
        (AUDIENCE) WOOD
    what did we drink to stay mellow
        (AUDIENCE) WINE!

Hey bopsies!
The golden morning sun found us
    shivering by still waters
So we scrounged dregs of wine for breakfast
    and cruised out to cop some more
The cat at the counter clued us
    to a cool groove called
        r a f t i n g
So we scarfed down thick buttermilk pancakes
    and brandy laced coffee
Then we laid out the sawbucks for
    river rafts that took us
        D O W N
The River of Life
    on magical waters
Where we floated blissfully
    between earth and sky
Let me hear you dig that scene
    how did the water look
        (AUDIENCE) SPARKLY
    who was on those rafts
        (AUDIENCE) BOPSIES
    what kept us floating
        (AUDIENCE) WINE!

Hey bopsies!

Mean old Monday trashed our groove
>out there in the dappled redwoods

We drowned our campfire
>with sacrificial waters from the lake

The dark shadow of the real world
>cast us out of the holy forest to go
>>b a c k   h o m e

We blew grateful kisses
>to the River of Life

And piled in for our
>laughing journey back to the big
>>C I T Y

The clouds in the sky quivered
>as we roared down the coast road

Singing songs that shimmered
>like the River of Life

Let me hear you tell it like it was
>did we want to go home
>>(AUDIENCE) NO

>what did we drink on those winding roads
>>(AUDIENCE) WINE

>and why are we here tonight ?
>>(AUDIENCE) MORE WINE!

Andy held the poem high, like a sports trophy after a championship game.

"Cynthia! Cynthia! Cynthia!" chanted the crowd.

Bopsie Lewis gave the signal and the band gave it their all.

"Bopsie! Bopsie! Bopsie!" shouted the audience. They were standing on chairs, wildly waving their arms in the flickering lights.

Wun had his eyes fixed on the mode-shifter. The portal began to shimmer. Andy felt the surge and went with the flow.

A scout from Jeshmol slipped through to make sure conditions were safe. All good. Jeshie colonists poured through, first by the hundreds, then by the thousands.

Andy blew kisses to the audience. The invisible horde flowed through the basement.

Dene could see clearly in jeshie world. Xen held up two fingers, which meant they were ready for the second test.

From the front seat, Wun readjusted the mode-shifter.

Emerging from the wooden phoenix, Dene took up a position behind Andy. Three evos were lined up perfectly, thanks to the guardians. Andy stood behind the microphone. Norbert sat sullenly at a table. Alicia was hanging out in the sound booth with Bongo.

Wun pressed the small red button.

Dene touched Andy's shoulders.

The little blue toy suddenly appeared on the dashboard.

Their wacky experiment had actually worked.

As the last of the jeshie colonists came shuffling through, Dene held Andy steady.

Suddenly, Xen and Wun both snapped alert in the front seat. Dene kept his hold on Andy but leaned forward so he could see the dashboard dome.

"replay" said Xen.

Wun looped the image. A bright green flash appeared, then vanished. They watched it again and again.

"what that" asked Dene.

"cloud wanderer" replied Xen.

"why" asked Dene.

"not know what they do" said Xen.

Wun closed the portal. Then he picked up his little blue toy and admired it.

Scene 21 - Ulta's Doubts

Ulta sat in her favorite chair, staring out the upper window of her elegant home. All was darkness. Her house sat on top of a rustic hill, overlooking the southern shores of the island of Tasmania. She watched whitecaps dance across dim choppy waters. Her icy inner control was beginning to crack.

Yesterday, the Special Board had ordered her to set up the portable portal so she could spy on Dene and Eberli. Riana had stayed away, for some reason.

From a purely technical point of view, last night had been a fabulous success. The Sylumini machine portal had performed better than ever. They had seen, in pastel detail, a stream of jeshies flowing through the basement. This was a testament to all the fine work done by her expert scientists, engineers, and technicians.

Somehow, Cynthia's old familiar soto yellow color could be seen in the data captured by the spy equipment. That would explain how they had been able to get the portal open. It did not explain how they managed to get that rare color. Cynthia was dead.

Ulta suspected that Dene had tricked her. The Special Board did not want to hear about tricks. They demanded answers.

Something bigger worried her even more.

For many years it was common knowledge that the jeshies had built a colony here on Earth, somewhere near San Francisco.

The terrans were involved in a big way and that was disturbing. It was well known that the terrans despised the Sylumini. Ten thousand new jeshie colonists had found homes waiting for them. The speed with which they flowed through to safety was alarming. Most of them appeared to be migrating east, which was bad news for the Sylumini.

What alarmed Ulta the most was how vast this colony seemed to be. Jeshie tunnels, which had been no more than speculation, now appeared in the spy dome as a vast underground network.

Potentially, that meant ten thousand new adversaries. How many were down there already? How many more would be coming? Why did they need so many? Who authorized this?

Looming over these grim statistics was a crisis which none dared say out loud. Big-K was going insane. Ulta and Lanmon had known Khaletora longer than anyone. They had worked together, as a management team, on their previous evo planet. When they reached Earth, they were good friends, on a grand adventure.

Impossible expectations had pushed Big-K over the edge. Ulta suspected that shadow agents from Andromeda were influencing her boss in the direction of a bad exit.

Hints were elusive. Her own career was being dragged into the abyss.

In the darkness of night, alone in her silent home, doubts began to bubble up inside her hardened exterior. Some other night she would have fired up her communicator dome to attack some challenging problem. This night, alone in the gloom, she allowed her mind to follow whatever path it confronted.

As the first faint glow of Darimia's rays touched the morning horizon, Ulta threw the pillow she had been clutching to the floor. Then she went downstairs to bed.

Scene 22 - Cami And Farli

Larush was Chief Executive Officer of the Valdarians at Chephra. She had met Dene only once, his first day on Earth, when Jenissen introduced him to the rival leaders of the portal community. Larush and Khaletora were about as different as two CEOs could possibly be but - on that very first day - both of them believed that Dene was doomed.

What a difference a few months makes.

While she was getting ready for work this morning, her taper device buzzed. It was Captain Behchel, the ultimate boss of all Valdarians. On Saturday night, at the Phoenix Poetry Center, a major test had resulted in a massive breakthrough. Riana's Plan was now officially approved at the highest levels. Dene and Eberli had guided this project through to phase one completion. The jeshie rescue was now back on track, after a depressing delay of several years.

Captain Behchel told Larush what he expected her to do. Now it was her turn to inform Gervaie about some organizational changes.

##

When Larush got to the Portal Analytics Department, Gervaie was already hard at work, even though her shift didn't begin for another hour.

"Oh, I didn't expect you this early," said Gervaie. "What can I do for you?"

Larush said, "There are going to be some staffing changes. Is anyone else in the office?"

"Not yet," said Gervaie, feeling nervous.

"Good," said Larush, shutting the door and pulling a chair close to the desk.

"I got a call from Captain Behchel at home this morning," Larush told her.

Lurking fear became near panic in Gervaie's unsettled mind.

Larush was so delighted by the good news that she didn't notice. "The Captain told me that Riana's Plan passed a major milestone. The next phase is to get it scaled up to industrial proportions."

Gervaie tried to keep her voice steady but it cracked when she asked, "How will that affect Portal Analytics?"

Larush replied, "Cami and Farli are going to be reassigned."

"I've been expecting this," sighed Gervaie, hanging her head in shame. "I shouldn't have let the Sylumini steal our trade secrets."

Larush was shocked at Gervaie's reaction. "Oh no, it's not like that at all. Everything is fine."

But Gervaie had been waiting for this doom for so long that she could not be consoled. "I understand. I let you down."

"Oh, I see. You're still worried about that bugging device, aren't you," said Larush. "That was never a problem."

Taking a closer look around Gervaie's office, Larush noticed that all of her personal items - which used to make it feel so comfortable - had been taken home. That's a sure sign that an employee either expects to get fired, or has already found another job.

Some reassurance was in order. "The Sylumini have bugging devices everywhere. Let me remind you that Celene threw them out of Ayamara because of that. Now her staff works in an office that they had to build with their own hands."

Gervaie glared at the barren shelves. "I suppose her problems are bigger than mine."

"Sit back, relax, hear what I have to say," said Larush. "An odd role reversal has taken place. Riana used to work in your lab as a consultant. Now, Cami and Farli will be working as consultants at the Ishmili Observatory. You'll get them back as soon as the rescue is over."

Looking bewildered, Gervaie said, "I try to do the best I can."

Larush addressed Gervaie's fears more carefully. "Think about it this way. Riana, Honat and Qusheem are all brilliant. They are also notoriously impossible to deal with. Can you imagine any one of them submitting a project proposal, requesting authorization for scarce Valdarian resources, then pushing the project through the system."

In spite of her inner pain, Gervaie couldn't help but laugh. "That would be absurd."

"That's why we need to send Cami and Farli in there," said Larush. "When they come back to you, they will bring the Observatory's new technologies back with them. That's why the Captain wants this transfer. We need to get our hands on what their hands develop. Cami and Farli are perfect for the job."

"I've always said we were under-leveraging the Observatory," said Gervaie.

"There's more good news that goes along with this assignment," said Larush. "Cami and Farli will be in daily contact with Xen and Wun."

"I don't believe I've ever met Xenunwun," said Gervaie.

"Xen and Wun are two jeshies," Larush informed her. "Ing combined both Observatory groups into one team."

"What about the language problem?" asked Gervaie.

"Cami speaks soto fluently," said Larush.

"Oh, I didn't know Cami had studied soto," Gervaie said. "It's a difficult language."

"We try to keep this quiet," whispered Larush, "but when Cami worked at the Lindar mode-tunnel, she became good friends with a soto named Beq. They worked together in the same lab. Eventually, they performed all of their day to day routine using only the soto language."

"Now that you mention it, I vaguely remember hearing something about that," said Gervaie.

"Unfortunately," whispered Larush, "Beq abandoned her post one day. Nobody has seen her since."

"Was there an accident?" asked Gervaie.

"That's been thoroughly investigated," said Larush. "Signs of instability had been building for a long time. Beq made an important mathematical discovery. Nothing can be proven, but apparently Beq disappeared into one of those nether regions, and has not been heard from since."

"That's horrible," said Gervaie.

"Anyway, hush hush about all this," said Larush. "We don't want any scandals."

"Of course not," said Gervaie.

"I think I hear someone out there," said Larush.

"That's probably Cami and Farli," said Gervaie. "They get in before the others."

"Let them get settled first," said Larush. "Then we'll tell them."

"While we're waiting, can you tell me more about this new breakthrough that got Captain Behchel so excited?" whispered Gervaie.

Larush shook her head. "When I asked the Captain about that he couldn't give me a solid answer. All he said was something about a little blue toy."

Chapter 9 - Paliyur

Scene 23 - Deadly Bazelium

Dene was waiting in line at the entrance to the Paliyur Tunnel. It was Tuesday morning, the last day of 1963, and commuter traffic was heavy. A long line of hovering anca waited in the thin sunshine of Greenland, edging toward the shadow at the tunnel's edge. Sometimes the line moved faster, sometimes slower, for reasons which made no sense. He had an appointment with Ing.

At the exit in Paliyur the crowd scattered. Zipping to the opposite side of the sphere, Dene entered a labyrinth of equipment rooms. Flying fast down narrow passages he came to a halt between a network switching station and an atmosphere filtration unit. In front of him was Ing's office. No sign was on the door. Visitors were not expected unless they knew where to find her.

"Good morning," she said. Ing never looked happy.

He sat in the only chair. "It is a good morning."

"Honat mentioned something about sealing the planetary bubble," said Ing.

"He gets involved with Lumbia's work sometimes," said Dene, trying to lead Ing into revealing what her motives were.

"Bazelium," Ing said, bluntly.

"A deadly mineral that is absolutely illegal everywhere in Nimulos," said Dene.

"What do you know about it?" asked Ing.

"Once upon a time, I used to work as a bazelium smuggler," replied Dene, relaxing, now that he knew what the issue was. "It was my cover for an operation to expose an unexplained epidemic."

"Why do you need this deadly substance?" asked Ing.

"The jeshies are the ones who need it," said Dene.

"For what possible reason?" asked Ing.

"To seal the planetary bubble," said Dene.

"You will now explain to me exactly what you mean by that," insisted Ing.

"Every time this rescue plan gets bigger, we have to expand our dual atmosphere requirements. All planetary bubbles are leaky. Bazelium from our side, mixed with a specialized jeshie compound, is the best sealant available. By the time their work crews get finished, everything will be perfectly safe. You can look it up on Ostramona.Net."

Ing looked it up. When deadly bazelium was properly compounded with jeshie minerals it was perfectly safe. She continued reading the entire article.

"It says here that there could be some serious side effects," said Ing. "In some cases, evos might get bubble fuddled."

"Oh yeah, they're gonna get bubble fuddled alright," said Dene. "That's a big part of our plan. When people get goofy like that, they produce a lot more of the dual atmosphere components we need. Just ask Lumbia. She can talk about it for hours."

"You still haven't convinced me to authorize your outrageous plan," said Ing.

Dene decided it was time to spring his big surprise. "Actually, an alien flash being is behind this crazy plan."

"Flashes don't deal with us. We don't interfere with them," she said, looking even less happy than before.

"When I was at the poetry jam, Xen and Wun noticed a jeshie flash slide over to our side," said Dene. " Flashes don't deal with us so I ignored it. Then Riana got involved."

Ing got a suspicious look. He was deliberately provoking with her. She didn't want to play his game. "Sit," she commanded. Turning away from him, she powered up her ishmili dome. Texting went back and forth for several minutes. "Tell me all you know," she demanded.

"An unknown alien flash being is somewhere in Roshomon. Riana says he needs to have the planetary bubble sealed tight. She asked me what I know about bazelium. I told her what I told you. That's all I know," said Dene.

Ing continued interrogating him, "How do you plan on smuggling this deadly substance in?"

"Nothing to smuggle," said Dene. "I hand it over to the jeshies."

"They're invisible," pointed out Ing.

"Riana says she knows how get around that," said Dene.

Ing sighed. "I'll let Chief Gromo know he should leave you alone."

"Much appreciated," said Dene.

"Moving on to the next subject - arrangements for your meeting with Captain Behchel have been finalized," Ing said.

"I saw the itinerary you sent over," said Dene. "Everything looks fine."

"In that case, I will approve your travel permit for the Roshomon star group," said Ing.

"I never bother with travel permits," said Dene.

"But I do," said Ing. "Jenissen left me in charge of you while he's away. I'm not taking any chances." She tapped away at the dome controller and submitted the forms.

"Thanks," said Dene.

"Is there anything you need from me?" asked Ing.

"One small favor," said Dene.

"Ask," said Ing.

"Can you arrange for an interview with Cynthia," asked Dene.

"Why would you want to speak with her?" asked Ing.

"At the poetry center last Saturday I saw how much Cynthia meant to Andy. Actually, she's very important to all of the bopsies," said Dene. "If Melona is going to play a new role, based loosely on Cynthia's original role, then I need to understand how we got into this situation. There are a lot of, you know, *stories* floating around."

"Cynthia was one of our most valuable assets," said Ing. "What happened to her was a crime. Give me one minute."

Ing brought up the calendar application and entered a task. "You have an appointment with Cynthia and Wendy, tomorrow morning at their school. I put you in the system as an interviewer gathering student opinions about career options for second lifers."

"I'll come up with some plausible interview questions at my hotel tonight," said Dene. "Is there something you think I might need to know before I meet with them?"

"Those two young women were murdered by the Sylumini, to slow Riana down, so they could catch up on their illegal portal project," said Ing. "As always, no evidence."

"Thank you for saying out loud what others will only whisper or deny," said Dene. His expression hardened. "Let me tell you something. There is no anca evidence. There was an ishmili eye witness."

"Noom watched the murder while it happened," agreed Ing. "She was sitting right there, in that chair you're in now, when she told me about it. Noom is not allowed to testify in an anca court."

"Noom can't testify but I've got a few leads," said Dene. "Maybe I can come up with something during this business trip."

"I hope you do," said Ing. "Our situation is desperate."

Scene 24 - Cynthia And Wendy

Next morning, Dene found himself in an empty classroom, sitting across the table from two young evos, Cynthia and Wendy. They had been on Paliyur for five years. Both of them giggled a lot.

"What did you think when you first got to Paliyur?" asked Dene.

"Oh wow," said Cynthia, "it was sooooo different from anything I ever imagined. I was expecting, like, you know, angels on clouds or something."

Wendy giggled, "I was expecting devils with pitchforks."

"Do you feel comfortable here now?" asked Dene.

"Oh yeah," said Cynthia, "This place is totally awesome. Sometimes we can see Earth through the windows. We don't know what's going on down there, unless somebody comes up the tunnel. Y'know, we were really young when we left first life, so our friends haven't started showing up yet."

"What do you miss the most about not being on Earth?" asked Dene.

"I miss Andy," said Cynthia. "I mean, like, I know he's gonna be here some day, and all that, and I hope for his

76

sake that he lives, you know, a full life, but I had a lot more fun when I was with him."

"What do you think you'll do when he finally gets here?" asked Dene.

Cynthia got a confused look on her face, "Well, uh, that depends on whether he gets married or not. I mean, he should, because he's a great guy and all that. But I've been here long enough to see what happens when romantic competition comes up the tunnel. It can get ugly."

"That's one of the reasons we're conducting this survey," said Dene. "New career opportunities are opening up. We'd like to place people who got along well on Earth in the same training programs."

Wendy, who had been quiet, got a perplexed look on her face, "Can I ask you a question?"

"Anything you want," said Dene. "I'm here to find out what's important to you."

"Um, here's what I wonder about," said Wendy. "When we first got here, they told us we had to go through orientation training. We graduated from that last year. Now we're in one of those career placement programs. They gave us, like, aptitude tests and stuff like that, y'know. Way boring. Anyway, my friend Cynthia here thinks that getting a job near Earth would be really awesome. She thinks Andy would like that. I'm not so sure. Anyway, here's my question. Can we really get a job in a different galaxy?"

"Of course," said Dene. "No matter what career choice you make, when you leave the Paliyur training sphere you'll be working in a new galaxy sooner or later. Lots of them in fact. This isn't something they emphasize during first life, but evos like you will mode-hop across the universe forever. Things will change constantly. It's a fascinating way to live."

Wendy got really excited. "Some of the older students say there's other universes out there. And we might be able to visit them some day."

"I suppose it depends on how you look at it," said Dene, "There's really only one universe. We're in the part we can feel. We have neighbors we can't see. For instance, when you were on Earth, you wouldn't have been able to see an anca like me. But here we are, sitting across the table from each other, having a pleasant little chat."

"This is so totally far out," said Wendy, clenching her hands. "I want to go to faraway places. It's just that - I don't want to leave Cynthia. We've been best friends forever."

"Let's ask Cynthia how she feels about this," said Dene.

"Yeah, well, y'know, they made us take these aptitude tests. They gave us one for travel," said Cynthia. "Wendy scored really high on moving far away. My score was like, go with what you know."

"There was something you said before," Dene mentioned casually, "something about Andy liking something. Would his opinion, or for that matter other friends of yours, affect your career choices?"

"Oh wow, I really think about that a lot," said Cynthia, "Wouldn't it be really cool if the bopsies came up here. I mean, can you imagine Bongo and Alicia doing their groovy thing at our school. I wonder if they're still together?"

Dene was not permitted to say that he had been with Andy, Bongo and Alicia last Saturday night.

"You'll have plenty of time to figure that out," said Dene. "By the time you graduate from Paliyur, everyone you knew down there, will be up here. You'll have some hard choices to make, when the time comes to move on to the career of your choice."

"I worry about that a lot," said Cynthia. "I mean, what if I make the wrong decision. From what our teachers tell us, the universe is a really big place."

"Your guidance counselors will help you with that," said Dene. "I'm just here to gather information about preferences."

"I see what you mean," said Cynthia, "I guess five years isn't very long. We've made a lot of cool new friends."

"If you don't mind me asking," said Dene, "how is it that you two came to be - what they call - 'early graduates' from first life."

"Oooh," said Cynthia. "That's, like, a huge problem for me. You see, I didn't exactly get along with my mom and dad when I was in high school."

"Lots of kids don't," said Dene.

"Well, my older sister was working in San Francisco. When I graduated I had a big fight with my parents so I went to live with her," Cynthia told him. "One of her friends knew Andy. As soon as I saw him I thought to myself, wow, I've seen this guy somewhere. And I had. He was at the library in my home town, the year before. They hired him to do a recording of a poetry reading, accompanied by a jazz trio, at our library. Wowzville."

"That's an interesting way to meet," said Dene.

"Oh yeah," sighed Cynthia. "Anyway, he worked at this bookstore my sister's friend owned. One thing led to another and after awhile Andy and I were living together. Needless to say, that freaked out my parents."

"They don't take these things lightly," said Dene, "and there are good reasons for that."

"Yeah, well, anyway, good-times bad-times, y'know, stuff happens," said Cynthia." Then Andy got a chance to go out on the road to record jazz music. I went with him. We hung out with some of the most awesome people."

"What happened next?" asked Dene.

"When we got back to Frisco my mom and dad wouldn't even speak to me," Cynthia said. "Eventually they warmed up but Andy wasn't allowed near our home."

"Do you understand why they felt that way?" asked Dene.

"I do now. But I couldn't then," said Cynthia. "Anyhoo, Wendy's parents threw her out a few days before Christmas. She drove down to Frisco to crash with me at Andy's pad. On Christmas Eve there was an argument. Andy said I should go see my parents to make peace with them. I said I wouldn't go without him. We'd all been drinking."

"Then what happened?" asked Dene.

"It's all crazy mixed up. I was in the back of Wendy's car, sobbing my heart out," said Cynthia. "There's, like, this dark stretch of road. Wendy was driving way too fast. Next thing I know - we woke up in Paliyur."

"How do you think your parents feel about that?" asked Dene.

"Heartbroken," sobbed Cynthia.

Wendy started crying too. She had always been the rebel in her family. Now she missed her mom and dad so bad.

"I apologize," said Dene, "I didn't mean to bring up such sad memories for you." He sat with them, talking to them, consoling them, and after a while they got their giggles back.

Dene was a hardened cynic but things like this made him really mad. He vowed that he would not rest until he got the anca who did this to them.

"Are you feeling better now?" asked Dene, not feeling so chipper himself.

"Yeah, yeah, I'm cool," sniffled Wendy - who started crying again.

Cynthia stopped sobbing just long enough to whimper, "It's not fair."

"That's why we need to work extra hard to keep things fair," said Dene.

Chapter 10 - Valdaria

Scene 25 - The Jump

Cami and Farli had been working at the Observatory for one month. They got up at the same time as always, in Brazil. They flew to work at the same place, in Egypt. They passed through the same security checkpoint. Then their regular routine got highly irregular.

At the Ishmili Observatory, there were no rules, no particular hours, and no project plans. When they asked, "What do you want us to do?" there was no answer.

It was easy enough to adjust to an unschedule like that. They did what they thought needed to be done.

On this particular day, Riana showed up at the Observatory when it was late in the regular work shift. She was obviously stressed out, or so it seemed to Cami, who had befriended her.

Cami knew from experience that when Riana was in one of her unpredictable moods, it was best not to talk to her. Continuing with her tasks, Cami kept her emotional radar on full alert.

Dene entered the room. "Have you told them yet?" he asked Riana.

"Told them what?" she muttered, without looking at him.

"When was the last time you slept?" asked Dene.

"I dunno," said Riana, "couple of days ago."

"Then I'll tell them myself," he said.

Floating over to Cami and Farli's desks, Dene said, "There's a journey I must make. I need to meet with Captain Behchel."

"Uh ... ," said Cami, starting to ask a load of questions. Then she held back. "Uh ... is there anything you want us to do while you're away?"

"Yes," said Dene, "you need to learn to work without me. When I come back from this trip I will be with you here

81

for awhile. Then I will be gone for a long time, delivering messages to Hamil and Hamine. No one knows what might happen."

Cami noticed that Riana was extremely withdrawn.

"When are you leaving?" asked Cami.

"Actually, I'm leaving right now," said Dene. "Would the two of you like to see me do the jump? There's not much to see, actually."

"Sure," said Farli, who had always wondered about this.

"Let's go to the big room," said Dene.

The four of them left the Observatory and floated out into the big room. This was the part of the lab where they worked on projects which were too enormous to be assembled in an ordinary room. It was two stories tall, with a large industrial crane attached to the ceiling.

Dene floated to the center of the big room. Cami and Farli hovered nearby. Riana lingered uncomfortably behind their backs.

"You won't actually see me do anything," he said. "One moment I'm here. The next moment I'm gone. Since I'm doing a low speed jump, it will take me a couple of days to reach Valdaria."

"That's a lot faster than a cruiser," said Cami.

Riana blurted out, "Stop at Zog on the way. You should see the Lindar portal beacon. That's what we're trying to mimic using Melona and Andy."

"Excellent suggestion," agreed Dene.

The jump requires a certain amount of intense preparation. He flexed his shoulders, waggled his taper, and prepared his mind.

Dene counted down, "3 - 2 - 1." Then he was no longer visible.

"Not much to see," agreed Farli, "but at least now I can tell the world that I've seen the famous jump."

"May as well get back to work," said Cami. Turning to Riana, she motioned for her to join them.

"You go ahead," mumbled Riana. "I'm going home."

Cami had never seen her ancient friend so troubled before. "Alright."

Scene 26 - Zog Reptans

Dene was hiding in a great jumble of boulders that had been hauled over to the edge of a farm field. The local star, Hurbu, had a rare color and it glimmered on strange flowers in the meadow. On the far side of the meadow was a modest farmhouse.

In the distance was the skyline of a reptan city.

Buried within the hills nearby was the Lindar mode-tunnel, which had the same design as Chephra. Construction had started earlier here and it was fully operational. Unfortunately, Lindar was too far away to be used for the rescue.

Riana's suggestion had been a good one. Observing the jeshie signal beacon had been a revelation to him. Now he had an enormously better understanding of what they needed to do with the people powered emergency portal that would be used for the rescue on Earth.

The sound of a Lindar security patrol was dangerously close. It was important to Dene that no one knew where he was, or when he would return. He shape-shifted to blend with the boulders.

On the back porch of the farmhouse a father and daughter appeared. They were Zog reptiles with delightfully colored scales. The daughter was young but her walk was steady. She saw the meadow with eyes which sparkled with wonder. Her father's eyes were worn with the cares of the world.

They spoke a language which Dene had not learned. He could tell from the way they moved that the mother had sent them out to find some sort of special food for dinner. With extreme caution, he slid a little further out so he could reach a better understanding of how the local evos behaved. Lindar and Chephra were two parts of the same Valdarian colonization project.

The daughter carried a dainty basket in her long fingered hand.

When the father found what they were looking for, he called the young one over. In tones which sounded educational, he explained what they were doing, then let her pick a few leaves, while he chose the best. She placed each leaf carefully in her basket, arranging them as they walked

83

along. When they were done, the two reptans went back to the farmhouse.

The daughter skipped. The father trudged.

While Dene was watching the reptans, he was himself being watched.

Beq and Vonso both kept their eyes on him. They sat on top of boulders.

Beq was the soto scientist who had worked with Cami when both of them were at Lindar. It was unusual, but not unheard of, for a soto and an anca to work in the same lab. One day, Beq disappeared from Zog. Later on, Cami got reassigned to Chephra on Earth.

Vonso was the cloud wanderer who had slipped through the portal at the Last Grand Slam Poetry Jam. He was a flash being, who are not at all like anca or soto. Riana and Zinxa had introduced Vonso to Beq. These four beings had big plans for the solitary anca who was hiding in the boulders.

Dene, for all his heightened skills, could not see either of them.

The instant Dene jumped away, Vonso followed. While it was true that Dene knew how to do the jump, this was a minor matter as far as Vonso was concerned. He could travel as fast as lightning. Or a hundred times faster, or a thousand. Whatever was needed to get to wherever he went. Vonso was a jeshie, green lightning, cloud wanderer, flash being - who stayed hot on Dene's trail.

Scene 27 - Conference Call

Beq raced home to Paroun. It was a pleasant little place, invisible to both soto and anca. Zinxa had taught Beq how to build a new life, in-between the realms of ordinary life.

Upon entering her house she raced down the spiral staircase to the basement. In the corner was her office. Hastily sitting at the desk, she fumbled with her brand new ishmili dome. Beq had only two contacts in her directory.

Putting Riana and Zinxa on conference call, she said, "The special ops agent just left. The flash being followed him."

"Then he should be in my area sometime tomorrow," said Zinxa. "I will find Vonso so he can tell me what he has discovered."

Beq knew that Vonso was a cloud wanderer from Jeshmol but she could not understand what he was doing here in Nimulos. "What's going to happen next?"

"That's up to him, not us," said Zinxa.

Riana remained strangely silent.

Zinxa had a clear understanding of this peculiar silence. As Riana's best friend, she wanted to bring what was being hidden out into the open. "Before worrying about our mysterious guest we should worry about our traumatized friend."

Beq was shocked. "What does that mean?"

"I can see that Riana has fallen in love with Dene," said Zinxa.

Riana blushed. "I don't know what you're talking about."

"You deny what is easy for an old friend to see," said Zinxa. "This new urbie sends ripples through you. No one has been able to reach you like that for such a long time, have they."

Beq felt like an unwanted guest at a private party.

"We must prepare Dene for the transformation," said Riana coldly. Her face was frozen with fear.

"That is why I made a decision," said Zinxa. "The full treatment, which Vonso strongly recommends, will be merciless. Riana is too weakened by love to oversee the ordeal. In our original plan, she was the one best qualified. But love has sapped my old friend's will power. When the time comes, it will be Beq and I who are Vonso's assistants. We will leave the healing of Dene to Riana."

Riana snapped. "Don't let him die. There has got to be a better way."

"A better way," said Zinxa, sarcastically. "Oh, I suppose *you* could travel to the Phorlom to speak with Hamil and Hamine. You would suffer no harm in that relentless void, nor would I. That is where the two of us learned how to venture into the nether regions, oh so long ago, when both of us were so much younger. But - let me see - there seems to be a problem. You're not a diplomatic courier, are you. They would never recognize your credentials. Dene is the only one who can gain for us the authority we so desperately seek."

"I know what Vonso is going to do to Dene," snarled Riana. "Don't let him do it."

"We've both been through the ordeal," Zinxa told her best friend. "It was you who put me through it. I finished your transformation for you. Both of us have worked on Beq, in small doses, with plenty of time for healing. Beq will also need to be readjusted by Vonso if our new JeshNim plan is going to work. We *must* bring Dene all the way over, or we will lose everything. Let me remind you - this is not just about us. The grand unfolding awaits our bold deeds."

"This is way too fast," hissed Riana. "What if Dene doesn't survive?"

"Ask Beq about Vonso's powers," suggested Zinxa, who was equally uncertain. "She is from Jeshmol, same as he is."

Beq hesitated, "Everyone back home has heard about the cloud wanderers. Personally, I had never met one before, or known anyone who had. The flash beings do big deeds in a big way. It is much the same with your star travelers, or so I have heard. We have faith in their bright powers. But I cannot honestly tell you that I understand what is happening in our situation."

Riana got that lost look in her eye, which took her places beyond the imaginations of others. When her attention returned she said, "There are many types of transformations. Which one does Vonso prefer?"

"Until Dene is thoroughly examined we will not know," admitted Zinxa. "Vonso told me he was hoping to find a star traveler who could provide advice."

Riana put her face in her hands and sobbed, "Why did Fevih do this to us? Why couldn't this have been some other time?"

"Beq and I will look into that," said Zinxa. "Turmoil clouds your mind."

Riana whimpered, "How can this be happening to me?"

"I will tell you," said Zinxa. "Love is not something you sought, it is something which snuck up on you. We both remember the joys and pangs of a few unsteady romances - before we locked ourselves away from an uncaring world - in order to achieve glorious deeds for the greater good of the grand unfolding. I envy you but I can no longer trust you."

A quivering turmoil shook through Riana as she whispered, "I believe this is what we must do. I desperately want to believe it. I believe. I believe."

"Hear out my plan," declared Zinxa. "Beq, come to my place as quickly as possible. Riana, you must stay at home to master the deep healing of the JeshNim other-siders."

"I will leave today," vowed Beq.

Riana could not speak. Her tongue would not loosen until she got hold of a tiny fragment of her legendary will power. "This is the only way."

"The time has come for Beq to learn how to prepare the minerals for the vaporous pit," said Zinxa. "I will consult with Vonso and we will find a common goal. This turmoil we face was unexpected but, in the long run, this new plan is better than our old one."

Riana found a firm voice. "Don't let him die. I would rather lose everything we have worked on for so long - than to lose him."

Scene 28 - Captain Behchel

The schedule called for Dene to meet with Captain Behchel for a total of six hours, during a standard six day work week, as time is reckoned in the Sagonish star system. This was more than other anca were given, because the stakes were so high. At these meetings the two of them spoke in clipped tones about tactical advantages and strategic opportunities. They also discovered that, in spite of huge differences in their personalities, they got along rather well. That is why the captain of industry invited the bold adventurer to visit his palatial home during the weekend.

Valdaria is an enormous mega sphere complex, a thousand times larger than Paliyur. It is home base for an industrial empire that has colonization projects spread throughout the Roshomon star cloud.

Anca spheres are round. They are built to withstand the harsh negative pressures of outer space. A planet sized office staff can work in a sphere, without the disadvantages of living on a troublesome evo planet. Valdarian architects had taken these engineering facts and designed them into a mega complex which impressed everyone who saw it.

In the outer ring were nine spheres, housing the offices of the nine industrial divisions of Valdaria Colonization Enterprises. Located in the center was the hospitality sphere, which featured hotels, entertainment and shopping services which visitors from the galaxy would expect. Extending from the central sphere were the north and south towers. Each tower consisted of three separate spheres, of decreasing size. The South Tower housed executive headquarters. The North Tower was Captain Behchel's personal domain. Every sphere could be reached through flexible commuter tunnels.

Dene was staying in a luxury hotel in the central sphere. At the appointed hour he heard a knock on the door. A messenger escorted him to the North Tower. A second messenger escorted him to the top.

Two splendidly tall doors, sparkling with perfectly matched crystals, opened silently at their approach. Facing them was the security team, seated at a wall of desks, blocking entry. They reviewed Dene's credentials and granted him access to Captain Behchel's private suite.

Upon entering this ornate domain, Dene saw what many had spoken of in awe. The entire upper sphere was surrounded by one continuous picture window. From it, guests had a grand view of the entire Sagonish star system.

Facing him was Captain Behchel, seated in a luxuriously appointed chair. Dene floated forward at a pace and style they had recommended at the hotel.

"Welcome," said the Captain, getting up to shake his hand. "There's a comfortable little niche over there where we can speak privately."

"My pleasure to be here," said Dene.

Nearby was a seating area which could accommodate a dozen anca, yet it was quite comfortable with only two. Staff attended to their preferences, then withdrew.

Captain Behchel opened the conversation. "I changed my mind about you in the middle of the week. There's certainly nothing unusual about the ishmili sending in a rough character to take on a few bad actors on a wayward planet. That was the character I expected to meet. After getting to know you better, I came to appreciate that you have mastered the art of applying force skillfully, and with good purpose. With that in mind, I want to mention that I approved your request for a star cruiser. Ulta needs to feel the sting of being challenged in the sky by someone like you."

"I appreciate that," said Dene. "When I return from the Phorlom I will set aside my diplomatic responsibilities. Then I have plans for Ulta."

"IF ... you return from the Phorlom," said the Captain, with an unchanging expression.

"From what you just said, I can tell that you have a realistic understanding of what I'm up against," said Dene.

The Captain folded his hands together. "Your soul-seed is going to curl up the instant you make your foolish jump into the Phorlom void. Unlike most anca, I have studied the jump. You need a stable gravity grid line. There are none in the Phorlom. That's why we perform our scientific research there."

"Everything you say is true," admitted Dene. "The reason I'm still here is because I never make a jump unless I have a clear understanding of my grid. I've studied the Phorlom. You're right, there are no stable lines, only small wavering ones near intruder objects."

"Then why risk throwing your life away?" asked Captain Behchel. "Even worse, from my point of view, why risk throwing away this fabulous opportunity for Hamil and Hamine to put Celene in charge of the rescue. Sarkon and Sarena have been a disaster. They allowed the Sylumini to lead them astray, which shows that they have faulty leadership values."

"As I sit here in front of you - I don't have a good answer," said Dene. "All I have is a hunch that something will turn up."

"Hunch," said the Captain, "is not a word in my vocabulary."

"I wouldn't expect it to be," said Dene, "which is why I came here today prepared to offer you some reassurance. If I actually do make it back from the Phorlom alive, with the diplomatic pouch safely in my pocket, I will send you a confirmation message over the anca network. Until then, you can hold off on the expense of my star cruiser."

"I accept your offer," said Captain Behchel.

"On a related subject, if I don't make it back, then I would like to leave Riana and her team in a strong position."

The Captain had been waiting for this, having discussed it at length with Ing, "What is it you have in mind?"

"The problem I face is that I will be gone for up to a year," said Dene. "The Sylumini will strike hard while I'm away. My goal is to make sure that Riana's team has everything they need to succeed, in the event that something bad happens to me. Keeping that in mind, I'm hoping that certain of my activities can be overlooked."

"I have already instructed Chief Gromo to turn a blind eye to what you're doing," said the Captain.

"Good. That gives me freedom of operation," said Dene. "When all this is over, I hope you will see the wisdom of my chosen course of action."

"I hope so too," said the Captain. "for your sake ... but mostly for my own sake."

"Enough said about that," said Dene.

"I agree," replied the Captain. "What I was really looking forward to is having an informal chat with you. Too much of my time is spent listening to engineers making technical presentations. You seem to have led a different sort of life."

"I've done it all," said Dene, "some good, some bad, but as I've gotten older there's one lesson I have learned to live by. If you don't stand up to the bad guys, they get worse. If you push hard enough on the bad guys, life gets better for everyone."

"I like the sound of that," said the Captain, "Now, if you don't mind, I'd like to hear how you learned how to do the jump."

"Long ago and far away, I was an architect on the way to my next assignment," began Dene. "I had some extra time on my hands so I decided to take an extended vacation in Zibbot. The next thing I knew ... "

... and that is how the captain and the adventurer spent a pleasant weekend afternoon, at the tippy top of the North Tower, reminiscing about their younger days.

Chapter 11 - Outlaws In The Asteroids

Scene 29 - Lunetor

"This bazelium isn't good enough," said Dene.

Lunetor the smuggler gave him a nasty look. "That's all I could find. That stuff's deadly. The urbie who mined it for someone else had a real bad ending. Anca aren't supposed to die like that. They're supposed to live until Nimulos fades away."

"I don't want anyone dying over a few chunks of bazelium," said Dene, "that's why I built this little machine." He pulled a sleek case from his side pocket. "How much bazelium do you think there is in this asteroid?"

"None," said the smuggler. "It can only be found deep inside a large planet."

"This particular chunk of space rock used to be deep inside a large planet," said Dene. "Watch this." He put the little machine on the surface of the asteroid and it burrowed its way into the stone.

A few minutes later the machine mysteriously popped back up between their two tapers. Dene picked it up and opened it. Lunetor flinched in terror.

"Everything is safely packaged," said Dene. "That's the beautiful thing about this. All you have to do is load it with standard mineral safety packets and it will continue to mine until it runs out of packets. Then it will come back to you."

Lunetor got a greedy look in his eye. "Bazelium is worth a fortune."

"Here's the deal," said Dene, "when you get as much of the best stuff as you can find, I'll pay market price and let you keep the machine. If you play nice with me, I'll even show you how to repair it so it will always be useful." Dene put the bundled bazelium in his pocket and handed the machine to the smuggler."

"Sounds like a fair deal," said the smuggler. "How'd an urbie like you learn how to do this?"

"That's a long story," said Dene, "which I am not going to tell you."

"Yeah, sure, whatever," said Lunetor.

"How would you like to double your profits at no extra risk," said Dene.

"Sounds too good to be true," said Lunetor.

"This has nothing to do with minerals," Dene said. "There's somebody I'm looking for. It's worth a lot to me to find him."

"Who's that?" asked Lunetor.

"Ever hear of Arhulio?" asked Dene.

"Arhulio got himself assassinated," said Lunetor.

"Who killed him?" asked Dene.

"One of Chief Gromo's detectives did the dirty work," said Lunetor. "Orders from the top. Put the cuffs on, didn't bother with no arrest. Took him far away. Dumped him in the void. No evidence. No blabbering witnesses."

"I've heard at least ten versions of that story," said Dene.

"Yeah, well, Arhulio had lots of enemies," said Lunetor, warming to his story. "For a long time he was Gromo's top detective. Jails around here are filled with urbies he brought in. Quite a few umbies too."

"Why did he go bad?" asked Dene.

"Hard to say," Lunetor told him, "but the story I heard goes like this. Detective work is nasty. Arhulio was doing a good job, so they promoted him into one of those fancy positions. You know, more prestige. Code breaker they made him. This guy could figure out anybody's dirty deal, just by looking at the data. Imagine that."

"Sounds easier than roughing up smugglers," said Dene.

"Eh, Arhulio was a lot like us," said Lunetor. "He likes action. Out here, no matter which side you're on, you don't report to no one. You're your own boss, take your own risks, reap your own rewards. Some of us just like it that way."

"What happened next?" asked Dene.

"One day Arhulio showed up," said Lunetor, "told us he was coming over to our side. Said he knew all the secrets. We didn't believe him, of course."

"I wouldn't believe him," said Dene. "Sounds like a trap."

"Yeah, well, I never would work with the guy but some of the other smugglers did," said Lunetor. "Made a fortune, those guys. Here I am scrambling for scratch and his pals are pulling it in big time. Anyway, you know how it ends."

"One day Arhulio is here, next day he isn't," said Dene.

"Nobody's seen him since," said Lunetor.

"Arhulio is out there somewhere," said Dene. "I need to talk to him."

"He's gone," said Lunetor.

"Double profit," said Dene.

"You gotta give me something to work with," said Lunetor.

"What do you know about poetry?" asked Dene.

Lunetor laughed at him. "Poetry? What I know about poetry is nothing."

"The only lead I've got is a poem Arhulio recited after they faked his death," said Dene.

"Whadda ya want me to do?" asked Lunetor.

"Get me some leads. I'll take care of the rest," Dene said.

The smuggler nodded his head. "I got a friend. I'll go see my friend."

Scene 30 - Grokar And Beemie

The poetry recital went well. Out here no one knew who Dene was so he could claim to be a wandering poet, no questions asked. The Roshomon star cloud is an odd appendage of our hefty spiral galaxy. Near where the cloud crosses a big arm there is a lonely star cluster. Dene had been told that Arhulio might be hiding there.

Those who lived in these parts were anca who didn't fit into those tiny organizational boxes that society likes to put everyone in. Free thinkers drifted out to this region. A few of them knew and loved Arhulio's poetry. Dene quickly mastered the nuances. His recitations were becoming quite popular. Introductions were made, a trail of clues was followed, and a rogue detective who was supposed to be dead left faint hints along a thin trail. These hints pulled Dene ever closer. He was already late getting back to Earth.

He had done a spoken word poetry show in a natural stone canyon. His voice echoed Arhulio's spiritual longings with resonant drama and deep mystery. Tales of the intense struggle to move beyond the limits of impure souls were popular with those who had moved out here to get away from it all. In a place like this, the only thing the locals wanted to exploit was their own vivid dreams.

As Dene's rhythmic words faded against the canyon walls, they were serenaded by a whoosh of evergreens waving in the night breeze. Among those gathered in this canyon were a couple, Grokar and Beemie, who had claimed an entire planet all for themselves. It was against the law for them to own Fenaron but no one stopped them. They invited Dene to spend the night at their place.

Near the top of a snow capped mountain, hidden in a deep valley, where the rays of the local star didn't reach until the middle of the day, Grokar and Beemie had built their dream home. The only evos on this planet were plants, fish, animals, and birds. No campfires or cities interfered with their view. Powerful winds, the howls of wild animals, and bird song played an endless symphony of natural sound.

In the morning he found his hosts sitting quietly on a wide veranda. Light from their star lit the tops of the trees on the distant mountain. Fresh air, and the sounds of scurrying animals, surrounded them.

"Good morning," said Grokar.

"May the wind be with you," added Beemie.

Dene took a long look at the dense forest, and the majestic birds soaring overhead, then he breathed deep the fresh clean air. "Nice to be here," he said.

Conversations in a place like this can take many a twist and turn. In the afternoon Dene heard the words he had been waiting for.

"So, where was Arhulio hiding when he taught you those poems?" asked Grokar.

"I never met Arhulio," said Dene.

This surprised both his hosts.

"Then how did you learn his poems?" asked Grokar.

"From other poets," said Dene. "Mostly they say Arhulio is dead."

Grokar laughed heartily. "We can take you to him. Beemie carves statues for The Retreat, where he found refuge. Tomorrow would be as good a day as any to make a delivery."

"Oh," said Dene, not wanting to rush into anything this important, "I'd like to see a few of those statues, if you don't mind."

There are few things as strong as the pride of a great artist. Beemie had mastered the skills of carving hard objects into uplifting forms. Her statues were scattered all across the mountainside. The three of them spent the rest of the day gliding through these rough terrains. Each statue had its own natural place. Dene, who had studied architecture, understood the vocabulary she spoke. Back at the cabin, their aesthetic exchange wandered far into the night.

Next morning, Dene found himself jammed into the back of their delivery cruiser, surrounded by three statues which were tied tightly to the walls. Grokar and Beemie raced their little cruiser toward a star that hovered at the remote edge of Roshomon. The couple in the cockpit joked endlessly with each other. Dene sat silently in the cargo bay, clearing his mind of what clogged it.

Scene 31 - Arhulio

Wakona was the last place anyone would expect to find a detective who was supposed to be dead. Rogue cops don't usually end up in religious retreats - but who's to say they shouldn't.

Strangers are not allowed within the sacred precincts of The Retreat on Wakona but Grokar and Beemie weren't strangers. After reciting one of Arhulio's inspirational poems, Dene was no longer considered a stranger either. They were invited inside and taken on a tour of the sculpture garden. Hospitality is a wonderful thing but, as the day dragged on, Dene began shifting the conversation in the direction of his hidden agenda.

It was not accepted practice for anyone to meet with devotees seeking the higher spiritual realms. In spite of these restrictions it made sense that Dene should meet his poetic master in the wild garden. A spiritual advisor was sent along to guide them.

The guide escorted Dene up a broad hill within the high walls of The Retreat. The Bells of Wakona sounded sonorously from the towers at the top of the hill. Grokar and Beemie had already gone back to their home planet.

"Good afternoon, Arhulio," said Dene. "Am I permitted to call you by that name?"

"Yes, for this purpose you may use my old name," he said.

Dene recited two of the poems. Arhulio taught him one more.

They were sitting on a bench in the garden, turned to face each other. The spiritual advisor wandered further up the hill. Whether his attention was diverted by higher matters, or more worldly concerns, Dene could not say, but the advisor's attention lagged.

While continuing to recite a poem, Dene popped an image into his palm dome. It was a coded signal beamed down from Ulta's spy cruiser. Xen and Wun had captured it during the Last Grand Slam Poetry Jam. Sylumini data is always heavily encrypted.

"I can break that code," said Arhulio, in a voice as soft and clear as the chiming bells on the hill.

Dene reached out to shake his hand, uploading the spy beams. All the while he recited a poem of cosmic praise in a steady voice. Arhulio looked excited.

When the allotted time was up the spiritual advisor came back down the hill. "How are the poetry lessons going?"

Dene recited a stanza he had just learned, in a voice resonant with numinous mystery.

"That's wonderful," said the advisor. "We can continue this later but it's time for the midday services."

"I am overcome by inspiration," said Arhulio, "and wish to seek realms beyond rituals."

The spiritual advisor nodded. Turning to Dene he said, "Would you care to join us?"

"I would be delighted to join you," said Dene, and he really meant it. He had lived a rough life and this place was a refreshing relief from the harshness of the world. The two of them left Arhulio alone, meditating in the wild garden.

They joined a quiet group of anca floating through the doors of a small chapel. Delicate aromas filled the air. Light filtered through colored windows. Dene, the worldly outsider, found himself among a dedicated group of urbies and umbies seeking unity with the great mystery.

At the midday service there was chanting and singing and prayer. There was one special moment which pierced Dene to his center. When he heard an old familiar song, which he had learned while very young, it touched him deeply. With vigor, he sang along to a tune he could never forget, repeating words he thought he had forgotten. That service in the chapel renewed him.

Afterward, there was an informal gathering in the vestibule. When the congregants began to disperse Dene asked for, and was granted, permission to learn one more poem from Arhulio before the gates closed at dark.

As Dene approached the wild garden Arhulio observed the way he moved. "The blessing has filled you."

"It's a marvel," said Dene. He glowed inwardly.

"Would you like to learn a new poem I've been working on?" asked Arhulio.

"One more," said Dene.

They sat on the bench facing each other.

The spiritual advisor said, "I have a few matters to attend to. I'll be back before dark." He trusted this gentle anca named Dene.

As soon as the advisor left, Dene and Arhulio shook hands. The decoded signal was uploaded into Dene's palm dome, along with detailed instructions revealing how the secret codes of the Sylumini were encrypted.

Arhulio said no more about poetry. He was back in the law enforcement game again and he was loving it. "What brings you here?"

Dene said, "The Sylumini have stolen important information from Captain Behchel. We can never get that information back but we want to know how they're using it. I must go away on a dangerous mission. Those who remain behind will need to know what the competition is up to."

"My life is here now," said Arhulio. "I won't return to the outer world until my inner world has been fixed. I want to thank you for keeping my poems alive out there. I would like to thank you even more for bringing me some good old fashioned detective work. In my former life I was the best code breaker Chief Gromo ever had. Working with this Sylumini encryption has enlightened me in new ways. They understand deception better than anyone. I am going to meditate on deception. It is a glorious path to the great mystery."

"Everything Tangled Into One," said Dene, repeating an old saying.

"Good luck against the Sylumini," said Arhulio. "I fought their dark agents for thousands of years. They always won."

Chapter 12 - Other Siders

Scene 32 - Ixchibo

Dene checked out of his luxury hotel in the Valdaria Mega Sphere and blended in as an ordinary business traveler. As he glided through the lobby, one of Chief Gromo's detectives followed, and two Sylumini agents went out by separate doors. He knew exactly what to do.

There was a commuter tube nearby and, at this time of day, it was packed. Mingling with the crowd he floated down from one level toward the next. As he glided along with the crowd, near the exit, he hunkered down and made his jump. Those near him didn't notice because they thought he got off when the crowd shifted. Those following figured he'd slipped away.

##

Far from Valdaria, barely within the Sagonish star system, was an anonymous asteroid. Popping out of his jump, Dene saw Lunetor waiting in the shadows. He flew over to the crater.

Lunetor's face was hard as stone. "Whadda ya got for me?"

As was the custom among mineral smugglers, Dene slowly removed a case from his side pocket, opened it for inspection, then waited for Lunetor's decision. The goods inside the case were all of exceptional value but you would never know that from watching Lunetor's face. After a few moments he nodded yes. Dene snapped the case shut and held it tightly under one arm.

Saying nothing, because a tricky deal can go bad over a few wrong words, Lunetor removed a case from his own pocket and held it out for Dene to examine.

Eyeing the bazelium with calculated care Dene said, "You brought me the very best. It's a deal."

They exchanged mineral cases and placed them securely in their own pockets.

"I've got one more thing," said Dene, "to pay you back for that favor you did me."

Lunetor got ready to fight.

Dene reached extremely slowly into his other side pocket, took out a second mineral case, and opened it for Lunetor.

"Whoooah," he gasped. Greed glistened in his eyes.

"You never saw me, I never saw you, nothing ever happened," said Dene.

"That's the way I don't remember it," said Lunetor, eagerly stuffing the second case into his pocket.

They shook hands and that was the last they ever saw of each other.

##

Betrayal is common everywhere but, in this remote region, it can lurk behind any chunk of space rock. Dene was on hyper alert.

In a flash of green lightning - Dene got kidnapped.

Coiling around him like a sky serpent, Vonso squeezed gently until Dene's mind went blank. After slithering through the stardust, the alien cloud wanderer took the unconscious anca to Zinxa's isolated lair.

Ixchibo is a protoplanet which has survived the gravitational flings of the unstable Sagonish star group for eons. No native life forms can flourish because it's too small for an atmosphere. The locals do not know that Zinxa lives alone in this barren place. She spends her time exploring the hidden worlds which surround us. Ixchibo is her home base.

Vonso morphed out of his lightning-travel form and created a communicator body. It was shaped like an egg, formed of green crackling fog. Dene clung to it in a trance. The two of them flitted through stone.

Zinxa and Beq waited in a cavern.

"i see the vapor pit has been prepared according to my instructions" said Vonso, in a voice which sounded like rumbling bells.

"We are ready for the transformation," said Zinxa.

Behind her stood Beq, staring at the green thing. It was unfamiliar. When she recognized Dene, she shuddered.

In the thin light they placed him on a gossamer hammock, which stretched across a pit of prepared minerals.

"we will wait until he is ready to question us" Vonso announced. It was a matter of honor. The green flash had captured Dene for good purpose. Kidnapping was wrong.

When Dene slipped back into consciousness, he saw a sparkly green fog hugging the floor, a short blue soto, and a tall anca with shadowy features. "To what do I owe the honor of meeting you under these circumstances?" he said. For Dene, this was a standard question when he found himself in a situation which made no sense.

"are you prepared to undergo the ordeal of transformation" asked the green fog.

"I am prepared to do whatever will make things better," Dene replied.

Zinxa introduced herself. "I am Zinxa, an old friend of Riana's."

Dene felt strong enough to sit up. "Jenissen told me that you were rumored to be around somewhere."

"This is Beq," continued Zinxa.

Beq peeked around Zinxa's floating body and said, "hello".

"Ah, Cami's soto friend who disappeared," said Dene. "She speaks highly of you."

"That is Vonso," said Zinxa.

"i am a cloud wanderer recently arrived from jeshmol" Vonso informed him.

"Never met one of your type before," said Dene. "On the other hand I have some friends, and a few enemies, among the star travelers. It is an honor to meet you." His clever eyes took in the situation with improved understanding.

Zinxa spoke starkly, "We are here to make sure you do not die in the Phorlom void."

"I had a hunch something like this might happen," said Dene, "but I had no idea it would look like this. What's expected of me?"

"We were working with Riana on a transformation for you," replied Zinxa. "Then Vonso arrived with a new plan."

"What transformation does Vonso have in mind?" asked Dene.

Vonso answered in a ringing voice, "jeshnim".

"Why such a radical change this early?" asked Dene. He knew that the JeshNim project had barely gotten off to a start in this remote sector.

Zinxa replied, "Opportunities arose earlier than expected."

Dene thought this sounded reasonable. "That suits me just fine. What next?"

Zinxa said, "Lay back in the hammock so we can heat the minerals. The vapors must do their work. Beq and I will prepare you. Vonso will guide us down the JeshNim path. Riana will be sent for when it's time for healing."

Dene smiled when he heard Riana's name. "I look forward to seeing her again." He lay back in the hammock.

There was a bustle of activity.

Soon enough, Dene was all the way under.

##

"Ready to make that call?" asked Zinxa.

"If you are," said Beq. Living in Zinxa's rough caves had given her a new appreciation of the many fine things she had left behind at Paroun.

They zipped down a fractured passageway until they reached the apartment. In the back room was a battered ishmili dome.

"We have Dene under our control," said Zinxa.

"How is he?" asked Riana.

"Unconscious," said Zinxa.

"Where is he?" asked Riana.

"Over the pit," said Zinxa. "Vonso is examining him."

Riana hesitated, "When will he be ready?"

"Tomorrow," said Zinxa.

"I will be there," said Riana. She quivered.

##

Two days later Dene woke up in the hammock, which had now been moved to the apartment. All of him hurt. A blurry form was by his side. "Why does everything look so pale?" he croaked.

"Because we placed you between the worlds," said Riana, softly. "When you're feeling better, I'll teach you how to reach a comfortable place."

"Where is that green wanderer?" he groaned.

"Vonso found an ally among the star travelers," Riana told him. "While you heal, they will talk."

"How am I doing?" wondered Dene.

"You now have the tip of your taper in JeshNim," Riana said.

Dene couldn't be sure if he still had a taper, but he understood that she was speaking in parables. "Is JeshNim where *you* want me to be?"

"JeshNim is where you *need* to be," said Riana. She touched his hand.

"Then I'm glad my transformation has begun," said Dene. He lapsed back into unconsciousness.

Riana gazed at his puffy face, squeezed his cold hand, and whispered, "Please don't die."

Scene 33 - Recovery

A few days later the patient was feeling stronger but dizzy. As his health improved, Riana's mood improved along with it. Dene knew that things were getting better when the three umbies went off to have a private conversation without him.

"Do you think he's strong enough to travel?" asked Zinxa.

"We've got to get going," said Riana. "He said he would be gone for three weeks and it's already been six. This one has powerful enemies and they're getting restless. Beq, would you mind if we spent some time at your house? It's much closer to home."

"I would be delighted to have guests in my place," said Beq, breaking into a magnificent smile. She looked forward to seeing Paroun again, with its soft lights and shimmering art.

"I will remain here," said Zinxa, "to wait for Vonso's return."

"We leave tomorrow," said Riana.

##

Paroun was named after a story that Beq had loved when she was very young. It was a place that only the main character could see. Others did not believe it existed. Now she had two honored guests in her very own Paroun.

103

Dene had no memory of how he got here. They had shifted him farther into that wispy region between worlds, so he would be safe during the dangerous journey. The place where he was recovering was strangely different.

As he continued to improve, he recalled fragments. Cami's soto friend at Lindar disappeared one afternoon. Beq hadn't gone anywhere. She had simply moved over to the other-side. Zinxa found her. Riana met with her. Noom presented her with an ishmili dome.

On the morning of the second day, Dene managed to sit up all by himself. He floated far enough to plop down on the couch. Riana sat by his side.

The way Beq decorated her singular home fascinated him. As a former architect, Dene was aware of form, style and space. In addition to her amazing math skills, and prodigious technical achievements, Beq was a genius at filling her home with wonder. Each item had been crafted from thin filaments of almost nothingness. Such were the possibilities of the grand unfolding.

A favorite of Dene's was Beq's music. She had been forced to abandon all of her old musical instruments. New music was needed in the new realm. While Dene sat on the couch next to Riana, resting and recovering, Beq would serenade them with the unique new sounds she had been discovering. Each instrument was assembled by hand, using theories from physics, with the resonant elements being shaped into artistic achievements. Her songs sped Dene's recovery.

On the morning of the fourth day Dene was able to pick out a few hesitant melodies of his own. It exhausted him.

Later that afternoon, Riana let it be known that they must leave tomorrow.

Beq would be alone again, in her dainty little fortress, but never again would she feel the horrid sting of intense isolation. Zinxa had taught her how to build this in-between place. Riana had brought friendship to this nether region. Dene had discussed the important cultural values of silence and emptiness. Life goes on and it is meant to be lived fully.

Early next morning, after the door had closed behind them, Riana supported Dene's arm so he could wave goodbye to Beq, who stood forlorn at her window. Then Riana shifted him deeper into the wispy regions. Hoisting him on her back, she held his arms securely, then flew away.

Beq waved bye bye from Paroun.

Scene 34 - Code Breaker

Riana hauled Dene to a place on the outskirts of Namoush, capitol city of Kemong Sector Forty Two. They were at the bottom of a cloud hill, overlooking the Emergency Services Warehouse District. On the other side of the fence, deep in a labyrinth of buildings, was the Hikli Laboratory where Xen and Wun worked with Lon and Trz.

Riana shifted into her jeshie form, took Dene off her back, then lay him down in a protected ravine. Skillfully making bodily adjustments, she reconfigured him to be in jeshie world. Placing his head on her lap, she leaned against the soft cloud hill to wait for his awakening.

Dene was severely disoriented for a long time.

When he regained his senses, and had been soothed, Riana asked him a question which had been nagging her. "Why did you visit that far star in Roshomon?"

Dene wasn't sure how she could possibly have known about that but he answered her honestly, "Arhulio taught me how to crack the Sylumini code."

Riana rarely showed any emotion. Now she laughed like a loony. "What did you just say?"

"I learned how to break the Sylumini encryption code," gasped Dene, still reeling from yet another shift into a separate reality.

"Well now, that changes everything, doesn't it," Riana said triumphantly. "What about the bazelium?"

Dene patted both pockets, "Still there."

"Let's get going," said Riana. She snapped her fingers and somehow they were inside the Hikli Lab.

##

Xen looked up from her work bench, "anca who speak our language visit us". Then she got a startled look on her face, "who that". Dene had been shifted between worlds so many times he was unrecognizable.

"this is dene" said Riana.

105

"ooooooh he not look good" said Xen.

"rough time realm shifting" said Riana.

"we glad you here" Xen said to Dene.

Dene nodded but could not speak.

Wun came over to find out what was going on.

"he got you bazelium" Riana said.

With trembling hands Dene managed to drag out both mineral cases.

Trz came around the corner to join them. It was evening so Lon wasn't there.

Xen opened the first mineral case, examining it with skilled eyes. She did the same for the second, "this best me ever see".

Wun and Trz crowded around to get a better look.

"we seal planet bubble super duper with this" said Xen. "vonso be bigly happy".

Dene flopped desperately into a chair, "me happy too".

"dene exhausted" said Riana, "him got one more thing tell you".

"rest" said Xen, "let him rest" "we got plenty time".

Trz raced off and came back with some medicine, "him take this".

Riana looked at it, "that should help".

After taking the medicine Dene shivered, coughed, and felt better.

"you tell when ready" said Riana, "no hurry".

Dene waggled one finger to let them know he wasn't ready. Breathing deep, he did a few chair exercises. "much better".

He placed both hands in his lap, palms up. The image projected from his right palm dome was the encrypted spy signal captured from Ulta. In his left palm dome was the same signal after being decrypted by Arhulio.

Dene had never seen two jeshies do the Fling Dance before.

One quick glance at the decoded signals made Xen and Wun shout, "huzzah". They grabbed each other by the forearms and performed an exuberant swirl around the NimuTrak. While dancing around the van they sang an ancient song, which nobody understood the lyrics to anymore.

"how you get that" asked Xen, after they stopped hopping and giggling.

"religious rogue detective" whispered Dene.

Xen looked at Riana, "what that mean".

"friend of his" said Riana.

"friend goodly to us" said Xen.

From that day forward, whenever Ulta spied on them, they spied back at her. The more she learned about them, the better they understood Sylumini technical limitations. In a conflict, the advantage goes to whoever understands their adversary the best.

Chapter 13 - Planetary Bubble

Scene 35 - Gheney Hospital

Lumbia was at the construction site for Gheney Hospital, monitoring air quality. The planetary bubble surrounding Earth had been given a fresh coating of sealant, compounded from the bazelium which Dene had brought back. Lumbia was a terran anca. The rescue colony was being built inside jeshie tunnels, which were located in terran territory. Maintaining the anca atmosphere in this vast underground region was Lumbia's profession. Now she had additional responsibilities for the dual atmosphere of their refugee guests.

Ush, the jeshie construction supervisor, came running up, "bigly atmosphere".

"That's what we wanted," said Lumbia.

"coating they put on" said Ush, "way thick" "we no need breathing gear now" "want you approve we not use heavy packs".

Lumbia took a look around. The work crews were carrying dual atmosphere tanks on their backs. Now they would be able to work in the open, without lugging those things around. "Let's go to my desk."

The hospital was being built from reconstituted Earth material, in the Jeshmol style. The atmosphere control room, however, was in traditional terran territory. It was filled with gauges, monitors and flow displays. Lumbia's desk was in a corner. She logged into her desktop dome and checked the readings.

"I've never seen anything like this before," she said. "We're already at three times the dual atmosphere levels we had yesterday."

"you give permission" "no heavy gear" suggested Ush eagerly.

Lumbia checked the log files. Jeshie management had already granted their permission. She added anca permission.

"You may now work in the open, as long as the outside doors are kept shut," said Lumbia. "Go ahead and make the announcement. I need to check on something."

Ush rushed out to tell the work crews that they could remove their heavy packs and uncomfortable masks. Cheers broke out while the workers set their gear on the ground. Life was starting to get a whole lot better down here in the eastern part of the colony.

Lumbia took out her taper device and called Dene, who was working at the Observatory with Riana, Honat and Qusheem.

"Hi Lumbia" said Dene.

"You asked me to call about the atmosphere levels at the hospital," she said."

"Indeed I did," he said, "how do they look?"

"We're up three hundred percent in one single day," she replied.

"That's great," exclaimed Dene.

"That's a disaster waiting to happen," complained Lumbia. "Your wacko plan is going to create a bubble fuddle overload that will drive people crazy all around the world. Humans just can't handle that much dual atmosphere."

"I totally agree," said Dene.

"Then why did you say it's great?" asked Lumbia.

"I shall share some recent information with you," he said.

"This better explain what's going on," she said.

"I was told that you and Fevih were good friends," said Dene.

"For ten thousand years," said Lumbia. "Then she and the other Thunderbirds vanished."

"Here's something else I heard," said Dene. "When Kemong first touched Roshomon, the TBirds flashed over to the other side. We don't know why. But at least we know where our star travelers went. Then, a few months ago, a cloud wanderer named Vonso flashed over here to our side. He had become an associate of Fevih's over there. For

109

reasons I do not understand, this has something to do with Grunda.

"Oh, him," said Lumbia, "Fevih and Grunda are enemies." She was unwilling to say more.

"Vonso recently teamed up with a Roshomon flash named Caelomi," continued Dene. "I had a meeting with the two of them a few days ago. Vonso told me that Fevih left something behind at Prairie Flats. For some reason, he wanted me to tell you it was green. Then he wanted me to hear what you would say."

Under any other circumstances, Lumbia would never have answered any question about the flash beings. "The thunderbird crystals," she replied, without hesitating.

Dene felt more confident. "The next thing Vonso wanted me to ask was what you believe might happen?"

Again, Lumbia did not hesitate, "The crystals will be gone."

"That's what he said you would say. I'm wondering if you could do me a favor. I'm a great believer in fact checking the real world," said Dene. "Would you mind going over to Prairie Flats to see how things look?"

"I'm on my way," she said.

Prairie Flats was near where Lumbia lived with Honat. The Thunderbird Room had been abandoned.

Ten minutes later Lumbia called him back. "The big green crystal is gone. The smaller ones are still here." She was in shock. She had watched these grow slowly for thousands of years.

"Vonso told me he would return for the smaller ones when he was ready," said Dene.

"Ready for what?" asked Lumbia. She toured the room. Nothing had been disturbed, except that the big crystal was missing.

"Here's what I was told to say," said Dene. "Fevih asked Vonso to take the crystals when conditions were right. The Planetary Bubble got sealed yesterday. Dual atmosphere levels rose quickly. Vonso acted quickly.

"Coiling his lightning-body around the largest of the thunderbird crystals, he carried it up to the sky, just below the bubble. At that high altitude he crushed it with his mighty coils, zapping the larger pieces with his lightning powers. As of today, those tiny fragments are being blown by the winds all around the world. The goal is to have the green bits dissolve in the dual atmosphere. That's why the bubble was sealed tight. That's what Fevih sent Vonso here to do. And that, my dear Lumbia, is why I am so happy to hear that the dual atmosphere readings are abnormally high."

"So *that's* what Fevih was trying to say," gasped Lumbia.

"What should we do?" wondered Dene.

"I know who to ask," said Lumbia. "I will be hanging up now." There was silence.

Dene slid his taper device back in his lower pocket.

Riana had listened to every word, "You handled that well."

"What's going to happen?" asked Dene.

Riana glanced over at Honat and Qusheem. Both of them were lost in their own little techno worlds. In order to answer Dene's question, she needed an ishmili dome, but the one here at the Observatory was occupied. "Follow me."

Scene 36 - Glastonbury Plan

A year earlier, Dene had met Riana for the first time at her apartment in England. From there she had brought him to the Observatory to meet Honat and Qusheem. Many interesting things had happened since then. This time they went in the opposite direction, from the Observatory to her apartment. The living room looked exactly the same.

At the back was a hallway. Dene had heard about it from Cami. First door on the left was the lab. Second door on the right was the spring room.

They floated down the hall and entered her personal laboratory. Riana put her hand on the wall next to the door, then quickly zipped to the opposite corner. Dene followed. This place was legendary. The first Earth portals had been designed here, forty thousand years ago.

She pulled up two chairs and sat down in front of her ishmili dome. Dene took his seat. The dome was incredibly old, with vivid displays. The gear surrounding it packed the wall with high tech options.

Deftly sliding her hands across the control surface, she brought up a five dimensional display. Dene recognized it immediately. The map showed North America from a tectonic plate view. This terran administrative region was Lumbia's atmosphere domain.

"This view is what it looked like in 1954," Riana said. "That was right before the rescue was called into action."

Dene saw caverns and tunnels and ventilation networks in 5D. Nothing seemed out of the ordinary. Terrans cope with endless planetary styles.

"Same view, as it is today, in 1964," Riana said.

Dene was fascinated. He studied the image in the dome for several minutes.

"Without me saying a word to you, what comes to mind?" she asked.

"The Nebraska Kid Highway, which I used to think of as a road, appears to be a gigantic antenna," he answered. "It's perfectly shaped, and you can see the network connections at both ends."

"You are correct. Now, what do you think Grunda would conclude if he was shown the same map?" she asked. There was a hint of teasing in her voice.

"Grunda would never be allowed to visit the North American underground," said Dene. "His administrative region is in EurAsia."

"What you say is true, but that's not what I asked."

Dene scrunched up his face and thought hard. He had heard rumors about Grunda's extreme powers and massive ambitions, but the rest was guesses. "I suppose he might wonder why anyone would need an antenna that huge?"

"Why would they?" asked Riana. She was definitely teasing. He was such a smarty and she had him stumped.

"It can't be Jeshmol," said Dene. "Their network connections don't look like that."

"If it's not for Jeshmol," said Riana, "and there's no need for such a thing here in Nimulos, then ... "

Dene looked at his hands. Somehow that seemed to be a clue. His hands looked different after the transformation. "Oh right, now I get it, JeshNim."

"Good answer, she said. "Now, who else was recently transformed into JeshNim form?"

"Ooh ooh - Beq," he answered.

"You're getting warmer," said Riana. "Think of it this way. She is JeshNim. You are NimJesh. We have a three thousand mile long antenna hidden deep in terran territory ... "

" ... which will connect us to JeshNim.Net when it gets built," he finished.

"Right. When is it going to get built?" she asked.

"After Hamil and Hamine get here," he answered.

"Wrong," said Riana. "We wouldn't need to hide this huge antenna if that was the case. The basic network node has already been built at KCE. All we need to do is connect. We're waiting for you to get authority from Hamil and Hamine so we can proceed."

"Are you sure?" he asked.

"That's what Noom told me," Riana said. "She spoke with the co-leaders last week They were in the Phorlom, traveling in the void cruiser. We are expected to have this project up and running long before they arrive on this planet."

"That's a huge change in plans," said Dene. "Why?"

"Grunda has some sort of nefarious plan in the works with the Sylumini," she said. Her tone of voice got serious. "None of us are sure what it's about. Vonso was sent by Fevih to stop Grunda."

"And I got caught up in this spectacularly insane mess," said Dene.

"You got caught," agreed Riana, smiling.

"I love this planet," said Dene, "it never gets boring." Then he grew silent.

"What are you thinking?" she asked. Her voice was hopeful.

Dene sighed. "While we wait for this peculiar craziness to work itself out, there is something else that's been on my mind lately. Perhaps we need to talk."

"We should talk," agreed Riana.

##

Dene's facial expression knotted, "I want to say something that I hadn't planned on bringing up until after I got back from the Phorlom. Please hear me out. When I was sent here to Earth it was just one more in a long line of

113

adventures. I figured I'd rough up a few bad guys and then move on. Now I've changed my mind."

"You have," said Riana, expectantly.

Dene hesitated. "Let me put it to you this way. I love adventure. But I want the next part of my adventure to be with you. This lovely little planet will be our entry point into an unknown series of shifting realities which will shape our future. If we do things right, and our luck holds out, we will be able to build our special contribution to JeshNim. That will be the safe haven which takes us through the next segment of eternity."

Riana was well pleased, for she had similar thoughts. "Maybe it seems silly, but Zinxa and I sealed ourselves away in a world of idealism. We were the advance scouts for the pioneers seeking cosmic survival through the planetary portals of Roshomon. She in her space rock, me in my high tech lab - we struggled for a noble cause. Then Beq came along, quite unexpectedly. She brought adventure back into our lives. You have joined forces with us. It seems to me that the time has arrived when I must rejoin the world, with all its ugliness, so that we may accomplish the great deeds which await our valiant efforts."

"I want to share in your adventure," said Dene.

Riana shifted her hand so that she was holding his.

Chapter 14 - More Jeshie Colonists

Scene 37 - East Coast Portal

Sitting on top of Melona's desk at work was a professional camera, which had come back from a fashion shoot at one of the big museums. Her job was to make sure everything that went out with the crew, came back to the office, and got safely locked away in the equipment cage for the night. The glorified title that went with this humble job was inventory control clerk. She was diligent and the managers at Impress Magazine had taken notice.

On a whim, she took the pawn shop camera out of her purse and placed them side by side. The big expensive camera was perfect for a slick fashion magazine. Her personal camera was ideal for an urban photo project. It was her latest hobby and she had taken to it with a passion.

Wandering the sidewalks of Greenwich Village were bohemians, tourists, weekenders, residents, and a parade of freaks whose lifestyles boggled the imagination. Each of them had developed their own unique fashion statement, their own familiar style. Melona captured these expressions of personal flair with her camera. Then she sorted them into photo galleries. After that she hit the streets again, searching for the next fascinating shot.

Sitting next to Melona was Noutashi, happy to see that the hobby she had chosen for her client was getting such positive results. Vint had told them that the two evos were needed for a portal experiment today. Some sort of fancy equipment was in the works. Noutashi and Eberli had both been issued hand held devices, called soto color mappers, for today's experiments.

As a way of focusing the attention of the portal guides, a camera for Melona had been chosen by Noutashi.

Eberli would continue working with Andy's passion for audio recording.

Today would be Melona's first portal. Noutashi was absolutely thrilled.

##

After work, Noutashi was sitting on a tree branch in Washington Square Park. Below her was Melona, sitting on a park bench, pawn shop camera in hand.

Noutashi held a brand new soto mapper in her hand. What amused her was that she could see what people looked like in soto colors. The crowd displayed on the small screen looked like a surrealistic painting done by a deranged artist.

Ulta's spy cruiser circled overhead. She could see something in Noutashi's hand but couldn't tell what it was.

Riana sat on the rim of the fountain. What amazed her was how efficiently the denizens of Greenwich Village had adapted themselves to the excessive amounts of dual atmosphere in their neighborhood. People power glowed like mountain wildflowers on a warm spring day.

Parked in the center of the fountain was the NimuTrak. Wun was busy calibrating the mode-shifter so that he could synthesize new portal tuning colors from the crowd. Xen was having a fun time decrypting Ulta's spy signals.

"what you think" Xen asked.

"anca spy baddie busy on us today" said Wun.

"what she do now" asked Xen.

"search same yellow we reveal her at phoenix" said Wun.

"we got pattern match for that" asked Xen.

Wun scrutinized the crowd, "that one right there".

Xen leaned over to take a look, "close enough".

Wun sent two codes to Noutashi's hand held device.

Noutashi followed the instructions she had been given. Two colored dots were displayed. The red one was Melona. The yellow dot represented a young woman who was sitting on a park bench, directly across from them. That girl had blown into the big city from Ohio last winter. She had been hanging out in The Village ever since.

Melona felt a sudden surge of intuition, beamed down to her by Noutashi. Ooh, wouldn't that be a perfect picture

116

to add to her folk singer collection. Putting the camera to her eye, she clicked off three carefully framed shots. Sixties girl with wavy hair, sitting on a park bench, strumming a twelve string guitar. The Arch rising majestically against Fifth Avenue. A crowd of anonymous pedestrians adding downtown flavor.

These pedestrians were essential to Xen and Wun's plan. The young woman with the folk guitar was a decoy to trick Ulta.

Not only did the jeshies have new gear, the human crowd in the park was severely bubble fuddled. For some people this was super cool. For others the air mix made them extra grouchy. Most were unaware of anything. Xen and Wun carefully selected those who felt enlightened after getting pumped up from a heavy jolt of jeshie air.

This crowd would be used to synthesize two portal colors. Melona would be their standard soto color. It was essential that none of this be revealed to the sky cruiser.

Ulta saw that something big was about to happen. Her equipment locked in on Melona, plus this other evo who was having her picture taken. Hopefully, this would confirm the data she had already collected.

The sweet thing for the jeshies was that Ulta's spy beams let them know exactly what she was looking for. Yellow showed up prominently. The two colors they were going to synthesize were beyond the range of Sylumini search algorithms.

The cast of characters in Washington Square was just what they needed. In this shifting urban parade were longhairs, ethnic residents, uptown curiosity seekers, urban tourists, brightly dressed islanders, suits down from midtown, every imaginable immigrant, daring artistic innovators, as well as whatever weirdos The Village had to offer.

After tweaking adjustments, Wun pushed the small red button.

Fresh powers flickered. Riana knew right away that the test had worked. The edges of a portal began to glow. She held her thumb up as a signal to Xen and Wun. Ulta saw her arch-rival's signal and beamed down every spy trick she had in the cargo bay.

While Wun concentrated on opening the portal. Xen concentrated on decoding Ulta's search parameters. They would need this data for the second experiment they were going to run out in San Francisco later today.

Right on cue the portal opened. A jeshie scout stepped through to make sure everything was safe for those who would follow.

Ulta got giddy.

Xen could tell that anca spy baddie had taken the bait.

In the midst of this spy versus spy contest, Noutashi was about as happy as a guardian anca could be. Her girl had done it. Looking at the hand held device, she watched the portal open. Then she saw the jeshies come streaming through. Her Melona had made all this possible and she didn't need any help from that old Andy.

As for Melona, she sat quietly on the bench, waiting for the next photo opportunity.

##

Jeshie colonists marched through in orderly fashion. They were lined up along Fourth Street, all the way past Broadway. As the alien immigrants descended through the fountain they entered their new home territory. There was no going back. Nimulos is where they would live from now on ... until JeshNim got built.

Ulta watched the count as they disappeared into the fountain. "Exactly five thousand," she muttered.

Right before the last colonist made it through, Xen waved for Riana to join them. She slid through the side of their van and said, "bubble fuddle bigly success".

Wun pointed at the dashboard dome, "hefty portal power".

"awesome" said Riana.

"ready for underground" asked Xen.

"look forward" replied Riana.

Xen shifted the van into transform-gear, then eased it down through the fountain, which put them in terran territory. Wun closed the portal behind them.

Ulta had watched Riana glide through the side of that jeshie van, then disappear, with no apparent scientific explanation. Next she saw the NimuTrak drive into the fountain. The portal snapped shut. There was no more to see.

"We lost track of them," said Ulta, over the intercom to Yori. "Head out to San Francisco. I'm sure we'll find them out there somewhere." She shut down the spy gear and took her regular place in the copilot's seat.

##

Instead of driving to California across the drifting Kemong cloud island, which they had always done before, this time the NimuTrak would drive down the Nebraska Kid Highway. This was the first time any of them had been granted a visitor's permit to enter the jeshie colony. During the long ride they planned on checking Vonso's scheme.

Taking the old Terran Tunnel beneath the Hudson River, they traveled under New Jersey, took the Loop onto the Nebraska Kid, then headed west.

Three friends in high spirits roared down the new highway, surrounded by delivery vehicles, passenger buses, and the occasional jeshie limo. Gliding into the high speed lane, Xen drove as fast as traffic conditions permitted.

When their speed steadied, Xen called out, "switch it on".

Wun touched the panel and several bright beacons of invisible light were powered up on top of their van. Riana leaned forward to watch the display on the dashboard dome.

The tunnel in front of them looked like a speeding circle, coming straight at them. The monitor images showed patches of bright green on rough walls. Sensors on the sides of their van measured coverage patterns.

The NebKid tunnel would have been little more than a jeshie hole in the ground - if it wasn't for that green residue collecting on these walls. After the colony permit expired, that coating would be solid. Then, the huge antenna would connect the terran underground to KCE, the permanent colony between Earth and Mars. With any luck, Grunda and his Sylumini minions would know nothing about any of this.

For one entire year these walls had been soaking up that green mist. It looked like the project was off to a promising start.

119

"Is that the band you were telling me about?" asked Bongo.

"Yeah, that's them," said Andy. "The Far Outs. They come to the park around this time of day."

"They look like cowboys with girl's hair," sneered Bongo.

"Shhhh," said Andy, "we don't want to upset their delicate artistic sensibilities."

"Yeah right," groused Bongo, "they're a delicate rock band."

Andy had hauled his little red wagon up Groovy Hill. They were in Golden Gate Park on a fabulously beautiful day. In the wagon was a reel-to-reel tape recorder, a car battery with an AC adapter, and some microphones. While they were setting up to make a recording, the band started their sound check.

"How do they get that strange sound?" asked Bongo.

"See that kid over there. He glued a microphone inside a ceramic whiskey jug. Then he blows across the top of the jug and runs that sound through a distortion box, into an amplifier," Andy explained.

"Why would they do something like that?" asked Bongo.

"Nobody else has that sound," said Andy.

"Uh, does anybody need that sound?" asked Bongo.

"The audience went wild for it last Wednesday," Andy told him. "I've never seen anything like it. That's why I wanted to come back here to get this down on tape."

"Seriously," said Bongo, "we do jazz recordings. Distorted whiskey jugs are not musical instruments."

Andy gave his long time audio friend a hard look. "We record the sounds that people want to remember. When you and I were young, jazz was called the devil's music."

"I don't know, man," said Bongo. "You're asking a lot if you want me to get involved in this crazy project of yours."

"There's more to it than that," explained Andy, in desperation. "You've got a degree in electrical engineering. It's easy for you to bounce from job to job. I barely made it out of high school, got injured in the lumber camps, and now I work part time in a failing bookstore. When they close those doors, Diane's family will send her off to some fancy rehab center overlooking the Pacific Ocean. I don't have anyone in my corner except you."

"Sorry man," said Bongo, "I didn't realize things were that bad."

"Yeah, well, they are that bad," shrugged Andy.

Bongo put his hand out to seal the deal. "I'll tag along for your little adventure."

"Stick around," said Andy. "You'll see what I'm talking about."

Xen and Wun had learned several important lessons from their New York experiment. The bubble fuddled people made opening the synth portal so much easier. Ulta was scanning for their fake yellow color. And, most important of all, using only one human worked perfectly with the synth. During their road trip here they had also shown that Vonso's antenna was looking much better than expected.

Now they were going to run a different set of tests out here in San Francisco. They needed to seriously expand their range of color options. If they could do that, then so many other things we be that much easier.

From the combined frequencies of this crowd, Wun rebalanced the portal parameters. This time, Andy would be their human standard. Strolling through the park, as characters in an endless west coast drama, were peace freaks, citizens from the hill, native originals, descendants of the conquistadors, meandering touristas, businessmen on break, a measure of asians, poet masters of absurdity, and whoever rolled into Frisco with a few dollars and a fool's dream.

"what we got" asked Xen.

"that yellow one close match new york" said Wun, "got crazy bigly power".

"we take that one" said Xen.

Wun adjusted the mode-shifter, then sent the data to Eberli, who held a soto mapper in his hand. It beeped. Ulta tried to get a close-up. Eberli shielded it so no one could see. There was a blue dot and a yellow dot. He knew the blue dot was Andy. The yellow dot was the whiskey jug musician.

121

Eberli beamed it into Andy's imagination that he should get a microphone up close on that jug player.

The band started playing one of their most energetic original tunes.

The spy equipment in Ulta's star cruiser was calibrated to perfection. As the portal began to open, she watched everything in exquisite detail. When the colonists started streaming through, her equipment counted each and every one. Exactly five thousand.

With that taken care of, Ulta turned her attention to analyzing the data. A fuzzy image caught her eye. She discovered that a powerful neutralizer field surrounded the big blue NimuTrak. They were hiding something from her. Quickly replaying the New York data, she saw the same neutralizer field, which she hadn't noticed earlier.

Suspecting a trap - she switched all her spy gear to standard auto-scan. She didn't want to reveal any technical secrets to the competition.

Xen said, "oooh she mad at us now".

Riana said severely, "good" "we want anca spy baddie feel badly" "she have bigly trouble with special board".

Scene 39 - Celene And Dene

Dene had never been to Ayamara before. When he was young, designing capitol cities along the lines of Hoshambelan and Ayamara was the type of work that had gotten him a solid start in life.

It looked eerie as he approached the future capitol of the Earth Anca Corp. Many years ago an enormous foundation slab had been laid down, deep in an isolated region of the Pacific Ocean. At the center were abandoned buildings, a few completed, most unfinished. Exotic ocean creatures - who could survive under crushing pressure, extreme cold, and endless dark - were the only inhabitants.

Celene had thrown the Sylumini out of Ayamara.

In a far corner of the foundation was one single building.

When Celene first arrived on Earth, she brought with her one thousand trusted staff members. Those thousand were the only ones who now worked inside that one building.

These executives and office workers had constructed their new headquarters with their own hands. Celene had ordered a preassembled office building kit through Ostramona.Net. That was the only way they could be sure there were no Sylumini bugging devices hidden in the walls.

One single building for an entire future capitol city. This couldn't go on much longer. That's one of the reasons why Celene and Dene needed to talk. Next year, he was going to make his jump to carry messages to and from her bosses. They both needed to make sure they were ready.

First they discussed the newly developed portal techniques - mode-shifters, synthesized guide beams, dual atmosphere levels, weight limit parameters. Dene explained that five thousand new colonists had been brought in for the east coast hospital, as well as an additional five thousand for the west coast shuttle terminal. Celene was very impressed when she heard how the Nebraska Kid Highway was speeding up the construction of this essential infrastructure for the rescue colony.

Nothing was mentioned about Ulta or Vonso.

After the immigration status was made clear, Celene wanted to pin Dene down on a few troublesome tactical items which bothered her.

"Let's review the fundamentals," said Celene. "Suppose you've delivered both sets of code cubes to Hamil and Hamine. What happens next?"

"That depends entirely on the co-leaders," said Dene. "At the most basic level, I'm nothing more than a courier. My job is to carry information to them, then return here with their replies. There is no compelling reason why any of that is any of my business."

"What if it becomes your business?" asked Celene.

Dene said, "I will bring my own personal opinions with me to Cazouni. If your bosses ask me a question, then I will explain to them what I believe to be true."

"What if your recommendations run at cross purposes to my needs?" asked Celene.

"You have an opportunity to build a diplomatic code cube that tells your side of the story," said Dene. "Sarkon and Sarena have the same opportunity. What I say will express my own views. My beliefs could easily run at cross purposes to you, or anyone else."

"That's how the game is played," agreed Celene. "Now, what if you don't get there?"

"There are two main reasons I might not reach my destination," said Dene. "The first is that I'm an impetuous space tramp who decides to jump to a more interesting adventure. The second is that I die in the Phorlom void because I'm an overzealous fool."

These were not the answers Celene had been expecting. "Why would you risk *my* diplomatic mission?"

"I wouldn't," said Dene, "but bad things do happen. A third possibility is that your bosses decide they can't trust me, so they refuse to hand over any code cubes at all. A fourth possibility is that I reach the void, decide it's too risky, and return here as a failed diplomat."

"Life's a gamble and then you get reassigned to a different part of the universe," said Celene, repeating an old saying. "Let's suppose you don't make it back for any number of reasons. What then?"

"I made sure that Riana has everything she needs," said Dene. "The Observatory has a dozen backup plans. The Hikli has access to hundreds of options. Ing and Jenissen are agile and tough. The Terrans are sworn enemies of the Sylumini. A jeshie colony is thriving here on Earth. Anca and Soto Guardian teams are working together to provide enough dual atmosphere for long term success. Nobody needs me."

In the privacy of her own thoughts, Celene agreed with most of what Dene had told her. That last point was something she disagreed with. Someone did need him. From what she had heard, Riana needed him.

Chapter 15 - The Edge Of Gomonish

Scene 40 - Broken Token

A large crowd had gathered at the Greenland Planetary Terminal to watch Dene make his famous jump. Some said he could do it, some said he couldn't. Nobody much cared about the reasons why he was being sent on this mission. They just wanted to say they had witnessed the jump.

Arcal was prime minister of the Hoshambelan Administration. Sarkon and Sarena had chosen him to officiate. Celene would be the next prime minister on Earth, after the Ayamara Administration got sworn in. The prime minister, and prime minister designate, hovered next to each other, waiting for additional dignitaries to come down the tunnel from Paliyur.

The ceremony being performed today was to guarantee that the messages being sent and returned were fully certified, according the ancient method of the broken token. Among anca, this is the only way to prove that a diplomatic exchange carries the full force of law. Networks can be hacked. Messages can be tampered with. Couriers can be compromised. The pieces of a broken token will only fit together one way.

Emerging from the tunnel exit, Jenissen and Ing arrived with a large group of prominent officials. The chief protocol officer showed each of them to their places. After the dignitaries were assembled, the ceremony began.

"We have gathered to inaugurate an exchange of diplomatic messages between two administrations," intoned Arcal. "The purpose of this exchange is to resolve the uncertainties surrounding the emergency rescue of our neighbors from Jeshmol. We will begin with the ceremony of the broken token."

Celene moved forward to the testimonial stand. "When I parted company with Hamil and Hamine we performed the first part of this ceremony. As their Chief Transition Officer, they provided me with a set of half tokens for official use here on Earth. The other half of these split tokens remain in their hands. A quarter token will be left here with the Hoshambelan Administration as security. The other quarter token will be carried by the courier. If the co-leaders at the remote location agree, their half piece, along with the courier's quarter piece, will be returned here. If those two pieces match the local security piece then the instructions in the diplomatic pouch will carry the full force of law."

She held her half token high for all to see.

It was well known that these tokens are color coded. What the colors represent is known only to those who control each half. This particular half token was a bold shade of red. The public would remember this.

Arcal called out, "I have been appointed guardian of the local security token."

Celene called out, "Who will validate the credentials of the courier."

Jenissen came forward to the testimonial stand, "I have certified Dene's diplomatic credentials with the Nimulos Expansion Region Administration at Hierashu."

Ing came forward and stated, "I affirm that the laws of the anca, the laws of the ishmili, and the laws of the soto, as they apply in this case, have been communicated to the galactic authorities, and they have granted their approval."

When these public proclamations were concluded, Arcal and Celene faced each other so that everyone had a clear view of everything they did.

Celene held the red half token in front of Arcal. "This half token was given to me by the incoming Ayamara Administration of Hamil and Hamine. They retain possession of the other half. I present it to you in the exact form that it was given to me."

Arcal raised the half token high. "In full view of the public, I break this half token into two quarters." He snapped it lengthwise, separating his hands so that the two pieces remained far apart.

Dene moved forward. He opened the diplomatic pouch and displayed it to the public so they would remember its form. Facing Arcal, he said, "The pouch is open."

The Chief Protocol Officer moved to the testimonial stand. While reciting a lengthy legal statement, at fast pace, he took a quarter token from Arcal's hand, sealed it according to Celene's protocol, then ceremonially placed it in Dene's pouch.

The Chief Protocol Officer then moved over to the other side and took the other quarter token from Arcal's other hand, sealing it according to Sarkon and Sarena's protocol. This he turned over to the Archivist.

Celene moved forward to place her diplomatic code cubes inside Dene's open diplomatic pouch. Arcal did the same, on behalf of the Hoshambelan Administration. Dene had not touched anything.

Once again the Chief Protocol Officer moved forward. The pouch was sealed according to current administration practices. Celene added special seals of her own, which would be recognized by Hamil and Hamine.

When all this was accomplished, Dene placed the double sealed pouch in his pocket, where it would remain undisturbed until it was turned over to Hamil and Hamine.

Dene declared to the crowd, "It is with a profound sense of responsibility that I embark upon this mission. A meeting place has been determined and a time has been set. I will be away for many months. If I have not returned within one year this mission will be considered a failed diplomacy. When I do return, the current administration, and representatives of the incoming administration, will determine what course of action shall be taken."

With that said, he placed his arms at his side, glanced left and right, then vanished.

In the crowd some said he really did make the jump, others said it was just a cheap magician's trick. Those responsible for diplomacy knew that the broken token would guarantee the results.

Scene 41 - Commander Udintav

In this sector of the Gomonish gravity group only one thin grid line extended a short distance into the Phorlom void. Connected to the other side was the Penezha sphere. Dene watched fearfully with practical eyes. This would be the last jump he could make without facing instant death. He waited until that flickering connection seemed strong.

Adventurer Dene overcame an icy wave of fear and jumped.

##

"Looks like that urbie they were telling us about actually got here," said the pilot of the Penezha sphere.

Some crazy anca was out there in the void, wildly waving his arms at them.

The copilot laughed. "Look at that idiotic expression on his face. Something's gotta be wrong with someone who lives like that."

The pilot motioned for him to go around to the void lock.

Twenty minutes later the door opened and Dene floated inside. "Your hospitality is greatly appreciated," he said to the Commander, extending his hand.

Commander Udintav refused to shake his hand. "I am confining you to quarters until we can send you back to Ostramona."

"No you're not," said Dene, with a sneer on his lips that made the crew quiver. "I made it this far. I can jump through the walls of Penezha anytime. Unless you want my death on your hands, you'd better show me your best maps so I can reach Cazouni."

A ferocious three day screaming match erupted between the Commander and the Diplomat.

To the surprise of every member of the crew, it was Commander Udintav who gave in. Calling his top officers around him he said, "The lives of everyone on this sphere are my responsibility, including this so-called diplomat. I received direct orders from Imbotil a few minutes ago. This irresponsible lunatic must be allowed to leave the safety of our sphere. Orders are orders. It is beyond my control. Show him the most recent maps and answer his every question."

128

When Dene was told of this he graciously extended his hand toward the Commander and said, "This will be a great honor for you when my mission succeeds."

Commander Udintav hesitated, then reached out to shake the hand of someone he was absolutely certain no one would ever hear from again.

Scene 42 - Beq's Bungalow

Five days later the void lock opened. Dene, well rested and filled with facts, jumped into the void. Beq was nowhere to be seen. Without her, the surface of this sphere might be where he died.

It was of no cosmic consolation to Dene that if his soul-seed did curl up, out here in the merciless emptiness, then it would eventually revive - perhaps millions or billions of years hence - when the universe would be in a vastly different configuration. He needed this now.

Commander Udintav watched through the small view port until Dene was out of sight. "Enter it into the logs that our visitor is no longer on board," growled the commander. "This incident is over. Return to your quarters."

Dene hadn't gone very far. He was trembling in desperation behind a massive support structure bolted to the hull. This was far worse than anything he had ever imagined. After reviewing every desperate trick he had ever learned - he came up blank.

"Over here," came a disembodied voice.

Easing his grip on a thick bolt, he looked around.

"Turn your head in this direction," said the voice.

Doing what he had always found to be useful in impossible situations - he relaxed. Faint tinges of color appeared.

"Oh, hi Beq, How long have you been here?" asked Dene.

"A couple of weeks," she said. "I wasn't sure when you would be ready."

"How did you get here so fast?" asked Dene.

"Vonso flew me." Beq looked proud. "What an awesome ride."

Dene clung tightly to the hull bolt. "Tell me what to do."

"I built a cute little bungalow at the top of the sphere," she said. "Follow me."

Feeling wobbly, Dene slid himself along the outer surface of the hull, while she skated gracefully to the top. Sure enough there was a small bungalow. The windows in front were decorated with frilly curtains. She opened the door. Inside, he could breathe easily.

"This is awesome," said Dene, after catching his breath.

"Your room is on that side," said Beq. "Mine is over here. We can hang out in the living room until I teach you how to jeshnim skate."

"This is a whole lot better than anything my buddy Udintav would have offered," said Dene.

Three days later they reached the lost planet Cazouni, feeling refreshed from the gentle exercise of skating through the golden clouds of JeshNim. These two were well pleased that they had gotten a chance to learn more about each other's interesting lives.

The outer surface of the lost planet was dull dust brown. No wind, no weather - only the relentless nibblings of the flickering void. Far below the lifeless surface were tiny one celled organisms. They had lived here since life first evolved on Cazouni. They knew nothing of the void. They had known nothing of the upper world when it was teeming with civilized life. For as long as there was internal heat, and a supply of nutrients from minerals, these tiny beings would live as they had always done. It was from these tiny specks of life that anca extracted atmosphere for the Cazouni Research Station.

Beq brought him to a massive door. "Here's what Riana told me. You are going through that door. I am not. I have other business."

"You saved my life," said Dene. "I hope to see you again when this mission is over."

"You will," said Beq. "Another thing Riana told me was this. On your way home we want you to visit us at Paroun. That's important. We need to finish your transformation before you go back to Earth."

"I will honor your request," said Dene.

Beq skated away on glimmering golden clouds.

130

Gliding through seven massive void lock doors was easy for Dene.

Inside the research station he felt desperately ill. The healthy anca atmosphere was like a choking poison. Falling down on his curled taper, he slowly sank to the floor. Before his mind blanked out, Dene muttered a prayer of thanks.

##

After adjusting to normal atmosphere he explored the research station. There was a large scientific research area, crew quarters, guest quarters, a recreation room, the cruiser repair shop, and a long tunnel leading down to the atmosphere mines. He chose a bunk in crew quarters for himself.

It turned out that the most valuable thing was the clock on the wall. Without it there was no way to count the days. In the void there is no regular movement. A lost planet, flung there by the whims of gravity, does not tumble according to a fixed schedule.

Sometimes he watched the clock. Other times he studiously ignored it.

With no one to talk to, nothing to do, nowhere to direct his intense energy, Dene shifted from his usual outgoing self, to his long neglected internal self.

Layer by layer, what used to seem important was replaced by what was actually important. After allowing his natural instincts to turn inward he discovered obvious surprises.

Before this enforced silence, his thoughts had always started with his own needs and then worked outward from there. Now he began to understand that a parallel approach yielded better results. Starting with a larger view of whatever needed attention, he working inwards from there, toward his own abilities.

With no action to keep his hands busy, his mind meandered, searching by small steps, and this inevitably led him to seek the source.

Not even those who achieve great wisdom can fully understand the one true source of all. Between each of us and the source is the veil of mystery. On our side of the veil is action. On the other side of the veil is upholding.

Always before, Dene had pushed against what was bad so that the good would have a chance to prevail. Now he sought out what was genuinely worthy so that he could project those powers into the world.

One day, while considering these intense musings, his mind shifted suddenly to something closer to home. With vivid inspiration he felt the presence of a place. That place seemed near. After sleeping and waking, he had a hunch.

##

In the equipment room, halfway between the research station and the atmosphere mines, was a ventilation shaft. Pipes rose up through the ceiling. Those pipes had to go somewhere. There was enough room for one anca to float up the narrow shaft.

At the top he discovered The Lookout.

This was a medium sized room with a circular shape. The pipe shaft was at the center. A thick domed roof, supported by massive walls, protected it from the void. It must have been here since the earliest days of the research station. Automated equipment pushed the stale air out into the void, while fresh air was kept circulating.

Whoever designed this place had provided features which turned it into a meditation center. Five thick windows had five hard benches. Floor, walls, ceiling were featureless.

When first he looked through those thick windows his eyes saw only pale brown dust. In the distance was lightless horizon. Every direction seemed the same.

With practice he began to see.

Five directions teemed with faint jeshnim. The Phorlom was slowly filling. Elemental structures - not Jeshmol, not Nimulos, combining both - could be perceived through his new jeshnim sensations. Vonso had been wise.

One day, while meditating, a flash of inspiration rolled over him like an enormous wave. Riana and Zinxa and Beq had left him here so he could discover for himself what had already illuminated them. Four lives had been thrown together. Whether it was raw chance, or planned fate, was unimportant. Somehow each of them was now part of something larger. It would be here, in the former nothingness named Phorlom, where they would become citizens of a durable world.

132

Staring through thick windows, into unfolding emptiness, he heard the Bells of Wakona chiming in his mind.

Chapter 16 - Diplomacy In The Void

Scene 43 - Rakari And Jagh

Living inside a slowly eroding planet, wrapped in utter solitude, had been refreshing. The incessant sound of the atmosphere pumps provided a daily rhythm for life. The clock on the wall kept his mind focused on the real world.

Four years ago Dene had been on Eetor when Hamil and Hamine asked him to be their diplomatic courier.

Four years ago Hamil and Hamine had strapped themselves into passenger seats for their journey to Cazouni.

Today they were scheduled to meet.

The research station was the same way he found it. Dene hadn't changed anything, except for his own bunk, which he kept tidy.

His personal appearance, on the other hand, was doubtful. Dene had been sent here as a diplomat. Three weeks of meditating upon the grand mysteries of the boundless universe had refreshed his soul and enlivened his mind.

But - one must keep up appearances.

At the Academy of Diplomacy in the Hierashu Capitol Region they had taught him the proper way to hover at attention, hover at ease, salute, bow, shake hands and display stylized expressions of generosity or animosity. He reviewed these lessons thoroughly. Of greatest importance, he felt, was vocal presence. For several days he practiced speaking clearly in a sonorous voice. Firmly but politely refusing to accede a point. Exchanging sensitive information in a conspiratorial whisper. Obscure protocols, which had seemed of little value during his student days, were reviewed with exacting attention.

When Dene heard the first rumblings of the void cruiser, as it made its way through the seven void locks, he went to the greeting place he had chosen. Assuming the position of devotion to duty, he hovered with dignity until his services were requested.

##

"Auto system off," said Jagh.

The cruiser was in the first lock. Pumps from the atmosphere mines switched on. The tractor mechanism slowly pulled them through. The inner gate began to open.

"Give me a visual confirm," Captain Rakari said to Copilot Jagh.

"An anca is hovering at attention," said Jagh.

"Any sign of hostile intent?" asked Rakari.

"Nothing more suspicious than a diplomat's smile," said Jagh.

The Captain initiated a special sequence where the cruiser engine remained ready and steady. The copilot would be sent out to investigate. If there was trouble they could escape.

Over the intercom Rakari announced, "Someone is in the research station."

"Is it the courier?" asked Hamine.

"We won't know until we ask," said Rakari.

Until this moment the four of them hadn't believed this would actually happen.

"We will wait for your report," said Hamil.

Jagh crawled back into the passenger compartment and went out the side door.

"State your intention," said Jagh.

"Diplomatic courier from Earth," said Dene.

"Your credentials please," said Jagh.

Dene reached slowly into his pocket and handed the sealed diplomatic pouch to the copilot. Reaching carefully in his other pocket he turned over his credentials packet.

"Wait here," said Jagh.

"On duty and awaiting orders," said Dene, saluting smartly.

##

After an extended wait, while his credentials were being checked, and the code cubes were given a quick review, the Captain shut off the engine. The four of them emerged through the side door.

Years of being cramped inside had left them feeling wobbly. During their long journey each of them had performed their daily exercises rigorously. But the body has its limits. It felt great to be out in the open again. According to custom, Dene waited patiently until they recovered their sense of balance and movement.

The captain and copilot took up positions directly behind Dene. The co-leaders hovered in front of him, just beyond striking distance.

Hamine said, "We accept your credentials."

"I am honored," said Dene, bending politely.

Hamil said, "The amount of information in the code cubes is enormous. We will need to conduct a thorough review."

"I am prepared to do as you request," said Dene.

The co-leaders were shown to the guest quarters.

Dene informed the Captain that he had occupied one of the bunks in crew quarters. Rakari confined him to his bunk. They searched the research station. Sitting with his taper coiled on the bed, Dene felt an inward glow.

Rakari and Jagh came back.

"Congratulations on not being dead," said Rakari. "I look forward to hearing how you did that."

"When the time is right," said Dene, "I will tell my tale."

Jagh added, "I checked the Phorlom.Net terminal while we were securing the area. There was a message from Commander Udintav. He wants an update on your status. Do you have anything you'd like to report?"

"Send my warmest regards to the dear Commander and tell him I appreciate his generous hospitality," said Dene.

Rakari and Jagh laughed raucously. They knew rough old Commander Udintav all too well.

Scene 44 - Mode Controller

When Hamil and Hamine asked Dene questions, these sessions would sometimes go on for hours. Their private conversations in the guest quarters usually lasted longer. That meant Dene had plenty of time to hang out with Rakari and Jagh.

Pilot and copilot understood how things really worked around here. Most of the time Dene didn't say much. The important thing was for them to repair their cruiser. If something went wrong, that was their only way out. Every now and again, he would hand them a tool, or run an errand. Mostly he sat, listened and watched.

After a few days, Dene decided to ask a question. "When I visited Captain Behchel, he had his scientists explain how a void drive works."

"That's nice," said Rakari, who had her head stuck in the engine compartment.

"What you're working on isn't a void drive," said Dene.

"Hmph," mumbled Rakari, straining on a wrench.

Dene remained silent until the engine was humming smoothly.

Rakari wiped her hands on a shop rag, "It's a mode-drive."

"Never heard of a mode-drive before," said Dene.

"Good to know," said Rakari, "we don't want word to get around."

Tossing the shop rag on the work bench, Rakari whispered something to Jagh.

Jagh nodded and opened the front panel of a large piece of equipment tucked away in the corner. Uncoiling a thick cable, he attached it to the mode-cruiser.

"We've got a little surprise for the co-leaders," said Captain Rakari. "They get nervous sometimes. Don't get them irritated. Let me do the talking."

"On it," said Dene.

Jagh powered up the mystery machine. A green light went on.

A short while later, Hamil and Hamine emerged from the guest quarters, all flustered.

"Oh there you are," said Hamine, "we have another list of questions."

"Pardon me," said Captain Rakari, "sorry to interrupt, but we have visitors we'd like you to meet."

"Visitors?" gasped Hamil. "How could anyone get in?"

"You already know one of them," said Rakari. "Noom is waiting for you."

Both co-leaders got really excited. Meeting with an ishmili, at such an exotic location, was a great honor.

"Follow me," said Rakari.

They floated down a long hall toward the atmosphere mines. On the left was the equipment room. Dene had been there many times. You would not notice it when you first floated through the door, but the exhaust shaft was connected to the watchtower.

Noom appeared in her communicator body. "Greetings and good fortune to you. I have made this journey to Cazouni so that I may introduce you to your colleagues."

"Oh my, what a pleasant surprise," said Hamine. "It's so wonderful to see you again."

Dene noticed that Jagh floated to the back of the room, opened a cabinet, then powered up a large machine. A green light went on.

Noom called out, "Jagh, please activate the mode-controller."

In the blink of an eye the dim equipment room became well lit. It was filled with exotic furniture. Three alien beings sat at a table. They stood up for introductions.

Hamil said, "Oh my, we didn't expect so much to happen all at once."

Hamine was amazed, "What a fabulous surprise."

Dene kept a neutral expression on his face, in spite of what he saw.

Noom explained, "You are now in a combined other-sider world. This is what our research teams have learned how to do out here in the Phorlom. Let me introduce you to your peers from Jeshmol."

Three jeshies stepped forward. Two of them were soto and the third was an evojesh.

Noom introduced the nimulon co-leaders first, "I would like you to meet Hamil and Hamine. They will be working with you here at the station during this research season. Accompanying them is their courier, Dene."

Noom introduced the jeshies next, "I would like you to meet Professor Fro, who is head of the Phorlom Research

Foundation on the Jeshmol side. He is the soto counterpart of Professor Obolon, who you met at Imbotil."

"pleased to meet you" said Fro. He spoke anca fluently but with a heavy accent.

"An honor to make your acquaintance," said Hamil.

"Next I would like to introduce Imi," said Noom. "She is our Senior Data Analyst. Imi now occupies the position which was first chaired by Riana."

"We've seen many of your reports," said Hamine. "How pleasant to meet you face to face."

"we schedule time soon" said Imi. She spoke anca in clipped chunks. Imi was a dark reddish-brown evojesh, with a thin body and angular features.

It is our special pleasure to introduce you to our most recent employee," said Noom. "This is Beq. She signed on with the Foundation a few days ago. We're negotiating to get her a position at the Zog Center For Interface Analytics. She is a good friend of Dene's."

"What a surprise," said Hamil.

Both co-leaders looked at Dene differently.

"You two should go ahead and say hello," said Noom. "I can imagine what a thrill it is to meet under these circumstances, after all the amazing adventures you two have been through."

Dene floated over and gave Beq a warm hug. "How nice that we meet again in such a pleasant place. Congratulations on your promotion." He winked at her.

"It's a dream come true," said Beq. holding both his hands. "I look forward to working with you again on Zog."

Hamil and Hamine were stunned that their courier was on a first name basis with a soto on Noom's team.

Scene 45 - On The Way

Time sped by quickly after that. The break room was filled with animated conversation all day long. Hamil and Hamine learned more in two days than they would have by studying the code cubes for two months. After the second day, Noom returned to her regular assignment in Roshomon. Fro, Imi and Beq discussed recent scientific breakthroughs with Hamil and Hamine. That's what this research mission was all about. Before the co-leaders accepted responsibility for Earth, they needed to understand the cutting edge research which would give their administration the tools they needed for success.

Dene took note of something very important during all this chatter. Not one thing was ever mentioned about Vonso. Nothing.

Then one day what had been obvious all along became clear to them.

Celene must be put in charge of the rescue. Sarkon and Sarena wanted nothing to do with its rigorous high tech demands. The Sylumini were seriously abusing their position as government contractors. Proper authority must be restored. Once that decision was made, everything else was easy.

Dene was quite happy. He didn't dare show his face at Hoshambelan too early or his enemies would accuse him of fraud. The extra time he now had presented him with a magnificent opportunity to explore Tromolea. This small local group of galaxies is where their contribution to JeshNim would become a reality. Ostramona, Andromeda, Phorlom - those were the major places in this plan. Exploring this geography was essential.

At the departure ceremony, Dene hovered inside the research station with the freshly sealed diplomatic pouch in his pocket. Rakari and Jagh hovered at attention next to their cruiser. Hamil and Hamine faced Dene with all the dignity inherent in their office.

"Your diplomatic mission was a success," said Hamine.

"May your return to Earth be safe," said Hamil.

"I will obey your instructions," said Dene.

Then he vanished from sight.

Rakari and Jagh shifted to the at ease position.

Hamine whispered, "This was certainly more than we expected."

"I have a confession to make," Hamil whispered back. "I was wrong. Not every anca who knows how to do the jump is a fraud."

Dene didn't go far. He and Beq had agreed to meet at the Watchtower. After shifting into his JeshNim form he

140

glided above the dusty surface of the lost planet. Beq sat on the curved top of the low tower. Golden clouds shimmered across the horizon.

"This is a lot more comfortable than when we met at Penezha," said Dene.

"We have learned to live within our JeshNim forms," agreed Beq. "How did your diplomacy go."

Dene patted his pockets. "Got the cubes. Got the verbals. It's all good."

"Will you visit us at Paroun?" she asked.

"Wouldn't miss it for anything," he said. "Sarkon and Sarena expect me back late in the year. I'll visit you two weeks before."

"That will give us plenty of time," said Beq. "We must finish your transformation."

"What are your plans?" asked Dene.

"Professor Obolon got me that job at the Zog Center For Interface Analytics," said Beq. "I'm going over to Imbotil to get the support I need to finish the transition."

"It must feel strange going back to the ordinary world, after experiencing the other-side," he said.

Beq got serious, "Ordinary feels so strange."

Dene had spent half his life struggling with this. "Eventually the new becomes the ordinary."

After a gentle hug, Dene skated away on golden clouds.

##

At the edge of Gomonish the golden clouds faded away, where they withered in the gravity field.

Dene had promised to send a confirmation message to Captain Behchel.

From the maps he had seen at Penezha he knew the location of a small galaxy nearby. They would have an anca network.

On the surface of a beautiful planet, at the edge of gravity's grasp, Dene popped out of his jump. A crowd of anca saw him suddenly appear out of nowhere. All of them reached for their taper devices at the same time. Law enforcement got flooded with calls.

The authorities took a skeptical view of his claim that he was a diplomat who knew how do the jump. What was he doing here? Who had sent him? If that was his story then why had he chosen this planet?

After checking his outrageous tale with the authorities at Hierashu, the local authorities reluctantly agreed to his request. Dene would be allowed to send one message over Anca.Net. Then it would be best for everyone if he moved along.

Sitting at a modest desk, in a small library, located in an anca community center, he took his taper device out and looked up the message number which Captain Behchel had given him. Entering the number, followed by the authorization code, he got an anca operator on the line.

"Valdaria Security, how may I help you?" the voice said.

"I have a Code Q26 message to deliver," said Dene.

"One moment please," said the voice.

After an irritating delay, an automated voice came on the line. "You are now connected. Please enter your pass code."

Dene had memorized the pass code, which he was glad he could still remember.

"At the tone please leave a message."

"Hi, this is Dene. I have a message for Captain Behchel. Phorlom mission a success. I am safely back in Gomonish. I will return to Earth at the end of the year. Please proceed with the plan we discussed before my departure. It's great to be back."

After signing off the communicator dome, he put his hands behind his head and leaned back in the library chair. A security guard kept an eye on him.

Ever since the ishmili decided to make use of his unusual talents, he'd traveled farther than any anca he had ever met, faced more enemies than he could count, and done things which seemed genuinely impossible. Now all he wanted to do was go home.

There was a new frontier out there. He'd known about it all along, even when he worked as an architect. Now he had seen and smelled and touched that frontier.

In a remote library, at the edge of Gomonish, the Bells of Wakona chimed in his mind.

Chapter 17 - Home Base

Scene 46 - Conference At Paroun

At the root of a hill, in the farm lands of Zog, was a little house called Paroun. Dene came out of his long jump, popped into the star cloud of Roshomon, got his bearings, and made a short hop to that hill. In front of him was the door to Beq's house. He knocked. No answer.

Faint whisperings could be heard inside.

Feeling frisky, he flung the door wide open and yelled, "Surprise!"

Riana, Zinxa and Beq all jumped.

"Gotcha," said Dene, floating inside.

Three umbies giggled.

Riana glided toward Dene, then froze.

He hesitated, wondering what might be percolating in that umbie mind of hers.

Zinxa roared, "Go ahead and do it."

Abandoning her natural shyness, Riana flung herself into his arms. Before they even said hello, they kissed.

Zinxa and Beq slapped their hands high and shouted, "Woo hoo!"

The diplomatic mission was almost over - and these two anca were almost a couple.

##

A couple of days later Riana and Dene were sitting on the living room couch, happy to be together in a safe place. Zinxa had her taper curled on the floor. Seated in her favorite chair was Beq. Next to her were several instruments but she was not playing music.

They were trading tales about their younger days. Riana and Zinxa regaled them with stories about when Captain Behchel was actually the captain of one of those old style void cruisers. Dene avoided recounting his adventures, but chose instead to spin out recollections of the marvels he had seen. It was Beq's memories of her youth which moved their conversation down an unexpected path.

That is because Beq was older than all of Nimulos. Her youth was not their youth.

By way of comparison, Riana was by far the oldest anca among them. She had emerged into life when Nimulos was still very young and that made her one of the ancient ones. Dene came next in age, followed by Zinxa. Both of them were considered old by anca standards. It was also true that Qusheem, who was an evo born of mother and father on a life planet, was nearly as old Zinxa.

If you added up all four of those ages then Beq was still ten times older than the sum.

Dene asked Beq, "Before getting involved in our JeshNim project, had you ever worked on assembling a survival region before?"

"Of course," she replied. "The most extensive experience I had was a survival region which you anca would call JeshSpel. That is where I learned to discipline myself for the inevitable. Each of our node-jewel beginnings will have slowly decaying ends. Without these survival regions - built with many hands, guided by enlightened minds, influenced from the great beyond - we are relegated to boring hibernation, until some shift in cosmic conditions revives our dormant soul-seeds. When the JeshSpel project reached beta testing, I requested a transfer."

"Do you mind if I ask why?" wondered Dene.

"Not at all," said Beq. "I had not yet learned enough. I was not yet strong enough. I adore mega-problems.

"JeshSpel, while challenging, was too easy. After that, my personal goal became wandering through the universe until I found myself at the wavering edge of epic disaster. This JeshNim project I share with you enthuses me because I am no longer in my old home region.

"But after working here, for a well apportioned amount of time, I will inevitably move on. Someday, I will find myself at an edge where there seems to be no further place to go. That should focus my mind."

"Sounds sort of like what mode-hopping is for evos, except we would have to call it region-hopping for admins," commented Dene, whose imagination was now soaring with new visions of what was actually possible in our multi layered universe.

Zinxa, who had mostly been quiet, entered into this conversation, "I once met a scout from one of those JeshSpel pods. The scout had slipped over to an in-betweener realm to survey resources for their pod. Both of us were quite surprised to find someone else in such a wispy environment. We forged a brief friendship and then moved on."

"Do you remember their name?" asked Beq.

"Faz it was," said Zinxa.

"I don't recall knowing them," said Beq.

"There were thirty billion in that pod," said Zinxa. "Nobody can remember everybody."

"Except the great mystery," mused Dene. The enforced isolation on Cazouni had shifted his thinking to enhanced levels of grandeur. It is widely believed, but of course impossible to prove, that the great mystery remembers everything about all of us, even when we forget.

The four of them, despite their varied backgrounds, felt this to be true.

Scene 47 - Triumphant Return

The security guards surrounding Hoshambelan Tower went on high alert when they saw a sparkling trail of light streaking straight at them. Dene went from hyper speed to full stop an arms length away from the elite guardians of the gate.

"Please inform Sarkon and Sarena that the courier has returned," he said, in a formal diplomatic voice.

A crowd quickly surrounded them to gawk. Dene and the guards remained perfectly still. Questions spread rapidly. The wanderer had returned. Was it really him? He looked so different.

The wheels of government grind slowly, no matter who you are, or where you live. The guards continued to stare at Dene. Troops of law enforcement officers were sent out to control the crowds. Rumors spread like a meteor shower.

Dene had come straight to the gates of Hoshambelan because any other act would have been pounced on by his enemies. Patiently he waited to guarantee that the first anca he reported to would be Sarkon and Sarena.

After countless procedural delays, Dene was sworn in at the testimonial stand, in front of the full court, assembled in special session. Calmly he stated his case, "Hamil and Hamine evaluated the code cubes which were sent to Cazouni. In my diplomatic pouch are their replies."

The Chief Protocol Officer floated forward. With grand pomp and ancient ceremony, Dene took out the sealed diplomatic pouch and presented it. After examining the form, the seals, and the hidden codes, a decision was made to call forth Prime Minister Arcal.

The quarter piece held at Hoshambelan, the quarter piece carried back and forth by Dene, plus the half piece sent here by Hamil and Hamine, all matched perfectly. The information in the code cubes now carried the authority of legal instructions.

One set of cubes was turned over to Sarkon and Sarena. The other cubes were presented to Celene. According to established practice, the leaders would review the instructions, discuss these matters as they deemed appropriate, then a political decision would be reached.

Dene relaxed ever so slightly. He had done it. A journey that many said he would never survive was now an accomplished fact. What a liberating feeling that was. His face showed no emotion but inside he was filled with everlasting joy.

He knew perfectly well that the moment he flew beyond the protection of the Tower things would get rough. For that reason he cherished this one precious moment.

Getting into Hoshambelan had been hard. Getting back out again turned into a major spectacle. The crowd outside had grown to millions.

Most anca hadn't spent even one moment wondering where Dene had gone during all that time. Groupthink is a power which is difficult to control. A mob of anca were curious. Something big was happening and they wanted to say that they had been there, had been part of it, had seen it with their own eyes.

The Chief of Security was brought in to discuss this vital matter with the leadership. Dene offered to jump from

Hoshambelan to his apartment in Antarctica. That would be the simplest solution. The politicians didn't like that. An enormous crowd was milling around outside. Another huge crowd had formed near Chephra. Clusters of rumor mongers had assembled all around the world. The anca government needed something to satisfy their idle curiosity.

Two squadrons were formed from an experienced cadre of the best officers. One gathered around Dene on the rooftop of Hoshambelan tower. The other was sent over to Chephra to form a protective corridor.

No public spectacle is complete without a speech. Arcal was sent to the rooftop, along with his peer Celene. Each of them delivered an oratory worthy of the history chronicles. Millions ignored their words. Much later, the scholars would study their speeches and call them a turning point.

A hive of security agents surrounded Dene on the roof. The Chief of Security boomed out, "Deploy the escort."

It took only ten minutes to fly from the deep waters off the west coast of Australia, to the desert sands west of the Nile River in Egypt.

The flying escort joined forces with the Chephra corridor. In less than a minute Dene was inside the main gate.

At the front desk Dene palm badged in, saying, "I am returning to work at the Observatory, after an extended absence."

Scene 48 - The Reunion

Dene opened the door from the hallway. Everything was quiet. Floating to the Observatory door he opened it.

"*Welcome Home*," they all shouted. A huge sign was hung across the ishmili dome, saying the same thing in gaudy letters.

Zipping inside, Dene said, "Hey everybody, it's great to be back."

Riana flew over and gave him a hug. "Hello again." Right there in front of everybody - they kissed warmly.

Qusheem was wearing a silly party hat, tilted at an odd angle, which made him look even more ridiculous than usual. "Yadpelr."

147

Honat said, "Glad you made it back alive."

Farli gave him two thumbs up, "Yo."

To Dene's surprise, Cami and Beq had renewed their interrupted friendship. Beq was sitting on Cami's desk.

"Nice to see all of you again," said Dene. "I can't tell you how great it is to be home."

After things got settled, Riana placed her hand on Dene's arm. "There's a welcome home gift we made for you."

"Seeing all of you is the best gift I can think of," said Dene, "but I look forward to getting this small token of your appreciation."

Grabbing his hand, Riana said, "Follow me."

They went out to the big room.

Near the floor, hanging from the industrial crane, was an enormous engine.

"Can it be?" gasped Dene. "How is this possible?"

Floating over to it, he touched it. The others joined him. They all floated around the big machine, laughing.

"This is it. This really is IT. Where did you get this?" asked Dene.

"We built it for you," said Riana.

Everyone giggled with glee.

"You built this?" said Dene. "This is a mode-cruiser drive."

"Rakari and Jagh sent us the designs," said Riana. "Beq brought them back with her. While you were out there exploring Tromolea, we were in here assembling this thing."

"What are we going to do with it?" asked Dene.

"Captain Behchel is in on the deal," said Riana. "He ordered his engineers to start building your star cruiser the moment you left Valdaria. The Captain told me that he had a hunch you were going to make it back alive. By the time he got your Q26 message, the major pieces were already in place. They sent a special crew of mechanics over to the special ops landing strip in Greenland. They're going to take out the star cruiser engine that flew it here. Then they'll replace it with this mode-drive."

Dene was stunned. When surprised by something this enormous he had learned to keep his mouth shut. Floating in slow circles, examining the design, he commented, "This isn't the same as what Rakari and Jagh were using. How does it work? We won't be flying this in the void."

"Two big things are happening," said Riana. "The first is what you asked for in the first place. We can challenge Ulta up in the sky. This star cruiser looks a lot like hers. Ours will perform stunts she can never achieve."

"I like the sound of that," said Dene.

"The other part has been in the works for a long time," said Riana. "You know that mode-shifter which Xen and Wun carry around in their NimuTrak?"

"Of course," said Dene, "that's what makes our exotic portal design work."

"Xen and Wun installed a new version of their mode-shifter in the NimuTrak. You and I are going to have a Jagh mode-controller in our new cruiser," said Riana. "That's the technology we're going need to get all those AmbuTraks through."

"Tricky tricky - very tricky," said Dene.

Qusheem slapped Dene on the back and said, "Hmdekpucs."

"I agree," said Dene. "All the pieces we need are now in place. All we have to do is make them work together."

They gathered for a group hug.

"You guys are the best," said Dene.

Chapter 18 - Under New Management

Scene 49 - Celene And Riana

"It's been such a long time," said Celene.

"During the darkest days of World War Two," said Riana. "Those were bad times. You and I had a lot to talk about back then."

Celene got up from her desk and gave Riana a hug of friendship. "Please be seated."

"What did you want to see me about?" asked Riana.

It amused Celene that she was dealing with someone who got right to the point. In her line of work, politics, double dealing was far more common. "The diplomatic mission was a spectacular success. Now what?"

"Dene is no longer a diplomat," said Riana. "He will be staying here as full time special ops until this rescue mission succeeds."

"I need to understand your plans," said Celene. "They put me in charge."

"Captain Behchel sent us a brand new star cruiser," said Riana. "We're going to challenge Ulta's spy cruiser with it. That will shift things around."

"Nothing was mentioned about that in any of the code cubes," said Celene. "How did something that huge escape notice?"

"Dene didn't know about it when he met with Hamil and Hamine" said Riana. "We surprised him after he got back. This is a deal between Captain Behchel and Captain Rakari. It's been in the works for a century. Jenissen and Ing are in on it too."

"You'd better be careful with Ulta," cautioned Celene.

"Maybe it's Ulta who needs to be careful with me," stated Riana. "Her minions stole priceless data of mine and that's what got the Sylumini in the portal game. It's payback time."

"I never thought I'd hear you say something like that," said Celene, with a sly smile.

Riana grimaced. "I used to wrap myself in protective silence. A big change came over me while Dene was away. To be honest, I wasn't sure if he would make it back alive. If something bad did happen, then he would have wanted me to finish what we started. I've changed."

Celene had some serious concerns. "The numbers are running against you. Ulta has a million top technical anca reporting to her. The Observatory has two full time employees and you're a part time consultant. I'm not sure where Dene fits in. What makes you think you can compete against such overwhelming odds?"

"That's what we want anca to think," said Riana. "Let's take a look at the real numbers. In Kemong, there are half a million jeshies working on this rescue. Our Earth guardians have made a strong comeback against the Sylumini. The Valdarians provide us with support throughout Tromolea. We have other things in the works, as well. It's Ulta who should be worried."

"What you say has a ring of truth," admitted Celene, "but Ulta can exploit any type of situation. Unlike most of the softies who have drifted into the orbit of the Sylumini, she's tough. The early eons of her life were dreadful."

"Risking the lives of hospital patients to gain valuable contracts is dreadful," retorted Riana. "Our biggest challenge is getting a fleet of ambulances through. Those infirm jeshies cannot make it over here on their own. I will never allow the Sylumini to get their filthy hands on our technology."

"Easier said than done," advised Celene.

"We're getting ready for a new set of tests," said Riana. "The time has come for us to send real ambulances through a new type of portal. Ulta will soon understand what an awesome thing we have done. The Special Board will understand nothing.

"That's impossible," snorted Celene, who had worked with portals for a billion years. "Beings from parallel expansion regions can make it through a people powered portal but heavy equipment cannot. A mode-tunnel is required for the big stuff."

"I will not reveal any details but here is the essence of our secret technique," said Riana. "We're going to combine a unique people powered portal with two new technologies which have been developed for industrial strength mode-tunnels. One research team is in Cazouni and the other one is in Kemong. Ulta cannot spy in either the Phorlom or in Jeshmol."

"That would probably be true" Celene had to admit. "What are your timelines?"

"Three years from now the Wamilla Medical Center will line up with the Gheney Hospital for the second rescue opportunity," said Riana. "Three months from now we'll know if the preliminary AmbuTrak tests worked. That gives us plenty of time to work on any problems."

Celene leaned back in her chair. "Maybe you really can pull this impossible project off. You and Dene are fabulous together."

Riana's billowing colors turned blush.

"Do you mind if I ask a question?" asked Celene, with umbie innuendo.

"Go ahead," said Riana. She knew.

"After this rescue is over - what are Dene's plans? Is he going to jump away from our planet, to hustle off on his next adventure?" asked Celene.

Riana's billowing colors darkened. She said firmly, "Dene is going to stay right here. He's not going anywhere."

"What makes you so sure?" asked Celene, as casually as possible.

Riana tapped the tips of her fingers together. "I've got big plans for Dene. He knows about some of them. This planet is where he belongs."

At last Celene had heard what she had been waiting for - juicy gossip.

The rest of their meeting was off the record.

Scene 50 - Hangar Nine

Getting into the top secret security area of Hangar 9 was easy. Dene jumped. He had never been to this place before, although he had heard a lot about it.

Wardel, the security guard, was sitting comfortably on a folding chair, carrying on a rambling conversation with the mechanics. When Dene jumped in, he inflated like a ship's sail, with huge muscular arms, and a bulked up taper, ready to surround and crush the intruder.

"Good afternoon, Wardel. I'm Dene. My name should be on the list."

"Good afternoon, Dene," said Wardel, deflating, and sitting back in his chair. First thing this morning, his boss had warned him that something like this might happen.

Dene drifted over to talk to Dirdri.

From the outside, Hangar 9 looked like any other star cruiser repair shop. It had a half circle profile, was long enough for the largest cruiser, and was plenty wide so that heavy equipment could move around. Jenissen used Hangar 9 for extra special projects. Over the past few days, Sylumini spies had taken up positions nearby.

Along the side wall was the old star cruiser drive. The crew had just finished installing the new mode-drive. The hood of the engine compartment was shut. Two mechanics were cleaning up. Everything about the cruiser shined the way brand new things do. It was painted white, like an ambulance, with the red and blue symbol of Kemong Emergency Services painted on the sides and front.

"How's it going?" Dene asked Dirdri. She was the crew chief.

"Got it hooked up but haven't taken it out for a spin yet," said Dirdri.

Riana was mysteriously next to them. Wardel bounced up from his chair but didn't inflate. He had known Riana for centuries.

"When do flying lessons begin?" asked Riana.

"Gotta get clearance from Jenissen first," said Dirdri.

Riana asked, "how long will that take?"

"A week, maybe less," said Dirdri.

Dirdri and Riana knew each other well.

Dene then asked, "Who's going to do the training?"

"That would be me," said Dirdri.

153

"Sounds good," said Dene. His mind was running fast. "How'd you learn to fly this thing?"

"I run the flight school," said Dirdri.

"Mode-cruiser flight school?" asked Dene.

"In Sagonish. We've got a landing strip out there in outlaw territory," Dirdri told him. "We don't bother them. They don't bother us. Everyone else is afraid to go out that far."

"I've heard about that place," said Dene.

"And we've heard about you," said Dirdri, "bazelium smuggler."

"I have another question," said Dene.

"You can ask," said Dirdri. "Doesn't mean I'll answer."

"Was this mode-drive engine, in a star cruiser body, already in the works before I went to Cazouni?" asked Dene.

"I am authorized to inform you that Behchel and Rakari had this project in the works long before they even knew you existed," said Dirdri.

"Does that include this cruiser design with that engine type?" asked Dene.

"Yup," said Dirdri.

"You just made me a very happy anca," said Dene. "Test pilots pull off all sorts of crazy stunts with new designs. I'm an experienced pilot, and so is Riana, but a mode-cruiser is something else again. Rakari told me they're really hard to handle. Flight training would be greatly appreciated."

"I'm a top notch test pilot and the best flight instructor you're gonna get," said Dirdri.

Riana had a few questions of her own. "I was on the team who assembled this mode-drive. Is it safe?"

"Kaga, come over here," called out Dirdri.

The mechanic stopped working in the wheel well and drifted over to them, wiping his hands on a shop rag.

"What's up?" asked Kaga.

"You ever build a mode-drive before?" asked Dirdri.

"Coupla dozen," said Kaga.

"What'd you think when you saw this one?" asked Dirdri.

"All the pieces were assembled just the way the instructions called for," replied Kaga.

"What else?" asked Dirdri.

"Your machinist did a fantastic job," said Kaga.

"Three of us worked on the extra parts," said Riana. "Now, give me an honest answer, how much rework did you have to do?"

Kaga was a little nervous about this question. Anca with excellent skills, and gigantic egos, can be bad trouble. "Not a whole lot."

"Real world," snapped Riana. "I want a real world answer. Just tell me the truth."

Kaga glanced at Dirdri. She nodded yes.

"Here's the deal," said Kaga. "Assembly instructions are nice, but plans that come from a communicator dome just don't have what a good mechanic carries around in their head. Your major assembly work was real good, but we had to tweak it a bit, if you know what I mean."

Riana reached over and shook his hand vigorously. "Thanks for those tweaks. We're going to challenge Ulta with this thing."

Kaga and Dirdri both broke into enormous smiles.

"You're going up against Ulta with our cruiser?" asked Dirdri.

"Oh yeah," said Riana, "it's about time somebody took her down a notch or two."

"That changes everything," said Dirdri. "We're putting the crew on overtime. This thing will run faster than a meteor and be smoother than a politician's lies."

Riana was by far the oldest anca in Hangar 9. With her ancient bearing, withdrawn manner, and subtle color swirls, she exuded an air of deep wisdom. What she said next was completely out of character.

Rubbing her hands together, Riana growled, "Ulta, we're coming to getcha."

Chapter 19 - Human Be-Ins

Scene 51 - Empty AmbuTrak

Human Be-In, Polo Field, Golden Gate Park, San Francisco, January 1967. Big media had gone wild. Last year the media invented the term hippie, as a way of describing a certain type of people who had gotten bubble fuddled. This year they were selling newspapers and magazines by hawking the wacko ideas that these hippies believed in. Humans should behave decently. Being human should be a life fulfilling experience. Human dignity should be the norm. The future of our planet is the responsibility of human civilization.

Andy and Bongo were sitting in back of the Be-In stage. Both of them were getting paid to run the sound system. That was pretty cool. Because he had worked in the audio biz for so long, Bongo had brought along two lawn chairs. If you're a sound contractor, you have to get to the gig early, lift heavy equipment, be on call, then do the load out. That's why lawn chairs are essential.

The rock band was hanging out in the psychedelic school bus. Dignitaries of the counter culture were speaking earnestly about the problems we had created for our planet. The audience was grooving in the pacific sunshine. Little kids were running around on the lawn, playing the same games that have always been there for the young.

The stage manager came over to Andy. "Five minutes until the rock act goes on."

Andy nodded. "We're ready."

"More than ready," sneered Bongo. He had grown weary of listening to intellectuals mumbling monotonically into a microphone.

As soon as the stage manager was gone, Andy glanced over his shoulder again.

"What do you keep staring at?" asked Bongo.

"Nothing," said Andy, snapping his head back. He tried to look casual.

"Don't mess with me, man, I've known you for a long time," said Bongo.

"There's a large white box parked next to us," said Andy.

"I always thought you were crazy but now I know for sure," said Bongo, looking around.

"They need us to guide the audience so we can levitate that box," said Andy.

"Suuure they do," said Bongo.

"But it won't rise up in the air unless we get the audience tuned to the right frequency," said Andy. "That's why they brought us here today."

"Whatever you say, bro," groused Bongo. Hey, he was getting paid to sit in a lawn chair.

Ulta had plenty to worry about. Her spy equipment had gotten so sophisticated that she could see into jeshie world better than ever before. The familiar blue jeshie van was nowhere to be seen. It had been replaced by a white van, of exactly the same shape. She could tell that this replacement was empty. Until now there had always been a driver and a passenger sitting in the front seats. The Special Board wanted reassuring answers. Ulta found only disturbing questions.

Below ground, beyond the range of Ulta's airborne spy gear, was a mode-bunker. It had replaced the blue NimuTrak as the operations center for this advanced style of portal. What they learned today would help them decide how to use the brand new mode-cruiser which was waiting for Riana and Dene.

"me think we ready" said Xen.

Dirdri had joined them from Hangar 9, "Looking good on my side."

"when you want me spy on anca spy baddie" asked Beq. She was in her soto-anca professional form but was waiting to shift into her other-sider form.

"you go now" said Xen. "low energy on stage" "watch what she do when energy get bigly".

Beq vanished from sight.

Backstage, Dene was hovering behind Andy and Bongo. He kept his eyes on the Guardians. Their teamwork was amazing.

The band sauntered onstage and got tuned up. The first few songs were wobbly. One of their more popular tunes got them in the groove. What started off as a quick instrumental break, evolved into an unanticipated psychedelic improvisation.

Crowd power began to surge.

Dene felt a short buzz on his taper device, followed by two longer ones. That was the signal from Dirdri. He scratched his right ear. That was the signal to Eberli. Guardians began tightening up their positions.

Ulta watched from the spy cruiser. This looked like the main event. She touched the controller to initiate a new search pattern.

Looking over Ulta's shoulder was Beq. She had shifted from her regular self, which the spy gear could detect, to her other-sider self, which was invisible to both Ulta's eyes and her fancy equipment. Beq was a super techie. She was very impressed by all the cool toys up here in the star cruiser. Their archenemy truly was as powerful and determined as the rumors had claimed.

Down in the bunker, Wun concentrated on the mode-shifter. When the meter reached the green zone he pressed the small red button on the side. As soon as she saw him do that, Dirdri switched on the new mode-controller. Both of them tweaked their equipment until the two machines were in synch. Then they locked in on Andy's human portal parameters.

The crowd set up a chant, led by the Guardians. "Aaaaaah aah a oh wah." "Aaaaaah aah a oh wah." "Aaaaaah aah a oh wah."

From his lawn chair, Bongo whimpered, "I think we're having some kind of weird earthquake."

"Shhhhh," whispered Andy. "Don't ruin my concentration."

Bongo's eyes were bugged out like ping pong balls. His lawn chair, Andy's too, were levitating off the ground.

Ulta's eyes were also bugged out, but for entirely different reasons. The big white box was rising up in the air, apparently by waves of human crowd power. This was totally unexpected. The box wavered, then stabilized directly above the musicians on stage. An unfamiliar style of portal began to flicker open.

The guitar player was the type who was sensitive to other worldly events. With the big white box directly above his head, he sensed its presence, so he looked up. That's when things turned bad.

As the big white box was sliding through portal, the guitar player stumbled over a cable and fell flat. The sound system burst into ear shattering feedback.

At first the audience thought it was all part of the act so they cheered. Then the shrieking roar made them cover their ears and stop dancing.

Andy and Bongo fixed the audio feedback in a flash.

What the two sound contractors could not fix was the force field surrounding the big empty AmbuTrak.

That white thing shot across San Francisco Bay, like a monster cannon ball, heading straight for Zacatra Island, which was the headquarters building for the underground jeshie colony. The box shimmied in the air because the audience had lost their groove.

Bongo and Andy's lawn chairs fell back to the ground with a thump.

"Thanks man," Andy said to his longtime audio friend, "we did it."

All that Bongo could do was point at the flying white object and say, "Uh, uh, uh."

##

High ranking jeshie officials were gathered at Zacatra to observe the test. The success of the rescue depended on the success of this test. For safety reasons, they were seated in a basement room, directly beneath the lobby, watching video feeds of the incoming AmbuTrak. A large target had been placed on the lobby floor.

Right above their heads they heard the front window shatter, then a loud thump, followed by a huge crash. Chunks of ceiling fell on their heads.

One horrified dignitary screamed, "eeeeeyyyyaaahh".

Thankfully, no one got hurt.

Taking charge of the situation, the jeshie Director of the Earth Colony stepped forward to make an improvised announcement. "we got test glitch" "demo goodly success".

Upstairs, as displayed in dome monitors all around the basement, they saw an upside down AmbuTrak. The work station where the receptionist usually sat had been obliterated. Two of the cloud tires on the van were still spinning.

Oops.

Scene 52 - Sky Challenge

Human Be-In, Sheep Meadow, Central Park, New York, March 1967. Yesterday, Noutashi had a delightful inspiration. Her boss had told her to get Melona powered up to extremely high levels for this second test.

She'd heard Eberli raving about the Be-In out on the west coast. She'd listened to Riana explaining the technology behind it. She'd looked attentive while Vint filled her in on the organizational roles of Xen, Wun and Dirdri. Vint really put the pressure on when he told her that Riana and Dene were going to be using their new star cruiser for the first time ever. Noutashi cared little about any of these technical details.

Her job was people power. That's why she brought Sandal Annie along with Melona to Central Park. Those two had been friends ever since the Beatnik Village days. Annie had copious amounts of people power.

##

Sandal Annie was in fine form today. "Where did they find all these freaks?"

Surrounding them were ten thousand long hairs, gathered together as a sixties tribe, in elegant Midtown Manhattan. Downtown in The Village you never saw this many shaggy bohemians in one place.

Melona agreed, "This is totally amazing. They must have been hiding them out in the suburbs somewhere."

Young women were scarf dancing, with beatific smiles. Young men faced the sky, as if seeking their destiny. An old couple wore tie-dyed t-shirts, bought from a wandering vendor. Little kids were running around on the lawn, playing the same games that have always been there for the young.

"Do you think we're here for a reason?" asked Annie.

Melona laughed lightly. "I don't know why we exist."

160

"Not that far out stuff," snarled Sandal Annie. "Do you think that you and I were brought here, today, for a special purpose?"

"Yes," admitted Melona. She didn't like talking about her odd intuitions.

"Follow me," called out Annie.

"Wait up," yelled Melona.

"Over here," yelled Annie. She brought Melona directly over the top of the invisible bunker, hidden in the ground below. Ulta circled above. People gathered around.

"Form a circle," shouted Annie.

In a flash, people formed a circle. First they danced in one direction, then the other. Smiles abounded. Others joined. The circle got bigger.

Noutashi felt so proud.

"What just happened?" Dirdri asked, down in the underground control bunker.

"see bigly signal" said Wun, "why".

Beq said, "me go topside take look". She shifted to her other-sider self. Moments later she came back. "sandal annie figure things out" "she got crowd tuned up" "this good as it get".

"awesome" said Xen, watching the monitors. "you send signal" "we scramble".

Dirdri signaled Riana and Dene, who were waiting in Hangar 9. Then she tuned in on Melona's soto colors to synthesize two humongous guide beams from the hyped up audience.

Xen and Wun opened the door to the underground bunker and trotted outside. Dirdri slammed the door shut and took control.

A brand new test AmbuTrak was parked outside. It was fully loaded. The cargo bay was packed with real hospital equipment. Laying down on the gurney was a test dummy. Standing next to it was another test dummy, outfitted with jeshie medic equipment. Data sensors would measure stress and strain.

After a short wait they got messaged. "Riana and Dene left Hangar 9. Three minutes. Portal opened by Noutashi."

Xen started the engine.

Wun messaged back, "we ready".

Ulta got a tiny surprise, then a huge surprise. The moment Xen started up the AmbuTrak, it became visible in her spy gear.

"So that's where they hid it. Underground," Ulta muttered to herself. From up in the sky she couldn't see that the van was white, not blue.

Ulta's attention was so focused on the portal that she jumped when Yori roared, "Emergency. Emergency. Star cruiser speeding straight at us." Ulta unbuckled her seatbelt and zipped into the cockpit. A star cruiser was about to crash into them.

Yori reached for the evasive action controls.

Before either of them could respond, the invading cruiser stopped short, in mid air, directly in front of them.

Star cruisers can't stop in mid air.

Yori calmly continued making the next loop. The unidentified cruiser came back into view. It was about the same size as theirs, painted hospital white, with red lightning in a blue circle. This flying machine did not move. As they flew past the cockpit, Riana and Dene waved at them, laughing.

"Jerks," snarled Ulta. "I'm going back to my work station."

"Affirmative," said Yori.

Ulta didn't see this, but the next time Yori circled around, she waved hello to Riana and Dene. They blew kisses.

Dene asked, "Portal conditions?"

"Noutashi did an awesome job," said Riana. "The portal is twice as wide as we need and amazingly sturdy."

"AmbuTrak status?" asked Dene.

"Engine running. Waiting for us," said Riana.

"Start the mode-controller," Dene said.

Riana touched the control panel. A green light went on. The industrial strength mode-controller was now linked to the redesigned mode-shifter in the bunker. This was the first time these were being used together.

The portal glowed in strange colors. It pulsated with an eerie sound.

"All systems go," said Riana.

Dene sent the signal.

Xen shifted the AmbuTrak into gear. Driving straight up in the air, she levelled it out directly in front of the portal. Everything looked perfect.

This brand new test vehicle was not equipped with a transform-gear. Xen and Wun had hot rodded their old blue NimuTrak with a customized transform-gear so they could easily shift between worlds. This standard issue ambulance had only a regular gear shift. Xen popped the clutch.

Ka Pow. With a bright glare of colors streaking behind, the AmbuTrak punched through to the earthly dimensions of the new jeshie colony.

"Follow them," growled Ulta.

"Affirmative," said Yori. Flying next to them, at precisely the same speed, were Riana and Dene, laughing.

Scene 53 - Need A Lift

"hi" said Beq. She had shifted back into her soto self.

Xen and Wun had forgotten all about her, being so hyped up about the portal.

"oh hi beq" said Xen. "where you been".

"visit anca spy baddie cruiser" said Beq. "she got nice toys".

"how she doing" asked Wun.

"she super mad at us" said Beq. "she use bad words".

"what you do here" asked Xen.

"hang out you guys" said Beq.

"you always welcome" said Xen. "hold on tight" "we fast turn at jersey loop".

Beq sat down on the gurney, next to the test dummy.

##

At the Jersey Loop they steered the AmbuTrak through a steep half circle. That put them on an entrance ramp to the Nebraska Kid Highway. They cruised beneath the Delaware River at high speed. At Exit Zar Qwa in Pennsylvania, they slowed down and made a fast right turn onto local roads. This forced the driver to slow down.

Up ahead was a large sign with red lightning in a blue circle, showing the way to Gheney Hospital. Their test AmbuTrak was painted the same way. Riana and Dene's new mode-cruiser was also painted like that.

Ulta was confused. She had lost track of the AmbuTrak at the Hudson River, which was to be expected. That rival star cruiser had been right next to them, going the same speed, when it simply vanished from sight and radar.

"Did you see that?" Ulta asked Yori.

"The mystery machine is no longer visible," said Yori.

"Good," said Ulta, "then I'm not the only one going insane."

Since nothing else made sense, Yori began flying reconnaissance loops.

Xen and Wun slowed to a crawl at the Ambulance Entrance. No staff was visible. Pulling up to the center door, the three jeshies got out.

Riana and Dene inched their enormous mode-cruiser across the parking lot. They got out and floated toward the others.

"Oh, hi Beq, we didn't know you were here," said Riana.

"me tag along for ride" said Beq. "we drive goodly fast" "nice to see colony first time".

Jeshies and Terrans began streaming outside. They had watched these momentous events on dome monitors, at a safe distance.

There was a grand celebration, of course. No matter who you are, or where you live, when things go well, you use that as an excuse to throw a party.

After the introductions, the spectacle, and the congratulations, they called on Xen to make a speech. Speeches made Xen nervous but, under the circumstances, it had to be done. "thanking you" "test go goodly" "we stay in colony now".

Colonists applauded. Terrans cheered.

Dene asked, "Why did you say that you're going to be staying here in the colony?"

Xen got embarrassed, right there in front of everybody. "ambutrak one way trip" "we this side of portal" "no way back".

"What about Lon and Trz?" asked Dene.

"they run hikli without us" said Xen.

164

Dene said, "Hmm, we should have thought about this before we ran the test. Riana and I can give you a ride back to the Hikli. Our mode-cruiser doesn't need a portal."

Xen and Wun were tremendously relieved.

##

An hour later the mode-cruiser was parked on the service road next to the Emergency Services Warehouse Facility. The bright lights of Namoush glowed on the horizon. Waiting at the back gate were an aging brown evojesh and a younger plum colored evojesh. Riana and Dene knew both of them but Beq needed introductions.

"Beq, I'd like you to meet Lon," said Riana. "She's the jeshie working with Vint."

"pleased to meet" said Beq. They shook hands.

"This is Trz," said Riana. "Trz, meet Beq."

"goodly honor to meet you" said Trz.

These seven varied beings spent a delightful evening at the Hikli - trading stories, trading boasts, revealing dreams.

When it came time to leave, Lon asked Beq, "what you plans".

"no have plan" said Beq.

"spare bedroom my place namoush" said Lon. "we do goodly shopping tomorrow" "me know best places".

"that be awesome" said Beq. She had a new home back on Zog, in the regular world, and it needed fresh decorations. Beq had also kept her other place at Paroun, as a weekend getaway.

Riana suggested to Beq. "We can give you a ride back to Zog whenever you're ready."

Beq said, "not worry" "me take shuttle home" "it between earth mars" "not far when you know how to skate".

Chapter 20 - Summer Of Love

Scene 54 - BeBop BookStore

The BeBop BookStore was closed forever. Brown paper was taped over all the windows. Andy was leaning on an empty hand truck. The Rishi family lawyer, Frank Delbarton, was comforting Diane Rishi, the way a pastor would offer solace at a funeral.

"Take everything," said Diane, with a dramatic sweep of her hand," I'm going back to my pathetic little apartment to have a nice stiff drink." She handed the keys to Frank, gave Andy a sobbing hug, then stomped out. The bells on the door jangled.

There had been an auction. Dealers had come in and scooped up books that Andy loved. Everything that remained was destined for the trash bin.

Frank turned to Andy, "You may now have what you desire."

Andy knew every book in this place by heart. Seeing this unruly mess was upsetting but he did what needed to be done. With brisk efficiency he piled books on his hand truck. Frank admired the methodical way he worked. Parked in front of the store was his old green delivery truck. In the mid fifties, Andy had bought it from a bakery in North Beach so he and Bongo could haul audio equipment around. Today it was going to be used for a book rescue. He wished he could take them all - but he already had too many.

"Thanks for everything you've done," said Andy. "It's been rough on Diane. I worry about her, now that the store is gone."

"Her family will take care of her," said Frank, "they always have. Don't forget, you and I have a little business we need to take care of, over at my office."

"Let me drop these off first," said Andy. "Should I meet you there in, say, an hour?"

"I'd like to go with you, if you don't mind," said Frank. "A big client from Los Angeles had to cancel. My work calendar is devoted to you for the rest of the afternoon."

"Wow," said Andy, "that's cool."

"Take your time, Andrew," said Frank. "I'm in no hurry. As a matter of fact, it's a good excuse for me to see what's happening out there in this fair city of ours."

"It's gotten really ugly out there," said Andy. "The newspapers call it the Summer of Love but I call it the Summer of Bummer."

"Let's go have a look-see," said Frank.

Andy bounced the hand truck down the steps, bowed his head reverently while Frank locked the place up, then mumbled a quiet prayer for all the lost souls who had ever walked through the doors of the BeBop BookStore. "Let's go."

San Francisco 1967. Summertime.

Kids who should have stayed back home were crowded on the sidewalks.

"Spare change, man," muttered a dude with vacant eyes.

"I mustered out of the Navy here in 1945," said Frank. "I liked San Francisco so I stayed. Once a year I go back up to Seattle to visit my family. Sometimes they come down here, especially the younger generation. In all my years I've never seen anything like this. Can you explain it to me?"

The long hairs, the ones the newspapers called the hippies, were out in force. Beads and bangles decorated second hand clothes. The streets were crowded, as if a hive of hungry insects had found a field of groovy grain, now stripped bare.

"We were footloose and fancy free when we were their age," said Andy, "but this beats anything I've ever seen. I don't know how to explain it. Somewhere deep inside I have this feeling that some powerful force has been unleashed, and we can't handle it."

Eberli nodded silent agreement from the invisible realm.

##

"Here we are," said Andy. There was a parking space right in front of his apartment building, which he took to be a good omen. He bounced the hand truck up the front steps and they entered the Kempton Sewing Supply store.

"Hello, Mrs. Kempton," said Andy. "I'd like you to meet Frank Delbarton."

"Pleased to meet you," she said. A hard life lined her face.

Andy said, "The bookstore closed and I got a few leftovers."

"So now you're out of a job," said Mrs. Kempton.

"I have your rent money," said Andy.

"If you don't pay the rent I don't pay the mortgage," said Mrs. Kempton. "It'd be a shame to lose this place - as much trouble as it's been - after all these years."

"I'll cover the rent," said Andy.

"I hope so," muttered the landlady. Business was slow, her husband was gone, and now her only tenant had lost his job.

"Would you like me to give you a hand?" asked Frank, as they started up the stairs.

"Nah, I got it," said Andy, "I move heavy audio equipment all the time."

Bump. Bump. Bump. Bump. Bump. The stack of books was heavy.

"How old are you?" asked Frank.

"Thirty seven," puffed Andy.

"You don't want to be moving heavy equipment when you get old."

"I can handle it," said Andy.

"Sure, you can handle it now," said Frank. "You're young. But you're already huffing and puffing. In a few more years, this won't be so easy. I can help you with that. We're going to talk about that when we get to my office."

Bump. Bump. Bump. Bump. Bump. "Sounds good."

Scene 55 - Elevator Of Lost Dreams

Andy's apartment was one large room, which took up the entire third floor of an aging waterfront building. After Cynthia died, he moved to this industrial district so he could leave his old life behind.

Frank took a look around and said, "This is a really nice setup you have here."

On the wall facing the street were two large windows. A warm breeze flowed through bamboo curtains. The kitchen area was in front. In the back corner was a bathroom cubicle. A single bed and a large chair were the only pieces of furniture. Everywhere else there were shelves piled high with books, records and memorabilia from life on the jazz road.

Centered along the back wall was a large door, surrounded by a massive wooden frame. Andy parked his hand truck next to it. "Have a seat," he said to the lawyer, waving his hand at the only chair.

He untied the ropes which held the books. As he wandered around the room, trying to find space on crowded shelves, he and Frank had a rambling conversation. After everything else had been put away, there was a small pile of books on the floor, next to the big door.

"What's in there?" asked Frank.

Andy opened the door. It was an industrial elevator. Long ago, when Mrs. Kempton's husband was still alive, the third floor was a warehouse for the dock yards hardware store he owned. An odor of old wood and thick grease wafted into the room.

"I call it the Elevator of Lost Dreams," said Andy. "A few of the books I got today belong in here. They're special. You know, signed by the author, or written by a friend."

"Are those the lost dreams of people who wandered off in search of a steady paycheck?" asked Frank.

"There's more to it than that," said Andy. "Oh sure, we all realized that we had to earn a living somehow. Most of my friends went back home to find a job, or moved to some crazy place, or whatever. Some, like me, figured out how to find enough work in the big city to support their dreams."

"What are your dreams?" asked Frank.

A deep silence, like the ocean on a still night, came over Andy. He thought about all those times he had felt connected to the powers-that-be, who seemed to have an unexplained need for his ordinary life. You don't speak of such things to your lawyer.

"Let me put it this way," said Andy, "lots of people want to make the world a better place to live but wishful thinking never gets anything done. I'm one of the little people in this old world of ours and that's fine with me. But, I like to imagine, there are a few small things I can do which might make things just a teensy bit better. If enough of us do that, then the world will slowly improve.

"Books, music, art - people everywhere need these things. In some mysterious way it connects us, one person at a time, to something larger than our individual lives. I've known you for almost twenty years, when you got money from the logging company for my injured foot. I've made a lot of friends since then. Most of them have moved away.

"When their dreams die, sometimes they give me something they've written, or recorded, or painted. I archive them in this old stalled elevator."

"We'll talk about holding onto your dreams when we get to my office," said Frank. "I'd like to help you keep on living this good life. Dreams, like everything else in this nutsy world of ours, need to be financed."

"What you say is true," agreed Andy.

"I don't mean to intrude on your personal life but, if you wouldn't mind, I'd like to see something from your special collection. That would be a wonderful way to spend a slow afternoon while I'm out of the office," said Frank.

"See this book here." He pulled one off the top of the pile. "The Art Of Bopsie by Alicia Hathaway. This is an autographed copy from a very dear friend. These are paintings she did of us, a small group of nobodies, who shared the silly days of our youth, back in the fifties. We really did believe we could build a better life. This book *belongs* in the Elevator of Lost Dreams."

Frank flipped through a few pages, sitting comfortably in an arm chair. To the lawyer's eye it was a few amateurish paintings, done in a modernistic style, that held no particular interest for him. The overall effect was one of friendly warmth.

To the bopsies, it was fading evidence of a way of life which was vanishing.

Frank handed the book back, which Andy tossed on top of the pile. That was the way of the world. What we have now, will soon enough be gone. And yet, without our foolish dreams, the world would be much worse than it is.

As he was closing the big door, Andy glimpsed Cynthia's curlicue handwriting. After the Last Grand Slam Poetry Jam, he had tossed the River of Life in here, along with everything else.

He shut the big door tight.

Now, phoenix like, he felt it was time for him to rise from the ashes.

"When one dream fades away, a new dream takes its place," said Andy. "That's what we need to remember. Follow your best dream. It might be better than your old dream."

"That's what we need to talk about," said Frank. "Somehow, you've managed to hold onto something which is important to you. I don't want this to get lost on this crazy planet of ours."

Taking a seat on a floor pillow, Andy said, "San Francisco has gone nuts this summer but the music is better than anything I've ever heard. I've put a lot of miles on the jazz road - San Francisco, Los Angeles, Mexico City, New Orleans, Chicago, Montreal, New York. I'm just the sound guy. Nobody notices me. While the audience is enchanted by the bright lights onstage, my job is tucked away in the shadows. You helped me get Bopsie Audio Productions set up. My pal Bongo is helping me get it started. Now my part time job is gone."

"I'm glad you turned to me," said Frank.

"I saw what you did for Diane," said Andy. "You protected her from the ways of the world, including her own bad behavior. A straight up city slicker like you even helped a former lumberjack like me. I'd be limping around on a bum foot if it wasn't for you."

"Let's go over to my office," said Frank, "I've got some paperwork I want you to see."

"I'm ready," said Andy. He felt a fresh flame flickering in cold ashes.

Eberli, who was sitting on the edge of the bed, was a very happy anca. He had his suspicions about what the Sylumini had done to Cynthia. He was aware of what they might do to Andy, or Melona, or both. Evos aren't the only ones who watch in despair while their precious dreams die. Eberli wanted his dream to come true. Andy was the key.

Scene 56 - Financing Dreams

The building was the same one Andy had entered, on crutches, back in 1949. Frank's office certainly had changed. Gone were the scuffed green filing cabinets and the cheap knotty pine paneling. Now he had a corner office looking over the street. Andy sat in a plush chair. Frank was seated behind his mahogany desk. On the wall were autographed pictures of entertainers and sports figures who used him as their lawyer.

Glancing at the talking points in the file folder, Frank said, "Do you remember when your grandfather passed away?"

"Yeah, it was October of 1952. I was working in the warehouse at Lectrindustries back then. That's where I met Bongo. I didn't have any vacation time but they let me take a week off, without pay, to go back home to Montana, so I could settle things up for my grandpa," said Andy.

"I have a question," said Frank. "How is it that you, his grandson, were the one responsible for doing this?"

"Ehhh - my mom and dad didn't get along," said Andy. "As a matter of fact my dad and my grand dad didn't get along either. I left home two days after I graduated from high school. There was nothing for me there. I haven't seen mom or dad since. The neighbors told me that after I went away, they got in a big fight, and wandered off. Grandpa was the only thing I had. Maybe I was the only thing he had."

"What do you have now?" asked the lawyer.

"My friend Bongo," said Andy.

"What does he do?" asked Frank.

"He's an electrical engineer. He's got a day job but he helps me out with my audio business. Bongo creates these wizardy electronic gadgets that give bands this new psychedelic sound." said Andy. "I wouldn't have much if it wasn't for his advice."

"Do you remember the value of your grandfather's ranch back in 1952?" asked Frank.

"Oh, it was something like twenty thousand dollars," said Andy.

"Who said it was worth that?" asked Frank.

"The real estate guy in Montana," said Andy. "Said he'd give me cash for it."

"And what did I say?" asked Frank.

"You said I'd be a fool to sell it for so little, even if that was more money than I'd ever had in my entire life," said Andy.

"What else did I tell you?" asked Frank.

Andy laughed. "You said the river that runs through it is worth more than all the cattle you can graze in those high mountain meadows."

"Did you believe me?" asked Frank.

"Well, sorta yes and sorta no," said Andy.

"I have an accountant who does some very fine work for me," said Frank. "I had him run the numbers, based on the current value of trout fishing property in Montana. The idea is for you to subdivide and sell small plots over many years. I have a client who wants to build a fishing lodge in Montana. He's looking to buy twenty acres. A small section of your property would be perfect for him. Take a look at these numbers," He handed Andy the accountant's report.

"Whoooeee," said Andy, "are you sure this is right?"

"Probably worth more," said Frank. "After you returned to San Francisco from your grandfather's funeral we sold 60 acres of your land, in 3 lots. That money has given you the luxury of working with books, art, and music - including travel on the jazz road. I have a feeling that what you're doing for society is worthwhile. I'd like to help you keep doing it. You have a small audio business. In my opinion, you're not a business man and it makes no sense for you to try and build an audio empire. I have a lot of clients in the music industry. It's ruthless."

"Yeah, I sorta figured that out the hard way," mumbled Andy.

"Next week I have an appointment with a lawyer representing the owner of an agribusiness down in Central Valley," said Frank. "He's getting to the age where he wants to retire. A fishing lodge is his retirement dream."

"So you want to sell my ranch to him?"

"Oh no," said Frank, "that's not how we maximize the value of your property. You inherited 840 acres of what you call mountain grazing land. That's worth a small fortune if we do this right. Some of your property is good for trout, some of it's good for hay, and the rest is what we like to call scenic. You never know what opportunities are going to come along but, let's say for the sake of argument, that you divide it up into 50 lots. There's money to be made on each transaction. Look at the second page of that accountant's report I gave you."

"Whoa," said Andy, "this really blows my mind."

"It's a lot to absorb," said Frank. "Take the accountant's report and the letter of intent to a good financial advisor. Find out what they have to say and we can go from there."

"Yeah, I gotta let this simmer," said Andy. "This is a whole different game than what I've been playing. I need to get my act together."

"With a deal like this you can benefit, I can benefit, and my client can build the trout lodge of his dreams," said Frank. "That way everyone will be happy - except the trout."

"Wow, this changes everything," said Andy.

"I'm meeting with the lawyer for the buyer on Wednesday of next week," said Frank. "On your way out, have my secretary make an appointment for the following Friday. We can take a fresh look at those numbers then."

"Awesome," said Andy, "I don't know what to say except thanks. I'll see you next week."

Andy made the appointment and walked out to his old green delivery truck. He knew a lot about bad luck but he'd never had much experience with good luck.

Eberli was following him, watching his natural colors, running plans through his mind. By the time they got to Andy's apartment he had come up with the name of a good financial advisor. The next problem was figuring out how to get the two of them together.

Chapter 21 - There's A Riot Going On

Scene 57 - Chicago Riot

Chicago was a city teetering on the brink of riot. The 1968 Presidential Convention had been planned as a showcase for the politics of progress. The sixties had pushed politics over the edge. Ten thousand radicals faced off against twenty thousand police and military.

This ugly development was being monitored closely by the anca government. It was not appropriate for the Hoshambelan Administration to take sides in any human conflict. The evos were expected to sort things out for themselves, with some individual promptings from the Guardians. What was important is that the government understand the situation well enough so that appropriate policies could be properly maintained.

What should have been easy had become an enormous mess.

When human population rose from millions to billions, the Hoshambelan Administration turned to its government services contractor for support. If the Sylumini were honest then things would have turned out differently. But they are not. They believe in always putting themselves first.

The visible face of this travesty were the Auxiliary Contractors, known to everyone as the Auxis. There were millions of them, none of them were permanent, and they would do what their anca supervisors suggested.

##

That's why Dene was sitting in a tree, across the street from where the protestors were gathered. He kept a close eye on the way that local events were unraveling.

The technique the Auxis used was as simple as it was impossible to prove in court. Almost all anca carry personal

175

taper devices. Auxis also carry company issued pocket monitors. Their job is to monitor human crowd behavior and report it to the authorities. By touching the pocket, while wiggling the taper, human behavior can be influenced. Their specialty is taking natural anger and amplifying it. This practice is totally illegal. Guardians have been complaining about it for thousands of years. The Courts have never been able to establish solid proof of wrongdoing.

Ulta designed the pocket monitor control system.

In Chicago the Auxis had been sent out to "monitor the riots." Malki was a squad leader. Some said he was a dumb thug. Others said he was a mastermind in disguise. Everyone knew that Malki was uncomfortably close to Khaletora.

Dene sat in his tree, studying every move that Malki made. He was careful to remain perfectly calm. That would irritate Malki. Dene simply sat there, doing nothing, waiting, watching, expressionless.

The police launched a barrage of tear gas canisters, then waded into the riot, billy clubs swinging. An angry young man, with a red bandana covering his face, picked up a canister and hurled it back at the police, hurting one of them badly.

That got Malki boiling mad. He gave the signal to his anca goon squad. Soon enough the cops were raining billy clubs down on this kid.

Dene flew out of the tree and got right in Malki's face. "Hey, you can't do that. You're interfering with human behavior. That violates the Code of the Guardians."

"Go back to diplomat school," Malki screamed. "Nobody needs you on this planet any more."

"At least I have a real job," Dene yelled. "I'm not a part time thug like you."

A dozen Auxis jumped Dene to defend the honor of their leader.

Twelve wasn't enough.

Dene whirled Malki around by his taper and knocked the goon squad to the ground. Malki came raging back. There was a ferocious ruckus, with loud screams and shrieks of pain.

"Ow, ow, ow, ow, ow," cried out Dene, in mock distress. Zipping away with one arm hanging limply, his taper quivering like a wounded anca, he barely managed to escape.

It was all an act.

Malki, who had taken a severe beating, strutted in the air like a champion. His goon squad shouted out cheers for their brave leader.

It wasn't until he got back to the supervisor's line, to report on this incident, that Malki realized his taper device was missing.

Scene 58 - New York Riot

Dene was not seen for two days after the Chicago incident. In his basement laboratory, conveniently tucked away in the diplomatic immunity of Antarctica, he worked with Jenissen's top cryptologist.

Arhulio's code breaking techniques revealed what Dene had been hoping for. Malki had been a few miles away when Cynthia and Wendy died in the car accident. The GPS system in his taper device showed that he had left it in a machine which wiggled it around, to mimic the natural movements of an anca's taper. Shortly after the two young women got hit by a logging truck, his taper device returned to its normal pattern. Circumstantial evidence. Not proof. It was enough.

After teaching the cryptologist how to break the Sylumini code, two deep cover agents were sent out to deliver these stunning breakthroughs to the Watchers and Special Ops. There was an enormous backlog of evidence.

With that out of the way, Dene went back to his regular line of work, which was making the Sylumini angry at him. Anger creates mistakes.

##

"What have you done now?" Noutashi asked, as soon as he drifted through the front window of Melona's new apartment.

"First you have to tell me what you think I did," replied Dene.

"You stole Malki's taper device," Noutashi said. "Everyone is talking about it."

177

"Stole is such a harsh word," said Dene, "Nobody saw me take anything. The only established fact is - we had a brawl at a riot."

"You're impossible," huffed Noutashi.

"I'll take that as a complement," said Dene. He took a quick look around. Melona's new railroad flat was much larger than her old studio apartment.

The young woman was sitting on the couch, watching a news review on television. She was enraged by what was happening in Chicago. The civilization she had been raised to honor and defend was collapsing.

Dene said, "Looks like Melona is ready to fight."

"She's been like this for two days," said Noutashi. "I tried to keep her away from the TV but it's the only thing people talk about."

"I'm going to teach her how to confront fear," said Dene. "A riot is about to start in the park across the street."

"Oh no you're not," snarled Noutashi. "We've got to protect her."

"Look out the window," suggested Dene.

Noutashi looked outside. Riana peeked over her shoulder.

Malki and his thugs were hovering in the air, mocking them.

Noutashi found this to be profoundly disturbing. She despised Malki and recoiled at his sneering face.

Dene continued speaking calmly, "Think about what they did to Cynthia. They can do that to Melona if it suits their purposes. You can try to 'protect' her all you want. I'm going to teach her how to face danger without flinching. That way she can shun evil, even if her invisible enemies saturate her with their evil powers."

"What makes you think you have a right to do that?" demanded Noutashi.

"Special Ops," said Dene.

"You work with Andy and Eberli," hissed Noutashi. "I told you to stay away from my client."

"And I did," said Dene, "until now."

"Why now?" whined Noutashi.

"Did Eberli protect Cynthia when she got murdered?" asked Dene.

"That was an accident," said Noutashi, weakly.

"*Was it?*" snapped Dene, harshly.

Noutashi got supremely mad. "Nobody I know thinks it was an accident. They think the Sylumini murdered that poor young woman, and her best friend, to gain advantage against Riana."

"And that worked perfectly for them, didn't it," retorted Dene. "Now they have their own portal. It's not quite ready yet, but it will be when the time comes for them to snap up a few valuable contracts. They will stop at nothing if your precious Melona stands between them and winning."

Noutashi shook her fists in rage. Then she caught hold of herself. Taking a deep breath, she said, "Give me five minutes."

Sitting on the couch next to Melona, guardian and client watched TV together. Footage of the police beating a young woman with billy clubs flickered across the black and white screen. Noutashi beamed a powerful emotion into Melona's imagination.

Melona jumped up from the couch, fists clenched, just the way her uncle back in Tennessee had taught her to do. "This in not *our* America anymore," she screamed. "*We* will not let you take it away from *us.*"

A moment later she was clomping down the stairs, camera bag in hand.

Chicago had been a city saturated with Sylumini. Greenwich Village was solid Guardian turf. Malki and his goons found themselves surrounded by hundreds of anca who despised these nasty intruders.

Tompkins Square Park has many moods and the locals know them well. It's a matter of survival in the slums. Mothers on park benches packed up their strollers and trotted home with their babies. The arts and crafts vendors waved to Camera Girl as they folded up their tables to rush away. Peaceniks with flimsy signs were overwhelmed by neighborhood ruffians bent on revenge. Men who looked like undercover cops took up strategic positions.

Melona circled the park. Dene flew close behind. Malki taunted them. Noutashi whispered signals to the Guardians.

Camera Girl stalked like a tiger in an urban jungle.

179

Snap. A young derelict with hate in his eyes.

Snap. A suburban girl with grungy slum attitude.

Snap. A cop methodically adjusting his riot gear.

Then Melona saw what she had been looking for. Three tough chicks arrived and they were ready to rumble.

Oh - those fabulous outfits these young women were wearing. Riot Couture with pink lace and black leather. Red bandanas wrapped tight around their wrists. Hats that your momma never wore to church on Sunday.

Melona pointed at her camera - as if to ask - is it alright if I take your picture?

The riot girls primped and posed, with tough smiles on their almost-pretty faces, shaking their hips with menace.

Melona needed to load more film. She didn't notice the cop stalking her. This officer in blue didn't want any evidence of what might happen next. Malki floated behind the policeman, with a lurid grin. Melona sensed Malki's invisible presence and found her strength.

Dene was in his natural element. He gave the nod to Riana. She glided over to one of the riot girls.

Street fighters clustered. Both sides felt tense. Then it popped. A rock got thrown. A billy club came down. The riot jumbled into action.

Looking through the lens, Melona clicked off shots of the three riot chicks as they jumped into the fray. They had battle cries of liberation on their ruby red lips.

Malki got the cop supremely riled up.

Just as the billy club was about to crush Melona's shoulder, Riana made her move.

The toughest riot girl made an impossible leap through the air. This young woman grabbed that billy club in midair, then whipsawed the cop to the ground with it. He couldn't see straight.

When his vision cleared, Roxie handed the billy club back to him and said, "I believe you lost this."

"Thanks," said the cop. She had bested him, fair and square. The policeman limped away, toward the first aid van. He would get bonus hazard pay.

Two Hundred Guardians escorted The Goons out of The Village.

##

In her apartment across the street, Melona found out why Roxie could wrangle that billy club out of the policeman's hands. She had grown up on a ranch outside of Gypsum Springs, North Dakota. With seven brothers, she grew up tough. They ran cattle where the wind howled like the gates of hell had busted loose. Summers were so hot the devil himself would have melted.

"Whuddoyou got to drink?" asked Roxie.

"Don't drink," said Melona, "but I don't mind if you do." She gave her money. Roxie came back with a bottle of whiskey.

"How'd you end up in New York City?" Melona asked.

"Kinda strange," Roxie said. "Last summer a coupla hippies in a microbus broke down near our ranch. We fixed it up for em. The girl kinda clung to me, cause she was afraid of my brothers. She kept talking about how there was 'something cosmic in the air.' What she said sounded sorta right, even to someone like me, all the way out there. So I came back east to see if I could find it."

"What did you find?" asked Melona.

"There's a lot of that 'cosmic stuff' going around," said Roxie.

"Why were you at the demonstration today?" asked Melona.

"I hang out with a bunch of chicks called The Now Sistaz," said Roxie. "They're the closest thing I've got to family. That was the drummer and their roadie with me. We think the time has come for big changes to be made."

"I've heard about them," said Melona. "I'd like to meet them. My hobby is taking photos of how women see themselves - not how the world wants to see them."

"I wuz wondering why you had so many pictures propped up all over the place," said Roxie.

"I develop them in the back room," said Melona. "Come on, let's develop the ones I took of you today."

"You can do that?" said Roxie.

"And you're going to help," said Melona.

An hour later, and a second bottle of whiskey, Roxie had pictures of herself with The Now Sistaz. They looked pretty sharp. Melona framed one for her new found friend to take home as a keepsake. It was Roxie, gripping the billy club, with the policeman being hurled sideways through the air.

Scene 59 - Khaletora And Lanmon

"Absolutely not," said Lanmon, the top Sylumini lawyer, at a meeting of the Special Board. It was the Monday after a bad week with Malki.

Other members of the board shifted uncomfortably in their chairs. No one ever spoke to the big boss that way. Ulta remained silent and apprehensive.

Khaletora smiled that splendid little smile of his. "Perhaps I didn't make myself clear. It would appear that this space tramp, Dene, has stolen the personal property of one of our contractors. Then he had him attacked during a reconnaissance mission. Dene must be brought to justice."

Lanmon, Khaletora and Ulta had been close friends before being sent to Earth. They were leaders of the Legal, Executive and Technical divisions. Lanmon was testing the limits of duty and friendship.

"Perhaps I didn't make *myself* clear," said Lanmon, firmly. "These Auxis are going to be our doom. They need to be disciplined - immediately."

"Your comments surprise me," Big-K hissed. "There is no evidence of wrongdoing on our part. We live in a highly competitive world and if we don't gain control of these valuable colonization contracts then someone else will. Their methods will be no different than ours."

"There have been complaints ... ," began Lanmon.

"Complaints are not proof," snapped Khaletora.

"As chief counsel it is my responsibility to provide the best legal advice possible," said Lanmon. "Dene is a special ops professional with the backing of the galactic leadership. The taper devices and pocket monitors carried by our Auxis are pure poison. When this thing breaks, all of us are going down."

Khaletora turned his hostility away from Lanmon and directed that splendid smile of his at Ulta. "Perhaps there is something in what Lanmon is trying to tell us. Would you care to report to the board if there have been any reports about faulty equipment our Auxis might have been using."

To show how serious he was, Big-K curled his own taper upward and took out his personal device. "See, everyone carries these things. Who knows, maybe mine has a bug in the operating system that hasn't been detected yet."

Ulta knew very well that disobedience rattled Khaletora's nerves. She replied in a crystal clear voice, "It is true that there have been some complaints about the Auxis. Every complaint has been logged and evaluated. No evidence has ever been found that constitutes proof of wrongdoing. I can bring up the log files if you want."

"That won't be necessary," said Khaletora.

Ulta was relieved. Her face showed nothing. There were over fifty million complaints.

Turning his attention back to the lawyer, Khaletora said, "What would your recommendation be?"

Lanmon's answer was well rehearsed, "That Malki be fired for losing sensitive equipment and the entire Auxiliary Contractor program be put under strict review by an outside panel."

"That is most unwise at this time," said Khaletora. "Reports of human misbehavior are rampant. This 'planetary bubble' is making people insane. The Hoshambelan Administration needs us now more than they have ever needed us before. Our job is to monitor, in a dispassionate and scientific way, the behavior of these humans. Look at the evidence. Ever since 1964, people all around the world have become unbalanced and rebellious. The government needs us so they can put a halt to this rampant abuse. Dene is a criminal. Our contract employees are the key to our success."

Lanmon took a deep breath and looked at Big-K with no fear, "The Auxis need to be brought under control. That needs to start at the top."

Big-K pasted that pleasant little smile across his face. "You're fired."

"Thank you," said the former top lawyer. "I want to be on a different planet when this thing comes crashing down."

Chapter 22 - At The Barricades

Scene 60 - Aiyoni's Artist Loft

The winter had been harsh and slushy. February 1969 seemed to freeze out the last rays of hope which had, once upon a time, defined the optimism of the sixties. These days, despair stalked the littered streets.

But, as they say, one person's bad luck is someone else's good fortune.

Sales of Melona's photos had never been better. Nobody trusted big media so dozens of underground magazines had sprouted up. All magazines, mainstream or radical, need words and pictures. Melona sold lots of pictures to the underground press because she captured the spirit of these troubled, yet strangely glorious, times.

She treaded her way through the ghetto slush with a portfolio tucked beneath her arm. A friend of hers had tipped her off about a new venture called Yellow Doggerel Magazine. They paid cash for pictures. On the spot. That's what her friend had told her.

Their office was a former bodega in the East Village. A large table, which was nothing more that a piece of plywood propped across two saw horses, was littered with mock-ups for the next issue.

Melona called out, "Hello, is anybody here?" No answer. Poking her head into the office she saw a shabby desk. No one was there.

Along the side wall was a park bench. Melona sat down to wait. Outside were the eternal sounds of sirens wailing. Somewhere a baby cried. The room smelled rotten.

Not long after, another young woman entered. She had radiant skin and a look of unimpeachable authority. "Have you been waiting long?"

"No one is here," answered Melona.

The woman said, "I remember you. You were at the Now Sistaz concert two weeks ago, over on Avenue C, with Roxie. That pink batik blouse you wore was adorable."

"That old thing," said Melona, "I got it at a thrift shop on Saint Mark's. I'm sorry, I didn't get your name."

"Aiyoni."

The name sounded familiar but Melona couldn't quite place it. "Pleased to meet you."

"Let's see how they're doing," said Aiyoni. They peered at the mock-ups. "These clowns are slackers."

Aiyoni started to walk out, then noticed Melona's portfolio. "Are you the one they call Camera Girl?"

"Some do," admitted Melona.

"You take lots and lots of pictures in Greenwich Village," inquired Aiyoni.

"Thousands," said Melona.

"You know what I need?" asked Aiyoni.

"I'd like to know," said Melona.

"I need starters," said Aiyoni. "When I get a commission for a work of art it has to start with something. A strong photograph works best for me. The ones I need are hard to find."

Melona remembered that name. Aiyoni was an internationally famous underground artist. "I'd be delighted to show you some pictures. They're sorted into galleries."

"Such as?" inquired Aiyoni.

"Hippie chicks, riot girls, tourist women, slum chic, teeny boppers, outre couture."

And that was how a fabulous collaboration began.

##

Hints of spring were in the air. In an old industrial building, south of Houston Street, was a battered door, leading up many flights of shadowy steps. The top floor was rented by Aiyoni as her artist's loft. Melona had trudged up these stairs every Saturday for more than a month. As always, she carried her portfolio with samples for the next project.

Two other women were already at work. Aiyoni had not yet arrived. She partied all night and worked in the morning. Afternoon's were for sleep.

Betty Lou had been with Aiyoni longer than anyone. She had perfected the art of looking dumb, because she had been born super smart. Almost nothing was known about Aiyoni's early years. Now, mainstream magazines featured her boldly designed covers, underground magazines grasped at her fame, and galleries clamored for her originals. Betty Lou had been there since day one.

Spaz was what Melona would call a motor head. Boys who have their head poked under the hood of a car are called motor heads. Rebuilding old junk cars is what got Spaz started. She had moved way beyond her younger days, with grease under her fingernails. Her hair was cropped and she had a tough girl attitude. Spaz was super sweet. Her job was to operate the studio equipment. In Aiyoni's art loft, there were lots of fancy machines.

"Let's see what you brought," said Betty Lou.

There was a large work table in the center. Long ago, when this had been an industrial manufacturing space, rows of windows had been slanted into the roof. Immigrant workers could toil at their sewing machines under free sunlight. Cold spring sunshine lit the big white table. Betty Lou and Spaz had cleaned and smoothed it, as they did before every new project.

Melona carefully set out twenty two pictures. She had heard that this was Aiyoni's favorite number. The two studio assistants eyed the works but said nothing.

The commission was a cover for Freaky Chic Magazine. It was dedicated to the ideal that you don't have to be born beautiful in order to feel beautiful.

The editor had a concept for the August 1969 issue called Summer in Slumtown. Aiyoni would create the cover art. The starting point would be one of Melona's photographs - IF - Aiyoni was inspired to use one.

Twenty two 8x10 pictures gleamed in cold sunlight, on a white table, at an artist's loft, high above the slums.

Aiyoni arrived. She didn't enter a room, she arrived in it.

Betty Lou joined her at the work table.

Spaz and Melona removed themselves to the side.

A silent decision was made. Aiyoni turned one picture upside down. Melona put the rest of them back in her portfolio. Then she found the negative for the one chosen. Spaz waited.

"Blow up the negative," announced Betty Lou.

186

Spaz took the negative to an industrial photo enlarger. When this first step was complete, the picture would be three feet tall, instead of ten inches tall. That was the starter. Countless small steps would transform it into a work of art. As a magazine cover, it would have to compete for the reader's attention in a colorful news stand.

The picture showed an uncertain young woman, wearing a black leather mini skirt, with bright flowers woven in her curly blond hair. A peace sign was printed on her blouse. Behind her, the city was burning in an urban riot. Flaming buildings outlined her figure. Looters sprinted down the sidewalk. The young woman's eyes had an odd expression of danger and exhilaration. It was a perfect statement for the turbulent times they lived in.

During the days and weeks ahead new ideas would be tested, old techniques would be applied. Some versions would get thrown out. Eventually something of value would emerge. Aiyoni squeezed hard on the art, until only the essentials remained.

Four guardian anca hovered in the bright loft with their four human clients.

"Do you remember the first day we saw Melona?" asked Spaz's guardian.

"She was this round faced youngster with a southern accent," Noutashi said. "I didn't know a thing about her but right away I wanted her on my client roster."

"I thought you tagged her as a writer," said Spaz's guardian.

"Still do," said Noutashi, "but we have to wait until this rescue is over."

"How's that going?" asked Betty Lou's guardian.

"Tense," admitted Noutashi. She had been told to answer such questions evasively, but they were friends. "They finally picked a portal place but the Sylumini are doing everything they can to delay it. The more they delay, the more secrets revealed during the permit process."

"I despise them," said Betty Lou's guardian. "How's Dene doing with your client?"

"Better than I expected," said Noutashi. "He really is an expert. Melona is enormously stronger than I would have gotten her. Dene didn't make her mean when he made her tough. I think she's actually nicer now."

"Maybe she'd be better off mean?" suggested Betty Lou's guardian. "Malki's squad has been tailing her. They want revenge."

"Like I say, it's tense," said Noutashi. "I can't talk about it too much."

Aiyoni's guardian got a hard look. "Now I see what's going on. Melona is safe here in The Village. When you take her out to the portal site, she'll be in danger."

"You got that right," answered Noutashi, with fear.

Aiyoni's guardian asked, "I hear the Auxis are going to be there in force. They're looking to turn the festival into a riot. I've got friends who despise the Sylumini. Want me to bring some along?"

"You'll have to ask Vint about that," said Noutashi. "That's not my decision. We need all the help we can get."

"Will do," said Aiyoni's guardian.

Four creative anca glanced apprehensively at their four charming clients. What a shame they had to live in a world of fear.

Scene 61 - Valerie's Photo Co-Op

Valerie was waiting for Melona at the People's Photography Co-Op. It was almost too late. These crazy picture galleries this young woman was obsessing about were going to get her killed. Riots were to run away from, not run into, waving a camera. What could possibly motivate her to face such danger? Valerie did have to admit, though, the drama and style were stunning.

Melona came dragging in - exhausted, frustrated, angry, hostile. She thumped two bags on the floor and slumped into a battered chair.

"Good afternoon," said Valerie, in a cheery voice.

"It was a lousy afternoon," said Melona.

"Why don't you let me develop your contact prints, while you wash the blood off your blouse," suggested Valerie. She had been involved in radical projects since the 1930s and had seen it all.

"Oh yeah that," said Melona, glancing down at her blouse. "I brought along a change of clothes, just in case."

Scrounging through her camera bag she took out four canisters of film. Her third pawn shop camera had an unfinished roll, which she wound up. "I only got a few shots on this last roll. Then I had to run for my life."

Valerie went off to make the prints.

Picking up the other bag, Melona headed for the ladies room. She came back a few minutes later, looked refreshed and clean.

"Several of them look promising," said Valerie.

"How many do we need?" asked Melona.

"Two is enough," said Valerie.

Melona pointed, "That one's for me. It doesn't go in the show. I'm going to keep it as a memento of the day I decided to never do this again."

Noutashi and Dene bumped knuckles.

A couple of hours later they sat in the conference room. Propped on wall railings, custom built for this purpose, were large format photos, professionally matted. This group had already been approved for the show. Phil, the owner of the Udjat Eye Gallery, was a good friend of Valerie's. He needed the complete set by Monday. Valerie got to choose the ones she thought were best but Melona had the final say.

The one picture Melona liked most would never be seen in public. It was Roxie being hauled away by two enormous cops. The rage on her face was perfect. The burly backs of the officers framed that rage. On technical grounds it was so-so, but as a souvenir it was priceless.

"You know what I worry about," Melona said.

"I find it impossible to imagine what you're thinking," said Valerie.

"I'm the reason my friend got hauled off to jail," said Melona. "If it wasn't for me taking pictures of her, she would have stopped going to these riots. She'd be sitting at home, with a bottle of whiskey, watching them on TV."

"You should worry about that," said Valerie. "Being an enabler for someone's bad behavior is morally wrong."

"Then what I did was wrong," gasped Melona.

Valerie moved so that she sat in the chair next to her young client.

"Why am I doing this?" Melona asked. Maybe she was talking to Valerie. Maybe she was talking to the wall.

"Because you have writer's block," Valerie explained.

"That's crazy," screamed Melona, jumping out of her chair. "I was at a street riot taking fashion photos."

"I've seen this before," said Valerie. "Creative types do many things well but only one talent brings fame. You're a writer, who takes pictures, so you can study character development. You told me that one day. On the desk in your apartment you have a dusty typewriter, with a piece of paper that has yellowed with age."

"I suppose," Melona grumbled. She sat back down.

Valerie sensed that she had violated Melona's delicate personal space. She pushed harder. "You know what's happening. Tell me."

"Maybe I'm crazy," said Melona, desperately.

"And maybe you're not," replied Valerie.

"You see ... they need me ... over there," confessed Melona.

From the tone of her voice, Valerie knew exactly what she meant. "You mean *them*," pointing at thin air. "The powers that be. The invisible ones. The guardians of order."

"Uh, yeah," admitted Melona, glancing up.

"Maybe they need each and every one of us," said Valerie. "Maybe we're all part of some grand scheme. Maybe they keep their plans hidden from us. How are we to know? I can't answer those never ending questions. But I will ask you one question."

"What?" said Melona.

"If they really do need you - then why not do the best you can - even if you don't understand," said Valerie.

That clicked. "Yeah. We don't have to know everything. We just have to play our role," said Melona.

"One of the people who was at the co-op, maybe twenty years ago, said this to me one day," continued Valerie. "What if 'they' also don't know everything - and rely on beings above them? And then Those beings rely on other beings above Them? And so on, until we run out of words that make sense."

Noutashi nodded her invisible head. Everything Valerie said was true. Dene caught her eye and agreed.

"Wow," said Melona. "Let's get those pictures ready." The first thing she did was put Roxie's photo back in the envelope. She would buy a nice frame for it tomorrow.

Scene 62 - Phil's Udjat Eye Gallery

Melona had stood, looking alert and professional, in the back room of the Udjat Eye Gallery, for two hours. A few people had shown some interest. One customer had even bought a print and told Phil, the gallery owner, how he wanted it framed. That made her feel good.

Noutashi was hovering nearby. Riana and Dene were out on the west coast, working with Andy. She was glad they were far away. In a few weeks this rescue nonsense would be over. Noutashi would get her Melona back. Some serious career redirection was on the horizon.

A wicked voice could be heard by anca ears.

"Heh, heh, heh," said Malki, "me and my urbies was out admiring the fine art you have here in good old New Yawk City. You don't mind if we take a little look around?"

Noutashi said, "Why would I mind. Seeing a bit of culture might do you some good."

It had been a long time since Malki had been in an art gallery. He squinted at some of Melona's photographs. "Not half bad," he said.

Three goons chuckled at their leader's humor.

"I invited some special guests," snarled Malki.

Melona heard voices she knew all too well. It was her boss Constance and their boss George. Everyone in the office knew they were having an affair. Riot pictures were not what she wanted them to see.

"May I help you," asked Phil, having seen both of them before.

"Just looking," said George.

"Feel free to browse. I'll be happy to answer any questions," said Phil. He removed himself from their presence, to give them personal space.

"This is interesting," said Constance, from the front room. When they 'worked late' they often went to galleries.

The painting she had pointed out did not have an identifiable subject, yet it managed to offend all artistic norms, without having any intrinsic value.

191

"Humph," said George. She was always needling him about something.

"Oh look," said Constance, "there's a new photography exhibit in the back room."

"Fashion at the Barricades," said George, in a sly male voice.

Malki and his goon squad chuckled from the invisible realm.

"Well hello there," said Constance, "what a surprise to see you here. Look George, it's Melona from work."

By this time George was also in the back room. All three of them felt uncomfortable. Riot fashion was not something Impress Magazine would approve of.

"So nice to see you," said Melona, feeling drained.

Malki did a little something to make Melona panic.

George, who was a take charge kind of guy, said, "Yes, we love going out to avant-garde galleries, as you may have heard."

Melona could not speak.

Constance asked, "What brings you here tonight?"

"I'm the featured photographer," she managed to say.

"Well," said Constance, "that's quite impressive. Look George, our very own Melona is having her own showing at one of our favorite galleries."

George was fascinated by these pictures of young women, in fanciful outfits, under hostile street conditions. He played that down in front of two women from work. "Excellent blocking, color and style but I'm not sure I understand the theme."

For the rest of her life Melona would never know where she found these words. "Well, as you have probably heard, our society is experiencing one of those periodic episodes of conflict which dot the landscape of history. One area of interest is empowering women. I photograph sub themes within that larger genre. The gallery owner thought that the public might be interested in seeing what women choose to wear while fighting for their rights. By the way, I'm not a rioter, just the photographer."

"You're not using any of our equipment, are you?" asked George.

"Legitimate question and the answer is no. Feel free to check," said Melona. "What I do is buy used cameras at pawn shops. Sometimes the police want to destroy my film because they don't want any evidence. A couple of times I've had to throw down my camera and run."

"*Well*," said her boss, Constance, "it certainly sounds like your weekends are more exciting than mine."

"This is excellent work," said George. "Not the sort of thing we could use at Impress, of course, but you have a keen eye and, I believe, a good future in our industry. Is there any other type of work you do?"

Melona felt a powerful surge of confidence.

"As a matter of fact there is," she said. On a chair was a stack of magazines which had published her work. She selected a few and handed them to George. "The graphic artist Aiyoni has used quite a few of my pictures for the covers. Look at these."

George was stunned. "Aiyoni. Her work is displayed in galleries all around the world. How did you meet her?"

Melona answered, "Personal connections in the arts community," thinking of Roxie.

George glanced at the magazine covers and said, "I'll like to take a look at these. I'll return them, of course."

"Keep them," said Melona, "I have more."

"Time for us to get going," said George, tucking the magazines under his arm.

"It *is* getting late," agreed Constance.

Then, with polite good byes to both Melona and Phil, they left the gallery.

"What was that all about?" asked Phil.

Melona whispered, "That's my boss and her boss. They're having an affair."

"Oh good," said Phil. "I'll remember that next time they come in. It's always easier to make a sale to a guy who's with his girlfriend, than a guy who's with his wife."

Melona returned to the back room and sat down. She was afraid she might lose her job over this.

Malki and his goons surrounded Noutashi. "Your evo looks worried. I hope nothing *bad* happens to her."

Laughing and joking, they drifted outside, into the dark glimmer of the decadent night.

When the coast was clear, Noutashi put her invisible arm around Melona's shuddering shoulders. They both needed a hug.

After a minute the young woman's head popped straight up. Wasn't that what liberation was all about? The freedom to win, the freedom to lose, the freedom to make mistakes and recover. Straightening her posture, she went and stood at the door to the back room, looking alert and professional.

Voices from a fresh wave of customers could be heard in the front gallery.

Melona didn't understand what had happened to her but she did feel that it was important. She had faced a menace and held her ground. As a young woman, she had found her courage in a fearsome world.

Chapter 23 - Pieces In Place

Scene 63 - Sub Sub Basement

Every week Eberli and Noutashi met with Vint to discuss their goals, frustrations and setbacks. They always met in Vint's office on Fridays. As they got closer to the rescue date their schedule was switched to Tuesdays and Thursdays, at a new location.

In the down shaft they dropped past the Headquarters lobby, past the basement, past the sub basement, to a level they didn't even know existed. In front of them was a red door marked "Do Not Enter" in bright yellow letters.

They entered.

A security guard blocked the way. "State your name."

"Eberli."

"Noutashi."

"State your purpose," said the guard.

"Meeting with Vint in Room 6SSB."

The guard peered into the communicator dome. "Palm-badge in."

Everything went smoothly.

"Third door on the right," said the guard.

##

"Oh good, I was hoping you'd be able to make it through," said Vint, after they entered a top secret conference room. "Sometimes things get a little tricky down here."

There was a narrow table with three chairs on one side. Opposite them was an ishmili dome. Eberli and Noutashi had never seen an ishmili dome before. Some sort of alien being, with luscious plum purple skin, faced them from the dome. It was Lon, seated comfortably in the Hikli laboratory.

195

"It is my privilege to introduce you to Lon," said Vint, "she is our Guardian contact from Jeshmol. One month from now we will meet each other, face to face, at the portal site."

"Wow, this is really cool," said Eberli. He had never seen an evojesh before.

"So exciting to meet you," said Noutashi, clutching her hands together. Even though they were different beings, from separate worlds, both of them knew instinctively that they were umbies and the other two were urbies.

"me hear good things about you" said Lon, in properly enunciated anca. "it pleasing to see you after many years".

Vint said, "Don't you think it's amazing that we nimulons can sit here at headquarters and talk to jeshies over there on the other side. There are three more - Xen, Wun and Trz - but they won't be attending this meeting. To give you some background, five years ago Riana used to translate for us through their ishmili dome at the Observatory. Now we do everything direct. Quite impressive, don't you think."

"they here yesterday" said Lon. "work on annie plan".

"They who?" asked Vint.

"riana dene" replied Lon. "they help xen wun on annie plan".

"I don't believe I understood you correctly," said Vint. "Are you saying that Riana and Dene were there at the Hikli?"

"at hikli" "yes" said Lon, nodding her head. "they talk xen wun nimutrak" "riana dene got sky cruiser" "new portal plan with annie".

"Sorry to sound dumb," said Vint, "but the Hikli lab is in Jeshmol. How could Riana and Dene be there?"

"riana teach dene move back forth with jeshmol" said Lon. "they no need portal".

"I didn't know that," said Vint.

Noutashi jumped in the conversation, "I'm not sure I heard you correctly but Sandal Annie is in the hospital."

"gheney hospital" asked Lon.

"Bellevue Hospital," replied Noutashi. "It's in New York City."

"hope annie do well" said Lon.

196

"I don't believe Annie is ever going to leave that hospital," said Noutashi, who felt sad about the prospect of losing her longest running client.

"you idea annie plan" said Lon.

"My idea was to bring Sandal Annie to Central Park that one time. Vint told me I needed to get Melona super powered up and Annie was perfect for the job," said Noutashi. "Nobody told me anything about her being involved in the actual rescue. Annie is not going to be able to make it. She won't be with us much longer."

Vint took over. "Sounds like another big setback for us. Are we sure this Annie you're talking about is the same Sandal Annie who is on Noutashi's client roster?"

"central park" "ambutrak" "gheney portal test" said Lon.

"That's the same one," said Vint. "I need to set up a meeting with Dene."

"me have goodly plan" said Lon. "riana dene be at hikli again thursday" "xen wun talk equipment" "we figure annie out" "no worry sylumini spy on us".

"That sounds perfect," said Vint.

Scene 64 - Noutashi's Revenge

"Circulation of our magazine has been going down because of all this hippie nonsense," said Jim. "At the next board meeting, we need to have some fresh ideas."

They were sitting in his plush office on the fortieth floor of Impress Magazine. Jim was George's boss.

"This hippie fad will fade," said George, "but I agree that we need to be on the ball when it comes to keeping circulation up."

"We're not in the business of thrown together fashion," said Jim. "Good style is always in style. Unfortunately, market forces are hard to control during turbulent times."

"Not all of the fashion statements of this younger generation are thrown together," said George. "Constance and I were out gallery hopping the other night and I acquired some quality photographs of these new styles. Strictly for research purposes, you understand."

"Heh, heh, heh," said Jim, "of course, you were only doing research."

"Let me get them from my office," said George, "I think you will want to see the potential of this trend."

##

From his file folder George picked two stylish pictures, taken from rival magazines, and placed them on Jim's desk. "These are not thrown-together styles," he said. "A great deal of thought and planning went into these creations. This is a downtown approach to fashion, and we have an uptown clientele, but I hope you can see what I'm driving at."

Jim examined them with the practiced eye of a fashion professional. "These are actually quite good," he admitted. "I was in Kurt's office the other day and he showed an interest in this music festival that everyone is talking about ... oh, what's that thing called."

"Woodstock," said George, helpfully.

"Ah yes, that's it," said Jim. "Kurt mentioned in passing that we might want to look into sending one of our photographers out there, with the idea of running a short 'special interest' section in the October issue."

"Take a look at these," said George. He placed four more photos on his boss's desk.

Jim picked them up, one by one. "The technique is similar to our Impress style guidelines, even though the subject matter is definitely downtown."

"Those pictures were taken by one of our employees," said George. "Not one of our regular photographers, mind you. Someone in the office staff."

"Who would that be?" asked Jim.

"Melona Geffion," answered George.

"Ah yes, I've heard of her," said Jim, "one of our best workers. I wish we had more of them like her. Is she stealing any of our equipment?"

"I checked into that," said George, "and the answer is no."

"Where'd you get these pictures?" asked Jim.

"I bought them in a bookstore over on Tenth Street," said George. "Their prices were a lot cheaper than what I would have paid at an art gallery."

"I'll hang onto to these, if you don't mind," said Jim. "I think Kurt might want to see them before the next board meeting."

"You can keep them for as long as you like," said George. "By the way, Melona has also done some very fine art projects with Aiyoni."

"That might be a good hook for the article," said Jim.

Sitting invisibly in a plush chair, thick black leather with bright brass tacks, Noutashi folded her hands together. All those nights spent working with George's feverish dreams. All those days prepping other guardians to reach into the dreams of Jim and Kurt. Those horrid hours worrying about the damage done by Malki. It looked like all that extra work might be paying off.

Staring out the window - skyscrapers in every direction - she wondered if her new plan was actually going work. She had promised Riana and Dene that she would find someone to replace Sandal Annie. It was a gamble. Life's a gamble. Somehow, they had managed to make it this far. Noutashi hoped she had chosen the right candidate to be the third portal tuner.

George went back to his office. Kurt turned his attention to the next task on his desk. Floating through the window, Noutashi hovered outside, watching traffic far below on the bustling streets.

One more week and she would get her client back. That's what she so ardently desired. One more week. Noutashi wished she felt more confident.

Chapter 24 - Entrenched

Scene 65 - The Bunker

Vint felt a rush of relief as he approached the site of the Woodstock Music Festival. After all these years, all those delays, this event was actually happening.

The farm country near here was pleasant, with rolling green hills and tidy blue lakes. As he approached the site, two things caught his eye. The first was the stage, still under construction, at the bottom of a hill. Across the way, on top of the opposite hill, he saw something which upset him enormously. Sylumini surveyors were taking measurements. Rumor had it that they were going to setup their portable portal here at Woodstock. It would be a grand propaganda coup. No doubt their real motive was to steal every secret they could get their hands on.

Landing in front of the stage, Vint looked at what was here - the performance area, the sound towers, the hillside where the audience would sit. Then he sank slowly into the ground. Directly beneath the stage was the Portal Bunker. It didn't look like much from the outside, a dull brown box, but inside it was a technological marvel. Vint palm badged in.

"Well hello there," said Cami. "Welcome to the command center."

"Hi," mumbled Farli. He was way busy.

"Looking good," said Vint. Every inch of space was packed tight with high tech gear.

Lumbia floated over and said, "Good to see you again, Vint. It's been quite some time."

"A couple of years," said Vint. "How's things with you?"

"I'll be glad when this is over," said Lumbia. "It seems like we've been working on this since forever."

"I was thinking the same thing on the way over," said Vint.

"You and I need to make sure our plans are coordinated," Lumbia mentioned. "We are no longer in the planning stages. This is crunch time."

"You got that right," said Vint, taking a deep breath.

"Let's go over to Lon's workstation," suggested Lumbia.

"I didn't realize Lon was going to be working here in the bunker," said Vint. He was looking forward to finally meeting her.

"She's scheduled to get here day after tomorrow," said Lumbia, turning the communicator dome on.

"Someone else mentioned that," said Vint. "Would you mind explaining to me how she can get here before the portal opens?"

"Oh that," said Lumbia. "It's like this. What you're looking at now is only half of the command bunker. Xen and Wun are going to bring their NimuTrak over to our side. That way all of the crucial technology will be in one centralized location. Lon is going to hitch a ride with them."

"I hope this works," said Vint. "This entire project feels like a thousand problems waiting to jump out at us."

"I worry about that too," said Lumbia. She was putting the finishing touches on an image in the dome. "Let's take a closer look what you and I are responsible for, which is producing enough dual atmosphere for the colony."

"Ah yes, our much delayed project with Lon," said Vint.

"This is the site map for the rescue operation," said Lumbia. "Over here is the Gheney Hospital. We are right here, at the first portal location, which is directly above our heads. Next to us is the second portal location, off stage right. Across the road will be the Sylumini Spy Tower."

"How can they get away with that?" asked Vint. "That would make sense if Sarkon and Sarena were running the show. But Celene is in charge now. Can't she put a stop to that?"

"That's the last thing in the world Celene would want to do," said Lumbia. "We've got the Sylumini right where we want them."

"Nobody ever gets the Sylumini right where they want them," grumbled Vint.

"That was then, this is now," said Lumbia. "Quick question. What do you know about the jeshie lawsuit filed against the Sylumini?"

"Dene was telling me about that," said Vint. "Ing won some sort of court case in the regionals and now there's a team of lawyers down there in your jeshie colony."

"I'm glad you know about that," said Lumbia. "I've been spending a lot of time with those guys. They just finished constructing an Office of Investigation Annex, directly below the Spy Tower. If the Sylumini make a mistake, the jeshie lawyers are there to catch it."

"I wish I could be optimistic," said Vint, "but I'm not."

"Here's what you and I are going to do," said Lumbia. "We are going to concentrate on one task. We'll work with Lon so these kids here at Woodstock can provide enough dual atmosphere for all the jeshies."

"That would be awesome," said Vint. "We focus on safety. Let the lawyers worry about the legal stuff."

"That being said," continued Lumbia, "we're going to have a front row seat for the biggest portal that's opened on this planet in a long time. Good, bad, or otherwise - we'll see it all."

Scene 66 - The Tower

Malki was enjoying himself immensely. Yesterday they had assembled the Tower on the Hill. This morning they showed Malki his desk on the ground floor. In his line of work, jobs were outside, in the open air, where crowds of people were gathered. Now he had his own desk, with his own communicator dome, and his own password. He knew better than to get used to it - but he was gonna make the most of it while it lasted.

Panoh, the on call technician, knew all about remote command centers. The engineering department would get a request to setup a temporary facility. Move the gear, set it up, run it until they told you to stop. Then haul everything back in the warehouse. This remote command tower just happened to have a portal to another world on the second floor.

"You know how many people are gonna be here in a coupla more days," said Malki. "One hundred thousand.

Ain't that something. We didn't even have that many in Chicago."

"Estimates are higher now," said Panoh.

"Whatever," said Malki. "This Woodstock thingie is gonna be a biggie. Just you wait and see. Oh yeah. Gonna be big. Real big."

Panoh said, "I do what they tell me."

Malki kept on talking. "Yeah, this is gonna be the place alright. This is gonna be where I do *exactly* what the big bosses sent me here to do."

##

Torley was on the second floor of the tower. The portable portal had been installed here. He had to admit that they had done an excellent job. Torley did not want to be at this remote site. He was second in command of the entire technology division, reporting directly to Ulta. He had subordinates who were supposed to operate equipment like this. This is what Khaletora told him to do, so this is what he did. Complaining got you fired.

The Portable Emergency Rescue Portal was only a few small steps away from being fully operational. It irritated Torley that the key features of their technology had been stolen by spies, or extracted from the system by creating needless delays. In spite of these concerns, it was a thrill to be on the cusp of such a major breakthrough.

Effrana had a question. "Which test bead do you want me to use?"

Torley said, "Let me see what you have."

A gleaming white tray was brought out. Exactly one hundred test beads were on display, each one a different soto color. Things had changed a lot recently. Unfortunately, data from Riana and Dene's latest tests was wildly inconclusive. Ulta had expressed her opinion, in private, that they were being tricked by Dene.

"Try this particular shade of soto yellow," Torley said. "It's the best fit for the scatter data."

Rinsing it off in a special solution, she placed it in a slotted tray, which was inserted into the portal chamber. "Ready when you are," she said.

"Proceed at your own pace," said Torley. "This is just a simple system check."

Effrana illuminated the yellow crystal bead with a beam of blue soto light.

Both of them were shocked when the test bead disappeared.

"What should we do?" gasped Effrana.

Torley was breathing heavily, fearing that he might make a wrong decision. "We know it was transported over to the jeshie side but we don't know where it went. Unless we can get it back, we should enter this into the log as 'system check positive' and leave it at that."

"That's a sensible suggestion," said Effrana, with a sigh of relief.

Both of them understood that there were serious legal implications.

##

Ulta sat at the hub of the executive suite on the third floor. Picture windows circled the entire upper floor, so that staff could watch everything happening here at Woodstock. The roof above their heads was crowded with spy gear.

Her political instincts were on maximum code red alert. Khaletora had been meeting with Malki a lot lately - in secret. Ulta had her sources. They reported where and when those meetings took place. No one knew what those two talked about. No matter what happened here at Woodstock, things looked bad for her.

Instead of paying attention to her assigned duties, she was searching the equipment database. The Sylumini were sneaky, and they did many loathsome things, sometimes even terrible deeds, but there was one thing they always did with the utmost accuracy - inventory control. Every piece of equipment they owned, or leased, or "appropriated", was always logged into the database. Always.

One tiny element in that vast mass of information had to be out of place. It would take at least one piece of equipment to bring Ulta down. All she needed to do was find it, before they used it against her.

Scene 67 - The Command Center

Lon was at the Hikli, sitting in a comfortable chair, a total nervous wreck. It was hard to believe that she had been working here for almost six years. Xen and Wun were doing what they did best - tossing great heaps of equipment into the van - getting ready for their next high tech road trip.

This journey was going to be different. Lon was going with them. The three of them were never coming back. Lon did not have to move to Earth. She had chosen to. Lon wasn't old, by Jeshmol standards. She had led a dull life. It was time for a change of scenery.

Trz walked up with two thick pillows.

"what these for" asked Lon.

"she crazy" said Trz, pointing at Xen. "she drive between worlds" "ours falling apart" "you need pillows".

Lon hadn't thought of this as essential travel gear but she knew Trz was the practical type. "thanks" she said.

"we go now" yelled Xen. She climbed into the driver's seat of the NimuTrak. Wun strapped himself into the techie seat.

Trz motioned for Lon to climb quickly into the back of the van. Now she realized why he gave her the pillows. There was no chair. No seat belt. Equipment was piled everywhere. Lon sat on the floor, adjusting the pillows for comfort.

Trz slammed the side door shut. With the clicker, he opened the big door of the Hikli building. A crowd had gathered outside. As the door was opening, Trz trotted over to the ishmili dome to act as navigator.

Xen drove the NimuTrak through a tight space between two buildings. Honking the horn to chase onlookers away, she gunned the engine and roared off at top speed.

Lon got slammed into equipment. She grabbed the pillows.

The area near the capitol city of Namoush had not been damaged by the mode-quake. When they got to the edge of the mainland, the Wamilla peninsula could be seen in the distance, drifting away into outer space. Xen raced the van off a broken road, at the crumbling edge, and plunged into the abyss between Kemong and Wamilla. She jammed it into transform-gear. That's when the ride got rough.

Lon clawed her way across the floor of the van, desperately clinging to anything that wasn't sliding around. If she tried to stand up, she got smashed down.

Wun tossed a pair of gloves back to her.

"what these for" cried Lon.

"kneel on pillows" said Wun, "grab side door supports with gloves" "look out window" "enjoy ride".

Somehow this desperate plan worked. If she wasn't wearing gloves, Lon would have hurt her hands on the door supports. Being able to look out the window did not make her feel better. They had left their old world behind but had not yet entered the new. The view was dominated by indefinite pastel swirls, whizzing by at tremendous velocity.

Wun tossed a pair of goggles back to Lon. "put on" "keep on".

Lon wedged her feet, took off one glove, adjusted the goggles. Putting the glove back on, she clung to the door in terror. The jeshnim goggles let her to see the other world they had now entered. It was dark with sparkling lights. Night time on Earth.

Many times, in the quiet of her home, or slow times at the Hikli, she had studied maps of Earth. In this moment of fear she recognized the outline of Europe. Sparkling lights were crowded cities.

Then everything went dark and she panicked. "aaaah".

"ocean" said Wun.

"me know that" said Lon. She had seen the Atlantic Ocean on maps. It was between Europe and North America. Now she was seeing the sea through goggle eyes.

Coming up fast was another familiar outline. The Atlantic Coast of North America loomed large.

"we near" yelled Xen, "hold tight". She applied powerful but steady pressure on the brakes.

Lon fell sideways.

"grab my arm" cried out Wun, trying to operate the dashboard dome with one hand, while rescuing Lon with the other. "back of seats" "hold back of seats".

After grasping hold of the headrests with weak fingers, Lon scooted her foot back and managed to drag both pillows under her knees. She was desperate. Maybe she was doomed.

"slow down fast" yelled Wun.

Lon watched through the front windshield. Flashes of light streaked by in a fog of double world reality.

Xen wrestled with the steering wheel, trying to keep it steady.

"target ahead" called out Wun. "slower" "slow down" "sloweeeeeeeer".

When they got close, Lon saw a large brown rectangle ahead. A string of lights was wrapped around one side. Lon remembered why. Before they left, Wun had wrapped the same series of colored lights on the side of their NimuTrak. Both sets had matching colors.

"docking station their left" "our right" confirmed Wun.

Xen slowed to a crawl.

As they made their slow crawl, Lon shifted her pillows, adjusted her goggles, and tightened her gloves.

Xen came to a stop, then shifted into side drive. Their van inched sideways in itsy-bitsy steps. The string of lights on the bunker lined up with the docking lights on the van.

"Rrrrrh rrhhr rnghgg" went the wheels.

"set lock sequence" said Xen.

"bunker grips locked" said Wun.

"confirm atmosphere" said Xen.

"readings goodly" said Wun.

"confirm intercom" said Xen.

A friendly voice, which Lon recognized immediately, came over the intercom. "confirm intercom" said Cami. "dual atmosphere goodly on our side".

The NimuTrak and the Bunker were now bound tight.

"you open side door" Xen called out to Lon. "front doors not work here".

It felt strange that nothing moved. On wobbly feet she stood up and stepped over to the side door. It opened easily.

The atmosphere on the other side smelled funny but it was not deadly. Taking a small gulp of this new air, she pushed the door all the way open.

"welcome to earth" said Cami, holding Lon's gloved hands to help her get out of the van. Both feet were on solid ground. This was earth ground, not jeshie cloud ground. Her feet tingled.

Cami gave Lon a gentle hug.

"thank for me be you here" said Lon, feeling dizzy.

"hi me farli" said Farli.

Lon limply shook his hand. It was a strange sort of solid.

Wun leaped out of the van and began dragging heavy equipment into the bunker as if their lives depended on it - which they did.

A few minutes later Xen and Wun had the atmosphere sealed and stabilized. Bunker Woodstock and NimuTrak Omega would be locked together for the next week. The five of them would share this inter regional, double wide trailer, as their home and work place.

Half an hour later Cami and Farli were sitting in their regular chairs. Xen and Wun had unbolted the seats from their van and positioned them in front of the ishmili dome. Two equipment cases had been rigged so that Lon could sit on her pillows in comfort.

Cami adjusted the ishmili dome and a familiar sight came into view.

Trz was sitting in his regular seat in front of the ishmili dome at the Hikli. "you have nice trip" asked Trz.

"it easy" said Xen.

Lon poked her head between Cami and Wun, so Trz could see her smiling face. "me want thank you for pillows".

Chapter 25 - Prelude To A Rock Festival

Scene 68 - Lumbia And Qusheem

Young people were showing up at Woodstock even though the concert wasn't scheduled to begin until tomorrow. Something cosmic was in the air - as they used to say back in the sixties. Many felt as if some invisible force was guiding them here. Guardian anca were that invisible force. These youngsters would never understand the reasons why.

Lon was sitting at her desk, in the back corner of the bunker, trying to figure out how the new operating system worked. They had given her an anca communicator dome. It was not at all like the soto domes she had used until now.

On the other side of the room, Xen and Wun were arguing loudly. Cami and Farli sat quietly at their workstations.

Someone was at the door. An anca floated in, an umbie with a sublime smile. With an air of grace, she pulled up a chair next to Lon.

"Hi, I'm Lumbia, I'm hoping that you are Lon."

"me lon" "pleased to meet".

"You and I will be working on the dual atmosphere," said Lumbia.

"vint mention that" said Lon. "looking forward".

"I'm also Honat's committed partner," said Lumbia. "You've seen him at the Observatory."

Lon was surprised. "me not know honat have commit".

Cami shouted out from the other side of the room, "Honat and Lumbia love each other madly but you would never know that from the way Honat acts at work."

"me see" said Lon.

209

"I'm the terran in charge of the atmosphere pumps," said Lumbia. "We should look at the flow diagrams."

"me never use anca dome before" confessed Lon.

Lumbia spent a generous amount of time teaching Lon how to use the applications on the unfamiliar desktop dome. The software had everything they needed for the festival. On the other hand, software can't do much if you don't understand the operating system.

"There, how's that?" asked Lumbia.

"better" "me thank you muchly" said Lon.

"Good," said Lumbia. "We can continue the training later. Right now, there's something I need you to do. Using that software app, I want you to identify two evos, one umbie and one urbie, who are the closest match to what you jeshies need for your air mixture. I need to calibrate my system."

"me trained for that" said Lon.

"Take your time," said Lumbia. "This needs to be accurate."

Studying the site map, Lon said, "those two".

"Let's go outside and take a look at them," said Lumbia.

The terran anca and the refugee evojesh left the portal bunker and poked their heads up through the ground. Terrans don't like to leave their familiar world inside a planet, although it's easy enough for them to do. Lon was seeing the surface of Earth for the first time. It was lush and green. How thrilling to admire its new colors and smell its fresh moist air.

A young couple was standing in front of the Woodstock stage, in awe, even though not much was happening right at that moment. He had long hair, a blue t-shirt, bell bottom pants, and hand crafted sandals. She had wavy hair, was wearing a granny dress, purple sunglasses, and her sandals were decorated with sea shells.

"I recognize that type," said Lumbia. "After the Second World War they started showing up in large numbers. We call them the children of the future."

"why you call them that" asked Lon.

"Because their dreams for the future of this planet are more to our liking than what we've seen in the past," said Lumbia.

"me gasping for air" complained Lon.

"Let's go back down," said Lumbia, "the dual atmosphere is more concentrated in the underground. That's why we need to get this Festival Bubble pumped up by tomorrow. We're going to have to support twenty thousand new colonists."

Back in the bunker, Lon took deep breaths. "me feel better now".

Lumbia said, "Now that I have a better understanding of what you guys require, I need to figure out how to make that work. The terran pumps need to be adjusted so we can get the mixture just right."

This was an enormously difficult problem to solve. With so many variables there were too many options. Lumbia crinkled her nose. Suddenly she looked pleased. "Let's get Qusheem over here. He'll figure this out in no time."

"me like qusheem" said Lon.

Lumbia reached in her lower pocket and took out her taper device. She called Honat at the Observatory.

"Hi," said Honat.

"Hello, sweetie," said Lumbia, "how are things at work today?"

"Busy," said Honat.

"I'm here with Lon," said Lumbia. "She's very nice."

"Good," said Honat.

"Would you please put Qusheem on," said Lumbia. "He never answers his own taper device."

"Sure," said Honat.

"Tsudfbic," said Qusheem.

"Lon found the two evos we were looking for," said Lumbia.

Honat's taper device got disconnected.

An instant later Qusheem was standing next to them in the bunker.

"Patrbov?" asked Qusheem.

Lon understood some of Qusheem's big-words. "those two" she replied, pointing at the site map in her anca dome. The couple was wandering away from the stage.

Qusheem gently moved their chairs aside, curled his taper on the floor, and began flipping through apps. Then he said, "Dwijhaktyg."

211

"If you think that will work?" said Lumbia.

Qusheem nodded yes, then vanished.

Lumbia said to Lon, "He says he'll adjust the people who are already here."

Qusheem is an evo, which puts him in the same general category as human beings. This gave him a good perspective on how they breathe. As an evo, Qusheem had been an extreme mode-hopper throughout Nimulos. By Earth standards, he was much older than our planet. There was a lot he had learned and little he couldn't figure out.

First he found the couple that Lon had identified. It was not Qusheem's role to influence their behavior, the way a guardian anca might do. What he was permitted to do, under these special circumstances, was influence the way they breathed.

Like all young beings, these two had latent powers which they were unaware of. Qusheem knew exactly what to do.

Breathe in. Earth air.

Breathe out. Jeshie mix.

Adjustments were made until Qusheem was pleased with the results. Then he tromped around the festival site, adjusting people as seemed best for his far seeing purposes.

When he got back to the bunker Qusheem said, "Czmoskimp."

"I'll take care of that," said Lumbia.

On Lon's dome they could see dual atmosphere levels rising. Lumbia switched over to the terran network. Obscure pump and valve data filled the screen. She slid her fingers across the control panel. "There, that should do it for now," said Lumbia. "When more people show up tomorrow, we'll adjust the atmosphere mix again."

Qusheem stood up. "Rhonux," he announced to everyone in the bunker

Lumbia said, "Oh, that's so nice of you. I'm glad you decided to stay with us until both portals are open."

Lon said, "me glad too".

Cami and Farli agreed.

Xen and Wun kept arguing.

Then Lumbia got a worried look on her face. "Wait. That means Honat will be all alone at the Observatory. The poor dear won't get enough rest."

"Gwubhenst," said Qusheem, who had worked with Honat longer than Lumbia had known him.

Lumbia sighed and said, "Yeah, I guess you're right. None of us are going to get much rest for the next week. May as well make the best of it."

Lon said "this what you guys call crunch time".

Scene 69 - Ulta And Malki

At the top of the Spy Tower sat Ulta and she had a plan.

One of the junior executives called out, "You have a visitor."

Malki came to her desk. As usual, he had a sneer on his face. "You sent for me."

Every executive seated near Ulta's desk could hear every word they said.

"How did the training session go?" she asked.

"Good," said Malki. "Real good."

"Have a seat," said Ulta, "I need to ask a few questions to make sure we're ready."

"Yeah sure," said Malki.

"Are all three squadrons fully trained for this crowd monitoring session?" asked Ulta.

"Five," said Malki. "The big boss wants five."

"We must be careful," cautioned Ulta. "The Watchers are sending agents to the festival. The Guardians are up to something. The Terrans have some sort of underground city going on down there."

"Yeah, well, we're always careful," said Malki. "That's what I told em at training today. I told em - be careful."

"There won't be any police presence here," said Ulta. "The security team they hired wasn't allowed to take the job because this site is not in their district."

Malki raised his hands in disgust. "They gotta buncha hippies running security for a bunch of hippies. How stupid is that."

"That's not for me to say," said Ulta.

Malki was wound up now. "Yeah and we got forecasts for heavy rain. And double the number of people are already on the roads There ain't gonna be enough food. There's no hotels out here in these hills. People are gonna be living in hovels, slopping around in muck. I'm telling you - and you can mark my words on this - this is a formula for big trouble. Oh yeah."

"And we don't want any trouble, do we," said Ulta.

"Heeeeey, you know what we're here for," said Malki. "They call us the peacekeepers."

"That will be all," said Ulta.

Malki left without even saying goodbye.

##

For a long while, Ulta worked diligently at her regularly assigned tasks. After the office chatter died down, and the staff was absorbed in their work again, she popped an image into the far back of her dome display. Nobody else could see it, unless they were hovering directly over her shoulder.

While Malki was sitting in the chair, she had spy devices capturing high resolution images of the equipment he was carrying. All Auxis have their own personal taper device, as well as a company issued pocket monitor.

Ulta ran an inventory control check on both of them. They were perfectly clean. All original parts. Correct serial numbers. Last year, Dene had stolen Malki's taper device, although no one had ever been able to prove he stole it. It seemed that Malki wasn't taking any chances.

This was bad news for Ulta. Somewhere in that mountain of data, some tiny piece of the puzzle was shifted slightly out of place. Ulta needed to find it.

Betrayal hovered over her shoulder.

Chapter 26 - All Together Now

Scene 70 - Helicopter

Melona was five minutes late for work. Most days, Constance would have called her out about that but her boss was nowhere to be seen. 'Thank goodness it's Friday,' she thought.

Sitting down quickly, amid smug looks from the other girls in the office, she put her purse in the desk drawer and opened a file folder. Her brain wasn't open yet but at least the file folder was open.

Constance and George appeared at her desk. "We would like to speak with you," said Constance.

The girls in the office snickered.

"Of course," said Melona, grabbing her steno pad and ballpoint pen.

"In the conference room," said George.

Melona was sure she was about to get fired. Seeing the two of them at the Udjat Eye Gallery three weeks ago had finally caught up with her.

The girls in the office were sure she was going to be fired. A few were gleeful. Most would be sad. None of them would stand up for her.

George hurried the two employees into the conference room and closed the door. "Remember that show you had at the Udjat ... " He saw the look of fear in her eyes and tried to calm her, " ... Nothing to worry about, this is good news."

Melona remained apprehensive.

"We just got out of a staff meeting," said George. "The big brass has caught wind of this Woodstock thing. There was, how shall we say, some discussion about this. Wouldn't you agree Constance?"

"To be honest, I'd call it a nasty argument, but I'll settle for discussion," she said.

"Getting to the point, you have been selected as staff photographer for Impress Magazine at Woodstock," said George.

Melona's jaw dropped. "You're sending me to Woodstock on a photo shoot?"

"That's right," said George, "I put my head on the chopping block for you. At any rate, the helicopter will be here in half an hour."

"Helicopter?"

"Apparently the New York State Throughway has come to a standstill because of festival traffic," said George. "We need to move you to the front lines as quickly as possible."

Melona stood at attention, saluted briskly the way her father had taught her, and said, "Reporting for duty, *sir*." It was a brilliant move.

"That's what I like," said George, "spunk. I used to have it in my younger days. Bring back some pictures. Impress might not run them but they want to have the option."

##

The helicopter landed in a small clearing in upstate New York. Still dressed for the office, Melona stepped into a dusty whirlwind. She carried a company camera in a fancy case, her own battered pawn shop camera in her purse, plus a large box of film. In her other hand was a stylish suitcase, filled with weekend clothes from fashion outfitter Ruthie's.

Standing in front of her with a clip board was a young woman. "Which act are you with?" asked Pamela.

Melona reached out to shake her hand, "Melona Geffion, from Impress Magazine."

"Aha," said Pamela, "I saw the helicopter so I figured you must be a rock star. Welcome to Woodstock. My name is Pamela. Your magazine has been very generous to us (surprise surprise, she whispered behind her hand) and I want to make sure you enjoy your stay. It's very crowded around here, so your overnight options are extremely limited."

"Don't worry about me," said Melona, "I've traveled all over with my camera, worked a few Off Off Broadway shows.

216

I'm tough. All I need is an old armchair, or a blanket on the floor."

Pamela said, "I know something you might be interested in. It's near the festival site. Stage hands downstairs. Farm daughter and a guest room upstairs. Momma don't allow no stage hands up there."

"I'll take it," said Melona, "I've got expense account cash."

"Everybody likes cash," said Pamela.

The farm daughter, whose name was Cathy, showed Melona the guest room. Neither of them could see Noutashi, gloating invisibly from a musty old chair.

"It's not much but everything else around here has been taken," said Cathy.

"This is a lot better than I expected," said Melona. The room smelled like old people but it was tidy. "How many others are staying here?"

"We got five stage hands down in the parlor," said Cathy. "The couch in the living room is still available but mom set the rent on that pretty high. Someone will take it."

"I'll take this room," said Melona.

"Nice to have you here," said Cathy, "if you need anything just ask. The festival's right over there through the woods."

"Let me get my things arranged," said Melona.

"Sounds good," said Cathy. She was glad to have a girl she could talk to. Those stage hands just looked at her.

Melona put the suitcase from Ruthie's on the old fashioned bed. Impress did a lot of business with them and Ruthie knew Melona well, from all the times she had picked up an outfit for a photo shoot.

Opening the latch, Melona took out several slinky dresses that would look fabulous on her ... if she'd been sent to a yacht club. Instead, she was going to an outdoor rock concert. Holding an adorable blue chiffon dress in her arms, she hugged it.

That's when Noutashi got to work. Now that her client was actually at Woodstock, her list of things to do suddenly got a whole lot shorter. What she needed right now was a half hour delay. Noutashi had big plans for her little girl.

Pressing her hands lightly on Melona's shoulders, Noutashi placed two powerful images firmly in the young woman's mind. Blue jeans. Expense account cash.

Twenty minutes later, Wanda pulled up in her brother's beat up old car, took a look at the new girl's hips, and got out with a grocery sack that had three pair of jeans.

"Howya doing today," said Wanda.

"I'm doing pretty good," said Melona. "Thanks for coming over. It's a long story but I desperately need jeans."

"I brought three pair over," said Wanda. "Try 'em on and see if they fit." They looked in the bag and haggled over price.

Melona went up to her room. Wanda was exactly her size in the hips but a bit taller.

"Those look alright," said Wanda.

Melona handed her cash for two pair and gave her back the bag with one pair. "That other pair is a size I will never fit into again ... ever."

Wanda counted the money, took the bag and said, "I'm never going to get back in these old jeans either. I just like to keep em around to remind myself that once upon a time they fit tight and the boys thought I looked real nice."

Three girls laughed.

Noutashi zipped over the tops of the trees and was overjoyed to see that Melona was still standing in the yard.

Some guy came walking through the woods. He carried a backpack and had a goofy expression on his face.

Tim asked, "Can you tell me how to get to Woodstock?"

Wanda pointed through the woods and said, "The festival is about a mile over there." She had a real cute smile.

Noutashi put the double whammy on Melona.

Melona stepped in front of Wanda and said, "I'm going over to the festival right now. On assignment. Let me get my gear."

When she came back Tim asked, "Would you like me to carry anything?"

"I've got this," said Melona.

"Have fun," said Wanda, with dagger eyes.

"Thanks for bringing that stuff over," said Melona. Then she said to Cathy, "Catch you later."

Cathy said, "Curfew's at ten."

Three young women chuckled.

Scene 71 - Sixties Fashion

Melona waved an uncertain goodbye. Tim had gone on across the road to find a camping spot for himself. He seemed nice enough. She had learned to take these things slow. Maybe they would find each other again in this vast gathering of the tribes.

In front of Melona was a fence. In the middle of the fence was a trailer. Inside the trailer was Harvey, the stage manager. He decided who got backstage, and who did not.

"Name?" asked Harvey.

"Melona Geffion, Impress Magazine," she said.

Her name was on the list. Pamela had told Harvey to be nice, real nice, when someone from the magazine showed up. He handed her a backstage pass. "All Access - 3 Days."

Melona put the lanyard around her neck and stepped into the musician's waiting area.

Dressing room trailers for the rock stars were on her left. Staff trailers were farther away. Because of massive traffic jams, only a few musicians had been able to get here.

An important lesson in life that Melona had learned was this. There are two kinds of women in this world. Some love to have their picture taken. Others hate to have their picture taken.

Using this valuable information, she kneeled on the ground. A small group of people were milling about. With deliberate flair, she took out the big company camera and loaded it with film. Then, with all the assurance of a pro, she slung the strap around her neck and walked toward them.

Attractive women, fashionably attired, began to appear.

After the first hour, she no longer had to go looking for style. It came to her.

A trailer park, even one filled with famous musicians, is not an appealing backdrop for fascinating young women, decked out in their best sixties finery.

One of these women, dressed in full psychedelic splendor, made a fabulous suggestion. Between the dressing room trailers and the backstage area was a plywood bridge. The stage hands had built it over a small country road so that the musicians wouldn't have to walk through the crowd to get onstage. Everyone called it the Rainbow Bridge.

At the top of this humble plywood construction was a spectacular backdrop. Stage on the left. Hundred thousand people on the hill. Sound towers rising to the sky. Unique women - creative outfits - spectacular backdrop. Melona's career as a Woodstock photographer was off to a solid start.

Noutashi was about as happy as a guardian could be. She had chosen Tim to take over where Sandal Annie left off. When Riana and Dene saw the results on the soto color mapper they agreed. Tomorrow they would find out if this was true. In the meantime, Tim had already made a good impression.

With these happy thoughts in mind she glanced over her shoulder. Auxis glared at them from the Spy Tower. The happy glow drained from Noutashi's face.

Scene 72 - Delusions Of Power

Khaletora was in a jovial mood. Members of the Special Board, plus invited guests, were packed into the executive suite on the third floor of the tower. They were sitting at the desks of regular staff, who had all been sent home early. Ulta was the only one at her own desk, because she was a permanent member of the Special Board.

"Urbies and umbies," said Khaletora grandly, "Welcome to Woodstock. We are here to demonstrate the amazing progress we have made. The Valdarians at Chephra have been unable to respond to the needs of this rescue. For reasons which baffle me, a small staff at the Observatory has been put in charge of the portal. Celene had been designated as leader of this rescue mission. They face enormous challenges. We are here to help.

"Our Portable Emergency Rescue Portal is the solution of the future. We won't be able to bring any refugees across today but our new technology is certain to be the long term winner. You will see a demonstration soon."

220

Enthusiastic applause followed this grandiose announcement. At any meeting with Khaletora, applause was mandatory - and applaud they did - with great vigor.

Big-Ks eyes got wider.

"The Guardians have been put back in the portal business. Why would anyone risk doing that? The days of people powered portals are over. Industrial strength mode-tunnels are the wave of the future. We have our prototype right here.

"Young people are pouring into this festival site. They have not been trained for portal duty, as citizens of the ancient world were. In addition to that, they are being forced to live under primitive conditions. Poor planning could result in a disaster."

His voice got shriller.

"Fortunately, we are the problem solvers. As they have done so many times before, our Auxiliary professionals will provide crowd monitoring services for the government. We are the peacekeepers. It is up to us to insure that this rescue is an inter-regional success."

At the sound of booming applause, Khaletora was well pleased with himself. "In a few moments we will go down to the second floor to see the portal. Are there any questions?"

One of the more prominent board members responded, "It is my understanding that something called Operation Groovy is scheduled to take place. Can you tell us about that?"

"Of course," Khaletora replied, confidently. "Look at the overcrowded conditions here. The festival organizers printed tickets for one hundred thousand people. Several times that number have already arrived. These are the types of human beings who have become disturbed by that planetary bubble. We call it Operation Groovy because these misguided folks believe a festival like this is what makes life groovy." He chuckled to himself. "Let's take a look downstairs."

Effrana was as nervous as she could be. She was the on duty technician. Her tidy world of settings and control panels had just gotten mobbed by high ranking executives.

Ulta glided over to reassure her. "I've got this. Just do what I ask." She began her prepared speech. "Portal technology has been available for billions of years. What you must remember is that no two portals are ever alike. Never. All worlds are always shifting. This facility is a testament to our ability to miniaturize sophisticated equipment and make it rugged enough to travel. Think about how enormous Chephra is. Take a look here. We can move this portal anywhere on the planet and set it up in one day. We deserve a lot of credit for that."

There were a few anxious glances. Board members didn't want Khaletora to think that Ulta was outdoing him.

"Now, I know it's very crowded in here," said Ulta. "You will be able to see a small portion of Jeshmol if you hover in front of this view tube, next to Effrana. She will be operating the equipment so be careful. Please keep moving so everyone has a chance."

Effrana adjusted the controls. A clear image of a dappled world appeared. Members of the board began gliding past.

One member suddenly gasped, "What's that?"

A little blue toy, in the shape of a miniature NimuTrak, had mysteriously appeared in the portal chamber.

Khaletora pushed everyone aside so he could see.

Ulta kept her cool and announced, "For safety reasons we must be cautious. This appears to be an unidentified object from an alien region. It might be contaminated."

Directly beneath the Spy Tower was the Jeshmol Special Investigations team. A soto named Yal observed the activities of the Special Board from the opposite view through the portal. The blue toy was in the foreground, Khaletora's big face was at the view window, and behind him were anca executives hovering eagerly. Yal was the lawyer in charge of gathering hard evidence against the Sylumini. Next to her was Riana, who grinned. The Sylumini were in big trouble.

A board member asked Khaletora, "Do you know what that is?"

"It's blue," said Big-K, with an engaging smile. "Perhaps someone from the technical staff can provide additional information."

Ulta took her cue, "It's never a good idea to speculate until the facts are in. It will be at least an hour before we can get this thing over to the lab."

She knew exactly what all of them were looking at. She had made a deliberate choice to reveal nothing. The legal ramifications of having that model of a jeshie van in their portal were horrifying. Someone from the other side had taken advantage of their mistakes. By law, this incident must be reported to the authorities.

Every executive in the room suddenly had a brilliant opinion as to what it was, and why it was here.

Effrana obeyed strict regulations and powered down the portal in safety-mode.

Ulta glided away from the crowd. It angered her that the others didn't seem to realize how serious this was. Their company had brazenly violated inter-regional law. That flagged them for all future contracts. To make matters even worse, this had blown their only chance to spy on Riana's portal. The big bosses in Andromeda would rage when they heard about this.

Vonso's enormous eye stared through a small window, at uncertain Ulta, with the wisdom of the flash beings rippling through his mind.

##

Down in the Special Investigations room, Yal and Riana were looking at something entirely new to both of them. A camera had been customized by Qusheem so they would be able to track the movements of the flash beings here at Woodstock.

As seen in the monitor, Vonso had his mighty lightning-body coiled around the entire Sylumini Tower. With power eyes gleaming, he had reared up to watch the green mist as it flowed through the festival bubble toward the terran underground. In the distance another flash being could be seen. Grunda crackled angrily at Vonso, challenging him according to their customs. Each felt a powerful urge to restore order.

"what they do" asked Yal.

"anca not know what flashes do" replied Riana. "we stick to what we do" "how you feel about legal case now".

"blue toy on they side" said Yal. "two way portal require two way permit" "none on file" "sylumini have tough time wiggle out this one".

Riana said, "there more you should know" "xen wun place evidence inside blue toy" "sylumini test bead there" "letter from ing included" "we take pictures as evidence".

"that goodly compelling" nodded Yal.

Scene 73 - Hotel Creakmore

Aiyoni was a force unto herself. In international art circles she had a global entourage who adored her. A couple of dozen of her followers were here at Woodstock. She had rented an entire hotel, some distance away, just so her people would have their own private party palace, at the biggest festival anyone had ever heard of. The hotel's decaying elegance suited their glitterati lifestyle.

When Aiyoni heard that Melona was at Woodstock, on assignment from stuffy old Impress Magazine no less, she sent a limo to stage hand house to have her brought over.

The Hotel Creakmore, as it had been dubbed, became Melona's fashion headquarters that Saturday morning. Musty furniture was brought down to the lobby as the foundation for fanciful sets. Mysterious props and fabrics began to appear, discovered by Aiyoni's clever assistants.

What inspired Melona most was that everyone in the entourage knew how to pose. Ask one of them to pout in pink and you've never seen such simmer. Ask another to languish in black and such gloomy ennui had never been captured on film before.

Amid this riot of excess, several of the pictures turned out to be quite remarkable.

While Melona worked, an endless party flowed around her, as if she was some solid boulder, caught in the middle of a cross cultural river, which had overflowed its traditional banks.

In between sessions there was some down time. Melona was sitting on the front porch, catching up on her photo notes, when a long black limousine pulled up right in front of her. The driver got out to open the door for a tall man.

"Oooh, that's Bob," someone whispered, "better go tell Aiyoni."

Another man got out on the other side. The rain slowed to a light drizzle. The two of them sauntered through the front door, walking right past Melona. She followed them inside. Aiyoni came traipsing down the creaking staircase to greet the tall one enthusiastically.

"Oh Bob, so fabulous to have you here with us, you look absolutely marvelous," said Aiyoni. "I saved a special room. You must stay with us." She squeezed his hand.

These two, attended by Aiyoni's perpetually flittering entourage, creaked their way up the stairs, chattering excitedly.

The other man looked around the lobby, as if trying to find his bearings. His eye took in the photo equipment and props. He glanced at the photographer, moved his eyes away, then quickly looked back at her face.

"Wait, wait," said Andy, snapping his fingers, "uh, uh - Melona Geffion."

She was quite surprised. "I don't believe we've met."

"We haven't," said Andy. "I recognized you from your picture on the back cover of Beatnik Village."

She laughed dismissively. "That old thing. No one remembers that anymore."

"We sold every copy in the bookstore," said Andy. "I have one."

"That was so long ago," she said, "I'm surprised you could still recognize me." She glanced down at her figure, which had betrayed her.

"I would never forget those eyes," he said, "they have a special intensity."

"Welcome to Woodstock," she replied cautiously, "what brings you here?"

"My buddy and I built some audio gear for Bob," said Andy. "We call it the Psychedelic GizmoTron. Bob brought me back east to make sure it works the way the guitar player wants."

"Is that Bob Shiller, record producer of the psychedelic sound?" asked Melona.

"Yeah," said Andy, continuing to look around. "Uh, I have a question. Bob is going to be staying here but I don't have a room yet. Would you happen to know of anything that's available."

"I'm staying at a place they call Stage Hand House," said Melona. "I can call over and you can talk to Mom. As far as I know, the couch in her living room hasn't been rented yet."

"Is someone named Jinks there?" asked Andy.

"Oh yeah, I know Jinks," she said. "He did a really nice favor for me yesterday. He built a storage locker backstage for my camera equipment. Gave me a lock and everything. That way I don't have to lug around all my heavy equipment."

"That's Jinks for you," said Andy. "He can figure out a way to do just about anything. We've worked a lot of shows together out in Frisco."

"First things first," said Melona. "Let's give Mom a call."

Ten minutes later Andy had a place to stay.

Noutashi and Eberli gave each other a congratulatory hug. After all these years they had finally gotten their clients together.

Chapter 27 - On Stage

Scene 74 - People Power Portal

"Well hello there Andrew, I am so glad we found each other in this amazing mob of people," said Bob Shiller. They were backstage. He turned to Melona. "I saw you earlier at Aiyoni's. I'm Bob."

"Hi, Melona, pleased to meet you." She went to shake his hand, but he gave her a west coast hipster hug instead.

"Aiyoni has such wonderful things to say about you," said Bob. "After I get a few things settled, you and I should have a little chat."

"I'll be here all day but tomorrow I need to get back to the City," said Melona. "I have to get my prints ready for Monday."

Bob turned his attention back to Andy, "I finally found out where my band is staying. Imagine this - sixty miles away - for one of the top acts in the world. They should be in their dressing room in about an hour. We'll have the guitar player test your gizmo then."

Andy patted the bag hanging by his side. "Got the Psych-O-delic Giz-mO-Tron right here."

"Great," said Bob, "I see the festival producers onstage. Let's grab them before they get away. C'mon Melona, you should be able to get some fabulous pictures from up there."

Bob's guardian anca gave the nod to Eberli and Noutashi.

The producers of the Woodstock Festival were having a weary conference. Last night it had been one crisis after another. Today looked like it was going be even worse. The moment Bob Shiller's foot hit the stage, they went right over to him. Without the psychedelic sound which Bob had hyped, out there on the west coast, this festival would not be happening, here on the east coast.

After a quick introduction, Melona was told she could wander the stage. She listened in on bits and pieces of their conversation, as she moved about, searching for the perfect picture.

" ... need to have a follow up festival like this out on the west coast soon ... "

Snap. Half a million people feeling groovy on a mud soaked hill.

" ... Andrew and Bongo will be able to handle that ... "

Snap. Stage hands protecting priceless electronics from the rain.

" ... no, no, no - we want new acts for the west coast - except mine, of course ... "

Snap. Those in the audience who had pushed themselves all the way up front.

Melona stopped and stared.

Tim was right there, trying to get her attention. He waved his arms and jumped up and down in the mud. Noutashi was right behind him. Eberli watched from the stage, ready to make his moves on Andy.

Melona waved to Tim and yelled. "Look at me. I'm up here."

Ten thousand boys looked at her.

Only one of them knew who she really was - Tim.

Noutashi zipped onstage. She gave Eberli the nod. They had both worked so hard for this one precious moment. Touching Melona's shoulders, Noutashi put her in a standing-trance, with Tim fixed in her gaze. Eberli held Andy steady.

##

Down in the bunker they went wild. The three portal tuners were in perfect position.

Wun adjusted the mode-shifter. The audience clicked into place.

"Show time," yelled Cami.

Vint and Lon rushed out the door. They surrounded Tim.

Powerful vibrations flowed in a dynamic triangle. Waves of transcendent energy rippled through the crowd. Soto colors began to brighten.

As has happened on gazillions of planets, throughout countless emanations of the universe, evo power was being transformed into portal power. A shimmering tunnel allowed two worlds to flow together.

In the bunker, amid a mad scramble, Cami boldly announced, "Portal lock is a go. We got two days to make this thing happen. Let's do it right."

They watched in awe while this grand procession unfolded. Centered across the stage, the first portal was wide open. Qusheem stabilized it on our nimulon side. Jeshie technicians stabilized it on the other. Anca Guardians worked in teams to bring the audience into alignment.

A signal was sent. A jeshie scout stepped through. The dual atmosphere inside the Festival Bubble was awesome.

With a wave of the scout's arm, disciplined lines of jeshies began marching through. First came the Soto Guardians. They were assigned to work with people who would create enough new air for the Earth Colony.

Next in line were the hospital specialists, colony administrators, and essential services personnel. More lawyers joined the team. On and on they marched, straight through the crowd, into the jeshie waiting room, which was built inside of Audience Hill.

Each group of new jeshies was greeted by other jeshies who were already living in the underground. Places were found in the waiting room or scattered among the audience. When all of them had been accounted for, the first portal was closed, but not powered down.

Noutashi released her hold on Melona, as did Eberli with Andy. Vint and Lon did the same for Tim.

##

Onstage, Melona felt as if she had been living inside of some incredible dream. Now she was back in the waking world. Looking around, she saw Tim and shouted, "I'll meet you out there."

Tim knew she meant him.

So did ten thousand other boys.

The audience was packed, so it took a lot of good old fashioned New York dash to bring them together. They looked into each other's eyes. This time they knew they were meant for each other. They had their first kiss.

Noutashi was well pleased. Opening the portal made her happy. That first kiss brought her joy. One more day. Then Melona and Tim would be hers. One more day.

Scene 75 - Tunnel To Gheney

After the jeshie colonists got settled, Lumbia came over to Lon's desk. "I'm going on a tour of the ambulance tunnel. Want to come along?"

"too busy" said Lon.

"I too, am busy," said Lumbia. "So is everyone else. That doesn't mean you won't do your job better tomorrow, if you look at facts on the ground today."

Lon peered into her desktop dome. She had been staring into it for three days straight. "me go tour with you".

"Right decision," said Lumbia. "Come on, I'll show you around. Besides, you haven't seen the colony yet."

"that sound good" said Lon. Reluctantly, she turned off her communicator dome. It was such a comfort. But - it wasn't the real world.

Lumbia opened the door and they left the bunker. The air was much fresher out here. There were crowd noises and a feeling of intense excitement.

"You need to see the terran pumps," Lumbia told Lon. They took a side door into the waiting room inside the hill.

A crowd of boisterous jeshies was there. After twenty years of delays, while living in a disaster area, they had reached their destination at last.

Above their heads was the Big Board. Each jeshie had been assigned a colony registration number. Getting them through the portal was quick. Moving them to their new homes was complicated. When the Big Board flashed your number, you went to the registration desk.

After pushing their way through this exuberant madness, Lumbia said, "Let's duck through this door." She palm badged in.

Down the hall they entered an ancient cavern.

"This is the pumping station control room," said Lumbia.

"me recognize" said Lon, "this feed dome".

"That's right, this is the place where your data comes from," said Lumbia.

The cavern was of modest size but it was packed with fat pipes, skinny pipes, gauges, controls, readouts, cables and a crisp crew of hard working anca terrans. Lon was the only jeshie in the room. She got several sidelong glances.

"You and I are going to follow the Ambulance Tunnel all the way down, so that our eyes can see, and our noses can smell, that everything is safe for tomorrow," said Lumbia. "There are also other things."

The tunnel was an impressive engineering feat. It was wide and well lit, with easy to read signs for the drivers. The most important feature was the road surface. Jeshies live in cloud islands, which have flexible environments. Earth is hard and uncomfortable for them. Their engineers had constructed a cloud surface road so the patients would have a smooth ride. Lon skated comfortably down this road.

A short distance into the empty tunnel they stopped. Lumbia whispered, "There is a secret you must tell to no one.

"me handle that" said Lon.

"Do you see the door?" asked Lumbia.

"no".

"Watch this." Lumbia pulled a hidden lever. A door in the side of the tunnel opened.

"what there".

"Step inside," said Lumbia. "This is the control room for a top secret flash being project which you and I will be working on."

"oooh exciting".

The monitors attached to the walls were standard. The data looked strange.

"What do you know about the cloud wanderer?" asked Lumbia.

"xen wun see green flash at phoenix" "they say cloud wanderer" Lon said softly.

"That was Vonso," said Lumbia. "Riana and Dene have met him."

"that unusual" said Lon. "flashes not talk you kind" "or our kind".

"Sometimes they do," said Lumbia, "when they need something from us. You and I will be working with these flash beings until this temporary colony comes to an end."

"twenty five years" wondered Lon.

231

"That long," said Lumbia. "When you guys move to KCE, Xen and Wun will take this project with them."

"what you me role" asked Lon.

"Air flow," said Lumbia. "A major decision was approved by the incoming co-leaders. They decided to start up the Darimia JeshNim project before they arrive. The idea is to get so far ahead of the Sylumini that they won't be able to catch up. Hamil and Hamine want to have these distractions out of the way before they reach our planet."

"that ambitious" exclaimed Lon, "how we do that".

"Vonso put something in the Planetary Bubble," explained Lumbia. "It is dissolving in the dual atmosphere. Later on today, when we power up the big pumps, the flow patterns will be different than what you and I originally discussed. Some flows will need to be diverted for the purposes of these flash beings. This room is the only place where we can monitor that."

"me cooperate gladly" agreed Lon. Until recently, her life had been dull. Now, all that had changed.

"If things go well, we will connect to a super high speed data network which the Sylumini will never be able to compete with," said Lumbia. "It sounds like such a wonderful plan. On the other hand, we have determined enemies."

The two of them left the secret room. Lon closed the door securely behind them.

"Let's see what's further down the road," said Lumbia.

Gheney Hospital was several miles away but the trip was easy.

In the parking lot, Lon blurted out, "me remember this" "xen wun drive here" "riana dene cruiser" "trz me watch from hikli".

A tear rolled down her plum colored cheek. She recalled how afraid she was that Xen and Wun would never be able to come back. Riana and Dene brought them home again. Beq became Lon's good friend after their shopping trip.

Inside the Emergency Room everything was sparkly and clean. Full staff was on duty. There was little for them to do today but here was great excitement about tomorrow.

232

The two atmosphere experts had a pleasant visit but they had to cut it short. It was time to report back to the festival site.

##

"There's one more thing I want you to see," said Lumbia.

At the entrance to the Emergency Room was a long platform where AmbuTraks would drop off respiratory patients. Today it was silent and empty.

At the far end of the platform, Lumbia took Lon to a small commemorative park, which had been setup for visitors. On a large pedestal was an artistic rendering of the familiar red lightning symbol. On the base was a dedication plaque. It read, in both soto and anca ...

This memorial is dedicated to those heroic pioneers who
opened the pathway from Wamilla to Gheney Hospital
March 26, 1967

Pointing her finger at the plaque, Lumbia asked, "Who do you see in this picture?"

Lon looked. She saw herself in that picture - along with Xen and Wun, Riana and Dene, and of course good old Trz standing next to Beq. "how this happen".

"I was going to ask you the same thing," said Lumbia. "What's the story behind this picture?"

"it selfie taken with ishmili dome" said Lon. "riana dene bring back xen wun" "beq tag along" "we celebrate at hikli" "ishmili dome only thing take all our picture goodly".

"You need to know this is here," said Lumbia, tapping the memorial plaque with her finger. "The official history of the Earth Colony calls you a heroic pioneer."

"me no hero" said Lon, blushing purple.

"Actually you are," said Lumbia. "We both are, in our own small ways. Brilliant beings, such as Beq and Qusheem, sometimes act heroically. Other times they do strange things. You administer guardians. I work with pumps. Our work is just as essential. We just don't happen to be as brilliant, or as charismatic. But brilliant beings don't always finish what they begin. It takes someone like us to carry things over the finish line. All of us are heroes."

Lon took a long look at herself, permanently pictured on the durable surface of this memorial plaque. "me glad you show this" "me feel muchly gooder".

Scene 76 - Bummer Zap

The portal room in the tower was crowded yet strangely silent. The Sylumini had failed. An alien object had dragged their spy mission down to an inglorious end.

Across the way, right through center stage, the bunker crew had opened a wide portal of astonishing durability. A huge host of dim beings had marched on through. Twenty thousand of them had vanished into the hillside where the audience sat. Another hundred thousand were spread out among the festival crowd.

Ulta and Torley were huddled at a communicator dome.

Khaletora entered. Torley twitched. Big-K made him nervous. Ulta remained perfectly calm.

"Would you provide a status update," Khaletora requested, politely.

Ulta had known him for a long time. When Big-K was polite, he was dangerous.

"Their stage portal is currently inactive but remains powered up. The alien object is at our headquarters under strict quarantine. Severe thunderstorms are predicted for Operation Groovy."

"Thank you," said Big-K, with sweetness in his voice, and venom in his eyes.

##

Khaletora pulled Malki into a conference room and locked the door. "Before Operation Groovy begins I need you to do something."

"Always ready to respond," said Malki, repeating the unofficial Auxi motto.

"We knew that they were going to bring colonists over," said Khaletora. "No one informed me that there would also be jeshies mingling with the festival audience. I need to know what I'm up against."

"I know who to ask," said Malki.

"Act quickly," said Khaletora.

"You can count on me," said Malki.

234

What a perfect piece of good luck this was. He needed a little break so he could test his plan. Flying away from the tower, Malki coasted along the edge of the festival.

A line of anca security guards were out on patrol. Malki went down the line until he saw someone useful to him.

"Hey Derol, what you doing all the way out here in the middle of nowhere?" asked Malki.

"This is how they keep us busy until you guys get the go on Operation Groovy," said Derol.

"Gotta check on something for the big boss," said Malki. "Have fun. Catchya later."

"Later," she said.

As Malki flew away, Ulta watched from her desktop dome in the executive suite. She had a MalkiWatch app. Everywhere he went, her SpyBots followed.

Malki was right handed. With company equipment, such as the notorious pocket monitor, he always operated it with his right hand. Malki had touched his left pocket - twice.

It didn't take long for Ulta to figure out why.

Sitting at the edge of the crowd was a young couple. Boy meets girl at Woodstock. They go to a quiet spot so they can talk. While these two gazed into each other's eyes, Malki flies by, stops briefly to chat with an acquaintance, then goes his way.

The first time Malki touched his left pocket, Derol's tracker was between Malki and the boy.

The second time, Derol's tracker was between Malki and the girl.

So ... this was something entirely new. It was impossible to know what was concealed in his left pocket, but it felt like the clue she had been searching for.

Before investigating further, Ulta programmed six SpyBots to follow the young couple around.

Two hours later she had the dreadful answer.

The boy had been taken to the emergency room of a local hospital, with apparent signs of severe psychedelic overdose. From the SpyBot spectrum, Ulta knew he wasn't on any drugs. That raised a host of suspicions.

The girl was in slightly better condition. She had been taken to the freak out tent, with knowledgeable hippies and concerned medics at her side, trying to talk her down from the bummer she was experiencing. She too had not done any drugs.

Some nefarious device was in Malki's left pocket. Ulta nicknamed it the bummer-zapper. By itself, what he had done was horrible.

But what if he did that to Melona and Andy? That would sabotage the entire rescue.

Leaning back in her chair, putting her hands behind her head, Ulta wondered what she had gotten herself into.

Chapter 28 - Operation Groovy

Scene 77 - Rain Chant

Operation Groovy was about to begin. Squads of Auxis were lined up, in strict formation, outside the Tower on the Hill. Malki, with rigid expression, hovered at their front ranks.

Khaletora was angry. On his left was Shing, head of the legal department. She had replaced Lanmon, who had gotten himself fired. On Big-K's right, no one hovered. Torley got called away from portal duty on the second floor. He replaced Ulta, at Khaletora's right hand.

"What happened?" whispered Khaletora, out of the side of his mouth.

"Ulta has discovered the secret of their portal," whispered Torley. "She's investigating."

Khaletora smiled that wonderful smile of his. He didn't believe a word of it.

Regaining his composure, Khaletora announced, "I would like to say a few words before we begin our peacekeeping mission. All of us are committed to the safe journey of our neighbors from Jeshmol. We have magnificent capabilities here at the rescue site. We are here to help."

Khaletora paused for applause.

There was none.

Big-K saw Malki nodding anxiously toward the festival site.

One hundred thousand Guardian Anca came flying over Audience Hill. They had been held in reserve. Within minutes, one hundred thousand human beings, specially chosen for this one mission, were joined by their home guardians. Invisible to Auxi eyes, but easily seen in the communicator domes, one hundred thousand Guardian Soto linked up with each team.

The Auxis knew right away that this was not going to be another Chicago.

Baiyoc, who was Planetary Director of the Earth Guardian Corp, flew to the Auxi front ranks and got right in Khaletora's face.

"We hear that you are the peacekeepers," said Baiyoc, in a booming voice. "That's a big job, with half a million people on this hillside. We are here to help."

"That's not your contract," snapped Khaletora. "The Sylumini are responsible for crowd control."

"Celene is in charge of this rescue," said Baiyoc. "She ordered us here. If you have a problem, take it up with her."

Khaletora pasted that winning smile across his face. "The safety of the refugees is our only concern. We will allow you to provide backup services."

Turning to the Auxis, as if everything had gone according to the plan, Khaletora grandly announced, "Operation Groovy will now begin."

Malki faced his troops. "Move on out." Half of them looked confused, the other half looked angry. All of them were seriously outnumbered. None of this had been in the contingency training.

Auxis need anger to control human behavior. Without natural anger, they can cause no amplified anger.

This Woodstock crowd was not angry. They had been hand picked to neutralize this gang of Auxis. The culture of competition faced off against the culture of cooperation. There would be no compromise. One side, or the other, was going to take the day. Game on and it was winner take all.

Baiyoc boldly announced to her guardians, "Operation Groovy Too will now begin. Move on out."

##

Thunder boomed across the dark sky - promising a ferocious summer storm. Onstage, an open microphone amplified that growling sky, sending low rumbles through enormous banks of massive speakers. The audience felt the deep bass reverberation of majestic nature.

Double guardian brigades were at their assigned posts. Auxi squadrons took up their positions. Detectives from the Watchers hovered strategically. Hidden in the underground was a team of jeshie lawyers.

A human voice could be heard onstage, "Hey, if you think real hard, maybe we can stop the rain." Hovering next to the announcer was his guardian anca, grinning widely with enormous enthusiasm. The guardian held both hands high, flashing peace signs. That was the signal to begin. The Groovy Too Crew began making their moves through the audience.

Lon moved to her assigned spot at center stage. Waving her hands, like the director of a trans world orchestra, she coordinated the rhythm of soto guardians with anca guardians. These teams played the natural powers of these human beings.

Spontaneously (or so it seemed to people in mud), the crowd began to chant, "No rain! No rain! No rain!"

Guardians reached out to every person who was willing to cooperate. On the anca side they swept through with feelings of peace. On the soto side they encouraged those gathered here to breathe in, breathe out.

"No rain! No rain! No rain! No rain! No rain!"

Chants ramped up people power like thunder.

No anger. No rage.

Breathe in. Breathe out.

"No rain! No rain! No rain! No rain! No rain! No rain! No rain!"

Joy spread through these mud soaked children of the future.

Hope surged through the ranks of the double guardians.

Confusion withered the will of the Auxis.

The rain did not stop, of course. Forces of nature care nothing about evos, or anca, or soto. In the deluge, people were drenched on the outside, but some felt a strange power tingling within.

Over at the Tower on the Hill the humiliation of defeat sank in hard. The bunker crew's stage portal was enduring. Their own portal had been unplugged.

Down in the Bunker beneath the Stage there was a strange quiet. The portal crew had finished their work for the day. Lon was busy onstage, bringing the rain soaked crowd up to peak capacity. Lumbia sat at Lon's desk, in the underground bunker, operating two monstrous dual atmosphere pumps.

All of a sudden, Cami called out, "Look at that."

Those nearby crowded around the ishmili dome. Lumbia turned around to look.

"Those two have returned," said Cami. She enlarged the image from the special camera built by Qusheem.

The Festival Bubble was a sphere, half above ground, half below. At the top was a vent hole. The mighty pumps controlled by Lumbia were pulling dual atmosphere out of the Planetary Bubble, through the vent, into two underground reservoirs. This would take a couple of days.

Doing a fancy dance around the vent hole was Vonso. Tiny flashes of brilliant green light showered all around. He was shattering the larger chips of crystal so they would dissolve faster.

Oooooh. Aaaaah. Shiny lights.

While some admired Vonso's brilliant moves, others watched Grunda in despair. His eyes burned with the powers of extreme observation. Now he saw what Vonso was doing. Grunda might not understand the reasons why but his subtle intelligence was reviewing facts.

Vonso danced furiously. Sparks flew brightly. When satisfied that his task was worthwhile, the alien flash being faced off against the earthly flash being. Mighty Grunda crackled angrily. Brave Vonso rumbled defiantly.

Both vanished into the thunder skies.

"Bakmulz," declared Qusheem.

"I agree," said Cami. "They will fight this out among themselves. When the flash beings need something, they know where to find us."

Scene 78 - The Forest

Bob Shiller sat in a comfortable backstage trailer, listening to the band he produced finish up their wet set on the Woodstock stage. The sound of rain tippedy-tapped on the metal roof.

"Gotta be with my guys," Bob said to his chums. Putting on his raincoat, he stepped outside.

240

Andy was huddled behind the amps, on a folding chair, in case something went wrong with the Psychedelic GizmoTron. No problems. Awesome performance. Ecstatic crowd.

"Andrew," whispered Bob, as the final note died away in the dimming light, "you did it. You guys are amazing. Give Bongo hugs for me. Tell him I'll drop by to see Alicia and the baby. You are free to go back home anytime you choose."

"Actually," whispered Andy, "Melona's boyfriend offered to give me a ride to the airport tomorrow. A dry night at stage hand house is what I need right now."

Bob had been wondering about this. Melona spent all her time with Andy but this guy Tim was always bringing her things - like a stylish rain poncho, and dry socks. Apparently the girl had taken sides with the guy who was the good provider.

"Take that ride," said Bob. "I can't imagine how I'm going to get out of this sloggy mess. All you have to do now is find that boyfriend in half a million people covered with mud."

"Oh, I know exactly where they are," said Andy. "They're right over there."

Offstage left was a fenced in area. Melona was clinging to the fence from the backstage side. Tim was hanging on from the audience side. It turns out that they lived six blocks away from each other in Greenwich Village.

"Don't leave tomorrow without seeing me first," said Bob. "I'm working on a deal that I want you to be part of."

"I told those two I would meet them in Food Tent Number Four for breakfast. Nine-thirtyish," said Andy.

"I'll meet you there," said Bob.

Andy walked over and told Melona he was heading back to stage hand house. Did she want to come along? Yes she did. Her feet were soaked. After a tender goodbye through the chain links, Tim trudged back to his lonesome campsite.

By the time Andy and Melona got across the Rainbow Bridge it was getting dark. Both of them had good flashlights, courtesy of Tim's bartering skills. Rain poured down from above. Roots jumped up from below. Soggy tree branches groaned in the wind.

Dene was first in line, with Andy right behind. Eberli protected Andy from the back. Riana was behind him to protect Melona from the front. Noutashi followed, with a wary eye on those gloomy trees. Scattered throughout the dark forest, like a flock of vigilant birds, were friends of Aiyoni's guardian anca.

Dastardly deeds waited in the dripping twilight.

##

Big-K, who rarely worked late, was alone in the executive suite of the spy tower. He had taken over one of the junior executive's desks. From this vantage point he had an excellent view of the stage. On the desktop dome were the latest and greatest apps for monitoring the situation over there at the festival portal site. As far as he could see, everything was peaceful and quiet.

All day long he had put on a brave face but in his center he knew that he had been humiliated. You can't win them all. The goal is to have the most robust long term strategy.

As a precautionary measure he had sent all the Auxis home. On the second floor, the portal had been shut down, pending an investigation. The first floor command center was dedicated entirely to the security guards on patrol around the tower.

Khaletora had chosen to stay because he wanted to be in charge. He was their supreme leader. After a really bad day he did not want any more mistakes. Diligently he kept his eyes on the dome.

Dene was acting as scout for their small group. An entourage of anca toughs flew through the forest to protect them. Khaletora was cheered when he saw one of his security patrols enter the woods to monitor the situation.

The patrol leader selected a position where they could follow Dene's line through the trees, without creating conflict. Both sides were comfortable with this arrangement. Those from the portal team had a right to escort their clients to their overnight lodgings. Those from the security patrol had an obligation to protect the perimeter of the tower.

Guard number five was dispatched to investigate the portal team at close range. He took the tracker out of his pocket. The audio/video feed was beamed back to the command center for analysis. Cautiously, he moved in closer.

On the desktop dome, Big-K watched.

##

Malki had been hiding inside the roots of a large tree for many hours. He was a master of disguise and deception. To anca eyes, and even the guard's tracker, Malki was not there.

In his left pocket was the special device he had tested earlier in the day. Soon his two targets would be lined up. Malki slithered to a new position so that guard number five's tracker device would be perfectly placed for his evil plan. Within moments he would finish the job which the big bosses from Andromeda had sent him here to do.

While waiting patiently inside the tree, Malki reviewed his secret orders. They had sent him to take out the entire top level of the company's leadership on Earth. Those weaklings would be replaced by stronger willed executives. Malki had almost reached his goal. Lanmon had gotten himself fired. Ulta had abandoned her post. Khaletora was now setup to take the blame for the foul deeds which Malki was about to commit. Guard five would be found guilty of aiding and abetting Khaletora.

Malki waited for Dene to move forward just a teensy bit more. Everything looked good for two fast shots. He placed his finger near the trigger.

##

"Arrrgh," growled Malki. Someone grabbed his neck from behind.

Ulta had been waiting in the forest longer than Malki. She too could blend with a tree. She too could be ferocious.

Guard number five heard screams and raced over to investigate.

The entire forest became alive with action anca.

Malki was a massive thug, who earned a living committing horrific deeds.

Imagine his surprise when he discovered that Ulta was enormously tougher than him. She had grown up in a supremely harsh environment. She had forgotten none of

243

those hard lessons as she clawed her way to the top of a better life.

Locking Malki in an inescapable knot, Ulta flew away as fast as she could, carrying his heavy load.

Dene's instincts were instant.

"Go, go, go," Dene yelled to Ulta, "I've got you covered."

The main body of the Sylumini security patrol flew toward guard five. Dene rushed at them and they fell to the forest floor from Dene's furious fists.

From her flight pattern, Dene knew exactly where Ulta was headed.

Khaletora pressed his face against the window of the executive suite, not understanding what he saw. In his center he knew this would not make him look good to the big bosses. His mind whirled with excuses.

Another dozen guards rushed out from the command center. Dene did his famous flying whirli-gig routine, knocking them down one by one. They fell in a line across southern New York State and then over northern New Jersey. The last one dropped into the Atlantic Ocean off the coast of Long Island.

A fresh supply of Sylumini agents came rushing over from Europe. They couldn't catch Ulta - who had Malki in her lock grip - because Dene flew backwards at top speed and took them out in ones, twos and threes. This group fell to the ground all across the Sahara Desert.

Two more groups were deployed from the Mediterranean contingent. They found themselves being hurled into the lush jungles of central Africa.

Ulta dove beneath the blue waters of Lake Victoria and carried Malki straight through the front door of Watcher Headquarters.

Moments later Dene came crashing through, with a phalanx of Sylumini security agents crushed around him.

When the fight was over, the Watchers found Dene, who was unconscious, under a pile of seventeen battered Sylumini.

Everyone got arrested.

Chapter 29 - Rainbow Bridge

Scene 79 - Food Tent

Breakfast on a soggy Sunday was more glorious than the rock festival itself - if you happened to be two young people captured in that golden glow of falling in love. Melona and Tim had found a comfortable place, at a long table, sitting with muddy people, in a groovy mood. The two of them may as well have been inside their own bejeweled sky gondola.

"I remember that place," said Melona. "I used to love going in there, just to look around. As a student, I couldn't even afford to read the titles on the books. But as someone who hoped to be a writer someday, it was heaven in that bookstore."

"My uncle had to shut it down," said Tim, with heartfelt sadness.

"I walk by there all the time," said Melona. "The doors have been locked for the past year."

"Talbot's Rare Books has been in the family for three generations," said Tim.

"I thought you said your last name was Hadley," wondered Melona.

"Hadley is my aunt's sister's married name," said Tim. "It's a long story."

"Sorry I asked," said Melona.

"That's alright," said Tim, uncomfortably.

##

When Bob and Andy walked into the breakfast tent they hesitated. It seemed wrong to disturb these two, caught in that delicate web of flimsy magic which steals hearts away.

Andy remembered what it had been like for him and Cynthia.

Bob was all about business so he strode boldly over and said, "Good morning, sorry to interrupt, do you have a moment?"

They were holding hands. Melona said, "What's up?"

Tim was shy.

"I need to get Andrew back to California," Bob said. "I made a deal with the festival promoters. What we did here on the east coast, we want to do out there on the west coast, later on this year. I heard that you offered him a ride to the airport. Is that still possible? If not, I can hire a limo, although I've been told that none are available."

"That would be cool," said Melona. "I need to get my pictures ready for Monday. There was a lot of flack about sending me to Woodstock. I need to protect my boss."

Bob laughed heartily. "I can believe that. Woodstock is not exactly the upper east side of Manhattan. I wish you all the luck in the world trying to explain this muddy mess to those old fuddy duddys."

"Maybe I'll get fired," said Melona, "but no matter what happens, I gave it my best shot."

"Which brings me to my other reason for coming to see you," said Bob. "I'm going to be in New York next month on business. There's a book agent I want to introduce you to. It's possible she might be interested in these lively new fashion galleries you've been putting together. She's a huge fan of Aiyoni."

"Why, thank you," said Melona. "I look forward to that. Thank you very much."

"Does Andrew have your phone number?" Bob asked

"Yes, he does," she said, "and I have his."

"Good," said Bob, "We'll put something on the calendar."

"What about you, young man," said Bob, turning to Tim.

"I'm just the guy with the car," Tim mumbled.

246

"Everyone has their own story," said Bob Shiller, "and I'm sure you do too. What kind of car do you have?"

"Uh, one of those urban black cars," said Tim.

Bob looked him over. "Black cars are what rich people get driven around in by someone else. You seem to be a polite young man but you don't appear to be rich, or a professional driver."

"Not rich," said Tim, hastily. "Uh, actually it's my uncle's car that we used for his business. Talbot's Rare Books."

"Talbot's," exclaimed Bob Shiller, "down on Fourth Avenue. I love that place. My bookshelves are filled with precious things I bought there. I'll have to drop by next time I'm in the city."

"Sorry, but we're going out of business," said Tim.

"Oh my, I am so devastated," said Bob. "That place was fabulous. Blame television, I suppose."

"Times change, you adjust," said Tim. "The auction people were in last week to calculate the value of the inventory."

"See, I told you everyone has a story to tell," said Bob. "Now I know yours. Come along, we've got things to do. I want Andrew on that plane."

"I need to get my gear from under the stage," said Andy.

"My cameras and film are in the plywood locker," said Melona.

"All I've got is this muddy back pack," said Tim, holding up a bag stuffed with festival memorabilia.

"Off we go," said Bob Shiller, and the four of them tromped out of the food tent.

The guard at the backstage gate stopped Tim with his big hand. "Backstage pass?"

"Oops, no, don't have one," said Tim.

Bob, who was already inside with Andy and Melona, said, "Is there a problem here?"

"I can't let him in without a pass," said the guy at the gate. He knew who Bob Shiller was but they were very strict about the passes.

"Harvey," yelled Bob, "get a pass for my guy."

A minute later the stage manager handed Bob an All Access pass.

The guy at the gate waved Tim through.

Bob placed the lanyard over Tim's head and laid a hand on his shoulder, "You've got good friends. Value them."

"I will," said Tim.

"Gotta go," said Bob, "things to do." Away he sauntered, searching for the next big deal.

Andy grabbed his gear. Melona emptied the plywood locker that Jinks had built. Tim hoisted his muddy backpack across his shoulder. These three set foot on the Rainbow Bridge.

Scene 80 - AmbuTrak Portal

Noutashi didn't know what to do. Dene was in jail after the Malki kidnapping. Riana had left to go get the mode-cruiser. Lined up on the other side of the Rainbow Bridge, the entire AmbuTrak fleet was waiting to be rescued. Never again would the Wamilla Medical Center be lined up with Gheney Hospital. It was now or never.

Without Andy, Melona and Tim inside that mode-cruiser, none of this was going to happen. Oh well, when life gets tough, make something up.

##

Shoof, supreme leader of the Watchers on Earth, told the jailers to release Dene.

The cell door opened. Dene was brought into the prisoner's office. His personal taper device was returned.

"May I?" asked Dene, pointing at his taper device.

"Do what must be done," said Shoof.

He sent Riana a message. "Out of jail. What next?"

Instantly she messaged back. "In Hangar 9. Come quickly."

"Leaving now," messaged Dene. He made his jump, calling out, "Thanks," as he vanished.

At Hangar 9 the mode-cruiser was ready to fly. Riana was in the pilot's seat. Dene strapped himself into the copilot's seat.

"We're waiting for the signal from Baiyoc," said Riana. "Things are tense over there."

When Andy, Melona and Tim reached the center of the Rainbow Bridge - Noutashi was in front - Eberli in back.

As she had done so many times before, Noutashi placed a thought in Melona's imagination.

"I want to show you something that's really important to me," said Melona. "This is where I got my start. My bosses sent me to Woodstock, all alone, on an assignment I wasn't qualified for. When I entered the musician's waiting area, only a few people were there. Believe it or not, the rock stars got stuck in traffic, same as everyone else."

Baiyoc rushed to the bridge. "Good. Keep them here." She messaged Riana, "Go."

Once Melona got started talking, it was easy for Noutashi to keep her talking.

"I was afraid at first," said Melona. "Everything seemed so much bigger than me. Then someone showed me this place." She pointed her finger down at the top of the plywood bridge.

"Look at that panorama," said Melona. They all turned around. "This is where it all started happening for me."

The three were enraptured by the background of stage, audience, sky.

Eberli went to work on Andy.

Andy said, "Ooooh, that reminds me. The photographer never gets in any of the pictures. Let me take one of you two. You'll want this later."

Melona handed him her pawn shop camera.

Bringing the camera to his eye Andy said, "Stand close together. Closer."

Andy knew that Tim was worried about him as a rival. The shy guy needed a boost in confidence, so he could get the girl of his dreams.

"Click."

##

A strange sight was seen, coming from the east, looming over the festival site.

What looked like an ordinary star cruiser was creeping along, above the little country road that ran behind the stage. No star cruiser can move that slow. It was painted ambulance white. On the sides and nose cone were the familiar red lightning bolt in a blue circle.

Every AmbuTrak lined up at the portal gate was painted that exact same way. As soon as the drivers saw this on their dashboard domes they felt a surge of hope. Cheers of glory rippled up and down the line.

Riana squinted her eyes. She inched the mode-cruiser forward until Melona, Tim, Andy, Noutashi, and Eberli were all safely inside the cargo bay.

"Portal check," called out Riana, as she brought the cruiser to a halt.

"Everything is ready," confirmed Dene.

Fading in from a fuzzy glow, Noom the ishmili appeared. "Greetings and good fortune to you. All systems go."

"Proceed," said Riana.

Dene pushed the big red button. A green light came on.

"Wait a second," said Melona, "what just happened?"

"We're in shimmer land," said Tim, in a spooky voice.

"Is this some kind of UFO abduction?" wondered Andy.

"I know what happened," said Melona, "this is why they brought us here."

Shimmer land began to take on form and substance.

Andy was the first to recognize one of them. Eberli hovered next to him, "I know you. You've spent a lot of time with me since I moved to San Francisco."

Eberli reached out and shook Andy's hand. For the first time they could do that. "I've been your guardian for a long time. It's nice to meet you in a shared realm."

Tim picked up on this cue. Staring at Noutashi he said, "Uh, uh, Washington Square Park. I was eight years old. A couple of bullies pushed me into the fountain."

Noutashi laughed. "Yeah, that was me alright. I taught you how to punch a bully in the face. They never bothered you again after that."

"Yeah," chuckled Little Timmy, "that kid had a black eye for a week."

"Oooooh, you're the one," growled Melona, when she recognized Dene. "You almost got me killed."

"I toughened you up," said Dene, "so you would be ready for what we need you to do right now."

"Right now?" gasped Melona.

Noom faced the three evos. She was fuzzy and strange but they knew they could trust her. Wrapping her enormous arms around them, she held them in her glowing trance.

The combination of the mode-cruiser, plus equipment in the bunker, snapped together into a single working unit. When the powers of Noom began to shine, everything was ready.

The Second Portal frame began to glow, right next to the Rainbow Bridge. The Festival Bubble began to sparkle. The ambulance portal whooshed open with a clear ka-ching.

A jeshie scout, carrying a Kemong Emergency Services flag, stepped through the portal. Breathing deeply, for all to see, the air was safe. The entire fleet revved up their ambulance engines.

Stepping to the side of the portal frame, the scout raised her red lightning flag high, then plunged it down dramatically.

A long line of AmbuTraks drove through the enormous portal, angled down the ramp onto the cloud island road surface, then continued on their super smooth ride to Gheney Hospital. As fast as the patients could be unloaded, the next ambulance took its place.

Reports from the hospital were encouraging. The fresh air of Earth, mixed with the dual atmosphere exhaled by the audience at Woodstock, cured most of their respiratory problems immediately.

When the last AmbuTrak made it through to safety, Noom released her trance on the three portal tuners.

Andy-Melona-Tim relaxed. Facing them was a magnificent ishmili. Surrounding them were four friendly anca. Nearby were thousands of jeshies. Clustered on the hillside was the magnificent festival audience.

The last AmbuTrak pulled to a halt near the bunker. The back door opened. Someone got out.

It was Trz.

The last ambulance drove away to the hospital.

Andy-Melona-Tim could not understand what they were seeing but they watched the whole panorama as it unfolded before their eyes. Each felt a wondrous joy.

Down in the bunker, Lon screamed. "it him".

Everyone was so busy they hadn't noticed.

"trz here" called out Xen.

They all rushed to the door.

"what you do here" asked Xen.

"no get rid of me that easy" said Trz.

Hugs brought this happy group back together.

On the Rainbow Bridge it was time for Tahra to return to her own version of reality. Riana and Dene flew their mode-cruiser back to Greenland. Noutashi and Eberli were left alone with their guardian clients.

Three people had their ordinary feet on solid plywood. Andy was still holding the pawn shop camera in his hand. A fresh breeze was blowing.

They were back in normal world. Everything seemed unreal.

A short while later, the NimuTrak had been unbolted from the bunker. It was now an ordinary van again. Lingering goodbyes lasted long.

"Kwefnoqxj," Qusheem suggested to Lumbia.

"That's a great idea," agreed Lumbia, enthusiastically.

Qusheem entered a message in the ishmili dome and sent it to the Observatory.

Five minutes later Honat came flying through the door. He grabbed hold of Lumbia and gave her an enormous smooch. "I missed you so much," he said, hugging her warmly.

None of his co-workers had ever seen Honat display emotions before.

More goodbyes, more stories, then all four jeshies were inside the NimuTrak van, the last vehicle still in operation from the decommissioned Wamilla Observatory Fleet.

As Trz was getting settled in the cargo bay, he felt Lon tap him on the shoulder.

She handed him a pillow, one of the ones he had given her at the Hikli. "you need this" said Lon, "driver crazy".

Everyone laughed - except Xen.

"Have a safe trip."

"visit soon".

Off they went, clattering down the cloud road, heading for their next adventure.

Scene 81 - Car Ride

The Talbot's Rare Books mobile was still parked in the same ditch where Tim had abandoned it two days ago. Local traffic was heavy, because lots of people were struggling to get back home, even though the festival was scheduled to go on for another day.

It was only after they got out onto the open highway that a sense of well being returned. They were going way too fast, surrounded by aggressive drivers, heading toward the concrete jungle. Ahhh.

Noutashi sat in the front seat between Tim and Melona. Eberli was in back with Andy. Both of the anca were admiring the leather upholstery, rare wood paneling and gilt door handles. All five of them were recovering from shock. None of them had ever experienced four realms at the same time before.

"All right you two," said Tim, "what did you do and how did I get involved in it?"

Andy had been thinking hard about this. "I don't know what we did but I do know what we should do next. Let's figure out if we all saw the same thing."

"Good suggestion," said Melona. "Right before things got strange, Andy was taking our picture. Things seemed almost normalish until then."

Andy said, "Normalish sounds about right. This whole thing has been kind of spooky, for a long time now. But when it went from feeling a bit weird - to seeing things which we all know are impossible - that's what I can't understand."

Tim said, "First it got shimmerish. Then it was like we were in some sort of alien airplane."

"Yeah," agreed Andy. "At first I thought it was one of those UFO abductions, like you read about in those crazy newspapers at the check out line in the grocery store. But you're right, it was more like an airplane."

"Let's see if we can agree on who those strange beings were," suggested Melona.

"I recognized one of them right away," said Andy. "This guy - I'm pretty sure it was a guy - has been following me around for twenty years. How did I know it was him if I'd never seen him before?"

Eberli did a silent bow in the back seat while Noutashi applauded from the front.

"Oh yeah," said Melona, "and then there was that tough guy. He was in the passenger seat. He almost got me killed. Maybe he was right, though. I do feel much stronger now."

"But he was there to protect us when that bad guy in the forest wanted to hurt us," said Andy. In some strange way, all of them knew this to be true.

"What do you think?" Melona asked Tim. "Do you think we're crazy?"

"If this was any other day, I'd be letting the two of you off by the side of the road right now," said Tim, "but I've known one of those strange beings all my life. I recognized her right away. I grew up in Greenwich Village, which has its own alien life forms. That one we saw today has always been there for me. This I am sure about."

"She's been there for me too," said Melona. "Ever since I got to college. Not back in Kentucky, though. That was a different one of those ... beings-from-over-there."

Andy suggested, "Let's see what else we can agree on."

"The two who were flying the alien plane didn't have feet," said Melona. "And their colors shifted around. That was odd."

"Then there was that big fuzzy who came around in front of us," said Tim. "We were under her control."

"Yeah," agreed Andy, "because they needed us to get those alien trucks through the tunnel."

"That's it," gasped Melona. "They needed us for the trucks."

"The big white trucks," said Tim. "Now it makes so much sense."

They all fell silent. This was too much.

"Well," said Tim, after an uncomfortable pause, "this isn't the kind of thing we can talk about in polite company. So what do you say, we never mention it to anyone, except each other."

"Yeah, that's the way to go," said Andy. "We need to stay in touch. We came into this not knowing anything about each other. Something big just happened. We don't know what it was. Probably never will. Somehow they needed us. It'll be like our own private club. The Tunnel Club."

"I like the sound of that," said Melona. "Three lifetime members of the Tunnel Club."

##

Noutashi turned to Eberli in the back seat. "They got it, they really did get it." She was hyper excited. Being a Guardian can be really frustrating. What just happened to all of them was such a thrill.

"I'm glad that's over," said Eberli. "Now we can get back to our regular lives. Twenty years for me, ten for you. Who ever thought Riana would need us for this long?" These words came out of Eberli's mouth, but as soon as he spoke them, he knew he didn't really mean them.

Noutashi continued with this line of thought, "Dene promised he would leave us alone after today. I thought I'd be overjoyed to get my girl back. Now I can find out if she likes that nice boy I introduced her to. On the other hand, there's got to be more. We can't just stop here. What should we do?"

"One of the guardians was talking to me about that this morning," said Eberli. "Half a million people were inside the Festival Bubble. That much dual atmosphere, with such a large group of people, hasn't happened since the ancient days."

"There's something else, too," said Noutashi. "For as long as those jeshies are living down there in those terran caverns, we need to take advantage of that."

We need to protect ourselves, too." cautioned Eberli. "The Sylumini have gone rogue ruthless on us."

"I couldn't agree more," said Noutashi.

255

"Let's see what Vint has to say on Monday morning," suggested Eberli. "I've got a few ideas I'd like to talk over with him."

"That's the way to go," said Noutashi, "we'll see what Vint has to say. We've got a brand new game in the works now. The old game has got to be replaced. We can't keep on living like this."

They knuckle bumped, the way they'd seen the stage hands from San Francisco do.

Chapter 30 - Consequences

Scene 82 - Judge Kloom

Judge Kloom read the list of charges from the bench: willful intent to harm an evo, evasion of inventory controls, abuse of public trust - the list droned on for ten minutes. Seated in the front row was Khaletora with twelve top Sylumini lawyers. Sitting on the other side of the court was Ulta, with her personal lawyer. Malki was in jail. The room was packed with those who hoped that, this time, justice would be upheld.

When the judge finished reading the list, Khaletora rose from his seat and boldly declared, "I object ... "

"Silence," roared Judge Kloom, banging down the gavel. "No one speaks in this court except under oath."

"Well then, place me under oath," demanded Khaletora.

"In my court, silence is enforced" said the judge. "Bailiffs."

Twelve lawyers squirmed in their seats.

Two burly bailiffs placed a firm grip on each of Khaletora's arms and led him away.

Floating down a long hall, gripped by powerful hands, Khaletora wiggled and whined. They came to a plain door. A duty officer saw them on camera and buzzed them in.

The Quiet Room was empty, except for one chair, in the exact center, bolted to the floor. Khaletora was placed firmly in this seat.

"In the quiet room you can say anything you want. In the courtroom you will remain silent, until ordered to testify," the chief bailiff instructed the chief executive.

Two bailiffs departed in silence. The thick door slid silently shut. Big-K was all alone.

For the first few minutes he sat perfectly still, with that splendid little smile pasted across his face.

##

Back in the courtroom, the judge had three pieces of evidence on the table. He called Ulta to the testimonial stand, where she was sworn in.

"Do you recognize these exhibits?" asked the judge.

"I recognize Exhibit A, your honor," said Ulta. "It is a taper device of the type the main office in Andromeda issues to their Auxiliary Contract Employees."

"Can you tell the court anything more about this device?" asked the judge.

"I'm afraid not, your honor," said Ulta. "I was informed that my services for the Sylumini Consulting Group are no longer required."

"If you hadn't gotten fired, would you be able to tell us anything about this device?" asked the judge.

"Yes, your honor. Inventory control used to be one of my main responsibilities and I take that seriously," she replied.

"We will have a number of detailed questions for you about this matter, in due course," said the judge.

"I am prepared to cooperate with the court," said Ulta. Now she could tell the truth without fear.

"What about Exhibit B?" asked the judge.

"I was head of the department which designed those units," said Ulta. "They are called crowd monitoring analytic units. We usually refer to them as pocket monitors."

"Quite a number of concerns have been expressed about these pocket monitors for a very long time," said the judge.

"I am aware of those concerns," said Ulta.

"What information do you have about Exhibit C?" asked the judge.

"From its outer form it would appear to be a type of device which is operated inside a pocket," said Ulta.

"Can you tell us anything more?" asked the judge.

"I do not recognize Exhibit C as being any type of equipment which was issued by my former employer," said Ulta.

"That will be all for now," said the judge.

##

Judge Kloom felt more confident than he had for a long time. The Watchers had informed him that they had learned how to crack the Sylumini encryption code. The report on Malki's old taper device was a treasure trove of indictable offenses. Several other high profile cases were waiting.

##

Formalities in a court of law are both time consuming and necessary. No additional testimony had been heard by the time the judge announced, "We will be taking a mid day break. Please follow the bailiff to the break room."

As the anca from the courtroom floated down the hall, they passed a door with no markings. Behind that door, a duty officer sat staring into a communicator dome, wearing headphones.

The screams bubbling from Khaletora's lips revealed much about his inner state of mind. With no one there to prop him up, Big-K had crumbled.

The duty officer had seen it all. Usually it wasn't until the second, or third, time they were sent to the quiet room that they began to weaken. This one had gone over the edge rather quickly.

Now Big-K was on the floor, pounding his fists on the ground, flapping his taper.

In the break room, idle chatter filled the air.

Scene 83 - House Arrest

Being under house arrest had made Ulta feel crazy for the first four days. After that she learned to like it. For the first time in a million years she was forced to take some serious time off. It was a good chance to take a long hard look at what she had been doing with her life. When you're working too hard to think, it's easy to ignore what others can see clearly. When you're all alone with your memories, hidden things move to the forefront of your mind.

Once a week, an officer from the court dropped by her magnificent home to make sure she was complying with their restrictions. Visitors were allowed, but only with court approval.

On this particular day it came as quite a surprise when the court officer said, "Riana has been granted permission by Judge Kloom to visit you."

"Riana," said Ulta. "Why would she want to talk to me, after all the bad things I did to her?"

"I wouldn't be able to answer that," said the officer. "Why don't you ask her when she drops by later today. The judge wanted me to make sure that you were comfortable with this request."

"I'd be more than happy to speak with Riana, or anyone else the judge sends over," Ulta said.

##

When the visitor tone sounded, Ulta glanced around her living room to make sure it was tidy. She opened the door and invited Riana in.

"It's so nice to see you. Thanks for dropping by to visit," said Ulta.

"You have such an elegant house," said Riana, "it's much larger than my apartment."

Each of these umbies lived on remote islands. England and Tasmania are on opposite sides of our planet.

"We may as well be comfortable," said Ulta. "Would you care to join me in the upper room. The view from there is rather pleasant this time of day."

"That would be fine," said Riana. The natural animosity between these two had softened slightly.

A wide picture window looked out across the Antarctic Ocean, from the southern shore of Tasmania. It was an extreme environment, stunningly beautiful, with fierce foamy waves and majestic dark clouds struggling in a turbulent sky. Ulta and Riana seated themselves in two large chairs, artfully upholstered.

Riana said, "I suppose you're wondering why I came to see you today."

"Let's just say I can't think of any reason why you would want to speak to me," said Ulta.

"I'm often criticized for being abrupt," said Riana, "but I'm going to skip the pleasantries and get right to the point. I'm here to offer you a job at the Observatory."

"They wouldn't let me through the front doors of Chephra," said Ulta. "Sylumini Office Services administers the security operation there."

"I don't care what they think," said Riana. "We want you there. We work for the ishmili, not the anca. Ing has already gotten your forms approved. Captain Behchel, who has been a close personal friend of mine for several billion

260

years, owns Chephra. Sylumini Security Services are subcontractors. They will bend."

"This comes as an enormous surprise to me," said Ulta, who had been daydreaming about which far away gravity group she wanted to migrate to, after she got out of jail.

"Your job position would be Technology Transfer Manager," said Riana. "That's several levels lower than your former position. It would also be a new beginning."

"You realize that I'm going to be spending a lot of time in court and might end up in jail," said Ulta.

"Not a problem," said Riana. "At the Observatory we come and go as we please."

"Why would you want someone like me?" asked Ulta.

"Two reasons," said Riana. "Here's the important one. Those at the Observatory don't like working with The System - if you know what I mean."

Ulta couldn't help laughing out loud. "That's a major understatement."

"During the emergency rescue we created hundreds of technical breakthroughs," said Riana. "If the Valdarians are going to take advantage of these, then someone needs to push them through the system. Cami and Farli are being transferred back to their old jobs. They were on loan to us."

Ulta thought very carefully about what she had just heard. "That was the first reason. What's the second?"

"No outsider understands our technology better than you," said Riana. "You stole our stuff and did great things with it. Now we want you to push our stuff through the system."

"What does Captain Behchel think about all this?" asked Ulta.

"The Captain says that sometimes a powerful enemy can be transformed into a powerful ally," answered Riana. "He's already signed off on this."

"This is all so sudden," said Ulta. "I thought my career was demolished."

"Look at what happened to Lanmon," said Riana. :You and Lanmon and Khaletora came here to Earth as an executive dream team. Then the Sylumini went rogue on you. Lanmon got fired because he didn't back down while defending our core values. He didn't have any trouble

261

finding a fabulous job at a new place. I hear he's quite happy."

"He is happy." said Ulta. "We stay in touch." She got lost in her own thoughts, which is a luxury she had almost forgotten. "Tell me more about this position you're offering."

"Dene counted 817 technical breakthroughs at the Observatory," said Riana. Each of them has some sort of haphazard documentation. The Valdarians won't need all of them but a few of these new designs are truly sensational. Figure out what's useful and get them into the system. Preserve what's leftover for future reference. Then you can figure out where you want to go with your next career."

Ulta got a quizzical look on her face. "What about Dene? He would be great for this type of work."

"Dene doesn't do day jobs," said Riana.

"Point well taken," said Ulta. Then she got a gossipy look on her face. "What about Dene?"

They were both umbies. They knew what she meant.

Riana changed her tone, "I've got plans for him. He knows about a few of them. These things take time, especially when you're as old as we are."

"If opposites attract, then you two definitely belong together," said Ulta.

Riana got a confidential look in her eye and whispered, "I'm going to tell you something but don't say a word about this to anyone. After the jeshies made it safely through the portals, there was a message from Jenissen. Special Ops doesn't need Dene anymore. He is free to go anywhere in the universe he wants. He said he wants to stay here with me."

Ulta wished someone cared enough about her to say something like that. She looked out the big picture window, admiring the choppy sea, as she had done countless times before. "I like this planet," she said, with a sigh. "I want to stay here and put things back the way they should have been all along."

"Your testimony in court is a good first step," said Riana. "After all, you're the one who designed the machines which turned things bad."

"Indeed I am," said Ulta.

Chapter 31 - Aunt Trish's Place

Scene 84 - Meet The Family

Melona caught herself doing it again. She was in her slum apartment, getting ready to visit Aunt Trish's charming apartment, which was only a few blocks away. That's where Tim lived with his aunt and uncle. Since she was going there to see Tim, it seemed logical that she should think of it as Tim's place - but she didn't. It was Aunt Trish's place. That's where she had been invited for dinner.

A month ago, after they dropped Andy off at the airport, he had driven past his building so she would know where he lived. Then he politely gave her a ride home, after those strange doings at the rock festival. Tim watched in despair as she disappeared through that dim doorway. Junkies ruled the slums.

Inside the iron clad door, triple locked, with a metal bar wedged into the floor, plus steel gates on all the windows, she was safe. Maybe. Three flights of stairs between her and the street was always a gamble. Each landing might be her last.

A phone was something she had not been able to afford until a few months ago. Earlier that year she had gotten a nice promotion, with a hefty raise. She'd paid her dues to the demands of society. The good things in life were starting to come her way. A clunky black phone, with a thick cord attached to the wall, was one of those things. It allowed Melona to investigate this new romance by telephone, without having to walk those ghostly halls.

The first week Tim had called her once. During the second week he called her again and then she called him back the next day. They enjoyed talking to each other.

The third week she finally met Uncle Brian and Aunt Trish. Last weekend she had been over to their place twice - just to say hello - before she and Timmy went out on the town.

Now she was going to dinner on a Saturday night.

At this particular moment she was holding two blouses on hangers. A nice pair of slacks lay on the bed. Dressing for a potential boyfriend was one thing. Figuring out what to wear for his aunt was another matter entirely. The problem was - what message was she trying to send?

##

After piecing together fragments of Tim's stories, about how he had ended up living with his aunt and uncle, instead of his mother and father, a narrative formed in her mind.

Trish and her sister, Natalie Edmond, had grown up on Long Island. Natalie was the wild one, not that Patricia was some sort of saint. After World War Two, Trish moved into an apartment in The Village with her boyfriend, Brian Talbot. Naturally her parents disapproved. Eventually they got married, but that was much later.

During the war Patricia's older sister, Natalie, married this guy, Owen Hadley, right before he shipped out overseas. You would never have known she was married, judging from the way she behaved. One day Owen showed up again, having fulfilled his military obligations. Those two settled into a hard drinking married life. Months later, Little Timmy was born. Natalie and Owen and the baby moved back in with her parents out on Long Island. That was bad.

Owen had trouble finding work so he enlisted in the military again, this time going to fight in Korea. He came back in a coffin, with full military honors. As soon as the death benefit check cleared, Natalie disappeared. Trish and Brian adopted Little Timmy.

Eight years later they got a letter from California. Natalie needed money. They did not send her any. Tim had no memories of his biological mom.

When he was fourteen they took a two week vacation to go out and visit her. Natalie was living in Venice Beach, where a part time job was enough to keep her in a cheap seaside bungalow. Tim had seen enough. His mom promised to visit. She never did.

Life keeps moving along. His aunt and uncle put him through Columbia University. Now they were trying to get it through his stubborn little mind that it was time for him to leave the nest. Not that Aunt Trish was suggesting anything to Melona. The youngsters would have to work things out for themselves.

For the past five minutes Melona had been holding up two blouses. Her arm got tired. She laid them on the bed, next to the slacks.

Noutashi had her taper coiled on the pillow, watching her client's inner struggle. This was so satisfying. Ordinary human needs filled the young woman's mind.

Melona got a determined look in her eye.

Putting both blouses back in the closet, she chose a different one. The slacks would have to do. After getting dressed, fussing with her hair, and putting on just a teensy bit of makeup, Melona grabbed a small package wrapped in pink. It was a little nothing for Aunt Trish.

Scene 85 - The Hilyers

Uncle Brian was very particular about his high-fidelity music. He had top of the line speakers carefully placed in the corners of the living room. His chair was at the sweet spot, where the sound field met his discerning ears. Cool fifties jazz played at low volume.

Early in the evening the four of them had all been polite. Trish sat in her upholstered chair. The young lovebirds snuggled on the couch. Brian listened to his enhanced sounds, seated in his plush chair. Keeping the conversation soft enough for jazz proved impossible. Trish hauled the kids into the kitchen and shut the door.

"How long have you been living in that apartment?" asked Trish.

"Almost a year," said Melona.

"When's the lease up?" asked Aunt Trish.

"Nobody has a lease in that neighborhood," said Melona.

"That's because you live in a hell slum," said Trish.

"I can't afford real Manhattan," said Melona.

"Can you afford to die young?" asked Trish.

Melona had been thinking a lot about this recently. Now that she knew how to look danger in the eye without blinking, maybe a safer lifestyle was worth considering.

Two stubborn women glared at each other.

"I don't want to die young," said Melona.

"And I don't want to make your business my business," said Aunt Trish, "but there's something you should hear about."

"What's on your mind," asked Melona.

"Last night I had a dream," said Trish.

Timmy nodded his head. His aunt's dreams were legendary in this kitchen.

"The Hilyers were in my dream," said Trish. "Three times."

"The Hilyers?" asked Melona.

"Ellie and Bill," said Trish. "They live across the hall."

"Three times?" said Melona.

"Oh, that's just dream stuff," said Aunt Trish. "That's how 'they' let you know you need to remember something out of your crazy dream. Anyhow, I saw Ellie in hall this morning. We had ourselves a little gab. She told me her husband had been given an opportunity to work at headquarters over in Europe for a year. This is a very big deal for both of them. Long story cut way short - they need to sublease their apartment. Ellie asked if I could recommend someone reliable."

The silence was thick.

Noutashi went to work on all three of them.

"How much is the rent?" asked Melona.

Trish leaned over and whispered in Melona's ear.

"Oh my gosh, that's only twenty dollars a month more than what I'm paying now," said Melona.

"This is a rent controlled building, dearie," said Trish. "We've gotta get you out of that place you're in. I don't want you getting stabbed before Timmy has a chance to do right by you."

There - she had done it - Aunt Trish had opened her big fat mouth and taken charge of everything.

Melona was stunned. "Wow. This is, like, a major life decision."

"You've got plenty more of those coming at you," said Trish. "Think it over. Mr. Hilyer starts his new job at the

266

beginning of the year. They're leaving in December so they'll have time to get settled over there. You could move across the hall and be safe."

Melona's eyes met Tim's. They had only known each other for a month. That wasn't enough time to make a major decision. A full year, on the other hand, would be plenty of time to figure each other out. They reached a wordless agreement with their eyes.

"Sounds like your dream tapped into something practical," said Melona.

"I'll tell Ellie next time I see her," said Trish.

Noutashi nodded her head solemnly. Dene had performed a lot of slick maneuvers to get that job for Mr. Hilyer in Paris. It was nice to know he was making good on his promise to reward Melona for all the trouble he had put her through.

Scene 86 - Talbot's Rare Books

"Wow, I haven't been here in a long time," said Tim.

"Unfortunately, I have," said Brian.

"I love this place," said Tim. He was surrounded by rare books, on shelves going all the way up to the ceiling. His entire life he had worked here part time.

"How's your new job?" asked Brian.

"I love it," said Tim, as he wandered through the stacks, with fond memories.

"You love it?" said Brian. "People don't love their jobs, they do them."

"I mean, yeah, it's just a job and all that," said Tim, "but I work at a sheet music publishing house, correcting and updating their catalog. When I was younger I worked here with rare books. Now I work down the Avenue providing music to entertain the City. If I'm going to take care of Melona I need a real job. Who knows what life might bring but at the moment I love it. And - I can walk to work in ten minutes."

"Then you have no excuse for being late," said Brian.

"So far I haven't been late," said Tim.

"I like what this new girlfriend has done to you," said Uncle Brian.

"By the way," said Tim, "did your brother sign?"

"Not yet," said Brian, "but I spoke to his lawyer and the pressure is on. I think they finally got it through his thick skull that if he doesn't sign now he's going to lose a lot of money. Holding out for that last penny is just plain stupid at this point."

"I hope this works," said Tim. "He's stubborn."

"I'm trying to swing this vacation place down in Florida," said Brian. "I need that money. I might have to hop on a plane and murder my own brother."

"Murders are for mystery novels," said Tim, repeating something he'd heard his uncle say. He looked around the family store. This place had been such an important part of his life. The smell of book dust was in his soul. It broke his heart to see it go.

By now the two of them had trudged down to the basement.

"Alright hot shot, I've got an ugly job for you," said Brian. "Now that I've become an old geezer, I'm not going to help you with it. She's your girlfriend, you do the dirty work."

"Sure, no problem," said Tim, looking at the huge mess piled in one corner.

"Sandal Annie owes money to everyone in The Village and always has," said Brian.

"How's she doing?" asked Tim.

"I visited her in the hospital last week," said Brian. "She's not getting out, except feet first, and she knows it. That's why she made me executor of her estate."

"Estate?" said Tim.

"You're looking at it," said Brian. "Other people might call this worthless junk, written by mad men and insane women, but this unholy mess is what remains of half a century of Greenwich Village life. I paid off a few of her debts and dragged her 'collateral' down here. She's been storing her crypto poetry at our bookstore for years. I don't know what's in this smelly heap and I don't want to find out. From what you've told me, this is the sort of thing Melona might be interested in."

"Annie was her unlikely guide into the world of being a published author," said Tim. "She's going to love this."

"How's that book deal going for her," asked Brian.

"That music producer from the west coast was out here last week," said young Tim. "He got Melona an interview with an agent who might possibly be interested in her Woodstock pictures. Or maybe some of that Aiyoni stuff. Who knows. Maybe something will come of it."

"Maybe, maybe, maybe," said Uncle Brian. "That's the book business."

"What do you want me to do?" asked Tim.

"Organize this mess so your aunt Trish doesn't freak out when we bring it into the apartment," said Brian. "Some of it stinks. Most of the boxes are crumbling. A lot of it's in brown paper bags that are falling apart. You are forbidden to bring any of this into our happy home until it's cleaned, boxed and deodorized. Anything that does not meet the high standards of my wife's keen sense of smell - goes in that pile over there."

"What does Aunt Trish think about this?" asked Tim.

"If this was my project she would never allow it," said Brian. "But since it's for her special girl, this messy pile will be welcomed as valuable treasure."

"I've been on the phone with Andy out in San Francisco," said Tim. "He's said he's going to ship some things to Melona from the elevator of lost dreams."

"What does that mean?" asked Brian.

"I'm not sure. Something about an island," said Tim. "The only clue I have is that somebody got stabbed at a concert."

"Your friends are crazy," said uncle Brian.

"It's better than not having any friends," pointed out Tim.

"Well, you're going to have to stop hanging out with your buddies until you get this dreadful pile of literary crap cleaned up," said Brian.

"Hmm," said Tim, looking at the heap, "I guess I know what I'm going to be doing with my spare time."

Chapter 32 - Refugee Shuttle

Inspector Oshika hovered outside the door to the Observatory. She had worked at Chephra since the first day of construction. In all those years she had never even once been sent to the Observatory. It was classified as an Ishmili area, not Valdarian or Sylumini.

After opening the door, one quick glance confirmed all her suspicions. This place was a permanent code violation. Oh well, not much she could do about it.

Cami got up from her desk and said, "It's so nice to see you again. It's been several years."

Inspector Oshika always held a CertPad cradled in her left arm. Looking at the display, she said, "I am here to certify the new JeshNim Network node."

"That's in Ulta's office," said Cami.

Oshika didn't like what she saw. Ulta's office was hanging from the ceiling, on an enormous hook, suspended from an industrial crane. The door to the office was a jagged hole cut through the wall.

"Why is that located there?" asked Oshika.

"Office space is tight," said Cami, trying not to giggle. "There are no rules against hanging a spare office module from the ceiling."

Oshika checked. There were no rules against hanging an office from the ceiling. But there should be. She made a note of that in her CertPad.

"Why don't you sit at Ulta's desk," said Cami. "I'll sit here and answer questions."

The office was completely empty except for one sparkling clean desk, a brand new communicator dome, two chairs, and a barren bookcase.

Cami and Oshika had worked together on hundreds of certification requests. Cami always began the same way, "Would you like me to explain the background of this request."

"Please do," said the inspector, adjusting the CertPad and dome controller for ease of use.

"A new employee will be assigned here at the beginning of the year," said Cami.

"Would that be Ulta?" asked Oshika.

"That is correct," said Cami. "She got fired by the Sylumini, hired by Ing, and approved by Captain Behchel."

Oshika looked in the CertPad to confirm each of Cami's statements. Since Captain Behchel was the big boss of every Valdarian employee, including Oshika and Cami, that settled the matter. Oshika detested Ulta.

"Check," said the inspector.

Cami wasted no time. "There are a number of high security risks associated with this project. Next generation, high speed connectivity to the colonies is being developed. Before launching this experimental system, four JeshNim Nodes must be certified. You are testing the first one."

"Node names?" asked Oshika.

"Ishmili Observatory at Chephra, Hikli Lab Two in the Terran Colony, Kemong Colony Zog in their main data center, and Kemong Colony Earth using a temporary setup," answered Cami.

"The system accepts those values," said Oshika.

"Glad to hear that," said Cami, with a sigh of relief.

"What needs to be done?" asked Oshika.

Cami yelled into the other room. "Hey Farli, send that coded message to Ulta's address."

"Sent," said Farli.

Inspector Oshika flipped back and forth between the CertPad and the JeshNim terminal. This took several minutes. "Node One has been certified."

"Excellent," said Cami.

The next three nodes should be a lot of fun for Cami and Farli. Their boss, Gervaie, had told them, "Log this in as a business trip but treat it like a working vacation. You deserve it." She was looking forward to getting her two best employees back on the team. If Ulta didn't get certified, they were stuck.

Next morning, Cami and Farli left their house in Brazil. They had shiny new travel bags slung over their shoulders. First stop was the jeshie rescue colony.

Flying up the Atlantic, with the Caribbean Islands on their left, they went back to the Woodstock site, where they had worked so frantically two months ago.

A shiny new gateway center had been built to allow anca visitors limited access to the jeshie tunnels. There was no access to the terran caverns. A huge sign, hanging from the ceiling inside the main entrance, read ...

Wamilla Colony Security Checkpoint
Have Your Permits Ready

They set their bags down at the security counter and presented their travel passes. Top level permits had been issued to both.

"You may proceed," said the guard.

At the information desk they got directions to Hikli Lab Two.

Starting at the old AmbuTrak road, they traveled south until they entered a new tunnel which connected them to the Nebraska Kid Highway. Near Chicago they turned left. A dual use terran/jeshie tunnel took them to Caboks.

The underground metropolis of Caboks has been a major hub in middle America for ten thousand years. It is close to where the three great rivers meet. Surface dwellers constantly crisscross this region on the topside world.

Honat and Lumbia lived out in the suburbs of Caboks. Xen and Wun had built their new laboratory in city center.

Following the interactive map from the information desk, it was easy to find Hikli Lab Two.

Without knocking, Cami opened the door.

"look who visit us" said Xen, getting up from her workbench.

Farli said, "Wow, look at this place. Everything is brand new."

Xen replied "we get new problems" "we build new toys".

272

Wun heard familiar voices and came over, "hey you drop by" "like you say you do".

Trz joined them. "me full time employee now".

"We're here to run the network test," said Cami.

"this for anca spy baddie" asked Xen. Anger was in her eyes.

"Riana hired her," replied Cami.

"why her" asked Xen. "she dangerous".

"Ulta risked everything to protect Melona and Andy," Cami explained. "She sacrificed her career to do the right thing. Besides, who knows more about our technology than Ulta. She's already stolen half of what we know."

Xen pondered this. "she not bad inside" "she do badly things".

"Besides," said Cami, "this is more for you than it is for her."

"how you logic that" asked Xen.

"Think twenty five years from now," said Cami. "The colony permit runs out. You are forced to move. You setup Hikli3 at KCE. The high speed JeshNim antenna you build here on Earth, will be what you connect to when you get reassigned to the permanent colony."

"you tricky thinker" said Xen. "me run test for you".

Farli, Wun and Trz were on the other side of the lab, talking tech jargon.

Cami asked Farli, "The test module, please."

He reached in his pocket and handed it to her.

She gave it to Xen, who connected it to the newly installed JeshNim terminal.

"if this pass test what happen" asked Xen.

"Ulta will be working at the Observatory with Honat and Qusheem," Cami told him. "Your Hikli2 node connects to them, plus the permanent Earth and Zog colonies. Ulta can only connect to you. She has zero access to the colonies."

"if me give her nothing" "then baddie got nothing to steal" Xen said.

"You can do whatever you want," said Cami. "After Ulta gets certified, Farli and I will be going back to work for Gervaie."

"no promotion" asked Xen.

"We both got big promotions," said Cami, "same department, fabulous new jobs."

"what riana dene do" asked Xen.

"Same thing they have always done," said Cami, "which is whatever they want."

"sound like us at hikli" said Xen.

"Ulta's role will be to transfer old rescue technology from the Ishmili Observatory to the Valdarians. She will fill out the forms we don't want to fill out, go to the meetings we don't want to attend, and prepare reports that we think are a waste of time," said Cami.

"me like ulta now" said Xen.

Scene 88 - Inspector Nar

After spending a pleasant evening in Caboks, they took the Nebraska Kid Highway out to San Francisco. The Mositey Shuttle Terminal was west of the city, where the mountains rise up from the coastal plain.

There had been regular shuttle service between Kemong Colony Zog (KCZ) and Kemong Colony Earth (KCE) for a long time. This rescue mission meant adding a third stop at planet Earth. The permit was temporary. There was a yearly quota for transferring jeshies from Earth to KCE, which was halfway between Earth and Mars.

The shuttle service catered to jeshie migrants and nimulon officials. All shuttles were supplied with dual atmosphere. For those on the go, this was an important way to make new contacts and expand your network of enterprises.

Cami and Farli visited the shops in Mositey Terminal. They bought a couple of small souvenirs, since they were traveling light. By the time they reached the gate they still had plenty of time. It was nice to be sitting comfortably.

"Over here," called out Farli, in a loud voice.

Cami got startled by the shout. She had been playing a game on her taper device.

A few travelers were annoyed at the noise.

Lon recognized the voice and came running over, "so glad me find you" "very crowded".

"Have a seat. They haven't started boarding yet," said Cami. "How do you like living on the west coast?"

"muchly different" said Lon. "work at colony headquarters" "no more guardian" "not get you message until morning".

"We were at Hikli Two yesterday," said Cami. "Xen and Wun and Trz say hello."

"me say hello back at them" said Lon.

"We're going on a business trip to KCZ and KCE," Cami informed her.

"that impressive" said Lon.

The Shuttle will now begin boarding. Please have your tickets ready.

Lon apologized, "wish me get message earlier".

"Oh, we've still got time to visit, said Cami. "Stay in line with us."

They got up. Cami and Farli adjusted their luggage straps. Lon waited with them while the line moved forward. They spoke in low voices.

Cami said, "Farli and I have a lot of vacation time built up."

"you work hard" "you deserve" said Lon.

"We'd like to visit you when we get back," said Cami. "Can you get some time off?"

"got lots days coming" said Lon. "when good for you".

"How about week after next," said Cami.

"me check" said Lon. She looked at her calendar app. Making a few entries, she said, "that my vacation".

"Wonderful," said Cami. "There are some things we need to talk about. Not enough time today."

By now, there was only one soto in front of them so they said their goodbyes.

"bye now" said Lon. "safe trip".

"See you soon," said Cami, "thanks for dropping by."

##

"There she is," said Cami, who had been looking all around the KCZ Night Club. They had gotten the third node certified earlier in the day and were looking forward to an evening's entertainment with a close friend.

Farli glanced up and saw Beq, who had obviously seen them first. She was treading her way through the crowded tables.

Cami and Beq had been the best of friends when they worked together at Lindar. Beq had wandered off, seeking the mysteries of unknown worlds. Now she was back on Zog, in a new capacity. They had agreed to meet out here at the jeshie colony.

"Sorry I'm late," said Beq.

"Not a problem," said Cami, "we're on working-vacation."

"I can tell," said Beq, who had never seen Cami this relaxed.

"How are things these days?" asked Cami.

"My new job is a fabulous challenge," said Beq.

"Tunhi runs a tight group," said Cami. "She's tough but fair."

"I get a lot of super dome time," said Beq, with a gleam in her eye.

"Use it wisely, this time," said Cami. "Last time you wandered off after making some calculations."

"Professor Obolon made that perfectly clear to me," said Beq. "She made certain I understood that she put her reputation on the line to get me this job."

Cami got that gossipy look in her eye. "Are you going to be able to make it to the commitment ceremony?"

"Wouldn't miss it for the world. Zinxa will be there too," said Beq, breaking into a broad grin and rubbing her hands together. "Isn't this exciting."

"Shhh," said Cami, "not so loud. Everything's not settled. We were with Lon yesterday and I couldn't tell her yet."

"How's Riana taking this?" whispered Beq.

"Oh my," said Cami, putting her hand to her mouth, "you absolutely cannot believe how she's behaving. The Ice Umbie has turned into Miss Mush."

Beq giggled, "Noooooo."

"Yeeeees," whispered Cami, "I told her that - as guide of honor - I was going to throw a color billow party for her. She screamed that she would never ever - no never never never - go to a billow bash. After that she broke down and cried. Then she said yes, of course she'd be there."

"That's hilarious," said Beq.

Right then the stage lights flashed on and off, on and off. The nightly show for business travelers at the Zog Colony was about to begin.

The Master of Ceremonies strode onstage. He was wearing a cape that sparkled under the bright lights and a hat that was wider than his shoulders. Waving his arms grandly, he blew kisses to the audience. "urbies umbies" "me proud to announce damosel umbie aun" "all way from mozopama" "she sing dance you pleasure".

Cami and Beq moved their chairs closer together, so they could gossip.

Farli shifted his chair so he faced the stage. He wanted to watch Damosel Umbie Aun do her famous Shooki Tooki Foo.

Kemong Colony Earth was a no nonsense kind of place. It was still under construction between Earth and Mars. The planned startup date was still a hundred years away. Then along came this emergency rescue. All of a sudden everybody wanted everything done yesterday.

Inspector Nar held certain core beliefs. He was an inspector. New worlds are dangerous. Safety first. There was physical safety, there was network security, and there was cultural integrity. All of them must be rigorously upheld.

He had a work request in his soto dome. Certify JeshNim Network node. Ulta's name was on the request. At the KCE site, Ulta was notorious for causing delays and creating needless problems. That had been bad, very bad, for meeting construction deadlines.

Cami had been warned about Nar. She and Farli had a plan.

"welcome to kce" said Nar. The walls of his office were decorated with safety posters.

Cami apologized, "sorry to interrupt" "we here certify jeshnim node".

Inspector Nar was deliberately noncommittal. "see request in dome".

"do you have concerns" asked Cami.

Nar said, "not trust ulta".

"did you read watchers report" asked Cami.

"long report" said Nar. "me busy".

"we stay as long as need" said Cami.

Farli, who was in on the plan, took the certification module out of his pocket and placed it on Nar's desk - label side up. Three certification stamps could easily be seen.

With obvious reluctance, Nar brought up the Soto Watchers report. He glanced at the executive summary.

Ulta had protected the lives of two evos, enabling the rescue of all jeshie hospital patients. Ulta had sacrificed her career to achieve these goals. She was cooperating with the authorities. No one else was better placed to right the wrongs which had been done.

Nar looked Cami in the eye. "if anca baddie steal then we doomed".

"true" said Cami. "look page twelve cert request" "read access section".

Nar did this. Ulta was allowed to connect only to Hikli2. KCZ and KCE were off limits to her.

"who this xen wun" asked Nar.

"make rescue bigly success" said Cami. "same level riana dene".

Nar studied the certification request with a perfectionist's attention to detail. With suspicion in his eye he looked over at the test module. Three approval stamps glared at him. Only one space remained blank. "me run this for you" "not trust ulta".

"we wait" said Cami.

An hour later, Nar ejected the test module and placed it on his desk. Reaching in a drawer, he took out a rubber stamp. Holding it up for them to see, it read "APPR KCE" in bold backwards letters.

"you tell ulta she owe me big time" said Nar. The rubber stamp was in his hand but the ink pad was still in his desk.

"me handle that" said Cami.

Nar took out the ink and stamped the label. After letting it dry he initialed it. "you have nice trip home".

"thank you muchly" said Cami. Now she and Farli knew for certain that they would be moving on up to their new profession as JeshNim executives.

Ulta, on the other hand, would have a lot of time on her hands to learn the ways of Honat and Qusheem.

Chapter 33 - The Big Day

Scene 89 - Bride Guides

The big day finally arrived. Riana hadn't been this nervous since she was young. Her hand rested on the knob of the front door. When she left this apartment she would still be a single umbie. When they came back home tonight she would be a spouse.

Setting her resolve, she opened the door and ventured forth.

Cami was throwing a color billow party for the bride guides. Riana hadn't been to a billow bash in a billion years. On the other hand, this sort of nonsense meant a lot to Cami. Casting aside her doubts, Riana decided that if she was going to do it at all, she was going to do it all the way.

From her modest home in western England she flew south across the Atlantic Ocean. At the eastern tip of Brazil she saw Cami and Farli's cute little house, perched on a hill, overlooking the tropical ocean. She landed on the veranda and sounded the visitor tone.

"Eeeeeeeeeeeeeeeeeeeeeeeeeeeh. She's here."

Flinging the door open, Cami announced, "Come on in."

Their house was stylish and modern. The living room had ample space for guests. Cami and Farli entertained often and well. In the far corner was a fantastically decorated billow cot. Sitting primly next to it was Saluf, the color maestro of Brazil, and some say all the world.

Saluf had rescheduled two well placed clients, and angrily driven away another, just so she could get her hands on Riana. The ancient one had the rarest colors of early Nimulos billowing within her body. This was the ultimate fashion opportunity and it could not be passed up.

The custom was that a theme for the bride guides would emerge from the billowing colors of the bride herself. It was the skill of the billower to determine which design would work best for the entire ensemble. One by one, Saluf considered the eight members of the bridal party.

Riana was the only primebie living on Earth. She had emerged into life just as the blaze of primordial expansion cooled. Those extreme powers had brought her profound awareness and persistent misunderstanding. As Saluf would soon learn, Riana also lived as an other-sider.

Cami was typical of the clients Saluf was familiar with. She had a galactic reputation for being brilliant, was well poised, polite in good company, fierce when defending her interests, and aware of the need to support and improve upon tradition.

Noutashi was the true hero of the emergency rescue. Her determination and judgement had brought pride to all citizens of Earth. Others may have made bold plans but it was Noutashi who made the hard choices which carried them through.

Zinxa was unique in Saluf's professional experience. Emergent as an anca, she had become an other-sider by choice. As the ultimate pioneer scout, Zinxa worked in the nether regions to reveal to Captain Behchel the life options available for our future survivor worlds.

Beq was truly stunning to Saluf. A soto, who had learned to live as an anca, then wandered off to seek the mysteries of the other-sider realms. The story of her guiding Dene to Cazouni had not yet been told, but the colors imprinted on her were clearly visible.

Lumbia was a terran - rarely seen among surface dwelling anca. In Brazil, a few terrans had been Saluf's clients but this one was different. Not only did she have that North American thing going - she had perfect presence, posture and dignity.

Xen was a soto and they are blue. Not much to work with - unless you are Saluf the Magnificent. That tough exterior - truck diver, mechanic, lab wizard - provided a solid foundation. By the time Saluf worked her special magic, the allure was mesmerizing.

Lon was pure delight, as far as Saluf was concerned. This evojesh was older than the entire Nimulos expansion region, yet she exhibited the freshness of youth in all she said and did. Those natural plum colors were an incredible new addition to the palette.

Three other-siders, two anca, one terran anca, a soto, plus a rare evojesh. What an opportunity to enhance a commitment ceremony by putting each and every one of them on finest display, to the best advantage of all.

Having finished her evaluation, Saluf invited Riana to approach the billow cot.

Scene 90 - Groom In The Sanctuary

Tristo tapped his fingers on the desk. Dene had made a valid point but his answer didn't quite fit. The Chapeltarians have answers for each of the major questions in life, plus a ritual for everything. It was all in the Green Book. There was some leeway, of course, but the pieces were solidly in place.

As minister of the Chapeltarian Assembly at Pofraisson in Paris, it was Tristo's duty to make sure that those who received their commitment ceremony here, shared the core beliefs of the assembly. He had asked Dene, "Why did you say that music is more important than doctrine?"

"Because music communicates the cosmic force to everyone," Dene had answered. "Doctrine delivers it only to the few."

This was an interesting, if obscure, point. There was a doctrine check list in his communicator dome. That particular answer was not included.

While pondering his ministerial responsibilities, Tristo glanced up and was shocked to see two additional anca sitting in his office. The door was firmly closed. On closer inspection, only one of them was an anca.

Dene had been waiting for Tristo to notice. "I'd like to introduce you to Zinxa and Beq. They're good friends of Riana. They'll be participating in the ceremony today."

"I don't recall seeing their names on the guest list," said Tristo. He and Laffise had been through that list at least a dozen times. Every seat in the chapel was taken. Hovering room only areas were going to be packed.

"There are two guest lists," Dene reminded him, "locals and aliens. Check the invited aliens list."

Tristo could never remember where he kept the files in his dome - so he left all of them open - which made it hard to find anything.

"Ah yes, there it is," said Tristo. "Hmmm. Right you are. On the aliens and others list."

"We're here to decorate," said Beq.

"Well, er, our committee has already taken care of that," said Tristo.

"How could your committee decorate the soto balcony?" asked Beq. "They wouldn't have been able to see it until a few minutes ago."

Tristo got a shocked look on his face.

"Same document," said Dene, "scroll all the way down to the bottom. Look under Alternate Seating."

Tristo grew irritated, "Soto balcony above the anca balcony. What does that mean?"

"Come out and take a look," said Beq.

"Why do these things happen to me," moaned Tristo.

Lafisse was in the sanctuary, staring with disapproval at the alien balcony above their normal balcony. Tristo held the title of minister but anyone familiar with how the Pofraisson really worked knew that it was Lafisse who kept things running smoothly.

"Are they authorized to do this?" demanded Tristo. Strange blue beings, and a weird assortment of oddly shaped evojesh, were hanging unrecognizable symbols over the front edge of the second balcony. None of this had been there a few minutes ago.

"Our special guests seem to think so," said Lafisse, pointing toward the pulpit.

In the sanctified area, next to the pulpit, were two bright fuzzy ishmili, Tahra and Noom. They were looking at the tape markings on the floor, to make sure they knew where they were supposed to suddenly appear, when called upon to do so during the ceremony.

"Greetings and good fortune to you," said Noom. "Thank you for letting us participate in this blessed event."

"Greetings and good fortune," said Tahra, "the jeshie balcony seems to be making you feel uncomfortable."

Lafisse put her hand beside her mouth and whispered to Tristo, "Ishmili. You invited them. They're in the ceremony."

"Ah yes," said Tristo, who had never seen an ishmili before, "welcome to the Pofraisson. We are so excited to have you here with us today."

Dene called out to Tristo, "I'm going to go help with the soto decorations." Turning to Lafisse he whispered, "Follow me. We need to talk."

Lafisse, Dene and Zinxa flew up to the second balcony, because they were anca. Beq took the stairs because she was soto.

"Have you met Trz?" Dene asked Lafisse. "He helped us at Woodstock. Trz is in charge of the decorations committee."

Trz shook Lafisse's hand and said, "you have goodly sanctified environment".

Lafisse had no idea what he was talking about.

Dene whispered low. "We've got anca, evonim, soto, evojesh, ishmili and other-siders at the ceremony today. Stay calm and go with the flow. The ishmili placed a force field around the Pofraisson. After the ceremony, the force field goes away."

Staying calm was not in Lafisse's nature. Folding her hands together, she gazed beyond the ceiling, "Please make this work," she whispered to some unseen power.

##

After Lafisse adjusted to her new normal, Dene turned to Zinxa and Beq, "I thought you two were at the billow bash. What happened?"

"Eh, we bailed," said Zinxa. "They were playing stupid games. We told them we'd meet up with them here."

"You two look fabulous," said Dene. "Who did your colors?"

Zinxa, who lived in a dark cave and avoided the normals, looked down at her taper. "Saluf is a genius. Anyone who can make me look this good deserves a major award."

Beq watched her hands shimmer. "I used to think I was blue. Now I know I'm so much more than blue."

"Hey Trz," called out Dene, "put these two to work. I just thought of something I need to do."

Trz said to Zinxa and Beq, "get ladder" "follow me".

Dene flew down to one of the pews in the sanctuary, where Lafisse sat.

"Sorry to bother you again," said Dene, "but when Tristo noticed Zinxa and Beq in his office he got flustered and forgot to finish his task."

"What now?" asked Lafisse, who had heard about Tristo's forgetfulness a million times.

"I passed my Doctrine Test but I don't think he entered that into the system," said Dene. "We can't go through with the ceremony today unless it gets approved."

Lafisse brought up a new display in her Chapel Tablet. Chapeltarian Doctrine Test. Dene. Approved. "You're good to go," she said.

"Thanks," said Dene. As he slowly drifted away he couldn't help thinking - he didn't do day jobs, and he didn't do doctrine - but he *had* seen the eternal light, and he lived by it. That had to be worth a few extra credit points.

Scene 91 - Commitment Ceremony

The ceremony was scheduled to begin at 3:00 in the afternoon, Paris time, but as was his custom Tristo waited a few extra minutes. The sanctuary was packed and the hallways were overflowing. This was the commitment ceremony that everyone wanted to say they had been invited to.

Tristo was in his office, peeking out the small window in the side door. Everything appeared to be in proper order.

"One more minute," he muttered.

The um-spouse procession was ready on one side of the chapel, behind closed doors. The ur-spouse procession was waiting on the other side.

Beel gave the hand signal.

Tristo opened the side door and entered the sanctuary, his sacral colors billowing majestically within him. Lafisse zipped back to the front office to take care of a few last minute details. All heads turned to watch the two doors opening in the middle of the chapel.

On the um-side, Riana floated in. From the opposite door Captain Behchel entered. He would escort her down the aisle. Everyone gasped at how magnificently stunning Riana appeared. Her ancient age glimmered with dazzling glory.

On the ur-side, Dene had not been allowed to see his commit-to-be until this moment. He knew he had fallen in love with Riana but had not seen her in full radiance - until now. Opposite him was Ing, who would glide along with him. Cami floated in next, to be accompanied by Farli. So it went, two by two.

The commitment procession was afire with the glow of ceremonial anticipation. The inner-fires of the procession sparked the memory-fires of those seated in the congregation. Ceremony repeats and repetition renews.

The rebel bride and her close friends swayed down the aisle - accompanied by the wayfaring groom and his jolly companions. Two individuals, supported by their group, would soon celebrate the binding power of cosmic love.

This commitment would not only bind them to each other, it would bind them to their community as well. That community had jumped across invisible boundaries. Many beings, many worlds, one love.

Through the majestic powers of the ishmili these combined groups could now see and feel what had formerly been invisible and untouched.

Tristo raised both his arms and a hush fell over the chapel. Casting his gaze from side to side, then outward to the eternal presence, he invoked the wordless blessing.

Then he said, "We are gathered here today to celebrate the partnership of Riana and Dene. Each of us owes our being to the great mystery. Today is their day to celebrate our consecrated connection to the mystery of life. Let us pray."

In unison, they chanted, "Oh great mystery, fill us with your divine presence. Guide us to live in the essential way, every day. We ask your blessings on those who have chosen to share their lives among us. May they be a blessing to our world, may our world be a blessing to the grand universe, we praise you for the gift of life. Amen."

"It gives me great pleasure to perform this ceremony today," said Tristo. "In addition to my ministerial duties, I have the honor of having Riana as a close friend. It is a tremendous pleasure to welcome Dene into our family of celebrants. We wish both of them our best as they seek to connect our limited lives to the limitless forever. To confirm their commitment, I ask them to join me at the crystal chalice."

The chalice, placed on an ornate stand, was filled with clear liquid, which symbolized the fluidity of life. Riana and Dene dipped a hand into the chalice, connecting the solidness of their beings to the ephemeral flows linking each to all.

Tristo extended his arms and said, "I confirm that the customs of the anca are being respected by those at this ceremony today. What do each of you wish to confirm?"

Riana said, "I confirm that the two of us working together will bring greater blessings to our community than each of us working alone."

Dene said, "I confirm that we as a couple are committed to transforming the natural limits of our first world into a sustainable home for our cosmic future."

They removed their hands from the chalice, dried them ceremonially, then faced the congregation.

After a litany of readings and songs - two majestic beings faded into view.

Tahra and Noom chanted in unison, "Greetings and good fortune to you. We are blessed by the dedication of these two anca to connect your worlds to a vigorous future. We thank the evos of this planet, the anca assigned to guide them, the jeshies who are their guests, our ishmili peers, the wulem who guide us, and our Lengtor life patrons Ur and Um. We reserve special praise for the one source of all, who touches each being everywhere, throughout the eternal changes of limitless life."

Tristo invited the anca couple to join him at the pillar of affirmation. They placed their hands on the pillar.

"Do you affirm that you will care for each other amid the challenges of life?"

"I do." "I do."

"Do you affirm that you will support our community with your shared lives."?

"I do." "I do."

"Do you affirm that you will honor the world with all its imperfections?

"I do." "I do."

"Do you affirm that you will obey the laws and customs of Nimulos?"

"I do." "I do."

"Do you affirm that you will seek to create a better future for our eternity?

"I do." "I do."

"Do you affirm that you will seek inner guidance from the great mystery?"

"I do." "I do."

They moved from the pillar and the celebrants faced the congregants. The binding ceremony was about to begin.

"Riana, do you take Dene to be the anca you will commit to. Supporting him in good times and bad, through togetherness and separation, when faced with happiness or sadness, during times when love is warm or love has cooled, throughout whatever life may bring your way?"

"I do."

"Dene, do you take Riana to be the anca you will commit to. Supporting her in good times and bad, through togetherness and separation, when faced with happiness or sadness, during times when love is warm or love has cooled, throughout whatever life may bring your way?"

"I do."

"You may now perform the binding ceremony," said Tristo.

These two faced each other. Raising their left arms to shoulder height, they encircled the wrist of the other with their right hand.

The minister intoned, "Let the blessed powers flow through you. May your lives flow into the blessed powers. By the powers vested in me, the two of you are bound to the ineffable unfolding of life."

Riana and Dene raised their left arms high for all to see.

Glowing golden around their wrists was the binding billow. The circle of commitment had been placed there by love.

Tristo intoned, "I now pronounce you um-spouse and ur-spouse."

The assembly sang a song of praise and joy.

Those who loved Riana most, the ones who had known her the longest, who had felt her stinging sharpness, who had been hurt by her brusque behavior - had tears in their eyes. She was beautiful, she was loved, and she was theirs.

Scene 92 - Crystal Sky Hall

Above the ancient rooftops of Paris the Crystal Sky Hall glistened in the crisp autumn air. It was the finest reception hall floating above the city of lights. How he managed to do it was a deep dark secret but Dene had contracted all of it for their reception. Paris glittered beneath the shimmering crystal floor. Guests mingled with familiar friends and fresh acquaintances.

What surprised many was how graciously Riana accepted her new role as um-spouse. Saluf had crafted her stunning outer appearance but there was so much more going on. Some deep seed inside of her had sprouted through to the surface. Always before, Riana had been the true believer, attempting to gain what she desired by sheer willpower. On display tonight were elements of her personality which had been tucked away. With the swashbuckling adventurer Dene projecting a shield around them, she could afford the luxury of putting her better self before the world.

With each shake of her hand, each nod of her head, each glide to the next table - every guest felt as if they were special - and they were.

##

The orchestra played softly, allowing the conversations of the guests to rise above their superb musicianship. Beel floated to the front of the bandstand. Three times he clapped his hands to get their attention. "Urbies and umbies, the new couple will now have their first dance as commits."

Dene glided over to Riana, extended his hand, and escorted her to the center.

Beel raised his voice so it rang strong and clear. "Urbies and umbies, please welcome to the dance floor, for the first time ever, Um-Riana and Ur-Dene."

Applause broke out, then cheers of pure joy. As if by common consent the guests rose for a hovering ovation. The jeshie refugees were safe. Earth's honor had been upheld.

Riana had been taking dancing lessons from Cami. She made an anca curtsy to her new partner. He bowed in respect. Her colors shone bright and clear - like the lights of Paris glittering beneath their tapers.

The orchestra struck up the song. The audience hushed.

Dene swirled Riana skillfully around the dance floor. Her colors billowed like a whirlpool of rainbows. She grasped his hand and off they twirled, pure wonder radiating from their glowing faces.

As their first song glided toward a shimmering end, other couples eagerly crowded the dance floor to join with them.

At every reception there is always a table for guests who don't quite fit into a tidy category on the seating chart. Sitting at this table was Ulta. When Riana approached she was glad to see how happy all of them were. Each of the odd guests had warmed to the other members of their company.

Riana glided over and put her hand lightly on Ulta's shoulder, "How nice that you could be with us tonight. I hope you're enjoying yourself."

"We all are," said Ulta, extending her hand to everyone seated there.

"I'm happy to hear that," said Riana. "We've had our differences in the past but I look forward to moving beyond all that."

"We will find a way," said Ulta. "Congratulations to you and Dene."

"Congratulations to us all," said Riana, with a polite gesture of acceptance.

Scene 93 - Two Living As One

It was after midnight and Riana had done more socializing in one day than she usually did in a year. Dene wouldn't say she was grouchy but he would say she needed some down time. The staff at the Crystal Sky Hall were well prepared for this eventuality. Getting them on their way was done with style and grace.

From the sparkle of Paris, to the stately tor of Glastonbury, was a short hop. They entered the vestibule.

Before opening the front door, she squeezed Dene's hand and gave him a sweet little kiss.

"I've been keeping a secret from you," said Riana.

"Oh, and what would that be?" asked Dene.

She looked him in the eye. "You've guessed, haven't you."

"Actually, I don't believe I have," said Dene.

"What did you think when we were in my laboratory?" she implored.

Umbies can be difficult sometimes, so Dene answered cautiously, "I thought it was nice that you trusted me to be there."

"Good," she said, with a shake of her head, and a hint of triumph.

They entered what was now their apartment. Down the back hallway were the same two doors that Dene had seen before. The one on the left led to her personal lab. Dene had been there a few times. The door farther down, on the right, was one he had never entered.

She took him by the hand and led him through the far door. In the middle of the room was a natural spring of slow flowing water. Over the eons, that trickle had carved out a small cavern in the stone. She had built her apartment around this spring room. The gentle seeping water fascinated her. The smell of aromatic minerals was strong.

"I want to show you my secret," she said.

In the shadows was an alcove. As they approached, Dene saw the dim outlines of an ornate door.

"Go ahead - open it," she said, waiting anxiously.

Turning the knob, Dene beheld a splendidly decorated room.

"I built a new apartment for you. It's an extension of my old apartment," said Riana, "I hope you like it."

In stark contrast to the minimalist style which Riana preferred, she had built his suite according to his tastes. As a matter of fact - most of the things in this room were his property.

"May I ask a question?"

"Of course."

"Where did you get these things?"

"Beel sent everything to you that he was allowed to take," said Riana. "Government property had to be left behind in Antarctica. While you were with Tristo in the chapel, a crew of Beel's moved your things here. My neighbor Harlond picked out the rest of your necessities. He loves collecting English furniture but his spouse won't allow him to bring anything more into their home. This was a splendid project for him. You'll meet him tomorrow. Or maybe the day after."

"This is so awesome," said Dene. "I knew we were going to have a new lifestyle but this is truly a pleasant surprise. Thank you."

She took him on a tour of the other rooms. There was a large bedroom. Next to it was a spacious office which was decorated like a meditation center. Then there was a parlor where guests would feel comfortable in a smaller setting than the living room. And of course there was his workshop, where all his tools from Antarctica had been brought over by Beel's crew.

"You need to see one more thing," said Riana. "See that door in the middle of the living room wall?"

"Yes."

"Open it."

He did. "Oh wow. It's your lab."

"That's my big secret," said Riana. "My laboratory used to be twice as large as it is now. Early on, I decided that you were the one for me. I had no idea how I was going to snag you but I built that wall through the center of the room - just in case. The first time I allowed you to visit, this was a new wall."

"The circle comes back on itself," said Dene.

"Enough of this talk about furniture. Let's go relax in the pool," said Riana.

"I was hoping you would ask," said Dene. "Cami told me about it."

The difference between his place and her place was stark. Leaving the door to his new residence wide open, they went back to the natural cavern. Along the back wall was a tiny sleeping cubicle for Riana. It had barely enough room for her to lay down. A few simple belongings were stored in rock crevices.

291

In the cavern itself, pretty little things had been carefully placed on stone ledges. A few of these were mood lights, which Riana illuminated one by one. A delicate glow filled the room, showing tiny ripples in the water.

The two of them sat at the edge of the pool, letting their tapers dangle.

"I have a way which I prefer," said Riana.

"Show me your way," said Dene.

She slipped into the pool, snuggling her taper down into the cool stone below. Her body was immersed in the slow flow. She kept her head in the moist cavern air.

Following her example, Dene joined Riana in the pool. Their hands found each other in the stillness.

This had been a day of words. Now it was a night of dreams.

Chapter 34 - Life Goes On

Scene 94 - Sandal Annie

Sandal Annie's funeral was packed. Melona took pictures of aging bohemians whose poems and paintings she had studied in college classrooms. At one point or another everyone in Greenwich Village had been Annie's friend. None of them were surprised that she was gone. All of them were amazed that she had lasted this long.

"A testament to be body's ability to survive self inflicted foolishness," one old geezer had remarked.

Melona owed her thin writing career, and thick life style, to Sandal Annie. Without the small endowment of cash from Beatnik Village she would have been just one more girl graduating from college, with a desperate need to find a husband, because mom and dad didn't plan on supporting her anymore. Now she was an empowered woman with good prospects. A seriously flawed human being named Sandal Annie had helped make that possible.

Pastors in this church had been forgiving Annie's sins for more than fifty years. She'd outlasted them all, except this latest one. A young liberal minister, with leather patches on the elbows of his tweed jacket, recited her funeral oration.

After the ceremony there was a repast in the basement of the community center. One incident amused Tim enormously because he knew something she did not. A cork board with pictures from Annie's long life had been placed on an easel. Melona took a photo of every one. Tim and Uncle Brian had brought these over from the archives at the bookstore. Tomorrow they were going to give the collection to Melona as a New Year's Eve gift. He wasn't allowed to tell her yet. Tim giggled behind the back of his hand.

Two of these pictures fascinated Melona. She took multiple shots of each - just to make sure at least one came out right.

There was 12 year old Mary Anne Olcott at her first communion in Boston. It seemed impossible that this frilly youngster, with golden curls, could have transformed herself into rip roaring Sandal Annie.

The other was of 18 year old Annie being dragged into a paddy wagon by two bulky New York cops. It was 1917, during World War One, and dissent was not tolerated, especially by a woman. Her crime was shouting out loud, in public, that war was not the answer. She wore sandals. The rage on her face reminded Melona of Roxie.

The fascinating part, as far as Melona was concerned, was that Annie was being arrested at exactly the same place where her father had snapped a picture of her as a young college freshman, back in 1959. They were the same age, at the same location, forty two years apart. In an eerie way, it felt like some sort of connected sisterhood.

Melona had always thought of Sandal Annie as old. Trying to imagine Mary Anne Olcott, the black sheep of a distinguished Boston family, living in Greenwich Village as a teenage rebel, simply astounded her.

While Tim waited patiently, he saw someone he recognized from other pictures that Melona had shown to him. Tapping his girlfriend on the shoulder, he said, "Let me get a picture of you," reaching for her camera.

"Not now. I need to finish," she said, grabbing the camera away from him.

"Why don't you look behind you," he suggested.

Melona turned around. "Ohhhhhhhhhhh my gosh, it is sooooo good to see you again." She rushed over and gave Roxie a humongous hug.

"Hi," said Roxie with a relaxed smile.

"You look great," said Melona. "Healthy, happy, what's been going on."

"Yeah, well, you know, things are better," said Roxie. "Uh, I'd like you to meet a guy. His name is Dwayne."

Standing next to her was a street kid. He didn't talk much. Dwayne wore a black leather jacket.

Melona took his hand, "Hello, nice to meet you."

He shuffled his feet.

"Let me get a picture of you two. For the collection," said Tim. "You stand over here. I want you right there. Yeah, that's it." He snapped three pictures. Melona, Roxie, and Sandal Annie posing with a paddy wagon.

"What are you doing these days?" asked Melona.

"Last time you saw me I was in one of my bad girl moods," said Roxie. "They kept me in jail for six months. I assaulted a police officer. Two, actually. It was the best thing that ever happened to me. Six months with no booze. Straightened me right out. I haven't had a drink since I got out of the slammer. Then I met Dwayne. He doesn't drink."

Dwayne shuffled his feet.

The two women talked for twenty minutes nonstop. Tim and Dwayne wandered off into their own little worlds.

Suddenly, Melona remembered that there was something Tim might be waiting for. Phone numbers were exchanged. The two gals rounded up their two guys. Then they went their separate ways.

"We should get going," said Tim, looking supremely nervous.

She understood and said, "I have an idea. Let's take a walk through Washington Square Park."

Tim smiled, "Hey, that's a great idea."

Scene 95 - Under The Arch

After sauntering through the park they found themselves standing beneath the Washington Square Arch. Melona took a deep breath and stood at the exact spot she had always imagined.

Tim was so nervous he couldn't move.

Noutashi lost her temper. All of the anca around Washington Square thought it was hilarious when she whirled around, did an upside down flip, and whomped Little Timmy in the head with her taper. His guardian anca knocked some sense into that boy.

In a deep voice, Tim said, "Ahem. I was hoping that you would consider marrying me." He looked down at his shoes. Then he looked into her sweet face. A delightful sparkle was in her eyes.

She grasped his hands in hers. "It would be wonderful to share our lives together. Thank you for asking. I accept your proposal of marriage."

With a smooth move he took a small velvet box out of his pocket. "This is for you, in commemoration of our future."

"Ooh, this is very nice," said Melona, "thank you so much."

With a fancy flourish, she slid the diamond onto her finger. The ring fit perfectly.

They kissed the way each had dreamed.

Tim was enormously relieved. "I was afraid it wouldn't fit."

"Oh my, it's a perfect fit," said Melona, waggling her new ring in the winter air.

Two girls in the park were jealous.

"Uncle Brian told me what size to get," whispered Tim.

Melona knew a slightly longer version of this story.

Tim confided his aspirations to Brian. Not knowing what to do, he sought out Trish. She knew exactly what to do. Striding across the hall she had a pleasant little chat with her future daughter-in-law. Then Trish went back to their apartment and told Brian what Melona's ring size was.

"I can't believe how wonderful this is," squealed Melona, doing a little dance. Imagine that, she was the kind of girl who got giggly over diamonds.

A middle aged woman, who had watched with a warm smile while this tender moment unfolded, asked, "Would you like me to take a picture of you two sweethearts."

After the film was developed, Tim had a look of goofy relief on his face. His bride-to-be beamed a confident smile. That picture would eventually become a family heirloom, mounted in a substantial silver frame.

Scene 96 - BeBop IsLand

Andy loved the old motorboat that came with the island. Growing up in Montana, boats had been for recreation but out here, where the land meets the sea at

Seattle, a boat was like an automobile. He was on his way back from the grocery store, with two sacks of food and some high priced champagne. Tomorrow was New Year's Eve.

That wizard of a city slicker lawyer, Frank Delbarton, had come through with a buyer for the trout fishing property. When Andy heard how much money he had made - he joked that now he could afford to buy his own island. It turns out that Frank had grown up in Seattle. Up there, you could do just that. So he did.

The boat was old but the previous owner had kept it in perfect condition. Before checking himself into the old folks home, he explained to Andy how everything worked - boat, dock, windows, doors, roof, emergency radio - everything. Islands are wonderful places to live, when the weather is good.

Andy renamed his new home BeBop IsLand.

As the motorboat puttered toward the dock, he slowed the engine and pulled up against the tires which were lashed to the pillars. The smell of moss was strong.

His house was a log cabin. Not the old kind like the pioneers had hewn from the forest with their axes. This was modern logs shipped in from a factory. There was the original box house. Three additions had been added on, over the years, in more or less the same log cabin style. The roof had been replaced three years ago, so that should be good when the weather got bad.

On the mantle above the fireplace was the old wooden phoenix, from his coffee house days. It looked really cool up there, with the sunlight flickering across it. The moose head which used to be there was on the floor. Next to the glass eyed moose were boxes and boxes of books and books.

##

Eberli and Lartel were waiting for him in the kitchen. He couldn't see them, of course, but by this time in life he had developed a sixth sense which let him know when he was "on" and when he was "off." Andy definitely knew he was "on."

Lartel was his new guardian anca. Not only had Andy been moved eight hundred miles further north but the guardians had put him on a new project. The people up here were a lot like the ones Andy had left behind in

Montana. They were independent minded, take care of yourself, give your neighbors a hand, type of folk.

That's where Lartel came in. He was a Seattle guardian and his department worked with these modernistic frontier types. Andy had been selected so they could try and figure out how to strengthen human connections with the planetary powers of the terrans.

Eberli explained. "This guy is real easy to get through to. Whether he's wide awake, or you want to reach him in his dreams, he just cooperates. We've never had him make a major mistake. He's got a real strong presence with other people but he's the quiet type."

"Why did they move him up here?" asked Lartel.

"That's a combination of bad and good," said Eberli. "Andy was working at a big rock concert when someone in the audience got stabbed. They brought the guy backstage, where Andy watched him die. Andy used to work in the lumber camps, so he'd seen plenty of knife fights before, but this shook him up. The Auxis were out there in full force and they wanted revenge. When my boss heard about this ugly incident he suggested we repurpose Andy's skills. We didn't need him for portal work anymore. Upper management had just rolled out this new project for your team. Vint asked me to come up here and transition my client to you."

"How long have you been working with this guy?" asked Lartel.

"Twenty years," said Eberli. "Now, let me show you something."

Andy was taking food out of the bag. Eberli projected an image of Lartel into his mind. Andy stopped. He looked Lartel straight in the eye. "Hi, nice to meet you." Then he went back to unpacking the groceries.

"That was spooky," said Lartel. "My clients don't even know I exist."

"That's what this is all about," said Eberli. "In the ancient days, people used to recognize us anca a whole lot better. They told many a strange tale about who they thought we were, but at least they knew we shared the planet with them. It's not like that anymore. People deny us."

"What's your opinion about that?" asked Lartel.

"There are so many different ways of looking at it that I can't give you a correct answer," said Eberli. "Let me fill you in on a few things that I do understand. Number one - the Sylumini got humiliated by the Guardians."

A cynical chuckle came from Lartel. "There's gonna be big trouble."

"Big trouble," agreed Eberli. "While the Guardians and the Sylumini fight it out above ground, the Terrans are going to be working quietly in the underground."

"Is this part of that jeshie colony thing?" asked Lartel.

"Totally separate projects," said Eberli. "Jeshie colony far away. Lartel and Andy up here."

"That makes me feel better," said Lartel. "I don't want the Sylumini pestering me. They're nasty."

"I don't have all the details but here's a couple of things for you to think about," said Eberli. "Noutashi will continue working with Melona over in New York City. She'll be running a bunch of terran experiments with the urbans. You're assigned to work around here with the rurals, on the same project. The goal is to get people back in touch with the fundamentals of this planet."

"My personal opinion is that the terrans can't reach the urbans at all, and trouble is surging because the rurals have been ripped away from their roots," said Lartel.

"You just mentioned two excellent reasons for wanting to make this project work," said Andy. "After you and Noutashi report back on your preliminary findings, the bosses want to startup related experiments all around the world."

"Worth a try," said Lartel. "We can't keep on going the way things have been."

"How about I stop talking and start listening to what you have to say," Eberli suggested. "What worries you the most?"

Lartel thought about this. "Things got pushed too far, too fast. I understand that we had to rescue those jeshies. Honor required it of us. But all that wild stuff they pumped into the air is driving people all sorts of crazy. I see problems around here that are going to be with us for a long time."

299

"The problems that got stirred up have already been plaguing us way for way too long," said Eberli. "Humans are gonna sink this planet if we don't do something fast."

"I'll do my best," said Lartel.

"Say, I've got to get going soon but I want to show you something first," Eberli said.

"Go for it," Lartel replied.

"Like I was telling you before, Andy does his best work when he's behind a tape recorder," Eberli explained. "At the New Year's Eve party tomorrow, you told me that one of your clients is a Hawaiian style guitar player."

"He's real good," said Lartel. "Recorded a few songs over in Seattle. Gets a lot of gigs with the local bands around here."

"What was it you were telling me about the local terrans?" asked Eberli.

"Terrans don't usually talk to us topsiders but, from what I hear, they have a lot of respect for my guitar guy," said Lartel. "I was told that they say he's the type of musician who feels all that deep earth stuff and knows how to bring it into people's hearts."

"That might be a starting place," said Eberli. "Get Andy and this guitar guy in the same room. See what happens. Then tell your boss about it."

"Can't hurt," said Lartel.

"Let's do a little experiment, said Eberli. "Earlier you were saying that putting his tape recorder in the boat is a bad idea."

"Salt water spray is rough on electronic stuff," said Lartel. "Andy needs to put it in one of those water tight boat cases that are down in the basement."

"Here's what I want you to do," said Eberli. "Project two images into his imagination. One of his tape recorder. The other of a travel case it will fit in. Just do it."

Lartel did what had been suggested.

Andy finished putting the groceries away. He was heading into the living room when he got a quizzical look on his face. Taking a detour, he went down into the basement.

On a shelf were several waterproof cases, lined up by size. Andy picked one that looked about right and carried it upstairs.

In the TV room was his audio gear. Setting the travel case down on the floor, next to one of his reel-to-reel tape recorders, he said, "Aha." Then he headed back to the living room.

"Told you so," said Eberli.

Chapter 35 - Settling In

Scene 97 - Across The Hall

Melona finally found that old picture she had searched for everywhere. It wasn't in the box it was supposed to be in. Somehow that envelope had ended up with homework from her freshman year. Ten amazing years had passed since then.

Her mother and father had driven her to New York City to get their daughter settled in the dorm. They couldn't afford NYU but Melona deserved better than community college. As they were walking down the street there was something about the iron fence in front of a brownstone building which captured her dad's imagination. She put on a vacation pose, with a cute little smile, and a country girl dress that came down two inches below her knees.

It seemed impossible that she could have ever been so young, so fresh, so perky.

She would have forgotten all about this picture if it hadn't been for Sandal Annie's funeral. Seeing Annie being dragged into a paddy wagon, at exactly this same spot, when they were each eighteen years old, triggered something deep inside. Melona wanted to rush across the hall to show it off, but Aunt Trish had asked her to stay away so they could get their apartment sparkling clean. It was bad luck to begin the New Year with a dirty home. At midnight, the decade of the seventies would begin.

Reaching over so she could prop up the picture on the end table, the lamp made her diamond throw sparkles. Camera Girl was getting married. Wiggling her hand, she admired the brilliant dance of light. Oooooh - bright shiny object. She laughed at herself.

Noutashi was sitting on the couch next to her. This had been a trip down memory lane for both of them. Her special girl had gotten engaged. The Hilyer's apartment was safe. Searching through boxes from freshman year had reminded Noutashi of her original plans for Melona. Unexpected events had changed everything. And yet, the fundamentals stayed the same.

Idle time is opportunity time - as they say in the guardian business.

Leaning over, Noutashi projected a thought into Melona's mind.

An image of her old typewriter appeared. It was in a box somewhere.

Noutashi knew exactly where it was but she decided to let Melona search for it on her own. Remembering forgotten things would be good for her.

"There it is," said Melona, twenty minutes later.

Taking it out of the box, a rush of memories flooded in. This typewriter had been given to her as a junior high school graduation gift. Her parents told her that she would need it in high school if she was going to get into college. They were right.

Bill Hilyer had been courteous enough to clear off his desk for her while they were away. Setting the case down, she unlatched the top.

In the typewriter was a yellowed piece of paper, permanently curled where it had been wrapped around the platen.

Now she needed typing paper. Mr. Hilyer probably had some but she didn't think it was right to use his. By the time her search was over, the tidy stacks of boxes she had neatly arranged were scattered everywhere. In her hand was a ream of paper.

Putting a blank sheet in the typewriter, she lined up the edges, clamped the platen shut, and rolled the paper down to the starting position.

"Good," thought Noutashi. "A blank page, a fresh mind, a new year, and a big surprise."

Scene 98 - Rent Control

Tim had been sent out to buy champagne for New Year's Eve. He and Uncle Brian had finished moving the archives from the bookstore to the back room. Brian told Tim to spend his own money on the champagne. He was a big boy now. He had a job. He was engaged to a fine young woman. It was a brave new world for young Tim Hadley.

While Tim was away on his errand, Brian and Trish were in the kitchen, trying to settle up on their plans.

"Ian tells me the deal is done," said Brian.

"Ian says lots of things," said Trish.

"I called the real estate broker as soon as I heard but nobody picked up the phone."

"It's the holidays. We'll have to wait until their office is open," she said.

"This is going to be so great," said Brian.

Trish said, "Much as I love New York, I can't wait to move down to Florida."

"They don't have good bagels down there," Brian said.

"With my waistline, I don't need more bagels," she said. "What I need is a warm ocean a brisk walk from our condo."

"We'll be living laaaarge," he said, doing a tropical hula dance.

"Don't live too large," she said, "we've got a mortgage to pay now."

"Mortgage schmorgage," he said, "let's live the life of beach bums."

"You live the life of a beach bum," she said, "I'll find a rich widower and throw you a dime when I see you picking up spare change in the sand."

"A dime," he said, "not even a quarter?"

"Well, for you, maybe a quarter. But you have to promise to be nice."

"I don't think I know how to be nice," he said.

"Sometimes you do, you stinker. But not today," she said. "By the way how's the deal on the bookstore going?"

"Mel took a look at the contracts. Or, should I say, he had one of his young up and comers do it for him. Everything looks fine," said Brian. "Coupla little things to iron out, but now that my brother has signed, everything is moving in the right direction."

Just then they heard footsteps in the hallway. It was Tim. They heard him walk across the hall and knock. There was a profound silence which left Trish and Brian in state of suspension. Two sets of footsteps came through the front door.

"I'm back," announced Tim.

"Hello dear," said Trish, "is your sweetie with you?"

"Hiya, Aunt Trishy-poo," said Melona. "Howya doing today?"

"Peachy keen," she said. It amused her to say old fashioned things like that because it irritated the youngsters.

Tim set down the bag from the liquor store with a triumphant flourish. First he took out a bottle of champagne. Then he took out some really fancy champagne. Last he took out a bottle of extremely fine brandy. "I thought we might like to have a little toast before the festivities begin."

Brandy snifters magically appeared. Glasses were raised. "Here's to the four us, to the sixties gone by, to the arrival of the seventies, and to life lived well," said Tim.

"Cheers."

When they set their glasses down Trish said, "Sweeties, your Uncle Brian and I have something we need to talk to you about."

Melona got a worried look.

"It's alright, honey," said Trish. "We want you lovebirds to take over this apartment from us."

Tim choked on his brandy, "What! You what!"

"We're retiring to Florida," said Brian.

"But, but ... you're too young to retire," said Tim.

"I would have retired when I was your age if I had enough money," said Brian, "but that's not the real world. Let me say something serious here. We're moving to Florida. You can take over this wonderful rent controlled apartment in The Village if you want it."

Tim glanced nervously around, "This would be fabulous for us. But I'll miss you. You're my family." A tear formed in the corner of his eye.

Aunt Trish said, "Did I mention that the deal includes keeping our bedroom exactly the way it is, so we can visit anytime."

Melona looked around the apartment with new eyes. "I can't believe this. Wow. This would be so wonderful."

Trish said, "Now that he got around to popping the question, you can set a date for your wedding and move in here all nice, neat and legal."

Melona looked serious, "My mother and father will appreciate that."

Trish quickly grabbed the lasagna out of the fridge and put it in the oven. Then she said, "We have a little surprise for you, sweetie pie."

Melona blushed. "Ooh, sounds like fun."

They escorted her to the back room. It used to be where they tossed things they were "going to get around to some day." When Melona started coming here, they cleaned it up and turned it into her office. On the desk were ten copies of Impress Magazine, which featured three of her pictures from Woodstock.

A musty smell was strong in the room. Boxes were piled high. She didn't understand. Then she saw the cork board from the funeral, with pictures from Sandal Annie's life.

"Oh my gosh," said Melona. "I found my picture. I'll be right back." She raced across the hall, grabbed it, and trotted back. "Look at this."

After they admired the two photos of Annie and Melona, at the same place in The Village, when they were each eighteen, Uncle Brian pinned the recent one next to the old one.

"How did you get these pictures?" Melona asked.

"They're yours," said Brian.

"What do you mean?" asked Melona.

"A few weeks ago, I mentioned to you that Sandal Annie had left a few items at our bookstore," said Brian.

"Yes, I remember that," said Melona.

"Well, I decided to take matters into my own hands and, after some discussion, I was made executor of Annie's estate. What you have is everything I could find of hers in Greenwich Village."

"So now it's yours?" asked Melona.

"No, actually, the entire collection is yours," said Brian. "I'm giving it to you as a gift. Sixteen boxes of memorabilia from her life. To be honest, I don't really know what's in here. Writing. Art. Photographs. This is where we found all those pictures for the funeral."

"This is a writer's dream," said Melona.

"Actually, it's probably more like a writer's nightmare," said Brian. "Bohemians do some of their most hideous writing when they're drunk. They must have swilled an ocean of cheap wine to crank out some of this nonsense. Anyway, happy treasure hunting."

"Timmy has something he would like to add to your collection," said Trish, pointing to a separate pile of tidy boxes, neatly stacked.

Tim cleared his throat and spoke in a formal voice, as if he was giving a lecture at the university. "You know Andy."

"Of course," said Melona, "we were a team. None of us know what we did but it seemed important at the time."

"Well, I've been on the phone with him these past few months. He left San Francisco and bought his own island up in the Puget Sound," said Tim.

"His own island," said Melona.

"Some sort of real estate deal," said Tim. "Anyway, he owns an island now. He moved there recently. Before he moved, he shipped his San Francisco collection to you. Something about an elevator of lost dreams. Andy wanted me to tell you that he kept all of Cynthia's memorabilia for himself - but he typed out copies of her writing so you could read her work."

"She died in a car crash," said Melona. "He's still in love with her."

"We're sorry to hear that," said Trish.

"I need to sit down," said Melona.

"Sit. Sit. You've got a lot to think about," said Trish.

Melona sat at her very own desk. The smell of old paper surrounded her.

"You youngsters stay here," said Trish. "The old married couple is going to finish making dinner."

Melona reached out and took Tim's hand. "Thank you so much. You have no idea how much this means to me."

"Maybe I do know how much it means to you," said Tim. "I like listening to your hopes and dreams. My goals aren't as big as yours and maybe it's better that way. We're going to get married. We're going to live here. I'm going to support you while you reach for your dreams."

Melona said, "You know what bothers me?"

"No I don't."

"You've given me all these wonderful things and I don't have anything for you."

307

"It's not a competition," said Tim, "You've given me a reason to live. You've given my aunt and uncle a reason to hope. We've given you a place in our hearts."

Noutashi cried when she heard this.

Chapter 36 - The End Of The Sixties

Scene 99 - Urban And Rural

When dinner was done, Melona got up to help clear the table.

"Sit," said Aunt Trish. "In my house women cook, men do the dishes and take out the garbage. I've got young Timmy trained. Don't spoil him. Men will take advantage of you if you let them. It's in their nature."

Melona could never imagine her mother saying something like that in front of her father.

When the dishes were done Melona said, "We were going to call my parents to wish them a Happy New Year."

Yesterday, they had given her mom and dad the Big Call to announce The Engagement. Renee and Larry were as happy as they could be that their daughter was *finally* getting married.

"Oh yeah," said Brian, "Now let me see, is it an hour later there, or an hour earlier? I can never remember."

"Earlier," said Melona.

Aunt Trish placed the big black phone on the table. Melona's hand trembled as she dialed. The place where she had grown up was in a different time zone. Holding the receiver in her hand, listening to the beep beep beep, she felt like she was calling into a different culture zone.

"Hello," said Renee, in her mid-south accent.

"Hi, mommy," squealed Melona. She couldn't help being excited.

"Larry, it's our daughter, pick up the other line."

"And the Talbots," said Melona.

"And the Talbots," her mother called out.

After all the hellos and how are you doings and has the date been set and that sort of thing - Uncle Brian finally got a chance to speak with Larry.

"Yes, yes everything is fine here," said Brian. "No, no we're not going to Times Square for New Year's tonight. Just a quiet evening at home. That's right, just the four of us. Wonderful daughter you raised. We really look forward to having her in the family. When are you coming out for a visit?"

"We were talking that over last night after we got the good news," said Larry, in his deep southern accent, which made Brian want to fall out of his yankee chair. "Renee teaches down at the college, so spring break would be best for us. Where would you recommend we stay?"

"Across the hall from us," said Brian.

"Excuse me, I think my phone crackled, what was the name of that place?" asked Larry.

"Let me explain," said Brian. "Our neighbors across the hall went to Europe for a year. That's right. Uh huh. Well, actually his company sent him over there to work at their main headquarters. Yes. It should be a very good opportunity for him. Anyway, more to the point, Melona has arranged to sublease their apartment while they're away. That's right. She'll be living across the hall from us, in her own place. Oh yes, it's very safe. When you get to New York there's a comfortable room waiting for you. No. No. It's not going to cost you anything. Here, let me put your daughter on."

"Hi daddy," said Melona.

Mommy decided it was time for her to get to the bottom of this. "What's this I hear about an apartment?"

"I'm renting the place across the hall from the Talbot's," said Melona. "Yes, I agree, that is very *convenient*. Right. I know. I get what you're saying. Everything is *fine*. This is a much nicer place than where I was living before. Well, I've been thinking about that a lot lately and I agree. Now that I'm going to get married I do need to be more careful. Oh yes, this is definitely a move up for me. It was very gracious of the Hilyer's to do this. Of course, it's good for them too, they don't have to worry about some stranger. Actually, they have a son but he's out of college and is a successful lawyer in Charlotte. I'm staying in his old room. There's a nice big room for you to stay in. Yes. Yes. Yes. And a Happy New Year to you as well."

"Happy New Year," the three Talbot/Hadleys shouted.

Larry wanted to speak with Brian again. "Well, let me tell you this - you've taken an enormous burden off our shoulders. We've been worried about her for a long time, what with all these riots and insurrections and so forth. If she's going to be over there by you that would be just fine. Thank you so much."

"You and Renee will stay with us whenever you visit New York," said Brian.

Renee broke into the men's conversation, "I just want to thank you all for the generosity you have shown to us. We can't wait to see our dear sweet little daughter again. We're looking forward to meeting you and young Timothy."

As soon as they hung up the phone, Trish got the brandy snifters out again. She divided what was left of the bottle into four equal portions. They raised their glasses high and she proposed a toast, "He's to our future-daughter-in-law."

They clinked and sipped.

Tim couldn't help opening his mouth to say, "Actually, from a purely academic point of view, wouldn't she be your future-niece-in-law."

Aunt Trish glared at her nephew, "You can call her anything she lets you get away with - but she's *My-Daughter-In-Law*."

Scene 100 - Renewal

"10 - 9 - 8 - 7 - 6 - 5 - 4 - 3 - 2 - 1. Yaaaaay."

"All right, time for the old folks to go to bed," said Uncle Brian. He shook his wife's shoulder. "Trish, wake up, it's time to go to sleep."

They shuffled off to their room.

Tim and Melona sat on the couch, holding hands, happy to be where they were.

As soon as the apartment got quiet, Tim stood up, took the jazz album off the turntable, and put on rock and roll music - at suitably low volume. Then he poured the last of the champagne and they clinked.

Noutashi sat in the guest chair. New Year's Eve was always a busy night for her. Riana and Dene had dropped by for a visit, so she had arranged her schedule to be with them. Riana was sitting on the couch, next to the young couple, amused by their happiness. Dene was reading the titles of the albums in Brian's collection.

"Happy New Year," Riana said softly. She looked so much healthier now.

Happy New Decade, said Noutashi. "How was the celebration in your time zone?"

Riana smiled, "Traditionally, I visit friends in Exeter on New Year's Eve. We watch the folk dancers along the river. This was the first time Dene had met them."

Dene said, "It was a real pleasure to meet friends who have known her for a long time. It gave me new insights into who she is."

"I envy you," said Noutashi. "I have fifty clients on my roster. Every New Year's they renew their vows of stupidity and excess. Before I got here tonight, two of them were taken to hospitals. Another one got hauled off to jail. And the night is still young."

"We'll be heading out to Caboks in a little while," said Dene. We wanted to drop by here first, to make sure Melona was doing alright. I promised aid and assistance."

"Getting that apartment across the hall was brilliant," said Noutashi. "Earlier this evening they gave her the Annie archives and the Elevator stuff. Thank you for your generous assistance on all three of those projects."

"You're more than welcome," said Dene. "On the way over here I was wondering if you could fill me in on what the Guardians of Greenwich Village are talking about these days. They have such a unique perspective on things."

"They think hiring Ulta is absurd," said Noutashi.

"Could be," said Dene, "but Ulta understands Sylumini weakness. We need that."

"An even hotter topic is how delighted everyone is that Khaletora got fired and Malki is going on trial for the deaths of Cynthia and Wendy," said Noutashi.

"That works to our disadvantage in several ways," said Dene. "Did you know that the big bosses from Andromeda sent Malki here to Earth so he could take out Khaletora, Ulta and Lanmon?"

That sounds absurd," said Noutashi, who was shocked.

"That's because the big bosses want to send in an entirely new leadership team. This new group will be much harder to deal with," said Dene.

"How so?" asked Noutashi.

"The recently announced management lineup have all been trained as cyber stealth experts," answered Dene. "They have mastered the methods of control by deception. This new group understands, with cunning ruthlessness, that if they are not thoroughly entrenched in the portal business before Hamil and Hamine arrive, they will get thrown out. We must be ready for them. This looks like it will be a spectacularly ugly fight."

"Will they threaten Melona?" asked Noutashi.

"She'll be on their watch list but I don't imagine she'll be in any danger," said Dene. "Harming her would be bad publicity. The specialty of these new executives is to weaken their competition at lowest possible risk to themselves. They will expand on Khaletora's policies with relentless determination. The planetary bubble will be shredded by the cosmic winds by the time these cyber warriors arrive."

"I don't like the sound of that," she said.

"We'll deal with them when we have to," said Dene. "In the meantime, what are your plans for Melona, now that her youthful adventures are drawing to a close?"

"I always had her tagged as a writer," said Noutashi. "Across the hall, she has a new sheet of paper in her old typewriter."

"Good," said Dene. "That's very good. Do you mind if I make a suggestion?"

"I would be delighted to hear your thoughts about her delayed career," said Noutashi.

"Have her write about characters who learn how to win big against bad people - without becoming bad themselves. That's always important," said Dene.

"Sounds like a workable plot line," said Noutashi. "I'll keep that in mind."

Tim and Melona stood up from the couch.

"Shhh," Tim whispered.

Two people and three anca listened to make sure the apartment was quiet.

"I'll get our coats," said Tim.

Tim knew the creaking floors better than anyone, having sneaked in and out of this apartment for most of his life. They put on their winter coats and went out to the balcony.

After Little Timmy and his Bride To Be got outside - Noutashi, Riana and Dene floated through the plate glass door to join them.

"I like being out here on the balcony at New Year's," said Tim. "I love the sounds of the city. Listen. We're hearing the opening sound track of the 1970s."

Cars honked their horns in the streets. Cheering tourists could be heard in the distance. Over on the Avenue, young rowdies shouted war cries of debauchery. Further east, where Melona used to live, came the sounds of gunfire.

The young couple snuggled in their winter coats, held each other's gloved hands, and basked in the bracing air of a new beginning.

"What are your plans after you leave here?" asked Noutashi.

"This is our second celebration of the New Year," said Riana. "We've got two more."

"Busy night," said Noutashi.

"Next will be Caboks," Riana said. "That's only one time zone away. We're going to Honat and Lumbia's place out in the suburbs."

"Sorry, but I have a lot of trouble imagining Honat living in a suburban development in the underground caverns," said Noutashi.

"So does Lumbia, sometimes," said Riana.

They laughed.

"Xen, Wun and Trz will be there, of course," said Riana. "Lon will be joining us from the west coast."

"What about Qusheem?" asked Noutashi.

"You never know with Qusheem," said Riana. "He doesn't like parties."

"I can understand that," said Noutashi.

"Two time zones later we're going out to visit Andy and meet Lartel," said Riana.

"Eberli mentioned something about that," said Noutashi. "I've spoken to Lartel a couple of times."

"After that we'll see what the new year brings," said Riana.

"Are we still working together?" wondered Noutashi.

"Not according to the organizational charts," said Riana.

"At the Guardians, everything goes by the charts," said Noutashi.

"But the Guardians are involved in this new urban/rural initiative with the terrans," said Riana. "Dene and I aren't assigned to that project but we'll get involved when the time is right. So the answer is - some day."

"I always thought I would look forward to this day," said Noutashi. "You two wouldn't be meddling in Melona's life anymore. Now I'm not so sure."

Dene gave his opinion on this, "We don't want to meddle. We want to set this wayward planet on a better path. A whole bunch of anca have suddenly realized that they have left too many important things undone. It's time we all started paying attention again. Otherwise, the bad guys win."

Three anca got lost in their own private thoughts, with different visions of what the seventies might have in store for them.

Two young people had hopes and dreams of their own.

For Melona, this peculiar silence was transformational. She had just been given two archives which provided structure for her return to the written word. What she needed was a spark.

An arc from eternity connected to her inner being.

This was not at all like a guardian anca influencing a human client. This was a direct link beyond space-time. Melona felt all of who she was connect with all of what there was. The great mystery lodged itself in her body, and in her heart, and in her mind, and in her soul.

Melona accepted.

Three anca saw this and bowed their heads.

Tim saw some deep change in the one he loved, "Is everything alright?"

Melona glowed, "All is as it should be."

Searching through her writer's heart, the young woman sought the essence. Ten years of mysterious frenzy jumbled through her memory. She touched the great mystery.

Tim watched her eyes.
Invisible anca listened.
She chose these words, "It is the end of the sixties."

The End

Glossary

Main Characters And Places

Administrative Beings
Beings such as anca (from Nimulos) and soto (from Jeshmol) emerge into life with the task of administering to the various needs of countless evolutionary beings.

Aiyoni
Human female. Internationally famous artist. She has risen to the top of the avant-garde pop culture scene. Her collaboration with Melona is productive.

Alicia Hathaway
Human female. Cynthia's best friend from their beatnik days. She is queen of the bopsies, a small group of hipsters living in San Francisco during the fifties and sixties.

Andromeda
In the Tromolea local gravity group the largest galaxy is Andromeda. The second largest is Ostramona. The big bosses of the Sylumini are headquartered in Andromeda.

Andy Baird
Human male. Portal guide number one. Male human protagonist. When the first rescue plan failed he learned new portal skills for the second rescue plan.

Arhulio
Anca male. Religious rogue detective. A rough life busting smugglers, and then joining them, left him in need of spiritual salvation. His code breaking skills helped Dene.

Avilia

Ostramona Special Ops goes after the bad guys. One of their many facilities is the Avilia sphere, between Ostramona and Andromeda. Dene meets Jenissen there.

Ayamara

In the future, the Earth Anca Corp will be administered from the capitol city of Ayamara by the co-leaders Hamil and Hamine. They are the incoming administration.

Baiyoc

Anca female. Leader of the Guardian Anca Corp on Earth. The rescue depends on double teams of anca and soto guardians. She leads them against the Sylumini.

Beel

Anca male. Diplomatic zone functionary. Working from a humble position he makes things happen. When Dene needs something big, Beel is there to help.

Behchel

Anca male. Industrialist building portals to transfer jeshie colonists. Merging two vast expansion regions into one is monumental and the Captain is up to those challenges.

Beq

Soto female. Brilliant scientist. After a distinguished career she made a mathematical discovery which transforms her into an other-sider.

Bob Shiller

Human male. Internationally famous record producer. The psychedelic sound of the sixties would not have reached such great heights if it wasn't for him.

Bongo Ribicoff

Human male. Andy's best friend from their bopsie days. He showed Andy how to survive in the urban environment of San Francisco. Bongo designs musical sound effects.

Bopsie Lewis
Human male. Leader of the Redwood Hipsters jazz band. The cool soundtrack inspiring the bopsie poets was provided by this group of local musicians.

Brian Talbot
Human male. Tim's adopted father. Talbot's Rare Books is where Uncle Brian taught Tim the things a young man needs to learn in life. Brian is married to Trish.

Caboks
A metropolis in the terran underground. It is near where the three great rivers meet. Unseen by topsiders, the wisdom of the deep is preserved in terran territory.

Caelomi
Flash being female. Star traveler from Nimulos. She teams up with Vonso to challenge the way colonization is being done for JeshNim in Roshomon.

Cami
Anca female. Design engineer who quantifies portal parameters. Intelligent, poised, and efficient - she gets thrown in with eccentric geniuses. Farli's commit.

Cazouni
Lost planet flung into the relentless void. The Phorlom Research Foundation built a remote research station there. Dene meets Hamil and Hamine here.

Celene
Anca female. Prime Minister for Hamil and Hamine. She came to Earth to prepare the way. What she found was a planet in turmoil. Then she set about fixing it.

Chephra
Chephra and Lindar are two mode-tunnels for colonization-cruisers. When the story opens, Chephra is still under construction and cannot be used for the rescue.

Constance

Human female. Melona's boss at Impress Magazine. Tough but fair, she mentors her young employee. When it's crunch time she makes all the right moves.

Cynthia

Human female. Andy's girlfriend who died in a car crash. The first rescue plan got cancelled because of her death. Was her passing an accident or was it deliberate?

Darimia

The anca name for our Sun is Darimia. Because of its location in a multi layered universe, a jeshie colony (KCE) is being built between Earth and Mars.

Dene

Anca male. Special Ops professional. Male anca protagonist. The ishmili sent him to Earth to challenge the Sylumini. He also has to get Riana figured out.

Diane Rishi

Human female. Owner of the BeBop BookStore. Former debutante from a wealthy family, her self-destructive life style wipes out Andy's part time job.

Dirdri

Anca female. Test pilot from Sagonish. Been there, done that, seen it all. She teaches Riana and Dene what they need to know about flying exotic mode-cruisers.

Earth

Our familiar home planet. One of billions in Ostramona. Unique opportunities for colonization flow through us every day. Sylumini greed upsets the balance on Earth.

Eberli

Anca male. Andy's guardian anca. He never expected the rescue to take so long. No matter how tough it gets, he hangs in there, totally mellow, through it all.

Eetor
Doomed planet. Because of the extreme conditions, Dene is unable to escape. When the ishmili finally get his new project ready, they send Dene to Earth.

Effrana
Anca female. Portable portal technician. She finds herself surrounded by babbling executives. When an alien object suddenly appears, she knows what to do.

Evolutionary Beings
Evos are the most populous beings in the known universe. By learning how things really work, from the bottom up, these evos understand what's really going on.

Farli
Anca male. Instrumentation specialist who builds portals. Others talk a lot. Farli gets things done. When it's time to improvise, you want him on your side. Cami's commit.

Fevih
Flash being female. Star traveler from Nimulos. She is a good friend of Lumbia, even though flashes and anca are rarely friends. Also an ally of cloud wanderer Vonso.

Fenaron
Grokar and Beemie aren't supposed to claim a planet. Nobody stops them. He creates poetry to challenge the mind. She crafts sculpture to uplift the spirit.

Flash Beings
Star travelers like Caelomi are from Nimulos. Cloud wanderers like Vonso are from Jeshmol. On Earth these two team up to rebalance colonization opportunities.

Fobimini
The Phorlom Research Foundation built this sphere between Imbotil and Cazouni. It is the supply depot for Rakari and Jagh carrying researchers into the void.

Frank Delbarton
Human male. Andy's lawyer. Dreams are free but supporting those dreams can get expensive. He shows Andy how to make the real world work to his benefit.

Fro
Soto male. Professor on the soto side. Peer of Prof Obolon. Without new scientific breakthroughs the colonization effort will falter. Both sides work to build JeshNim.

George
Human male. Melona's boss's boss at Impress Magazine. A seasoned corporate climber, he helps Noutashi make her plans for Melona come true.

Gervaie
Anca female. Cami and Farli's manager. Proper organizational practices don't work very well when your new team is crazy and your rivals are ruthless.

Gheney Hospital
For the first rescue Zacatra Hospital was built. For the second rescue they moved it to Gheney Hospital. Times may change but doing the right thing is forever.

Gomonish
While the fabric of space-time continues to expand, the most stable home we will ever know is Gomonish. Riana and Dene want to help us to survive after it fades away.

Grand Universe
Nothing ever stays the same. What is here now will someday be gone. Who you are will transform into who you will become. All this happens in the grand universe.

Gromo
Anca male. Chief law enforcement officer in Sagonish. Upholding the law is an honorable profession. Sometimes you have to know when to look the other way.

Grunda

Flash being male. Star traveler from Nimulos. Stubborn rival of Fevih. When Vonso moves to Earth he must continue the battle against Grunda's forces.

Hamil and Hamine

Anca male and female. Co-leaders of the next anca administration. Creating a JeshNim colony for our future is their career. Dene gets authority from them for Celene.

Hierashu

Headquarters of the Nimulos expansion region. Central authority begins here. Local control makes local decisions. Dene is an Hierashu certified diplomatic courier.

Hikli Laboratory

There are three different Hikli Labs. The first was near Namoush in Kemong. The second is in the terran underground city of Caboks. There will be a third at KCE.

Honat

Anca male. Design genius who visualizes portal conditions. Far seeing but ill mannered, the rescue of the refugees depends on his unique blend of skills.

Hoshambelan

The Earth Anca Corp is administered from Hoshambelan by Sarkon and Sarena. In the near future the capitol city Ayamara will become the center of anca power on Earth.

Hurbu

Zog orbits around the star Hurbu. In this star system is the fully operational Kemong Colony Zog (KCZ). The Lindar mode-tunnel supports new jeshie colonists.

Imbotil

A small galaxy in the Tromolea local gravity group. It is located near the edge of the Phorlom void. The Phorlom Research Foundation is headquartered in Imbotil.

Ing

Anca female. Leader of the Ishmili Colonization Bureau. Four worlds - ishmili, anca, soto, and human - come together in her tiny office on Paliyur.

Ixchibo

As far as other anca are concerned, nothing happens on Ixchibo. Hidden within this proto-planet is Zinxa. She is a pioneer scout searching out our JeshNim future.

Jagh

Anca male. Bold test copilot in the Phorlom void. In addition to flying a mode-cruiser, his inventions bring three mutually invisible worlds together.

Jenissen

Anca male. Leader of Special Ops in Ostramona. When life gets ugly they send him. Dene is assigned to Jenissen to oppose the Sylumini.

Jeshmol

Jeshmol is our neighboring expansion region. It is co-expanding through our Nimulos. They are old, we are young. The ishmili are combining both into JeshNim.

JeshNim

Every expansion region will eventually fade away. Surviving into eternity means building new stepping stones. JeshNim will be our next cosmic stepping stone.

Kemong

Billions of cloud islands are in Jeshmol. Billions of gravity groups are in Nimulos. Kemong flows invisibly through Gomonish. Chephra and Lindar will bring colonists.

Kemong Colony Earth (KCE)

Between Earth and Mars a colony is being built to house jeshies. Construction is not finished yet so a temporary rescue colony was also established on Earth.

Kemong Colony Zog (KCZ)

Near Zog, in the Hurbu star system, the KCZ colony recently went into full operation. Because of the Earth rescue, a shuttle service links all three locations.

Khaletora

Anca male. Chief Executive Officer of the Sylumini on Earth. Unrealistic expectations have pushed him beyond his limits. Galactic leaders have lost faith in him.

Kloom

Anca male. Chief Justice of the planetary courts on Earth. Judge Kloom upholds justice. Justice requires hard evidence. Sylumini are masters of deception.

Lafisse

Anca female. Secretary of the Pofraisson Chapel. The scatter brained minister, Tristo, would never get anything done if Lafisse didn't follow through on the details.

Lanmon

Anca male. Lawyer who stood up to Khaletora and got fired. Those at the top must sometimes choose between right and wrong. Lanmon chose what was right.

Larry Geffion

Human male. Melona's father. Raised with solid southern values, he finds his beliefs challenged when his daughter goes away to college in the big city. Married to Renee.

Lartel

Anca male. Andy's new guardian. After the rescue, new projects were organized. Lartel learns from Eberli what to do with Andy. He will work with Noutashi and Melona.

Larush

Anca female. Chief Executive Officer of the Valdarians on Earth. In addition to the high tech challenges of Chephra, she must face off against the ruthless Sylumini.

Life Zone, Lengtor
The only part of the grand universe we can see and touch is in the Lengtor life zone. Ur and Um are our life spark patrons. From them we are all called urbies or umbies.

Life Zone, Trogeln
Trogeln (Lengtor with letters switched) is one of countless "other" life zones in the grand universe. Ru and Mu (Ur and Um with letters switched) are "their" life sparks.

Lindar
Lindar and Chephra are two mode-tunnels for colonization-cruisers. When the story opens, only Lindar is functional. Lindar and Chephra share same design.

Lon
Evojesh female. Jeshie guardian in charge of the rescue. Peer of Vint. Resentful about getting involved, she has her grandest adventure. She works with Xen, Wun and Trz.

Lumbia
Anca female. Terran underground atmosphere expert. The terrans live apart from surface, and sphere dwelling, anca. The jeshie colony is in terran territory.

Lunetor
Anca male. Mineral smuggler. A shady crook whose illegal activities guarantee the safety of those in dire need of rescue. He knows where to find things on the dark side.

Majestic Beings
Ishmili and Wulem are two types of majestic beings. Anca and Soto are advised by the Ishmili. The Ishmili are advised by the Wulem, who report to Ur and Um.

Malki
Anca male. Skilled thug and master of deception. Sometimes bad things need to happen. When those things are really really bad, they send for Malki.

Melona Geffion

Human female. Portal guide number two. Female human protagonist. Her awareness grows that those vague hunches she feels are important to the powers-that-be.

Mical and Macel

Anca male and female. Co-leaders of the Ostramona galaxy. They are responsible for every life planet in their domain. They authorized Dene for special ops on Earth.

Mositey Shuttle

Temporary jeshie colonists need to be moved to the permanent colony when there is enough space for them. The shuttle takes them from Earth to KCE or KCZ.

Namoush

Capitol city of Sector Forty Two in Kemong. Governor Zeb and Lon both live there. When the mode-quake hit neighboring Wamilla, they got called into action.

Natalie (Edmond) Hadley

Human female. Tim's biological mother. When her soldier husband, Owen, got killed in the Korean War, she freaked out and abandoned their only child. She is Trish's sister.

Nebraska Kid

Human male. Farm boy selected by Xen and Wun. Early third portal guide testing the new design. He helped get the Little Blue Toy over to the other side.

Nether Regions

Nimulos and Jeshmol are ordinary expansion regions. Nether regions (in-between realms) can be inhabited only by unique beings. Riana and Beq are examples.

Nimulos

Nimulos is "our" expansion region. This is the anca name for what Earth scientists call the Big Bang Universe. Nimulos is co-expanding through Jeshmol.

Norbert The Poet
Human male. Eccentric street poet. How was he to know that invisible aliens needed him? All he wanted to do was read "The Death Of Hipness."

Noutashi
Anca female. Melona and Tim's guardian anca. Stubborn and excitable, she tries to protect her clients from Riana and Dene. Peer of Eberli, then Lartel.

Obolon
Anca female. Professor on the anca side of the Phorlom Research Foundation. Among the earliest researchers in the Phorlom were Obolon, Behchel, Riana, and Zinxa.

Observatory, Chephra
Chephra was built to be a colonization mode-tunnel. One special lab is the Ishmili Colonization Observatory, which operates under ishmili control, not anca or soto.

Observatory, NimuTrak
Linked to the Chephra Observatory is the mobile NimuTrak Observatory van. Xen and Wun (jeshies) are working with Honat and Qusheem (nimulons).

Ostramona
What we call the Milky Way has the anca name Ostramona galaxy. The alignment of Kemong, relative to Ostramona, creates the JeshNim colonization opportunities.

Owen Hadley
Human male. Tim's biological father. He meant well but things didn't turn out right. After surviving World War Two, he died in the Korean War. Married to Natalie.

Paliyur
Anca live either on a planet or in a sphere. Planets are natural places which anca administer. Spheres are artificial. The Earth's sphere is named Paliyur.

Paroun

Beq made cutting edge math discoveries which pointed her toward the nether regions. Zinxa found her. Beq's new in-betweener home is named Paroun.

Penezha

The Phorlom Research Foundation has two research spheres in the void. Penezha is along a direct line from Earth to Cazouni. Riana's lab is linked to Udintav.

Phil

Human male. Owner of the Udjat Eye Gallery. For rising young artists in the pop art scene of the sixties, Phil's gallery was a stepping stone to stardom.

Phorlom

In the Tromolea local gravity group is a medium sized bubble known as the Phorlom void. It's unique stillness makes it an ideal environment for scientific research.

Pika Pablera

Human male. Owner of the Phoenix Coffee House. For the San Francisco bohemians of the hip fifties, his place was the poetry center, as well as a portal for the jeshie colony.

Pim

Soto male. Leader of the Wamilla division of Kemong Emergency Services. Career politician who ends up living in a disaster zone. Xen and Wun "report to Pim."

Prairie Flats

Small town in middle America. Below ground is the Thunderbird Room, which is where Fevih led the conclave. The green crystals were left behind.

Qusheem

Evonim male. Instrumentation genius who builds exotic portal observation posts. An extreme mode-hopping evo who works directly with anca. Qusheem is a peer of Wun.

Rakari
Anca female. Bold test pilot in the Phorlom void. Danger is her constant companion. Her long term goal is to help build a secure region for our shared eternal future.

Renee Geffion
Human female. Melona's mother. She had big plans for her daughter in Kentucky. Her daughter fell in love with the big city and won't be coming back. Married to Larry.

Rescue Colony, East
With an additional ten years for development, the east coast plan is much safer than the west coast plan. Gheney Hospital replaced the original Zacatra Hospital.

Rescue Colony, West
On short notice, a limited rescue plan was put together near San Francisco. It was halted by Cynthia's death. Five years later they had a new plan to confound the Sylumini.

Rescue, Mode-quake
A mode-quake in Wamilla is like an earthquake in California. Hospital patients needed to be moved to the uncontaminated dual atmosphere on Earth.

Riana
Anca female. Ancient primebie seeking to build the survival region of JeshNim. Female anca protagonist. She is tragically misunderstood by the world she seeks to save.

Roshomon
Ostramona is a majestic spiral galaxy swirling in the sky. Earth is located in an oddly shaped cloud of stars, which the anca call Roshomon.

Roshomon Colonization
While Nimulos and Jeshmol move invisibly through each other, certain parts overlap. Earth and Zog are in perfect position for long term colonization opportunities.

Roxie

Human female. Ranch woman from North Dakota. Unlikely friend of Melona. Fate throws them together, in the mean streets of New York, during a riot.

Sagonish

A five star system in the Roshomon star cloud. Because of complex tugs of gravity it is easy to mine rare anca minerals. Captain Behchel founded Valdaria there.

Saluf

Anca female. Color billow maestro. When umbies need to look their best, nobody does that better than Saluf the Magnificent. Riana and her bride guides benefit.

Sandal Annie

Human female. Aging bohemian from Greenwich Village. Melona befriended Annie during an assignment for a college class. The two of them later opened a portal.

Sarkon and Sarena

Anca male and female. Co-leaders of the current Earth anca administration. The good old days, when nature could be dealt with naturally, has left them behind.

Sector Forty Two

Kemong is divided into many sectors. A mode-quake devastated the Wamilla peninsula, which is located in this sector. They requested help from Earth.

Tahra and Noom

Ishmili male and female. Majestic beings who provide guidance for both anca and soto. Tahra works with Lindar on Zog. Noom works with Chephra on Earth.

Tim Hadley

Human male. Portal guide number three. His guardian anca Noutashi selected Tim to help Andy and Melona. She also has plans for Tim and Melona after the rescue.

Torley
Anca male. Second in command at Sylumini Technology. He reports to Ulta. One of those at the top who does only what is expedient for his personal advancement.

Trish (Edmond) Talbot
Human female. Tim's adopted mother. Never shy, Aunt Trish takes one look at Melona and decides they will bring Little Timmy to the altar. Trish is married to Brian.

Tristo
Anca male. Minister of Pofraisson Chapel. Well meaning but absent minded, he is skilled at deep spiritual connections. Officiates at Riana and Dene's commitment.

Tromolea
Within the colossal Gomonish gravity group there is a small local gravity group known as Tromolea. The two largest galaxies are Andromeda and Ostramona (home to Earth).

Trz
Evojesh male. Trz is one hundred times older than Riana. Both are ancient in their respective worlds. Trz was born to evojesh mother and father one trillion years ago.

Udintav
Anca male. Strict disciplinarian in a supremely dangerous environment. Everyone on his Penezha crew obeys his every command. Dene challenges his authority.

Ulta
Anca female. Chief Technical Officer of the Sylumini. No one in the Sylumini is smarter or tougher than she is. Riana is her archenemy who holds portal secrets.

Ur and Um
Life Patrons male and female. Co-leaders of the vast Lengtor life region. In a limitless universe they are our links to the eternal. We have life because of them.

Valdaria

Valdaria is both a place and a colonization enterprise. Captain Behchel built a mega sphere complex for the Valdarians, at a placed named Valdaria, in Sagonish.

Valerie

Human female. Activist running the Peoples Photography Co-op. She instructs Melona in how to master photography. She also mentors Melona about life.

Vint

Anca male. Managing Director of the guardians in charge of creative types in North America. His detailed planning skills help make the rescue a success.

Vonso

Flash being male. Cloud wanderer from Jeshmol. He teams up with Caelomi to correct some big problems on Earth. Their enemy is the star traveler Grunda.

Wakona

Detective work can be rough. An anca detective named Arhulio decided he needed a break. So he went to The Retreat on Wakona to turn his life around.

Wamilla

A tiny section of Kemong is the Wamilla peninsula. Because of its precarious position it was devastated by a mode-quake. The peninsula broke off and drifted away.

Wamilla Medical Center

Medical Center famous for treating severe allergy cases. The plan was to send these patients to KCE for relief. When the mode-quake hit they got diverted to Earth.

Wendy

Human female. Cynthia's best friend from school. She knew nothing about the invisible portals powered by Andy and Cynthia. Wendy died in the car crash with Cynthia.

Wun

Evojesh male. Observatory technician who maps portal conditions. His sideline is creating new equipment which links the invisible. The Little Blue Toy was his invention.

Xen

Soto female. Design engineer who maps portal conditions. Without her stubborn determination, two worlds would not have been connected as quickly. She works with Wun.

Yal

Soto female. Jeshie lawyer in charge of investigating the Sylumini on Earth. She joins forces with Riana to collect evidence that will hold up in a court of law.

Yori

Anca female. Pilot of Ulta's spy cruiser. She is a true professional who flies with great skill. When surrounded by chaos, she remains cool, calm, and collected.

Zacatra

For the west coast rescue plan, Zacatra Hospital was built. Then the east coast plan was put in place. Zacatra Island was converted into Jeshmol Earth Colony Headquarters.

Zeb

Soto female. Governor of Sector Forty Two. When the mode-quake hit, she responded diligently. Zeb worked with Noom and Riana to create the Hikli Lab.

Zibbot

Gravity group where Dene learned how to do "the jump." The ishmili needed his latent talents. The Mysterians of Zibbot are famous for their esoterica.

Zinxa

Anca female. Other-sider pioneer scout. Among the strangest of strange beings. Six billion years ago Zinxa and Riana learned how to enter the nether regions.

Zog

A planet remarkably similar to Earth. Reptans are the top level evos on Zog. Humans are the top level evos on Earth. Valdarians built matching mode-tunnels.